About the Authors

Judy Lynn Hubbard is a Texas native who has always been an avid reader – particularly of romance. Judy loves well-written, engaging stories with characters she can identify with, empathise with, and root for. When writing, she honestly can't wait to see what happens next; she knows if she feels that way, she's created characters and a story that readers will thoroughly enjoy and that's her ultimate goal.

Melanie Milburne read her first Mills & Boon at age seventeen in between studying for her final exams. After completing a Master's Degree in Education, she decided to write a novel and thus her career as a romance author was born. Melanie is an ambassador for the Australian Childhood Foundation, is a keen dog lover and trainer, and enjoys long walks in the Tasmanian bush. In 2015 Melanie won the HOLT Medallion, a prestigious award honouring outstanding literary talent.

Taryn Leigh Taylor likes dinosaurs, bridges, and space, both personal and of the final-frontier variety. She shamelessly indulges in clichés, most notably her Starbucks addiction, her shoe hoard, and her penchant for falling in lust with fictional men with great abs. She also really loves books, which is what sent her down the crazy path of writing one in the first place. For more on Taryn, check out tarynleightaylor.com, facebook.com/tarynltaylor1 and twitter.com/tarynltaylor

Sinfully Yours

Sinfully Yours:
The Convenient Husband

JUDY LYNN HUBBARD

MELANIE MILBURNE

TARYN LEIGH TAYLOR

MILLS & BOON

First Published in Great Britain 2024
by Mills & Boon, an imprint of HarperCollins*Publishers* Ltd,
1 London Bridge Street, London, SE1 9GF

www.harpercollins.co.uk

HarperCollins*Publishers*
Macken House, 39/40 Mayor Street Upper,
Dublin 1, D01 C9W8, Ireland

ISBN: 978-0-263-32267-5

MIX
Paper | Supporting
responsible forestry
FSC™ C007454

THESE ARMS
OF MINE

JUDY LYNN HUBBARD

To my beloved sister, Carol. I wish you were here to see this day, but you'll live forever in my heart.

Prologue

Alesha Robinson took a deep breath and held it in for several long seconds before releasing it slowly. She continued the silent argument with herself to combat the foolhardiness of what she was about to do. She should turn around and go home. She started to do it—for the thousandth time, she started to do it—however, she kept walking, almost running toward her destination, as if she were eager for the impending meeting when nothing could be further from the truth.

Would he listen to her? Was there a chance in hell that he would understand and forgive her? Was she just fooling herself by thinking she could appeal to his good side? In the short time they had dated two years earlier, she had often been privy to his charm, wit and good humor. He had been a perfect gentleman, someone she had wanted to get to know better, but circumstances had not worked in their favor. For reasons he still was unaware of, she had abruptly ended their relationship without explanation. Would he hold that against her now?

He had a reputation of being fair and she knew firsthand that he was, or rather had been. But was she remembering a man from a lifetime ago? Did she dare hope that man still existed after the horrible way they had parted?

She mumbled a slight apology after nearly colliding with another pedestrian on the sidewalk, then continued on her way. She was almost there, and still she had no idea what she was going to say to him. She resolved to cross that bridge when she came to it and continued determinedly on her way to an unscheduled yet overdue meeting.

She pulled her light coat tighter around her as a biting blast of October wind forced its unwelcomed way in between the gaps of the coat's loosely tied opening. Absent fingers brushed a stray strand of shoulder-length curly black hair, which had been loosened from its clasp by the teasing gust. What was she going to say? How should she begin? She rehearsed one scenario and then another, and another, yet she still had no idea what would come out of her mouth when she opened it.

Her hesitant feet suddenly stopped outside the forty-story building that was her destination. Craning her head, she glanced up the tall, foreboding black glass frame. She wondered, would the foe she must now face be as formidable and as unyielding? Lowering her eyes to the front door, she took another deep breath and exhaled it before walking through the double doors to face the fire, uncertain she could evade the scorching that was sure to come.

Chapter 1

Derrick Chandler stared in exasperation at the man sitting across from him. Why did campaign managers always have to try to change your life? He listened in annoyance as Cameron Stewart continued to tell him what he must do in order to win the Senate race, which he had recently entered.

He wondered why he hadn't just stuck to corporate law instead of throwing his hat into the political arena. He decided the main reason was the city in which he resided—if you were a successful lawyer and lived in Washington, D.C., it seemed predestined that a foray into the world of politics would occur at some time or another.

Fingers absently tapped his chocolate-colored, clean-shaven chin impatiently and then brushed a piece of lint off the breast pocket of his immaculate navy blue suit. After Cameron talked until he was satisfied, then Derrick would have his say—the other man in the room would not be pleased with what he would hear. He disliked anyone telling him what he should and should not do, and Cam was treading on dangerous ground.

"Derrick, the simple fact is that you need a wife." Cam succinctly summed up his ten-minute tirade.

Derrick bolted upright in his chair, his gray eyes growing hard and cold. His voice matched his angry countenance. "And you need a psychiatrist."

Cam sighed audibly, not in the least put off by his friend's frigid tone. "Just listen to me…"

"No, you listen to me." Derrick held up a hand forestalling his friend's words. "I tried the marriage scene once, and we both know what a fiasco that was."

"Well, I told you before you married her…"

Derrick's darkening eyes stopped Cam cold. "You're treading on dangerous ground, Cameron."

"I know, Derrick, but just hear me out." He quickly continued before his friend could object, "You hired me to increase your chances of being elected and, whether you like it or not, I've got to tell you what I think."

"Well, I don't like it, but if you want to hear yourself talk, be my guest."

He scratched his lightly bearded chin. "We're doing great in all demographics except for women."

Derrick frowned. "I thought our numbers looked pretty good there."

"Pretty good, but if you had a woman in your life, one who could relate with and talk to other women, one on one, about their concerns, I have no doubt our numbers would double."

"Wouldn't a female member of my staff work?"

"Please!" Cam's look of disgust elicited a chuckle. "Man, this is America—the land of opportunity, the home of apple pie and baseball."

Derrick rolled his eyes. "This sure sounds like a commercial."

"With the election a little over a year away, now is the perfect time for you to be seen as someone who has deep ties to the community, someone who has something in common with his constituents, someone who shares their dreams and hopes. The best way to identify with them is to be seen as a family man."

"You're not married."

"I'm not running for public office, either." Cam folded his arms across his chest. "You are and you need someone, and not just any woman—a wife. Just think about it, a built-in hostess for parties and a date ready and willing to go with you whenever and wherever. I know I'm getting through to you." Cam carefully studied Derrick's purposefully unreadable expression.

"Wouldn't a German shepherd accomplish the same thing as a wife?" Derrick smiled slightly.

Cam closed his eyes in frustration before quickly opening them again. "Will you try to see my point of view?"

"No, you try to see mine. I am not going to marry anyone ever again!" He deliberately emphasized each word.

Cam opened his mouth to speak, but closed it again as a buzz sounded from the phone on the desk.

Derrick yanked up the handset impatiently. "Yes, what is it?"

He was more than a little annoyed—he had left instructions not to be disturbed.

"If she won't tell you, then tell her I'm in conference and can't be disturbed!"

He unceremoniously slammed the receiver back into its cradle. He made a mental note to apologize to Dorothy once Cameron left. He was in a foul mood, brought on by the other man's ludicrous suggestion.

Cam was shaking his head disapprovingly. "People skills, Derrick. People skills!"

"What do I pay you for?" In spite of himself, he almost smiled at his friend's dismayed tone.

"To tell you what others dare not."

"Well, you certainly seem to enjoy that part of the job." This time, a genuine smile tilted the corners of his frowning mouth.

"My mother always told me I love a challenge, and you certainly are that." Cam picked up his briefcase and prepared to leave.

"Are we done?"

"Yes, we're done. I'll try to sell you on getting a wife later."

"Oh, joy." Derrick rose to shake his hand.

"Do you have anything else you need to talk to me about?"

"No, please go." Derrick reclaimed his seat behind the desk.

"See you tonight at seven sharp."

As Cam walked toward the door, Derrick grimaced at the thought of another political dinner/debate—he loved the debates, but he detested sitting around with strangers, making senseless small talk over steak or chicken that tasted like rubber and vegetables that had much in common with plastic.

"How could I forget?"

"Just be there, and on time."

"Anything else, Mom?"

"As a matter of fact, yes. But I don't have the strength to discuss it with you right now." He ran a hand over his bald head. "I used to have hair before you and I became friends."

"Later, Cameron." Derrick's sigh turned into a chuckle at

the exasperated look he received before his friend left with a decisive click of the door.

Alone at last, he laughed out loud and ran a hand over his short-cropped hair. He enjoyed needling Cam, almost as much as he enjoyed his newfound career in politics. Best friends since law school, Derrick and Cam looked like brothers—each sharing the same dark coloring, height and build. They had been friendly rivals who had quickly developed a deep, lasting friendship.

Another chuckle escaped from his lips. Cam was right— Derrick could always count on him to say what others dared not to. He supposed that was one of the reasons he liked him so much. That and the fact that he had always been intensely loyal and dependable—two attributes Derrick valued greatly.

Picking up from his desktop a manila folder containing information on his running mate, he reclined in his plush black-leather chair as he began to leaf through the pages carefully, familiarizing himself with every detail—it was always best to know one's opponent better than oneself.

Curious as raised voices wafted through the closed door to his assistant's office, Derrick wondered what had prompted the argument. Seconds later, the door abruptly swung open to admit a woman he thought he would never see again—Alesha Robinson. Automatically, he stood and his icy eyes locked with her uneasy ones.

"It's all right, Dorothy. I'll see Miss Robinson."

He broke eye contact and nodded curtly in his assistant's direction. The woman glanced angrily at Alesha before firmly closing the door as she left.

He felt as if he had been punched hard in the gut, and it wasn't a pleasant feeling. Alesha Robinson was here, standing a few feet away from him, looking as beautiful as he remembered. Damn her! Damn himself for wanting to quickly close the distance between them, crush her in his arms and fuse his starving mouth with hers.

"What brings you to my door, Alesha?" He silently blessed his voice for sounding coolly controlled, when he felt anything but.

She looked lovelier than he remembered, dressed in a plain white sweater and black slacks. That silky light brown skin of hers begged to be caressed. His fingers itched to oblige. Her thick black hair was pulled back from her face, held in a clasp at her nape. He knew from experience that her hair was soft—softer than anything else this world had to offer. To keep from walking over to her he sat back down in his chair. His eyes then went to her left hand and he wasn't sure whether he was relieved or angered that no engagement or wedding ring rested there.

He continued to survey her hungrily. His eyes drank in every aspect of her face, afraid she was a mirage he had to memorize before she quickly disappeared. He had sometimes wondered if the predicament her brother had gotten himself into would force them to see each other again. He couldn't decide if he was glad or angry that outside pressure had precipitated her return to his life, instead of her own desire.

Her steps faltered as her eyes refamiliarized themselves with Derrick's extremely handsome face—she had almost forgotten the effect the mere sight of him had on her. Since their first chance meeting when they had both stopped to help out at the scene of a multicar accident, he had done strange things to her equilibrium. Although currently his face was hard and foreboding, she remembered how his infectious smile could send her heart racing frantically. He sat before her after all this time like a statue—a beautiful bronze statue, she amended. She recalled how unbending his body had been against the yielding softness of hers—they had been the perfect complement for each other in so many ways. That is, until everything had fallen apart by her own hands.

Her stomach churned queasily and her heart began beating faster and louder in her ears as she stopped just in front of the mahogany desk behind which he sat. Her heart leaped in her chest, but was it from anxiety or happiness at seeing him again? Anxiety, definitely. She was here for business—to ask him for a monumental favor—and for no other reason.

"Mr. Chandler, I need to speak with you." She was pleased with the steadiness of her precise and crisply articulated sentence.

"Why so formal, Alesha?"

"I'm here to discuss business, Mr. Chandler."

She made her voice curt, hoping the tone would end his unnerving inspection of her, which was causing every nerve ending in her body to silently cry out for what she knew from experience was his masterful touch.

He had an almost irrepressible desire to trace his fingers down that silky skin of hers—it couldn't possibly be as soft as he remembered. Yet, instinctively, he knew it was. And her full, faintly tinted brown lips—would kissing her still feel like exquisite torture? Pure heaven, that was how he remembered feeling with her in his arms, and he was sure that observation was still accurate.

She waited uneasily for him to say something, anything. He seemed content to just stare at her. Piercing eyes traveled leisurely over her. What was he thinking? Instinctively, she knew she didn't want to know. Was he as disconcerted by seeing her again as she was at seeing him? She couldn't tell—he seemed cold, almost frigid. She felt like fleeing. Why didn't he say or do something?

"Mr. Chandler?"

"I'm busy."

He was annoyed at himself for behaving like a moon-struck idiot. With great effort, he tore his eyes away from her lovely face and angrily picked up a piece of paper from his desk. It took all his self-restraint to totally ignore her.

She bit back the angry retort that sprang to her lips at his callous actions. One thing she didn't need was to put him on the defensive. She had come to him for help, after all—help that she really didn't deserve.

"Surely you can spare me a few moments." Her tone indicated she would accept nothing less.

He returned the paper to his desk and reluctantly looked at her once again. He mentally scolded himself as he felt his pulse rate increase as she ran her tongue over her upper lip.

"What do you want?"

She silently cursed him for asking a question he obviously knew the answer to. *You might offer me a seat first,* she silently fumed.

"I'm here about Robert."

At the mention of her brother's name, he closed the folder in front of him and motioned for her to be seated in the chair Cam had just vacated. She was painfully aware of the intense focus of his eyes and an emotion she dared not name hidden in their now-frigid depths.

"I was wondering when he would send you in to plead his case." In fact, he had been counting on it.

Her spine stiffened in the soft leather chair and quickly contradicted him. "He didn't. I came on my own to ask you not to press charges against him."

He smiled slightly at that. "You must be as mad as your brother is if you think I'm going to allow him to embezzle $100,000 from my campaign fund and just walk away, free as a bird."

"If you will just let me explain…" She squared her shoulders for a fight she had known was inevitable.

"There's no explanation you have that I am interested in hearing. He took the money—that's all I need to know."

"Regardless, I'm going to tell you the reason my brother *borrowed* the money from you."

His eyes narrowed at the slight edge evident in her tone. What did she have to be bent out of shape about? He was the one who had been wronged by her brother—and by her. What right did she have to treat him as the villain or even to be here asking anything of him?

"*Borrowed?* That's an interesting choice of words. Go on. Tell me, why did your brother *borrow* the money?" He crossed his arms across his broad chest, drawing attention to his muscular physique.

She had the feeling she was wasting her time, but she had to try, for her family's sake. Maybe he would be sympathetic once he learned why Robert had stolen from him. At least she prayed he would.

"Well?" he prompted. "Let me guess. He used it to bet on the ponies." At her blank stare he tried again. "The slots? Sports? Cards?"

"I don't approve of my brother's actions."

"Neither do I and I intend to make my disapproval a matter of public record by filing charges against him." When she remained silent, he continued, "I don't know what you hoped to accomplish by coming here." *Except to remind me of what you needlessly snatched away from me—from both of us—two years ago.*

At this moment neither did she. "I thought I could make you understand."

"Did your brother take my money?"

"Yes." The single word was spoken through gritted teeth.

"Was it his money to take?" He continued in the same no-nonsense courtroom tone.

"You know it wasn't!" She felt like a petulant child he was taking great pleasure in chastising.

Yes, Robert had been wrong to take Derrick's money, but couldn't he show a little compassion? She wondered how much of his unbending attitude had more to do with her past actions than with Robert's thievery.

He had been dreaming of and dreading this moment for two long years. Against his will, he noticed those heavenly eyes of hers sparkle as her temper rose, making her even more beautiful, more desirable. His inappropriate observations annoyed him, making his next words clipped and terse.

"By your own admission, and your brother's, he committed a crime—a felony. What more do I need to understand?" He opened the folder on his desk again, dismissing her.

"Robert's sorry."

He laughed without humor. "I'm sure he is, now that he's been caught."

She was favored with another of his piercing gazes. And somehow resisted the almost irrepressible urge to run as fast and as far from him as her legs could carry her. Even after two years, he still unnerved her completely while he seemed completely unaffected by seeing her again. No, that wasn't true. He was angry, but not at her brother.

"He knows what he did was wrong."

"Well, that's very touching, but it doesn't replace my $100,000, does it?"

He was tired of talking about her brother and would much rather talk about her. What had she done in the two years they had been apart? Had she missed him? Had she second-guessed and third-guessed her fateful decision that had ruined both of their lives? Had she spent sleepless nights wondering where he was and whom he was with? He hoped so. Because against his better judgment, he had thought about her often—about the satisfying relationship they could and should have been enjoying during that time, if only she hadn't destroyed things between them.

He was disheartened to learn that despite her betrayal, she still had the power to move him and make him want to rewrite their story to his satisfaction. Why couldn't they turn back the clock and be meeting coincidentally for the first time? Why did they have to be enemies by virtue of their past relationship?

She remembered him as caring, compassionate and passionate. He had made her feel as if she were the most important person in the world to him. He had made her want to lose herself in him. He had both thrilled and frightened her. Where had that Derrick Chandler gone? Had she somehow destroyed him? If she had, why did that thought disturb her so much?

"I have a lot of work to do."

He needed to get her out of here before he made a complete fool of himself. He didn't like where his memories were leading him or how hard he had to fight to keep himself from touching her. She had nearly ruined his life, and he shouldn't want anything to do with her, should he?

"We'll pay you back."

He sighed fully before giving her his full attention again. "When?"

"As soon as we can." At his dubious look she nearly shouted, "You don't need the money. You don't even miss it!"

"That's not the point."

The coldest eyes she had ever encountered locked on hers. She forced herself not to retreat from his frigid gaze—she knew from past experience he could utterly melt a woman's heart and resistance without even trying. After all this time, he still unnerved her. He made her feel completely raw and vulnerable.

"So, what is the point?"

"Your brother took something that belonged to me. No one does that without suffering the consequences—no one."

The darkening of her eyes let him know that his reference to their relationship was not lost on her.

"How can you be so heartless?"

"Look, I didn't ask your brother to embezzle funds from me, and I didn't ask you to come here today, pleading with me to show mercy to someone who should be—no, who will be—prosecuted."

Why didn't she leave and stop torturing him with her very presence? Lord, what had he done in his life to deserve this?

"I don't know what else to say." She closed her eyes as if seeking divine intervention.

Unable to bear staring at her beauty another second, he swiveled his chair to look out the huge wall-to-wall windows. "You can show yourself out."

She quickly weighed telling him the real reason Robert had embezzled from him. It had nothing to do with gambling, as he had suggested. If he knew Robert's actions were motivated out of love, not greed, would it change his attitude? Would the truth soften his hard heart? She didn't want to bare her soul to him, but if it would save her brother, she didn't have a choice in the matter.

"Won't you please just listen to me?" She faced the back of his head. "Robert's not what you think. He took the money because…"

He swiveled in his chair and held up a hand to forestall the remainder of her explanation. He'd had enough and needed her to leave.

"Alesha, I don't care why Robert took the money—all that matters is that he's an embezzler! Nothing you have to say will change that or make me change my mind about pressing charges against him. I've heard you out, now goodbye."

She quickly stood, realizing she was wasting her time. There was no use in trying to appeal to his better nature. His words made that perfectly clear and she had no intention of giving him the satisfaction of watching her beg.

She snatched up her purse. "What happened to you? How did you become so cold?"

"I am what people like you have made me."

God, she was torturing him. Her very presence tormented him; yet she also made him feel like he hadn't felt in a long, long time, and he was angry and unsettled by that.

"You are what you want to be." She was angry with herself and with her absurd reaction to seeing him again. "I'm sorry I wasted your time." She turned and walked toward the door.

"Alesha?"

He spoke her name softly, almost caressingly. She felt it run down her spine like soothing, exciting fingers of desire—the sensation stopped her in her tracks. She prayed he would stop being so informal with her because the way he said her name—intimately, for her alone—was destroying her. How could a man's voice stroke her in forbidden places so forcefully that she wanted nothing more than to be utterly immersed in him?

She was about to walk out. However, despite his better judgment, he didn't want her to go. What was it about Alesha Robinson that had always sent his blood simmering and then, just as quickly, boiling out of control?

She turned turbulent eyes on him. "We don't have anything else to say to each other."

"You started this, Alesha." He arrogantly lifted an eyebrow before deliberately adding, "And I'm going to finish it."

"We're done."

She turned to leave again, not just because he annoyed

and angered her, but because there was something about Derrick Chandler that was setting off small explosions of awareness within her entire body. Her legs felt wobbly and her heart ached for something that had once been within her grasp and now seemed light-years away. She needed some air; she had to get out of here before she made a complete fool of herself.

"What if I told you that I wouldn't press charges against your brother?" His unexpected words halted her departure.

Had she heard him correctly? She turned and her puzzled gaze encountered his.

"What did you say?"

"I think you heard me."

"Don't toy with me."

An arrogant half smile turned up the corners of his mouth at her chastising tone.

"I never play, unless I choose the game and am assured of victory."

She believed him. He was a man used to getting his way—always, except once with her. She slowly walked back until she was standing in front of his desk again.

"So you're serious about letting Robert off the hook?"

"Yes."

Something in his tone worried her, yet she stood her ground. She had the feeling she would regret her next question, but she had to ask it.

"What do you want in return?"

He stood and slowly walked until he was standing in front of her, so close that their bodies were almost touching. She resisted a strong impulse to turn and run or take the few steps necessary to bring them breast to breast. She faced him unwaveringly as she waited apprehensively for his response.

His eyes roamed over her from head to toe. His blatant

inspection made her feel as if she were a piece of prime meat he was preparing to devour with that wicked mouth of his. Her heart began to beat erratically, not from fear, but from another emotion just as strong.

"Something only you can give me."

"Which is what?" She tilted her head up his tall frame, staring at him uneasily.

He continued to subject her to his slow scrutiny, his eyes lingering long on her moist, slightly parted lips, before lifting to meet her eyes once again. His thorough examination was more disquieting than anything she could have imagined he would say. However, his next words proved her wrong.

"I want you," he answered truthfully.

Chapter 2

He was unblinking and serious as he continued staring into her huge, horrified eyes. After a few seconds of silence, he laughed out loud at her apparent shock. He knew his declaration was the last thing she had expected to hear—it was honestly the last thing he had expected to utter.

She didn't make a move as his brief laughter reverberated in the quiet office before silence returned. He said nothing further and she was unable to respond. Instead, she stared at him unblinkingly, a hand slowly going to her suddenly constricted throat while her heart thudded loudly.

When she finally found her voice it was hushed and strained. "You can't be serious!"

"Can't I?"

She searched his face for signs that he was being facetious, yet found none. Still, he had to be joking. Her other hand moved to her throbbing temple and she tried to laugh dismissively—she couldn't have heard him correctly.

"I must have misunderstood you."

"Did you?" His piercing eyes studied her face carefully.

"Did you say that you want…me?" She forced herself to repeat his ridiculous statement.

"You understand me correctly."

"What do you mean by *want*?" As she articulated the question, she was petrified of his response.

"Want. A transitive verb meaning to desire, to have need for, to crave."

Every word he used to describe his meaning brought vivid pictures to her mind. She swallowed hard to dispel the lump that had rapidly risen in her throat, but to no avail. She stared at the man in front of her, amusement still twinkling in his eyes. Yet, underneath the levity lurked something else—a seriousness that terrified her.

"Are you saying you expect me to…you expect us to… that you want…"

She couldn't force herself to finish that sentence.

"I want you to marry me."

"Marry you?" She sank into the chair she had vacated earlier.

"What did you think I meant?" He studied her distraught face carefully. "Alesha, you didn't think I wanted us to live together in sin, did you?"

"Why do you want to marry me?" She needed a cold compress for her head.

"Because I need a wife." He reclined against his desk.

"You *need* a wife?" She paused before continuing. "Why?"

"According to my campaign manager, it would be good for me to be seen as a family man, and having a wife would equip me with a full-time hostess and date."

He took no pleasure in reiterating Cam's earlier words. Although seeing the woman who had single-handedly ruined his life two years ago in acute distress was very gratifying, indeed.

"How romantic."

Her dry tones made his eyebrow rise slightly—he had no clue how she managed to be sarcastic at a time like this.

"You once made it clear that you didn't want romance from me. Has that changed?"

"Do you always do what others tell you?" She deliberately sidestepped his previous question.

"Never." He firmly shook his head.

"Then why start now?"

She couldn't marry him—or anyone else—under these circumstances. The very idea was absurd!

"I've already answered that question." His face was unreadable.

"Have you?"

Of course, he didn't tell her that until she had walked through his office door, he had no intention of agreeing to Cam's suggestion. Even having put the proposal on the table, he couldn't believe he had done so. Yet, there had always been something about her—something that sparked a chord inside him. He was dismayed to learn his reaction to her hadn't dissipated with the time they had spent apart—time she had forced them to spend apart, he angrily went over in his mind. Despite his better judgment, he still wanted her, and this time he was determined to have her—all of her.

"You don't even like me."

She waited for him to respond but he remained silent. Slowly, he smiled without humor and neither denied nor confirmed her observation. Lord, she wished she had never come here today! She had thought, prayed, that time would have healed old wounds. However, it was painfully apparent it had not. He obviously wanted nothing to do with her, but if that was true, why was he suggesting that they get married?

"'Like' is irrelevant, Alesha."

"How can you say that? How can you suggest that we get married?"

"I told you why already."

He sighed, his tone implying he had no desire to explain his reasons to her again or to justify them to himself.

She lowered her aching head into her hands and willed herself to wake up from this nightmare. However, when she raised her head again, the man in front of her had not vanished, as she had hoped. Rather, his presence was undeniable as he watched her closely.

"You're serious."

"I am." He nodded affirmatively.

"Is this about revenge?" She articulated the only possibility that made any sense to her.

"It's about fate, Alesha."

"Fate?"

Her disdainful, soft echoing of his single prophetic word caused a slight clinching of his jaw—or did she imagine that?

"Yes."

There was uncomfortable silence as each tried to guess what the other was thinking. Each one of them would have been surprised to realize their feelings were more in sync than not. Since parting, they had been destined to come to this point and now they were here. Where their lives ended up from here was a mystery to them both.

"If I agree to your proposal, what do you expect?"

She couldn't believe she was actually contemplating his unorthodox proposition. However, she didn't have a viable alternative—not if she wanted to save her brother.

"Model behavior, public affection. There'll be a great deal

of publicity and we will have to appear happily married and very much in love."

Intense dread spread throughout her entire soul as he rattled off his requirements for a wife as if he were reading from a shopping list. He seemed so hard—had she done that to him? Somehow she knew she had and that hurt more than anything.

"And privately?" She stared into those cool gray eyes of his.

"You'll have to be more specific."

His mocking smile showed that he knew exactly what she referred to. He was getting immense pleasure in needling her.

Taking a deep breath and releasing it on a sigh she elaborated, "This will be a marriage in name only?"

"No, it will not."

She stood up at that, her chest heaving rapidly. "You can't expect me to…for us to…" Her voice trailed off, unable to finish that sentence.

"I can, and I do." His eyes swept appreciatively over her slender, shapely body.

"This is ridiculous, and I'm a fool for even considering your absurd proposition!" She turned and walked rapidly toward the door.

She had a right to be angry at his suggestion. He would have been disappointed if she weren't. He could have picked up the phone and had ten women in his office within a matter of minutes, willing to do whatever he wanted. But he didn't want any other woman. He wanted Alesha. Damn her, he always had. He didn't want to desire her, but he couldn't help it any more than he could help breathing. She intrigued him and he wanted the chance she had denied them both two years ago—to get to know each other better, intellectually and intimately. And, God help him, he didn't care that he was literally blackmailing her to get that opportunity.

He knew he was treading on dangerous ground—he also knew there was absolutely nothing he could do to stop himself. He craved Alesha, and this time he was going to do whatever it took to get her and to make her admit that she wanted him, as well. He wouldn't allow himself to dwell on why her desiring him was of the utmost importance to him.

"You're a smart woman, Alesha." His words halted her progress toward the door. "I think you know this is the only way to save your brother from a sure conviction and a lengthy prison term."

She slowly retraced her steps to stand several feet away from him and tried one last time to reason with him. "Mr. Chandler…"

"Derrick."

"Mr. Chandler." At her refusal to use his first name, she received another one of his mocking smiles, which she had quickly grown to hate. "We're virtually strangers. How can you expect me to marry you and become your wife in every sense of the word?"

"First of all, we are hardly strangers, Alesha. Secondly, when you grow a little older and a little wiser, you'll realize a lot of people do things that they don't want to do every day because their survival or the survival of those closest to them requires it."

"Is that supposed to make your ridiculous offer easier to accept?"

"You might surprise yourself and actually enjoy being married to me." He silently promised himself that would be the case.

She glared at him. "Never!"

"Never say never, Alesha."

He pushed away from the desk and walked over to stand

inches from her. Reaching out his hand, he trailed a finger lightly down her soft cheek, and he nearly groaned at the contact he had longed for since she had first entered his office.

She shuddered at his touch. He merely smiled before his finger moved to trace the outline of her lower lip, causing her flesh to tingle uncontrollably—and not from revulsion. His intense gaze mesmerized her and she was unable to step away, even when he removed his finger from her face. Ravenous eyes slowly, carefully studied every inch of her from the top of her head to the tip of her toes.

It was difficult to take in enough air to properly expand her lungs. Where his fingers had lightly touched, she burned and yearned for something forbidden. The spicy scent of his aftershave wafted up to her nostrils, causing her mouth to water. Despite her qualms, she wanted to be pressed close to his hard body and feel his strong arms around her.

She remembered how those lips had felt against hers and longed to see if her memories were accurate. She swayed toward him slightly, and he smiled even more, yet he made no further attempt to touch her, much to her dismay.

His inaction and her bizarre reaction to him cautioned her to get as far away from him as possible, but her limbs refused to obey the silent command. What was the matter with her? Was he hypnotizing her? Why didn't she turn and run away?

As his eyes admired her beauty, he knew exactly how she felt—he felt the same way, too. It didn't make any sense. This strong attraction between them was the last thing he needed, yet here it was, and he was absolutely helpless to do anything about it, except try to assuage it in hopes of finally purging it forever.

He continued his perusal, eyes moving to the soft curls of her hair, which was pulled away from her face by a clasp. He longed to free the soft tresses he knew would be smooth and silky. Her face showed the barest traces of makeup, yet her type of beauty didn't require any artificial enhancements. Her brown eyes were distraught, her smooth brown skin begged to be touched, her lightly tinted full lips were made for kissing— an invitation he had accepted often in the past and almost consented to now. The bulky sweater she wore hid her attri- butes from his piercing gaze, yet he knew from experience that beneath it was a curvaceous, beautiful body that he was certain would give him the most intense pleasure.

She could barely breathe. His eyes thoroughly destroyed her equilibrium as they sensuously appraised her. She didn't allow herself to speculate on his thoughts—knowing instinc- tively that they would disturb her more than his blatant pe- rusal did. She felt hot, uncomfortable and something else she refused to put a name to.

"You're a beautiful woman, Alesha, but then you've always known that, haven't you?" His voice hardened per- ceptibly as his hand moved up to cup the side of her face, his lips mere inches from hers.

"How dare you!"

His condescending tone propelled her into action. She pushed his hand away from her face and moved several steps back, placing much-needed distance between them. She silently willed her wayward pulse to return to normal— impossible until she was no longer in his presence.

"You'll find that I dare quite a lot."

Silently, he promised himself he would taste those lips again soon enough. For, try as she might to find another way, his was the only course of action she could take to save her brother. He knew that and so did she. He was certain she would agree to his terms.

"What makes you so sure I will be around you long enough to realize anything about you?"

"Because your brother's life is in your hands. I think you'll do anything to save him—even marry me."

She was tempted to tell him to go to hell and take his demented proposal with him. Unfortunately, she knew it wasn't a question of whether she could live with his unreasonable proposal, but rather whether she could live with herself if she didn't even try. This was the only way to save the two people she loved most in this world.

He walked back behind his desk and sat down in his chair. He knew she loved her brother and would do anything to get him out of this horrible situation—her presence here was evidence of that. However, maybe this was too high a price for her to pay. But could she live with herself if she didn't try to help him? Could she live with herself if she did?

"If I agree to marry you, why can't it be a marriage in name only?" To her horror, Alesha blurted out a question that made it obvious she was considering his offer.

All she had to do was take one look at him to answer her own question. Derrick Chandler was a handsome, virile man. He wouldn't go without a woman for days, let alone months—he would never have to. Besides, their past relationship wouldn't allow him to marry her only for show. He wanted what she had denied him—of that, she was certain.

"Alesha, I expect our marriage to be real, because that's the way it has to be."

"Why?" She grudgingly admitted, "You're a handsome man. You can have any woman you want. Why me?"

"Thank you for the compliment." He smiled. "I'm running for public office. I can't be married to you and then be seen around town with other women." He felt compelled to add, "And I have no intention of living the life of a monk."

"But why me?"

"I think you already know the answer to that question."

He reclined in his chair, studying her distraught countenance.

"But…"

"I've got a lot of work to do."

His statement was true. However, more to the point, he needed to get her out of his sight so that his pulse could return to normal. This reunion was more upsetting than he had anticipated. Why, after the hell she had put him through, did she make him feel like a damn schoolboy asking a girl out for a first date?

"I'll give you twenty-four hours to decide. If I haven't heard from you by this time tomorrow, I'll take that as a no and contact the police."

He was proud his voice remained steady, when he felt anything but. He lowered his head and began to study the papers on his desk once again, totally ignoring her.

She opened her mouth to try to convince him to give up this ridiculous idea, but closed it again, realizing the futility of that gambit. He had set his terms and the next move was up to her. Without another word, she turned and left, slamming the door forcefully behind her.

He leaned back in his chair and let out his breath on a loud sigh. Tense fingers loosened his tie a bit. She hadn't left a moment too soon. Why had seeing her again affected him so profoundly? It was because he hadn't been with a woman in a while—that was it. That had to be it.

He shook his head in satisfaction and returned his eyes to the manila folder on his desk. After a few seconds, he gave up trying to concentrate on anything other than anxiously awaiting Alesha's return tomorrow, even though he already knew what her answer would be.

Alesha entered her mother's home and forced herself to appear happy and carefree, even though her heart was heavy, laden with the ultimatum Derrick Chandler had just issued to her a few hours earlier. Despite the dark cloud of gloom that hung over her, she could not risk letting her mother know she was upset—her mom had already had one heart attack a year and a half ago. Alesha would make sure she didn't find out about the events currently transpiring in her children's lives.

"Mom?" She searched for her mother as she walked through the house, throwing her coat onto a chair in the hallway.

"I'm in here, darling."

Following her mother's voice, Alesha made her way toward the bedroom. Once there, she was extremely glad to see that, for once, her mother was taking her doctor's advice, reclining in bed, though she was fully dressed.

Alesha walked over and kissed her mother's cheek warmly before perching lightly on the side of the bed. "How are you feeling?"

"I'm fine, darling." Barbara Robinson smiled as her daughter eyed her carefully.

Alesha marveled at what a beautiful lady her mother was. At age fifty-six, her black hair was sprinkled with gray and was cut short, attractively framing her oval face. Alesha smiled lovingly at her and silently vowed she would do everything in her power to make sure her mother stayed healthy and happy.

"What have you been up to today, dear?"

"Just the usual." She smiled. "Have you been following doctors' orders?"

"Yes, dear. I've been behaving." Barbara rolled her brown eyes heavenward. "Honestly, I don't know how much more rest and relaxation I can stand."

"Mother…"

"I know. I know." Barbara sighed heavily and then smiled slightly.

"You just continue to be a good girl, and Bobby and I will be around to make sure that you do." Alesha grasped her hand and surreptitiously took her pulse.

Before her mother could respond, the front door opened and closed and Robert's voice called out, "Mom? Alesha?"

"We're in here, Bobby." Alesha walked over to the bedroom door.

Seconds later her brother found them. He was about two inches taller than Alesha, though they both possessed the same café-au-lait coloring. Entering the bedroom, he bent down and placed an affectionate kiss on his mother's forehead, brought out a beautiful bouquet of colorful flowers from behind his back and handed them to her. Alesha noted and engraved in her memory the happy look on her mother's face. She would do anything to keep her that way forever.

"For the most beautiful lady in the world." He smiled as he straightened to stand beside the bed.

"They're lovely. Thank you." Barbara brought the bouquet to her nose and sniffed appreciatively.

"Let me get you a vase for them." Alesha took the flowers from her mother's hands and glanced pointedly at Robert, silently communicating that he should follow her.

"Is there anything sinful to eat in the kitchen?" Robert's brown eyes twinkled mischievously.

"Well, you know I'm not allowed," Barbara complained, "but, there is some chocolate cake."

"Perfect!" Robert smacked his lips in anticipation.

"Mother, what are you doing with a cholesterol-filled chocolate cake?" Alesha quickly returned from the doorway to glance at her mother disapprovingly.

"Relax, darling. I didn't eat any. Antonia came by today and left it. I couldn't turn her down, now, could I?"

"I suppose not." Alesha sighed before adding, "I'll be sure to take it with me when I leave—just to remove the temptation."

"Sorry, Mom, but you know how she is." Robert smiled sympathetically.

"I do, indeed."

"Don't you two start ganging up on me." She wagged her finger at them good-naturedly. "Come on and get your cake." Alesha pushed her brother ahead of her out of the room.

Robert's eyes focused on the cake sitting on the counter. "Mmm, this looks great!"

When the door was safely shut behind them, Alesha spoke slowly and calmly, "I went to see Derrick Chandler today."

"What?" He whirled to face her.

"Shh! I don't want Mom to hear you." Her voice was barely above a whisper, but firm.

"Why did you go see him? I thought you were going to stay out of this." He'd lowered his voice, yet his tone remained angry.

"You decided that, not me." She filled a vase with water. "I had to see if I could make him listen to reason."

"Did you?" He knew the answer before she replied.

Turning her back on him to cut a slice of cake, she replied cryptically, "In a way."

Robert walked around to stand in front of her, placing a finger under her chin and lifting her eyes level with his own. "What exactly does that mean?"

"He agreed not to press charges against you." She hoped he would leave it at that for now.

"If…" He knew there had to be an *if.*

She gave him his cake, took a deep breath and released it slowly before replying, "If I agree to marry him."

Robert nearly dropped the plate onto the countertop. He stared at his sister, horrified.

When he spoke, his voice was barely controlled. "Please, tell me you're joking."

She walked away from him to stare out the kitchen window. "I wish I was, but you know I wouldn't joke about this."

"Damn him!"

Alesha quickly walked to his side and placed a restraining hand on his arm. "Be quiet! Remember, Mom is just down the hall. We can't let her know what's going on."

When he spoke next, his tone was lower, but just as enraged. "I hope you told him what he could do with his idiotic proposal!"

She remained silent, lowering her gaze from his. Robert's heart skipped a beat at her demeanor.

"Alesha, you didn't agree to this insanity, did you?" He watched her closely.

She raised her eyes and responded truthfully, "He's given me until tomorrow to decide."

"There's nothing to decide. There's no way I'm going to allow you to sell yourself to him to save me! I knew what I was doing when I took that money. I'll suffer the consequences for it."

"Bobby, even though you were wrong to embezzle from him, I won't let you go to jail if there's anything I can do to stop it."

"I won't let you do this." He was equally unyielding.

"You can't stop me." She shook her head. "If Mother finds out what you did and you're sent to prison, the shock would kill her—you know that."

"But, Alesha…"

"No buts." She placed silencing fingers on his lips. "I can't risk losing either of you. If that means I have to marry Derrick Chandler, then I'll marry him." She wished she felt as calm as she sounded.

"You're a wonderful sister, but I will not allow you to marry someone you don't love to save me."

He turned and left the kitchen. She ran after him, but reached the front door only in time to see his car pulling away.

She closed the door and sighed. Her decision was already made—it had been the very second Derrick had made her the offer. She would do whatever it took to save her loved ones, even if it meant sacrificing herself in the process.

Cam's mouth was wide open in shock. "What did you say?"

Derrick laughed heartily before reiterating, "I'm getting married."

"To whom? When? How?" Cam shook his head vigorously as he fought to comprehend his friend's unexpected announcement.

"To Alesha Robinson and very soon." He chuckled at Cam's understandable confusion.

"Who?" He frowned as he racked his brain to put a face to the name he instinctively knew he should recognize.

"Robert Robinson's sister." Derrick played with the slender stem of his wineglass.

"Robert Robinson?" Then leaning closer to Derrick and lowering his voice so as not to be overheard, he asked, "The dude who embezzled from your campaign?"

"The one and only." Derrick nodded before bringing the glass of wine to his lips.

"Have you lost your mind?"

Cam's question was relayed so earnestly that Derrick couldn't refrain from laughing out loud again. He had laughed more today than he had in a very long time.

"You're the one who said I needed a wife." His gray eyes twinkled with merriment.

"I know, but…"

"Cam, this is perfect." His countenance was that of a kid set loose and given free rein in a candy shop. "It's a business arrangement, no emotional entanglements—just a plain, simple agreement that I will end once it's served its purpose."

It was also an opportunity he had waited two years for, a chance to exorcise the demons Alesha's abrupt departure had left in her wake. He was certain once he had some answers, and maybe even a measure of retribution, he would be able to permanently purge the tenacious memories of their past association from his mind and heart once and for all.

"Which is what?"

"To help me get elected, of course." Derrick sighed loudly. Boy, was Cam being dense tonight!

Cam's eyes took on a seriousness that was relayed by his next words. "Sometimes when we think we have something figured out, it takes on a life of its own and goes in directions we never expected."

"What am I going to do with you?" Derrick raised his eyes heavenward in exasperation at his friend's prophetic statement. "If I don't do what you suggest, I never hear the end of it, and if I take your advice, I get prophecies of doom and gloom."

"When I suggested marriage, I wasn't referring to the farce you're contemplating." Cam took a much-needed gulp of his wine.

"Never again." Derrick adamantly shook his head.

"Derrick, you're my best friend. I'd like to see you happy." He lowered his glass to the table.

"I appreciate that, buddy, and I am happy. I'm also going to marry Alesha—on my terms."

"She's agreed to this?"

"Not yet, but she will tomorrow." His voice was confident as he fingered the slender stem of his wineglass.

"How can you be so sure?" He couldn't shake the nagging feeling that there was more to his friend's inane proposal than met the eye.

"She doesn't have a choice. It's the only way to save her brother."

"She might surprise you. Maybe she'll decide the price is too high to pay." Cam played devil's advocate.

"She won't." His short response was delivered confidently.

"Why won't she?"

"As I said before, she doesn't have a choice." Derrick hadn't noticed his tone turn somewhat cold.

"I get the feeling you know this lady—very well. Have you met her before?"

"Two years ago." Derrick silently cursed himself for slipping up in front of Cam, of all people.

"Wait a minute." His eyes reflected understanding. "Is this the same Alesha you dated briefly?"

"She is." He didn't see any reason in denying it.

"The one you abruptly stopped seeing, which sent you into one of the longest and foulest depressed moods of your life?"

"You're exaggerating." Derrick took a suddenly much-needed swig of his drink. Cam wasn't exaggerating. If anything, he was being kind.

"No, I'm not." Intense eyes bore into his. "You wouldn't talk about her—not even to me."

"There was nothing to say."

"Really? I didn't believe you then and I don't now."

"Cam, we dated once or twice, it didn't work out and we ended it." He silently cursed the nerve in his jaw that was pulsing erratically.

"We both know there's more to it than that." He refused to be silenced. "I was there, remember? I know what happened to you shortly after the breakup." At Derrick's continued silence, Cam asked, "Are you out for revenge?"

"Don't be ridiculous." Cam's astute observations and Derrick's own contradictory feelings as far as Alesha was concerned made him uneasy, although his words appeared confident.

"I think you should reconsider this."

"There's nothing to reconsider. I'm going to marry Alesha and that's that." Derrick's tone was firm and final.

"Derrick, are you sure…"

"Yes, absolutely."

"How do you plan to pull this off?" He knew when it was useless to try to reason with his friend, and this, unfortunately, was one of those times. "Alesha will be in the limelight *all* the time. I assume you realize the public must perceive your marriage as real."

"Of course." Derrick shook his head in agreement. "In public, we'll appear as a couple very much in love. You, Alesha, Robert and I are the only ones who will know about our arrangement."

"And what about privately?" Cam leaned forward, studying his friend closely. "What do you expect, and—more importantly—want from Alesha privately?"

"Mr. Chandler, it's time for you to take your place onstage." Both men turned in the direction of the man who interrupted them.

"Certainly."

Derrick smiled and stood, grateful to escape his friend's last probing question.

Chapter 3

The following morning Derrick was engrossed in work when the intercom buzzed. Without being told, he knew who was here to see him and his heartbeat quickened.

"Yes?"

"Sir, Ms. Robinson is here to see you."

"Please send her in."

Standing, he walked over to the door seconds before it opened, admitting Alesha. She opened her mouth to speak and then closed it again. He remained silent. This was her show.

She took a deep breath, released it and, before she lost her nerve, said, "I'll marry you."

"I see."

"You don't seem very surprised." She raised an arched eyebrow.

He ushered her over to a chair in front of his desk and then perched on the edge. "I'm not. You didn't have much of a choice."

"No, I didn't."

She didn't try to hide the resentment in her voice before angrily lowering her gaze from his. She was uncomfortable with him so close and wished he would move away. Yet, even as the thought entered her mind, she realized she would have to get used to being in much closer proximity than this to him—after all, they would soon be husband and wife. At that thought, she shuddered visibly.

"Are you cold?" His hand rose toward her.

"No."

Sensing her discomfort, he dropped his hand to his side, stood up, walked behind his desk and sat down. He smiled slightly as she breathed a silent sigh of relief.

"Do you have any questions?" He leaned back in his chair and studied her somber expression.

"Such as?"

"In case you've forgotten in the time we've been apart, my age, religion, likes, dislikes, etc."

"Tell me whatever you want."

He smiled slightly at her tone, which infuriated her. Why did he always act as if she amused him? He was so frustrating!

"To refresh your memory, I'm thirty-six, born and raised in Washington. I was an only child. My parents are deceased. My favorite food is Italian." He rambled off facts she was mortified to realize she still remembered.

"I'll make a mental note of all that."

"You do that." He leaned forward. "Let's discuss specifics, shall we?"

What he really wanted to do was touch her—to experience the softness of her skin for a much longer duration than yesterday's brief contact. He wanted to release her bountiful mane from its clasp, bury his face in the feathery soft tresses and see firsthand if they were as silky and soft as he remembered. He wanted to devour those pouting, luscious lips…

"All right, but I have one condition."

He raised an eyebrow. "You're in no position to make any demands."

His arrogance was born out of desperation rather than disdain. He didn't want to be cold with her, but it was either that or make a complete fool of himself by acting on his longings.

The hair on her neck stood on end at his insufferable tone. However, her voice was measured when she responded. "I realize that, but I really must insist on this one."

"What is it?"

"My mother must believe our marriage is real. I don't want to upset her."

Did she imagine the softening of his features at her sincere confession? That was ridiculous. He hated her and marriage to him would be his ultimate revenge.

Much to her surprise, he agreed. "Fair enough. Everyone has to believe our marriage is real—that includes your mother." At her continued silence, he said, "Anything else?"

"Yes." She paused, trying to find the best way to phrase her next request.

"Well…" He drummed his fingers on the desktop, not out of frustration or impatience, but to keep them from trying to touch her.

"I'd like us to be engaged for a few months so that my mother will buy our relationship."

His fingers immediately stilled. "Impossible."

"Why not?"

"I have a little over a year until the election. We must be married as soon as possible." He paused, considering a compromise. "I can give you a month at the most."

What he didn't tell her was that he doubted he could wait longer than that to quench his burning desire for her—he prayed he wouldn't go mad trying. Damn her and him! Why, after all that had transpired between them in the past, did she still have the power to unnerve him the way no other woman ever had?

"This will never work, you know." She shook her head.

"It will work." He smiled confidently. "Wait and see."

"If you say so." Her tone belied her skepticism.

"Do I need to remind you what I expect from this marriage?" His gray eyes bore into hers.

Nervously wringing her hands in her lap, she warily met his gaze. "No."

"You're positive?" He stood and walked slowly toward her until he reached her side.

"I'm positive." She also stood to be on a more level plane with him.

"Don't say you didn't know what to expect."

"Is there anything else?" She unflinchingly met his determined gaze.

"Just three things."

He motioned for her to resume her seat, which she did reluctantly. He perched on the desk in front of her. He wished she would stop looking so sad, as if she were being handed a death sentence.

"What are they?"

"First of all, I don't know whether you're on birth control or not, but if not, you will need to start immediately."

She felt her cheeks grow warm at his intimate demands. How could he expect her to discuss such things with him! His words made her fully aware of what their relationship would be, and all she could do was stare at him in embarrassment.

"Since this is only a business arrangement, neither of us needs or wants any unnecessary complications."

She found her voice and whispered resentfully, "Why is it always the woman's responsibility?"

"Well, I can't speak for other men, but as for me, I dislike the feel of a condom. I don't want anything to come between me and…"

"I'll take care of it."

She blushed hotly at his blatant admission, wanting to get off this subject as soon as possible. She reached up to touch her suddenly constricted throat.

He smiled at her as his eyes moved down her face to rest on her slightly quivering, espresso-colored lips, before traveling slowly back up to encounter her distraught eyes, and his smile deepened. However, there was something else present in her eyes—a deep longing, an expectation, a need. He saw it there, silently admitting that it echoed similar smoldering feelings within him.

She really was delicious. He had a feeling he was going to enjoy being married to her very much—while it lasted. He forced himself to mentally add the last observation and forcefully reminded himself that theirs would only be a brief alliance to purge her from his life once and for all. He didn't want or need anything more permanent.

"What's number two?" Her voice was breathless as she brought a hand up to her suddenly burning cheeks.

"It concerns your job." His tones took on an ominous ring.

"What about it?"

"You'll have to give it up."

Her eyes changed from wary to disbelieving to angry as she glared at him. He felt an absurd desire to pull her in his arms and tell her everything was going to be all right.

"Give up nursing? Why?"

"The main reason for this marriage is so that I will have a ready-made hostess. You'll have to be available at a moment's notice. That's hardly possible for someone in your profession."

"I love my work. I don't suppose that matters to you."

"I understand, and I know that you're very good at it." The sympathy in his voice was overshadowed by the sacrifice he was asking her to make.

"How do you know that?"

"Have you forgotten that I saw you in action when we first met at the accident scene?"

She remembered everything about their intense first meeting. It had been a multivehicle accident that both had stopped to help at. He had been strong, unshakable at the sight of blood and torn flesh and had been very receptive to taking orders from a woman.

"No, I haven't forgotten."

He had watched the play of emotions flit across her beautiful face. He wanted to ask if she remembered every detail of their breakup, too, but that was unnecessary. Finally having her in his presence again, he wanted to know why she had shut him out of her life. To this day, her rejection still rankled him, and that was one thing he was fighting tooth and nail to keep from her.

"What else do I have to give up?"

"Are you agreeing to my second condition, or do we end this right here?" His hooded eyes watched her carefully.

"Yes, what's your third condition?"

Her words should have thrilled him, yet instead they cut through him like a hot knife. He didn't know why he had the urge to apologize to her or why her understandable unhappiness made him so unhappy. He reminded himself that this was only a business arrangement, not an emotional entanglement. Either she agreed to his terms, or he would call the deal off and have her brother prosecuted. He wasn't forcing her to marry him. She had a choice—one he knew she wouldn't take—but a choice nonetheless.

"My third condition is this."

Unable to hold himself in check another second, he stood and slid one strong arm beneath her coat around her slender waist, pulling her closer as his other hand moved to the back of her head, pulling her lips toward his.

"What do you think you're doing?" She pressed her hands against his solid chest, trying unsuccessfully to break free from his unwelcomed embrace.

"You'll have to do better than this, or you won't convince anyone that you're madly in love with me." He lowered his head toward hers.

She continued to struggle in vain. However, when his lips were mere inches from hers, one hand released her silky tresses from their confining clasp, allowing the shoulder-length tendrils to slide over his fingers as he pulled her mouth toward his. As he had known it would, her hair felt like silk against his fingers. His appreciative eyes swept her distraught face thoroughly.

"I prefer your hair loose, remember?"

"Mr. Chandler, I don't care what you prefer."

"Oh, but you will care." His softly voiced promise caught in her throat as he once again instructed her to use his first name.

"No." She strained against his ironclad embrace.

"You'll say my name on moans of passion in just a few seconds."

"Never."

She knew her denial lacked believability because her voice was breathless, and a strange feeling began forming in her stomach at his nearness.

"We'll see."

Before she could respond, determined lips closed over hers in a strong kiss. His mouth was warm and inviting, not cold and repulsive as she had hoped it would be. She had known from past experience that his lips would feel like this—wonderful and vital. Days, months and years were swept away by his sensual mouth as it thoroughly refamiliarized itself with hers.

Her heart began to beat rapidly—not in fear, but in arousal. She moaned in protest to her thoughts and his actions, and her mouth parted slightly in shock and surrender.

That was all the encouragement he needed. He took full advantage of her surprise, sliding his tongue between her lips to slip into the honeyed recesses beyond. He continued to masterfully taste every centimeter, every tantalizing crevice of the bounty he had uncovered.

Her hands moved to his shoulders to push him away, yet stopped there, resting instead. Did she really want to escape? That simple yet complex question rolled around in her dazed mind. A hundred confusing sensations bombarded her entire being as Derrick continued his mind-shattering caresses. She hadn't expected to be blown away by a simple kiss after two years. However, there was nothing remotely simple about Derrick's kiss, or her disheartening responses to the masterful, sensual onslaught he was unleashing on her.

One of his hands slid languidly down her back to rest on her hip, pressing her closer against his hard length as his mouth continued to plunder hers. Her eyes were half closed, as sensation after sensation—each an awakening, each frightening and intensely pleasurable—began to overpower her self-proclaimed resentment of the man whose arms she was nearly melting into. The hands resting on his shoulders flexed and then tightened their grip as she resisted an almost irrepressible urge to entwine them around his neck and press herself even closer against his hard length.

Never in a million years would she have dreamed she would be in Derrick's arms again, enjoying his kisses and caresses. Yet, here she was, wanting, almost reveling, in this intimate contact with a man she should hate for blackmailing her into marriage. She hadn't bargained for this. She hadn't expected to still be attracted to him physically. How could this be? Even as the question arose in her mind, she admitted that he was the only man who had ever elicited such thorough, satisfying, mind-boggling passion from her and, to her dismay, he had lost none of his skills when it came to arousing her hidden desires.

His lips slowly drew apart from hers, despite a slight moan of protest from her, and he huskily commanded, "Say my name."

"No."

Her voice was soft and tortured. For the life of her she didn't know where the strength to articulate came from.

Her refusal made him pull her closer, until she felt every hard inch of his wonderful body pressed intimately, maddeningly against her own. Unapologetic hands slipped beneath her sweater to touch the satiny heated flesh of her back, and she thought she would die from something very close to rapture when he pulled her yet closer.

Playful lips nipped at hers before sliding down her jaw to burrow into her softly scented throat. She gasped as he raked his strong teeth across her skin, and then his tongue traced the outline of her collarbone before he raised his head to stare into her confused, dazed, passion-glazed eyes.

"Say my name." As he softly repeated his previous command, one of his hands moved to her hair, his fingers entangling there.

He was as surprised as she looked at the shock of pleasure

holding and kissing her elicited within him. It was as if the damnable time they had spent apart had never occurred. He pulled her mouth to within centimeters of his. His tongue skimmed her lips lightly before retreating again, refusing to give her what she wanted until she yielded to his demands.

"Say it."

His warm breath intermingled with hers as the hand at her back moved to rest between her shoulder blades before sliding back down her satiny flesh. He needed to hear his name on her lips, whispered with passion before he muffled the sound with his ravenous, hungry mouth.

She closed her eyes briefly before acquiescing. She spoke so softly he thought he had imagined it.

"Derrick."

"Again." He softly kissed her quivering lips—lips that were as addictive as anything he had ever known.

"Derrick," she reiterated on a sigh, and then on a moan, as he had foretold, as his lips and hands continued to lightly caress her. "Derrick."

The last thing she saw was his smile—not of triumph, but of understanding—before her eyes closed once her mouth was finally, ravenously recaptured. He kissed her again and again and she prayed he would stop soon before she begged him never to. His lips were like a magnet, attracting her against her will, holding her mesmerized, unable to break away.

The last thing she wanted was to escape from this intensely pleasurable embrace. Her mind screamed out for her to put as much distance between them as possible, yet her body craved closer contact with his—much closer. How could she remotely tolerate kisses from a man who was single-handedly ruining her career and stealing her freedom? What in the name of God was wrong with her? She couldn't begin to formulate an answer anymore than she could deny that she craved and enjoyed his kisses, almost to the point of self-destruction.

After endless, sweet minutes of torture, his firm, strong, warm lips dragged themselves from hers. She fought the urge to pull his mouth back to hers and gradually opened her confused, embarrassed eyes to find him staring at her with an unreadable expression. Her cheeks were warm, her lips were trembling, and she could just die from the embarrassment.

He smiled slightly, one of his fingers trailing over her quivering, moist lips as he huskily said, "I think our arrangement will be very profitable and pleasurable—for the both of us."

She pushed away from him at his words, partly in anger and partly just needing to escape from his overpowering presence and from her own desires. She needed to get out of there! This time he let her go, and this time she nearly ran out the door, not stopping to look back—certain she would find him following her.

Had she turned to stare at him, she would have seen echoing arousal, disbelief and dismay etched on his handsome features. Her retreating pace accelerated until she was safely out of his maddening reach—for the moment.

A few days later, she sat beside Derrick in one of the most upscale jewelry shops in Washington. Even though she had insisted she didn't want an expensive ring, he had been adamant that she would wear a ring to be marveled at, for appearances' sake.

She hadn't seen him since the devastating kisses in his office, yet the time apart had done nothing to ease her mind, nor squelch her anticipation of their next encounter. She didn't know what was the matter with her or who she was becoming. Even more unnerving, when she was with him, she wasn't sure she even cared.

"What about this one?" He held up a three-carat brilliant-cut diamond solitaire, set in a split band of platinum.

"It's beautiful but…" She carefully took the exquisite ring from his fingers.

"But what?" He eyed her closely.

"It's too expensive—all these rings are."

She placed the exquisite ring back onto the black velvet cover on the table next to the matching wedding band, which was inset with a carat of diamonds halfway around it, and the man's wedding band, which was a thick circle of brightly polished platinum with scrollwork over its surface.

"Nonsense." He smiled at her assertion. "Besides, when this is all over, you'll have something to sell that will bring you a nice piece of change."

She turned hurt and angry eyes on him. When she spoke, her voice trembled slightly, "Why did you say that to me? You know I'm not marrying you for your money."

The somewhat mocking smile on his face slowly faded as he realized he had hurt her. Part of him had meant to, but he derived no pleasure from the fact that he had succeeded. Instead he felt miserable about it. He wasn't a cruel person and there was no reason for him to act like one.

"Alesha, I'm sorry."

He cupped her sad face between his hands tenderly—more tenderly than he would have imagined himself capable of.

"Are you?"

Her whispered words implied she didn't believe him. She was, however, oddly moved by his unexpected and uncharacteristic apology.

"Yes, I am. Very." Soothing fingers lightly rubbed over her cheekbones.

"You wanted to hurt me." Her voice was barely audible.

"Maybe I did," he admitted softly, eyes never breaking contact with hers.

Despite knowing the reason, she would have asked him why. However, his lips lowered toward and captured hers. He kissed her softly, soothingly at first, but as if the barest contact with her mouth inflamed him, the kiss soon became passionate, and the hands on her face pulled her closer to his ravaging mouth.

Her own hands slid up to rest on his chest as she allowed herself to enjoy the wondrous sensations washing over her body as Derrick's expert lips and tongue continued to mate hotly with her own. He had to be the best kisser in the world, she dazedly thought as, against her will, his mouth slowly lifted from hers.

"Why are you always kissing me?" Her question was formed breathlessly against his lips, which still rested lightly against hers.

"Because I enjoy it and so do you." He earnestly traced the outline of her moist lower lip with his tongue, feeling her quiver. "You always did, remember?"

She did, but she wouldn't tell him that. She realized she didn't have to articulate it. He knew—just as he knew she wanted him to kiss her again and again.

"Derrick, I…"

"What?"

"Nothing." She shook her head, not knowing what to say—or to confess.

His eyes bore into hers as he continued, "Your mouth is made for kissing—soft, moist, sweet and tempting—like a ripe, juicy, luscious strawberry. It begs to be stroked, caressed…consumed." He ended his erotic assertion on a ravenous whisper before his lips slowly tasted hers again.

His sensuous, hypnotic words stole her breath. Her heart

began to beat erratically at his nearness and the vivid imagery he had created within her head. She couldn't have responded if she wanted to, and it was just as well because, as if to prove his point, his lips pulled at hers, tasting them, before closing over hers again. Of its own volition, her right hand moved up his chest to his shoulder, to rest at the nape of his neck as he continued his exploration of her quivering mouth.

His hands moved to her back as his lips continued to kiss hers. She sighed in pleasure and her mouth opened wider as he continued to taste the sweet nectar he found within.

She had forgotten where they were and so had he, until a loud cough interrupted what had become a heated, passionate embrace. To her disappointment, Derrick's lips reluctantly slid from hers as they both turned toward the sound.

"Excuse me." The salesman's embarrassed countenance greeted them as they simultaneously turned passion-glazed eyes in his direction.

Alesha quickly lowered her gaze from his, so embarrassed she would have moved away, yet Derrick's hands on her back wouldn't allow her to. As always, he seemed completely in control of the situation.

"Forgive us—we're very much in love." He smiled at the salesman, who nodded in understanding.

"Of course, it's such a joy to see." The man beamed at the two of them. "Have you decided on rings?"

"Yes, we'll take these." Derrick handed the man the most expensive set in the case, the one with the trillion-cut solitaire. Then, turning loving eyes to her, he said, "Right, darling?"

"Yes." She was surprised anything audible passed from her passion-constricted throat.

"Excellent choice, sir, madam." The man barely contained his enthusiasm. "Shall I wrap them for you?"

"The wedding rings, but she'll wear the engagement ring." Derrick lifted the solitaire off its black-velvet base and placed it onto Alesha's finger before lifting her hand to his lips and kissing it as his eyes bore deeply into hers. If she didn't know better, she would think he loved her dearly.

"The perfect ring for the perfect fiancée." He lowered her hand from his lips, but continued to stare into her bewildered eyes.

"Let's just see how that fits." The salesman took Alesha's hand from Derrick's to inspect the ring. "It looks like an excellent fit. How does it feel?"

"It—it's fine." Alesha's eyes were still mesmerized by Derrick's.

He reclaimed her hand, kissing it again before he abruptly stood. "Darling, I'll be right back." Then he followed the ecstatic salesman over to the register.

Once alone, she placed sweaty palms against her burning cheeks. Uneasily, she contemplated what had just transpired between her and the enigma who was her fiancé. Trembling fingers lightly touched her moist, thoroughly kissed lips.

God, what was happening to her? With confused, forlorn eyes, she stared furtively across the room at Derrick, and she felt a twinge of longing in the pit of her stomach. Unashamedly, she wished he were still seated beside her, kissing and caressing her. She glanced down at the twinkling diamond on her left hand and, for a moment, wished her engagement to Derrick was real instead of simply a business arrangement. She shook her head to dispel the vivid longing that suddenly invaded her soul for something forbidden and terribly exciting, which she feared only Derrick could give her.

She was treading on very dangerous ground and must take extreme care not to think of Derrick as anything other than a means to an end. Marrying him would ensure her brother's freedom and her mother's continued ignorance of what Robert had done—nothing else good would come from their union. She had to keep repeating the suddenly distasteful truth that he was using her, as she was him. There were no emotional entanglements or involvements as far as they were concerned and she didn't want any. If only she could believe her silent assertions.

Why couldn't she hate him? She wanted to—things would be so much simpler if she did. But she didn't. Perhaps it was the realization that her still-unexplained actions were the basis for his angry feelings toward her. She understood his anger toward her better than he did.

In her mind, two years ago she had done what was necessary when she had ended things between them. Yet the decision still plagued her, even after all this time. Therefore, how could it not affect Derrick the same way? Besides, Robert had stolen an enormous amount of money from him, and he had a legitimate right to want to extract retribution from both of them, didn't he?

She knew he didn't love her. At times, she was certain his feelings for her leaned more toward hatred. However, there was no denying that he wanted her physically, and she instinctively knew he wasn't happy about that. She knew Derrick wanted nothing to do with her on a permanent basis, just as she wanted nothing to do with him. However, she was forced to admit to herself that she came to life in his arms as she did at no other time.

After two years, he still had a power over her body and sometimes her mind, but she silently vowed that she would not let that power extend to her heart. She couldn't afford to lower her guard with him because their relationship—although once very real—was now only a sham, a farce, an emotionless business arrangement. She must never let herself forget that, because if she did, she would truly be in danger of losing her soul.

Chapter 4

"Is your sweet young man coming for dinner tonight?"

Barbara Robinson smiled at her daughter as they sat in the living room of her house. Robert glanced up from his magazine with a scowl, but made no comment.

"Yes, Mom." Alesha grimaced slightly at her mother's choice of words.

Of all the adjectives she would use to describe Derrick Chandler, *sweet* was certainly not one of them. She would have chosen words like *gorgeous, enigmatic* and *arousing*. She grudgingly admitted she would also add the word *kind* to the list of adjectives. For he had been unbelievably kind to her mother in the past two weeks since she had been told about their imminent marriage and, if she were completely honest, kind to her, as well. Her mother had taken to Derrick remarkably well—too well for Alesha's taste.

"I'm so happy for you, darling." Barbara's sincere words broke into her disturbing thoughts. "I like Derrick. He's a good man—strong, dependable—and very handsome." She tagged on the last comment with a laugh.

Yes, he was devilishly handsome and sexy, Alesha admitted. Yet, there was also a hardness to him that hadn't been present years earlier. She knew she was the one responsible for its creation—a source of guilt to her. Now she wondered if she could also possibly be the one to eradicate it.

"Thanks, Mom. I'm glad you like him." She forced a lightness in her voice she was far from feeling.

"How could I not like him after seeing how he dotes on you?" Barbara beamed proudly.

Alesha smiled at her, but remained silent. Yes, Derrick certainly played the role of the doting fiancé very well—too well for her taste. The memory of the many kisses they had shared over the past few weeks made her cheeks burn with embarrassment. Kisses? That was a tame word to describe their passionate, near-consummated encounters since they'd become engaged. She blushed hotly at the memories.

He was *always* touching and kissing her, always raising her to a fever pitch, yet refusing to go any further. Though she should have been happy about that, she was disturbed to admit she was not. Irrationally, she wanted to know the fulfilling promise his smoldering kisses hinted at and truthfully believed he was trying to drive her insane with unfulfilled longing. Much to her dismay, she couldn't wait to experience the conclusion of Derrick's devastating caresses and kisses. Instinctively, she knew it would surpass anything she had experienced in her life.

Dear Lord, she couldn't believe her thoughts! What was the matter with her? What had he done to her in so short a time and what would he do to her sense of self once they were married? Married! Her mind slowly repeated that word. Soon, very soon, she would be Mrs. Derrick Chandler. Her life would definitely change then, but for better or for worse?

Alesha stood as the doorbell chimed. "I'll get it."

She reached and opened the front door to Derrick.

"Hello, sweetheart." He smiled lovingly at her.

His easy use of the endearment caused her heart to somersault. He handed her one of the bouquets of flowers he held in his hands. With his free arm, he encircled her waist and placed a firm, passionate kiss on her soft, moist, waiting lips.

When he released her, she was breathing erratically. He whispered in her ear before escorting her into the living room with his arm still around her waist.

"Try to look happy."

She nearly told him she didn't have to try to look happy—she *was* happy to see him. Of course, that was only because he had presented a reason to escape from her disquieting thoughts, wasn't it?

"Derrick, how lovely to see you again."

"Thank you, Barbara. It's nice to see you, too." He released Alesha and bent to kiss her mother's cheek while handing her the other bouquet of flowers. "Hello, Robert."

"Derrick." Robert's voice was clipped. "Excuse me. I need to make a call." He shook Derrick's hand before walking out of the room.

Alesha sighed as she sat down in a chair near her mother. She could see why her mother liked Derrick—he was absolutely charming. He did know how to make a person feel special.

"Thank you. These are lovely." Barbara sniffed the flowers appreciatively.

"I'm glad you like them." Derrick straightened and sat on the arm of Alesha's chair, his arm draped along the back.

She tried to listen to the small talk going on around her, but Derrick's nearness was making that impossible. His arm moved from the back of the chair to rest on the nape of her neck, absently massaging her tense flesh. Instead of sooth-ing her, it had the opposite effect. He lightly caressed her soft skin, driving her to distraction. She wouldn't give him the satisfaction of knowing how much his actions unnerved her. She didn't have to because he already knew—a fact that was confirmed when she glanced up into his eyes.

"Darling, you're wearing your hair down, just the way I like it."

"You like her hair long?" Her mother's query thankfully saved her from responding.

"Oh, yes." Derrick's voice was a potent caress as he con-tinued to lightly finger her silky tresses.

"I tried to get her to cut it, but she said it would be too much bother."

They continued to discuss her as if she weren't present, which suited her just fine. She didn't think she could for-mulate a coherent sentence if her life depended on it.

"I'm glad she didn't—I love it the way it is."

He bent down and brought a handful to his nostrils, in-haling its fresh scent. Then he let it trail through his fingers back against her warm cheek, his fingers still absently play-ing with a handful of strands.

She stopped paying attention to the conversation alto-gether at that point. Derrick's nearness and actions banished any logical thoughts from her mind, replaced by desires only for him. She wanted to reach up and bring his satisfying lips down to hers, and once again feel the burning ecstasy of his kiss.

"Isn't that right, darling?"

She glanced up at Derrick, who was smiling down at her lovingly and if she didn't know better, she would honestly believed he cared for her.

"I'm sorry, what?" She shook her head slightly as she forced herself to refocus on the conversation around her.

"Baby, were you daydreaming about our wedding again?" His finger lightly trailed down her burning cheek.

She swallowed the lump in her throat and forced a smile to her lips. "I'm afraid I'm guilty as charged, darling."

"Your mother was asking where we were going to spend our honeymoon, and I told her we had decided to go to my house in the country for a week and take a *real* honeymoon later on." His eyes laughed at her once again.

"Yes, Mom, that's right." She didn't know how she managed to make her voice sound cheerful when she felt anything but. "Excuse me—I think I need to check on dinner."

"Sweetheart, you just checked." Her mother frowned.

"I—I know, Mom, but it was almost ready. I'll be right back." She stood and hurriedly left the room, but not before she caught a glimpse of Derrick's mocking eyes as he followed her. No doubt, he knew exactly what she had been thinking and feeling. Damn him and herself!

A short time later, they were all seated around the dining room table. Alesha, of course, sat next to Derrick. Her mother and Robert sat on the other side.

"Sweetheart, tell me the full story of how the two of you met."

Her mother's question took her completely by surprise. She had assumed her brief response weeks ago had satisfied her mother's curiosity. She nearly choked on the piece of food she had just placed in her mouth and hurriedly took a sip of water before turning to Derrick.

"Why don't you tell her, darling?"

"All right, baby." He lightly kissed her lips before turning to her mother. "Well, Barbara, Robert sent Alesha to my office to pick up a check for a television spot." He glanced at Robert who was silently fuming. "I was floored by her visit, but more so by her beauty." He paused, this time to stare appreciatively at Alesha, and she grew warm under his burning gaze.

After he knew he had made her thoroughly uncomfortable, he said, "I was surprised when she wanted to discuss my campaign strategy. I had taken one look at her and my brains flew right out of the window. I asked her out to lunch, and she accepted." He kissed her cheek before continuing, "One meal with her wasn't nearly enough. I knew I had to see more of her, and we began to date. It became apparent that we were both swept away. The rest, as they say, is history." Derrick finished his tale and, much to her mother's delight, picked up Alesha's left hand and brought it to his lips.

"That's so romantic!" Her mother eyed them both with pure happiness.

"Yes, Mom, so much so that I almost can't stand it."

Thankfully, her sarcasm was lost on her mother. Derrick merely smiled and gave her hand a little warning squeeze. God, how she amused him! His eyes strayed to her tantalizing mouth and he resisted an almost irrepressible urge to capture those tasty lips with his own and spend untold minutes feasting on every sweet curve. He couldn't wait until they were married, until she was legally his wife and intimately his woman.

"Why did you wait so long to tell me you were seeing Derrick?" Her mother directed the question toward her.

"Tell her what you told me, darling." Derrick's eyes danced with mischief.

"Well, Mom, it was because…because everything happened so fast and we wanted to be sure about how we felt before we said anything." Alesha rattled off what she hoped sounded like a plausible answer.

"I understand." Barbara sighed as she glanced approvingly at the loving couple before her.

I'm glad you do, Alesha silently thought. Would this dinner never be over with? All she wanted was to get away from Derrick's disturbing presence, her alarming reactions to him, Robert's understandably sulky mood and her mother's glowing countenance as she bought into every shameful lie and half truth they fed her.

"It's partly my fault, too, Barbara. I was just getting to know Alesha, and I wanted her all to myself. I hope you can forgive me." He placed a lingering kiss on the corner of Alesha's mouth.

"Of course I can, Derrick."

Robert couldn't take another second of this nauseating display and quickly stood. "I hope everyone will excuse me, but I have to leave."

"So soon?" His mother frowned.

"I'm sorry, Mom. I thought we'd be through with dinner by now, and I have other plans." If he stayed here another second, he would surely throw up.

Derrick took everyone by surprise as he stood up, too, and said, "Robert, I was going to ask you this later, but since you're leaving, I'll just do it now."

"What is it, Derrick?" Robert tried to hide his dislike of the man for his mother's sake.

"Alesha and I have thought a lot about this, and we want you to be the best man at our wedding."

"What?"

Derrick thoroughly surprised everyone present. Robert and Alesha stared at Derrick in absolute shock.

"Oh, Derrick, how wonderful," Barbara said with great enthusiasm. "Isn't it, Robert?" She prompted him to respond to Derrick's offer.

"Are you sure, Derrick? Don't you have someone else you'd rather have stand up for you?" Robert tried to gracefully decline.

"Of course I'm sure. After all, you were instrumental in us getting together." Derrick smiled as he took Alesha's hand, causing her to stand before pulling her close to his side. "If it wasn't for you, we never would have become engaged."

"What about Cam?" Robert searched for a way out.

"He'll understand why I want you." Derrick refused to relent. "What do you say?"

"Sure." Robert glanced helplessly at Alesha who shook her head in resignation. "I really have to go now." He bent down to kiss his mother's cheek, and then dashed out the door.

"Derrick, that was so nice of you." Barbara continued to sing his praises, much to Alesha's dismay.

"It was nothing, Barbara. As I said to Robert, he's the reason Alesha and I are getting married. I can't think of anyone who deserves to be my best man more than he does."

Alesha stared at him, trying as hard as she could to hide the anger consuming her. He brought out such a range of emotions in her—one moment he could make her feel intense longing and desire. In a millisecond he could elicit a feeling of understanding and deep friendship. Just as quickly as he did now, he could spark a flame of anger, burning so brightly that she thought it would consume her. Her eyes blazed fury into the smiling, mocking depths of his.

At this moment, she was convinced that his sole purpose on earth was to bring chaos and disorder into her family's lives. His smile intensified, as if reading her mind, and somehow she resisted an urge to pick up her fork and use it as a weapon against him.

After dinner, Derrick sat on the sofa as Alesha paced angrily back and forth in front of him. Obviously, she was angry and he knew why.

She spoke to him in hushed, incensed tones. "You really enjoyed yourself tonight, didn't you?"

"Very much." His eyes followed her tense body as she walked away from him.

"How could you ask Robert to be your best man? You deliberately placed him in an untenable position." Her voice was angry, yet deliberately low enough so as not to disturb her mother.

"He could have said no."

"How? Momma would have become suspicious if he had."

"I hardly think Robert is the injured party in any of this."

"You're right about that." She stepped away and took several deep breaths. "Derrick, please reconsider. You don't want to marry me."

He stood at her words and walked over to face her. "On the contrary, I do."

"Why?" She was both flabbergasted and pleased to hear sincerity in his voice.

"Because you amuse me." He intentionally left unspoken the fact that she also inflamed, excited and captivated him.

"How flattering!"

"What do you want me to say? That I'm madly in love with you?" She remained silent and he continued, "You know why I'm marrying you, Alesha—it's purely business."

Even as he spoke the carefully chosen, cold words, he knew he was lying to both of them.

"How can I forget?" she hissed angrily. "You remind me every time I see you."

"You sound upset." He placed a hand under her chin and forced her turbulent eyes to meet the piercing depth of his own.

"Don't be ridiculous." She snatched her chin away, disturbed by his nearness and his insightful statements.

Despite her vehement denial, she knew he was right—she hated hearing him refer to their marriage as nothing more than a business arrangement, even though she knew that was exactly what it was. She tried to walk around him, but he grabbed her upper arm, stopping her.

"Maybe this is what you want to hear." He paused for what seemed like an eternity. "I want you, Alesha, very much. I've wanted you for a very long time, and this time I'm going to have you—all of you."

Her breath caught in her throat at his blatant, unexpected admission and arrogant assertion. She tried unsuccessfully to quash the vivid erotic images that sprang to mind as a result of his confession.

He moved closer until he was standing mere inches from her, causing her breathing to increase. Her heart thundered loudly in her ears as she continued to meet his scorching gaze. His hands reached out and grabbed her shoulders, pulling her body closer to his own.

"There's no one around to impress." She silently cursed her voice for sounding expectant and aroused instead of angry.

"I know that." He shook his head in agreement. "I'm doing this simply for my own pleasure—and yours."

He made her wait for an eternity until his burning mouth finally covered hers. She promised herself she would not respond. However, she soon found that her traitorous body had its own agenda. His hands moved to her lower back, pressing her intimately against the rock hardness of his own body. His tongue barely touched her lips and they parted, allowing him unlimited access to the hidden, inviting caverns of her sweet mouth. His hot tongue scalded hers.

Despite herself, she heard a moan of pleasure escape from her mouth and her arms slowly moved up his chest until they were entwined around his neck. He smiled slightly before pulling her up until she was standing on her tiptoes as he sucked her lips against his and massaged her tongue urgently with his own. Never in her life had she been kissed so thoroughly or devastatingly. Each kiss was different, yet achingly similar. When it came to arousing and satisfying a woman, Derrick Chandler was no novice, but then she already knew that. Without even trying, he could ignite her desire for him.

The hands at her back moved to trail lightly up her sides, resting at her breasts before sliding between her shoulder blades, pressing her closer as he continued his devastating assault on her mouth. She felt a similar sensation to one she hadn't known of until he had first kissed her, as the way he was now, building in pit of her stomach. It was a type of hunger, not for food, but for something entirely forbidden.

Her fingers fastened behind his head, holding him close. Her lips opened wider beneath the insistent, maddening pressure of his. Their kisses deepened. God, she wanted… What? What did she want? Something she was afraid to name, something she knew only he could give her.

Reluctantly, his lips slid from hers, and he stared deeply into her half-opened eyes. He studied the play of emotions dancing in their brown depths, and knew she was disturbed by her strong attraction to him. He himself was a little surprised and even troubled that, after all that had transpired between them, she still had the power to make him lose control.

The reason he kept reminding her about why they were marrying was that he needed to be constantly cognizant of that. Still, regardless of how they had come into each other's lives again, he couldn't wait for her to become his in every sense of the word. And though she would never admit it, he knew she was also anticipating the day when they would be husband and wife, but, more important, lovers.

His lips claimed hers again in another scorching kiss. Her eyes closed against the blinding passion mirrored in his, and she sighed in rapture against his bruising lips as they continued to devour hers. His fingers entangled in her hair, pulling her mouth closer still as he continued to savor her enticing lips. One of his hands moved to pull the hemline of the burgundy blouse she wore from the waistband of the matching skirt, sliding beneath to caress the warm, satiny skin of her lower back. She gasped against his mouth at the intrusion, but instead of moving away, she wantonly pressed closer, suddenly wishing their clothes would disappear, leaving only their bare bodies. She didn't know what was happening to her common sense, and at this moment, she didn't really care.

He felt her total surrender. He knew he could take her now and she wouldn't resist. For that reason, he also knew he couldn't, regardless of how much he longed to do so. He had silently promised himself not to consummate their relationship until they were married. He had convinced himself it was because he wanted to give her time to get to know him again, but the truth was that he was afraid that once he made her his, he would risk losing himself. He wanted… What did he want from her? Revenge, retribution or something simpler yet much more complicated and disturbing?

"I can't wait until we're married."

His admission was whispered against her moist lips. His mouth was so close to hers, she could still feel its imprint. There was no mistaking his meaning, and that prompted her eyes to flutter open as she stared at him, embarrassed by her actions and the fact that she hadn't wanted him to stop kissing or caressing her. Even now, her skin tingled from the light trails his fingers had blazed across it.

Unexpectedly, she pushed out of his arms and hotly responded, "Well, we're not married yet!"

She was angrier with herself for responding as eagerly as she had than she was with him for initiating the kiss. Turning her back on him, she prepared to leave him standing there alone. However, his hands prevented her from moving. He pulled her back and turned her around until she faced him again.

"But soon."

He placed a quick, hard kiss on her moist lips before he left her standing there alone, staring after him longingly, with nothing but her disturbing thoughts to torment her already tortured soul.

Chapter 5

Alesha sat in the hospital lounge, dressed in pale pink scrubs, checking the surgery schedule for the day. She tried unsuccessfully to ignore the envious banter of the four friends and colleagues who shared the lounge with her.

"Alesha, you're so lucky!" one of her friends cooed as she passed around a copy of *Time* magazine with Derrick's handsome face on the cover. She had to admit the eight-by-ten glossy photo from which the cover image was taken didn't begin to do him justice.

"How did you ever land such a marvelous catch?" the woman continued.

Returning her eyes to the schedule on her lap, she responded, "Just fortunate, I guess."

"I'll say you were!"

She sighed at the response. The slight sarcasm in her voice had been lost on her friends, who continued to salivate over Derrick's picture.

"Angie, you're on with Dr. Ryan at 3:00 p.m. in O.R. 12." She tried to redirect everyone's attention from her private life and back to work.

"Fine." The slender brunette with the short-cut hair nodded before returning to the subject that was on everyone's minds. "Come on, Alesha. Out with the dirt."

She looked up at her best friend, her exasperation evident. "What dirt, Angie?"

"How is he in the romance department? I'll bet he knows exactly what to do and does it expertly."

Alesha blushed at the explicit question, especially as she remembered the many ardent kisses she and Derrick had exchanged. What would Angela say if she told her she had never slept with Derrick—or with any man? She wanted to confide in her best friend. She could use some guidance in the romance department.

"Angie, leave Alesha alone. Can't you see you're embarrassing her?" said Linda, another one of her friends.

"I'll bet she could tell us all stories that would have our hair standing on end!" Angela picked up the magazine to take a closer look at the gorgeous man on the cover. "You'd better hold on tight—he's one sexy guy!"

"Why, thank you."

All heads turned in the direction of the door, to find the object of their conversation and desire lounging against the door frame, dressed impeccably in a charcoal suit, crisp white shirt and red tie.

"Derrick, what are you doing here?"

Alesha automatically stood and walked over to him. Dear Lord, how long had he been standing there and how much had he heard?

"I couldn't wait until tonight to see you, darling."

To the delight of her friends, he placed his hands around her slender waist, pulled her close and lowered his head purposefully toward hers. As always, they shared a breathtaking kiss. She clung to the lapels of his suit as she once again experienced the passion in his embrace. She didn't know how long he kissed her—time was suspended—however, when he finally lifted his head, she was more embarrassed than ever. She was sure that the blatant desire on his face, and hers, must be obvious to everyone in the room.

"Ahem!" Someone coughed loudly, making both of their heads turn in the direction of the other occupants of the room.

"Mr. Chandler, it's a pleasure to meet you." Never one to be accused of being shy, Angela walked up to shake his hand.

"Derrick." He smiled at them all in turn as they introduced themselves. "Please forgive me for interrupting your break."

His hand resumed its possessive position on Alesha's waist. He kissed her on the cheek.

She leaned against his chest and looked at him adoringly before plastering a stupid grin on her face, something she had gotten very good at in the last month. She hoped no one would ask her anything, because she didn't think she could trust herself to speak.

"It's no intrusion at all."

Alesha glanced at all of her friends as they nearly swooned at Derrick's feet. He could ask any of them all to jump out the fifth-floor window and they would do so gladly.

"I hope to see all of you at the wedding." At their gleeful promises, he added like a true politician, "And I hope I can count on your votes."

"Thank you. We wouldn't miss it for the world. And you definitely have my vote," Angela said, and the others promised to support him at the ballot box, as well.

"We can hardly wait for the big day ourselves." Derrick pulled Alesha closer. "Right, darling?"

All she could do was nod because, as always, his nearness was affecting her ability to think clearly. She wished he would let her go so she could breathe again. As if sensing her unspoken desire, and doing just the opposite, he pulled her even closer.

Everyone else reluctantly returned to work. Alesha would have gone with them, but Derrick refused to release her. Once they were alone, she turned to stare at him angrily.

"Was that really necessary?" She suddenly found her elusive voice.

"What?" He feigned innocence.

"You know what—that nauseating scene you just played."

"Weren't there a few parts you enjoyed?" His voice was slightly husky as he traced the outline of her trembling lower lip with the fingers of his free hand.

Despite herself, she felt a shudder pass down her spine to the tips of her toes at his touch and was certain he felt it, too. She longed for his lips to recapture hers once again.

His eyes shifted from hers to her slightly parted lips and back to her eyes again, yet he made no move to kiss her. Why was he toying with her? More importantly, why was she quivering in anticipation, craving another of his devastating kisses?

"Do you know what I want right now?" His voice was a whisper—his lips were a hair away from hers.

"What?" She fought to keep herself from swaying toward him.

Without answering her, his lips brushed against hers before he released her waist. Taking her hand instead, he led her out of the lounge into the busy hallway.

"Where are we going?"

They got onto the elevator. She glanced out to find all her friends watching enviously.

"To lunch."

"I can't leave the hospital. I have surgery in an hour and a half." She tugged against his hand.

"You'll make it. We're going to the hospital cafeteria." His smile widened as the doors closed.

After a brief stop at her office, which Derrick insisted on seeing, they boarded the elevator again. When it stopped on the twelfth floor, Derrick grabbed her hand and pulled her out.

"Where are we going? The cafeteria's on the first floor."

"You'll see."

He smiled and led her toward the doctors' conference room. A sign reading "In Use" was posted, but he disregarded it and began to open the door.

"Derrick, what are you doing?" Her hand covered his to stop him. "We can't go in there!"

"Of course we can." He swung the door open and ushered her inside.

She was still trying to reason with him when suddenly all her friends and colleagues ran toward them, yelling, "Surprise!"

They all beamed at her shocked face as she looked around the room, seeing for the first time that it was decorated with streamers, balloons and signs wishing her well. She quickly returned her astonished gaze to Derrick.

"You knew about this?" she gasped.

"Knew about it?" Angela walked over and hugged her tightly before continuing. "He's been a doll! We invited him, and he assured us he would be here, whenever, wherever."

"I—I don't know what to say." She stared at him in disbelief before quickly turning and adding to everyone, "Thank you all so much."

She was bombarded with hugs, well wishes and gifts. Someone shoved a glass of punch into her hands. Derrick was by her side constantly as she spoke with everyone. However, someone ushered him away to talk politics, and she was alone in the midst of another group of friends. Despite their good intentions, their words began to make her feel uncomfortable. She felt like a hypocrite, allowing people she had worked with for years to believe she was blissfully happy about her impending marriage, when nothing was further from the truth.

"Alesha, what's wrong?" Angela grabbed her hand in concern as she noticed the pained expression on her friend's face.

"Nothing, nothing." She forced a tearful smile.

"This is your best friend you're talking to. Tell me." She squeezed her fingers comfortingly.

"Oh, Angie, it's just…" She paused.

Even though Angela was her best friend, she had never spoken to her or anyone about Derrick—not two years ago, and certainly not now. How could she explain her inner turmoil to her friend, or to anyone here? No one could begin to understand what she was going through except…Derrick.

She searched for him, longing to be with anyone with whom she didn't have to pretend to be happy about leaving a job she loved in only two days. Her eyes encountered his as he stood across the room speaking with the head of surgery. He smiled at her reassuringly, and she automatically returned his smile. As odd as it sounded, she suddenly was very glad he was here. Her feelings were so complicated as far as he was concerned. Even though a part of her vowed to dislike him—a promise she had, thus far, been unable to keep—more times than not she enjoyed his company. That was a scary admission.

"What is it?" Angela's persistent tugging on her hand forced Alesha to refocus her attention.

"I'm just going to miss everyone so much." She hoped that would appease her friend.

"It's not as if you're never going to see us again. Besides, you'll be so busy with your handsome new husband and your exciting life that you won't give us a second thought."

"You may be right." She forced herself to assume a teasing demeanor.

She turned to respond to a question from another friend and, seconds later, felt a strong arm around her waist. She knew the arm belonged to Derrick. Her friends tactfully excused themselves, and she turned to face her soon-to-be husband.

He lowered his head and kissed her softly on the lips. "You looked like you needed rescuing," he whispered, his sympathetic eyes staring into her pained ones.

"I'm fond of all of these people—this is really hard."

"I know." He pulled her slightly closer.

Her hands automatically rested on his broad chest as she gazed into the compassionate depths of his eyes. In that instant, she felt that everything was going to be all right. To everyone present, they looked totally in love with each other.

"Why did you agree to come to this party?" She felt and heard him sigh as he studied her face.

"It was a good opportunity to test how others react to us as a couple." He deliberately chose his words to see how she would respond.

"I should have known," she hissed softly.

"If I had refused after being invited, it would have looked suspicious."

His words enraged and saddened her. She should have known he had only been thinking about his career! Anger darkened her eyes and she tried to free herself from his suddenly unwanted embrace.

"We certainly wouldn't want that." She tried in vain to free herself. "Will you let go of me?"

"Alesha, stop struggling before someone notices." His voice was low, but firm, commanding obedience. Yet she refused to comply.

"Let go!" She brought her free hand up to his chest and pushed. He moved his hand from her waist to her back, effectively sandwiching the hand on his chest between their bodies.

"There is another reason I came." He placed his free hand underneath her defiant chin and lifted her angry eyes to meet his.

"I don't care to hear it." She tried unsuccessfully to free her chin from his grasp.

She couldn't stand to hear any more of his heartless comments. She needed kindness from him, not taunting.

"I'm going to tell you anyway." He brushed a brief hard kiss on her lips, his hand moving from her chin to cup her jaw.

"Please stop, Derrick."

"I know it's hard for you to give up your career, even if just for a little while." His fingers softly caressed her cheek. "I thought today, of all days, having at least one person here with whom you didn't have to pretend to be happy about that choice—even if it was me—would make this farewell somewhat more bearable for you."

She immediately stopped struggling to free herself, but remained silent, unable to believe her ears. She searched his face for signs of teasing or deceit, and instead found only sincerity. He had articulated her feelings perfectly. How could he be so in tune to her feelings? How could he be both the cause of her pain and the only means to alleviate it? He never ceased to amaze or confuse her.

"What?"

"Contrary to your belief, I really don't want to make this any more difficult than it has to be." Fingers absently brushed stray strands of hair away from her eyes before he ruefully added, "I don't suppose I could expect you to believe that."

She stared at him, speechless, for a few moments before finding her voice. "I do believe you."

"Well, that's progress, isn't it?" He softly kissed her and she automatically responded to the warm, comforting pressure.

"I guess it is." She couldn't remove her gaze from the genuine tenderness reflected in his eyes, directed toward her.

"Did I tell you how beautiful you look tonight?"

"No." Her eyes registered surprise at his question.

"Well, let me remedy that." He took her hand and brought it to his lips. "You look gorgeous."

"Thank you." Her voice was wispy soft. "You don't look too bad yourself."

"Thanks."

He treated her to one of his devastating smiles before turning his attention to the traffic he was expertly weaving in and out of. They drove on in silence for a while. She had easily slipped into the role of Derrick's fiancée.

He pulled his sports car up to the restaurant and turned to face her. "Now remember, I told Cam that we met again…"

Alesha's fingers on his lips halted his words. "Derrick, you've told me a hundred times. I won't forget."

"I'm being a pain, huh?" He captured her hand with his own, refusing to release it.

"A little bit." She was breathless. Suddenly the close confines of the car became suffocating.

"I'm sorry." His eyes darkened.

"Um, I guess we should go in." Instead of moving away,
an invisible magnet drew her closer to him.

"I guess."

Though he agreed with her, neither of them made any
move to leave. Inevitably, they kissed. Lightly, at first, but
then the unexpected passion consumed them. Her hands
rested on his chest and he cupped her face, tilting his head
one way and then another, bringing her sweet mouth closer.

A cool blast of air forced them slightly apart. "I beg your
pardon sir, madam," A red-faced doorman apologized.

As always, it was Derrick who regained his composure
first, glancing over her shoulder. "It's no problem. We were
just getting out." Then, returning his attention to her, he
asked, "Ready?"

She ran her tongue over her slightly damp lips, tasting
him and nodded slightly. She didn't trust herself to speak.
He released her face and opened his door before walking
around to help her out. He continued to hold her hand as
they entered the restaurant, where they were to meet his best
friend.

As their coats were checked, Alesha used her fingers
to wipe off traces of her lipstick staining his lips. Their
eyes met and held for several suspended seconds before they
were shown to a table. At their approach, a tall man who
closely resembled her fiancé in build and height stood. He
was dressed like Derrick in a dark navy suit with a red tie.
He smiled easily, and Alesha instantly liked him.

"Well, well, I don't believe it. You're on time." The man
chuckled at Derrick and then turned to Alesha. "It must be
due to your good influence."

"Very funny." Derrick smiled. "Cameron Stewart, Alesha Robinson."

"Alesha, it's a pleasure." Cam shook her hand warmly. "Derrick said you were beautiful, but not exquisite."

"Thank you. I'm glad to finally meet you, Cameron." She smiled as he brought her hand to his lips briefly before releasing it.

"Cam. No one calls me Cameron except my mother—and Derrick when he's mad at me." He winked at his friend.

"Which you take deep pleasure in making sure is often," Derrick said as they were seated in the booth.

"Untrue." Cam shook his head. "I'm the easiest person to get along with you will ever meet."

"Hah!" Derrick snorted good-naturedly.

That was the way their dinner progressed. It was quickly apparent that Derrick and Cam were the best of friends, and could talk to each other only as best friends could and get away with it. Alesha enjoyed herself very much. She saw a side of Derrick that was completely relaxed—one she hadn't seen in a long time and one she liked very much.

Cam was a gem. He had a natural talent for making people feel at ease. Alesha took to him like a bee to honey. She felt a bit uneasy about deceiving him, but as Derrick had continually drilled into her head, everyone—including their friends and family—had to believe they were very much in love.

"Alesha, may I have this dance?" Cam stood and extended his hand in her direction after giving a chivalrous bow.

"I'd love to." She kissed Derrick's cheek. "You don't mind, do you, darling?"

"No, but you will once you experience his two left feet."

"He's just jealous because I'm a much better dancer than he is."

He *was* jealous, but not of Cam's dancing skills. Rather,

that Cam would be holding Alesha in his arms—something he himself longed to do.

"In your dreams." Derrick's words trailed after them as they walked away.

"Well, what do you think?" Cam glanced expectantly at Alesha as he twirled her around the dance floor.

"Very nice." Alesha smiled.

"You be sure and tell Derrick that." He winked at her and she laughed.

"I will." She returned his smile.

"You know, Alesha, I was blown away when Derrick told me he was getting married—and to whom."

"Were you? Why?" She feigned innocence, reminding herself to keep her answers short—there was less chance of slipping up that way.

"It was so sudden." Cam's words were an understatement. "Also, given your past relationship, it was the last thing I expected to happen."

"Our decision to get married is anything but sudden." Cam's dubious stare forced her to elaborate. "It took us two long years to realize we were destined to be together."

"Is that how you feel? As if you and Derrick were destined to be together?" Cam watched her with the attention of a hawk, studying its prey.

"Yes." She smiled at him and prayed for a change in topic.

"Really?" He twirled her out of the way of an approaching couple.

"Yes." She faced his piercing stare that was very similar to Derrick's. "I realize you don't know me very well, Cam, but believe me, I'm marrying Derrick because I want to."

"What's changed between now and two years ago?" He had skillfully maneuvered them into a relatively secluded part of the dance floor so that their conversation wouldn't be overheard.

She almost laughed out loud at his question. She wanted to ask how much time he had for her to list the monumental changes that had occurred in her life over the past two years.

"A lot." She silently cursed herself because even to her ears her voice sounded strained.

"I'm not prying just to stick my nose into yours and Derrick's business, Alesha." His voice was a little defensive.

"I realize that." And it made her feel all the worse for lying to him. "You're Derrick's best friend, and I know you have his best interest at heart."

"I do."

"For reasons I don't want to get into, Derrick and I weren't ready for each other two years ago. Now we are and we know what we want." Her words held shades of the truth and thus were spoken confidently.

"And that would be each other?" She felt as if she was on the witness stand and the case would be made or broken by her next words.

"Yes. Nothing else will satisfy either of us. We've finally realized that, thank God." She prayed for the music to end, because she didn't know how much more of this grilling she could take.

"Well, I suppose it's the romantic beginning and ending to a relationship any woman would love to have." Cam suddenly smiled and she heaved a sigh of relief.

"Yes."

"So it would seem that this time true love triumphed in the end."

He studied her closely—too closely. She realized this was the moment she would either sell the lie or destroy it.

"It has. I finally realized that Derrick is everything I want in a man and in a husband."

Her expression was appropriately dreamy as her eyes

sought out Derrick's from across the room. She sighed happily before returning slightly watery eyes to meet Cam's.

"I'm happy for you both." Cam smiled.

"Thank you." She gave a silent prayer. Apparently, he was buying her nauseating performance.

"No, thank you for returning to Derrick's life."

His words made her feel like a first-class heel. He was a nice man and a loyal friend, and she truly hated deceiving him. Even reminding herself that it was necessary didn't help salve her heavy heart.

"I like you very much, Cam."

"I like you, too." He smiled. "I see why Derrick jumped at the chance to marry you."

No, you really don't.

"Thanks." She smiled.

The song ended a few moments later, and they made their way back to Derrick.

"What were you two talking about so earnestly?"

"I was trying to steal her away from you." Cam winked at Alesha.

"Never happen," Derrick said.

Derrick placed a possessive arm around her shoulders and pulled her close. Absently, his fingers played with the strands of her hair.

"Sure of himself, isn't he?"

Cam smiled. He wondered if Derrick realized that he was always touching Alesha, or how his expression softened when he looked at her. His friend was in for a big surprise if he thought his marriage to Alesha was going to be a cold, antiseptic business arrangement.

"Very. But he's right, I'm afraid." Alesha joined in their infectious banter, placing a possessive hand on Derrick's chest.

"Man, have you done a job on her." Cam feigned disgust.

"It's called love," Derrick corrected, placing a brief kiss on her lips. "Right, baby?"

"Right." She willed her fluttering heart to be still.

"Now that you see how devoted she is to me, will you stop trying to steal my fiancée?"

"No promises." Cam displayed a devilish grin.

"Will you two excuse me?" Alesha said.

She rose, as did her dinner companions, and walked in the direction of the ladies' room. She definitely needed a moment to compose herself.

"You and Alesha are very good actors."

"Why do I feel a judgment coming?" Derrick took a sip of his coffee.

"No judgment, just an observation," Cam said with a smile.

"I know I'll regret this, but let's hear it."

"I don't think either of you is completely acting about your feelings."

"That's ridiculous." Derrick took a much-needed swig of his drink.

"Is it?"

Cam's razorlike eyes homed in on Derrick's. Derrick suddenly felt like an insect under a microscope.

"Yes, very. You know why we're getting married."

"Yes, I think *I* know." He leaned closer and added, "But I don't think either of you has a clue."

"Cameron..." Derrick's voice held a warning.

"Shh, here comes your fiancée." Cam laughed at his friend's scowling features.

"Did I miss something?"

Alesha sat beside Derrick once again. The atmosphere was noticeably thicker than when she had left.

"No, I've just made Derrick angry with me again, but

he'll get over it." Cam laughed and received a dark glare from his friend.

"Oh, I see." Alesha carefully glanced from one to the other.

"Alesha, it was a pleasure to finally meet you, but I have to go now." Cam took her hand and brought it to his lips.

"Thank you, Cam. I enjoyed meeting you, too." She smiled genuinely.

"See you tomorrow, Derrick." He continued to grin broadly.

"Goodbye, Cameron."

Derrick's stilted response made his friend laugh.

"See, I told you he was mad at me." He winked at Alesha, who chuckled as he departed.

"What was that all about?" She turned to face her still-scowling fiancé.

"Nothing. Just Cam being Cam." Derrick quickly dismissed a topic of conversation he didn't want to pursue.

"Are you angry with him?"

"Always." Derrick laughed, and she relaxed as his black mood seemed to suddenly dissipate. "You did a wonderful job tonight." He placed his arm alongside the back of the booth, bringing her that much closer.

"Thanks. I was nervous," she admitted with a slight laugh.

"You needn't have been. I told Cam you could do it." He impulsively hugged her shoulders.

"You what?"

She frowned at his words, and pulled slightly out of his embrace. She had been led to believe that Cam didn't know anything about their arrangement.

Chapter 6

"Cam knows." As her frown grew into a glare, he said, "Remember, we're still in public."

She forced a slight smile, though her eyes still shot daggers at him. "You lied to me."

"No. I never said Cam didn't know."

She was annoyed by his truthful reminder. She would have moved farther away, but his arm held her captive.

"But you insinuated as much." Her words were quietly hissed through gritted teeth. "What did you two do? Have a great laugh at my expense?"

"I didn't bring you here tonight to make fun of you."

"Then why?" She resisted an urge to empty the contents of her water glass onto his head.

"Because I needed to know if you could really pull this off with someone who wasn't a friend, a colleague or related to you—someone whose questions you couldn't anticipate, someone who would take you completely off guard. *You* needed to know."

"You still could have told me." Her voice had lost some of its edge as his words sank in.

"It would have undermined the purpose if I had." His logic was inescapable. He studied her closely. "You believe that I wasn't trying to make a fool of you, don't you?"

She studied his earnest expression, and the remainder of her anger dissipated. She might be an idiot, but she did believe him.

"Yes, I believe you." Her body relaxed noticeably.

"Good." He released his breath on a sigh.

"You sound as if you actually care what I think." She fingered the white linen dinner napkin, though her eyes never left his.

"I do."

"Why?" She stopped fiddling with the napkin.

"Do you know what I want to do?"

He didn't answer her question on purpose. It wasn't that he couldn't have, but rather, he wasn't sure she would like his response, or if he cared to hear the truth himself.

"No, what do you want?"

"I want to kiss you." He glanced around the room before returning his full attention to her. "But, unfortunately, we do have quite an audience."

"That's never stopped you before." Her whispered invitation surprised them both.

"No, no, it hasn't." He smiled slightly before his lips captured hers.

It was an earth-shattering kiss. One of his hands cupped her jaw, tilting her head until it lay over his arm as his mouth plundered. Her hand slid up his chest to rest at his nape as she kissed him back. She didn't know how long their mouths feasted, but when he lifted his head, she wished he hadn't stopped. As if reading her thoughts, his mouth settled against hers again and she sighed in pleasure. Her fingers fastened on the back of his head as she held his mouth closer. Long minutes later when he lifted his head again, they were both breathing heavily.

"I'd better get you home." His voice was thick with passion, his eyes dark with longing. She felt the same way.

"Yes." Her voice was barely audible.

His head lowered toward hers again and she waited for another kiss, yet it never came. Instead, he pulled back and summoned the waiter, to pay for their bill.

Neither spoke as they left the restaurant or once they were seated inside the car. Alesha silently contemplated their supposedly purely business alliance, which had quickly evolved into something completely different than she believed either of them had anticipated, yet it seemed that neither was unable or unwilling to arrest its unexpected evolution.

November 29 dawned cold and clear as Alesha and Derrick exchanged their wedding vows. She wore a white, sequined designer gown made especially for her, and her hair was covered by a headpiece and a cathedral veil that trailed behind her when she walked down the aisle. It was a beautiful formal evening affair that rivaled some of the most elegant weddings of celebrities and royalty.

They posed for what must be the thousandth picture of the day, facing each other, bodies pressing close, arms encircling each other as they smiled into the camera. She had to admit that all day they had presented the picture of a deliriously happy couple, very much in love. If she didn't know any better, she herself would swear they were crazy about each other.

Suddenly, the lights dimmed and a space miraculously appeared as people moved to one side in preparation for their private dance. Derrick took her hand and led her slowly onto the dance floor. She gathered the white lace veil closer to her as she went into her husband's waiting arms.

She gratefully buried her face in Derrick's shoulder and dropped the fake smile from her aching countenance. She was able to escape from the peering eyes and cameras for a few blissful minutes. As she moved closer to Derrick, her hand moved from his shoulder to the back of his neck.

"You're doing remarkably well. Don't stop now."

His whispered reminder in her ear annoyed her no end. Why couldn't he be quiet and let her fantasize about this being real?

"Raise your head and give me a kiss for the people like a good wife."

She almost refused—not because she didn't want to, but because she didn't like being ordered to play a part when everything that had transpired today had held special meaning for her. However, she complied and his lips slowly neared hers before closing warmly, firmly over them as they continued to sway slowly to the music. Through her closed eyes, the bright light of camera flashes was evident as more pictures were taken and she heard the hushed sighs of delight as people witnessed the touching scene before them.

Dear Lord, how long did he intend to kiss her? His lips continued to caress and take her breath away, which further delighted the crowd, who whistled and cheered the loving couple before them.

After what seemed like an eternity—and, if she were honest with herself, not an unpleasant one—he lifted his head, yet maintained eye contact with her. She was mesmerized by his gaze, unable to look away.

To onlookers, it must have seemed as if they were totally enamored of each other, impatiently waiting for this elongated celebration to end so they could escape and privately express their love. Of their own accord, her thoughts drifted to the time in the near future when she and Derrick would be completely alone together.

She was at war with herself—part of her wanted more than anything to finally culminate the desire that had been building within her and had gone unquenched since his first touch years ago. Another part of her wished that the reception would go on forever, even though she secretly hated every moment of it. Shamefully, she couldn't decide which part she wanted to win out, and oh, how that bothered her.

The song finally ended, and he led her off the dance floor with his arm still around her waist. She plastered the happy smile on her face once again as they approached her mother and brother.

"I'm so happy for you, dear." Her mother embraced her warmly.

"Thanks, Momma." Alesha smiled as her mother released her. She possessively placed her arm through Derrick's, who covered her hand with his own.

"Derrick, I'm so glad you're a member of our family." Barbara warmly kissed her son-in-law's cheek.

"Thank you, Barbara. You'll never know how much that means to me." He held Alesha close as he smiled at her mother.

Alesha resisted the urge to slap his face. It was one thing lying to all these strangers, but it was another thing doing it to her mother. But was he lying? He seemed genuine enough. She believed he liked her mother and she knew her mother adored him.

Derrick didn't like deceiving this nice lady. She had been nothing but kind to him since they had met, and he genuinely liked her. When she found out the truth, he hoped she would understand. Suddenly, he realized he would hate to lose the special friendship he had developed with Alesha's mother.

That surprised and worried him. He hadn't meant to become attached to Alesha again or anyone in her family. However, that's just what had happened—and in a very short time. What was it about his new wife that captivated him so? He had to be careful not to let himself become any more involved with his wife or her family. Yet, he feared it was already much too late to stop that from occurring.

"How about a glass of punch, Barbara?" Derrick spoke more to quiet his unwanted thoughts than anything else.

"I'd love one, Derrick." Barbara linked her arm through his.

"Excuse us, darling?" He kissed Alesha's lips lightly.

"Of course, sweetheart. I'll be right here." She smiled lovingly at him as he led her mother off.

She was alone with Robert, and she dreaded it. "Robert, don't start," she warned before he could utter a word.

"I don't have anything to say, except I can't believe this is happening." His response was somber.

"It's done. We'll all have to make the best of it."

"Can you do that?" He eyed her closely.

"I have to."

Truthfully, she feared that being Mrs. Derrick Chandler wouldn't be nearly as hard as having to stop being Derrick's wife.

"I'm so sorry."

"I know." She squeezed his hand. "I want you to know that I don't blame you—you know that I understand why you did what you did."

"I know you do." He suddenly grabbed and hugged her close, as if he would never let her go. "If he hurts you…"

"He won't."

She knew without a doubt that Derrick wouldn't harm her physically. However, she was afraid there had already been irreparable damage done to her emotionally. How much more there would be after months of living with him as his wife, she couldn't begin to guess.

"He'd better not."

"Smile." She forced herself to follow her own advice.

He tried, but the smile didn't quite reach his eyes. Her own eyes grew distant as she contemplated her immediate future. Soon, very soon she would have to leave here with her husband—with Derrick. She would have to be alone with him, and she would be expected to give herself to him totally, a prospect that didn't repulse her, but rather unnerved and, dare she think it, excited her.

Today marked the start of new life as Mrs. Derrick Chandler and in a few short hours, she would truly begin her life as his lover. She shivered at the thought. There was no longer any denying to him, and certainly not to herself, that she wanted him physically. In a matter of hours, she would have him and he would, in turn, have all of her with all that implied.

Derrick and Cam stood together watching as Angela, Alesha's maid of honor, and her bridesmaids surrounded Alesha on the other side of the room. Derrick watched his bride with mixed emotions—he had felt strange all day. He had been mesmerized as she had made her stunning entrance at the church. As they had recited their vows, an emotion he dared not name had assailed him. Of course, he knew their marriage was a carefully orchestrated arrangement, but he *really felt married* to her. It was unnerving and exciting. He wondered if she felt the same way.

"Well, you two did it—and very well, I might add." Cam slapped him on the back.

"Did you ever doubt it?" Derrick smiled, grateful for the intrusion on his disturbing thoughts. "Thanks for understanding why I had Robert as my best man."

"No problem. It looked good for the photographers."

"Spoken like a true campaign manager." Derrick chuckled.

"Alesha is a beautiful bride."

"Yes, she is."

Derrick's eyes easily found his wife across the room. She was smiling at something one of her bridesmaids had whispered to her—a beautiful smile, a smile he was sure could light up the world as it lit up his heart.

Cam studied his friend closely as he watched his bride. There was something in his expression that Cam couldn't put a finger on. He had watched the two of them all day, and as he had informed his friend weeks ago, he didn't think either of them was as aloof toward this marriage or each other as they insisted they were.

Derrick, aware of Cam's thoughtful scrutiny turned cool eyes toward his friend. "Don't start."

Cam smiled. "I wasn't going to say a word."

"Oh, yes, you were. But don't."

Derrick's eyes gravitated back to stare at his beautiful bride. Cam's eyes followed Derrick's and his smile widened; though, as his friend had suggested, he remained silent.

All too soon, Alesha sat alone in her dressing room. She gazed at her frightened expression in the mirror. Now that she was alone, she was finally able to let her happy facade fade. Her heart was beating frantically, and she knew if she didn't gain control of herself very soon, she would faint.

She stood and smoothed nervous hands down the front of the pale blue suit she wore. The long jacket almost reached the hem of her just-above-the-knee matching skirt, which had a half-inch slit up the right front side. She brushed her hair until some of the curls had disappeared, but left it loose, though it was brushed away from her face. She slowly sat down again, her wobbly legs unable to support her.

She knew the reason for her apprehension—soon she would be alone with her husband, and would, therefore, put an end to all the imaginings her mind had conjured up about the night that was rapidly approaching. She shuddered visibly as she thought of Derrick and her alone in the most intimate of situations and positions. Despite herself, her heart skipped several beats in...anticipation?

A knock at the door made her jump. Taking a last look at her nervous reflection, she stood, walked over to open the door and found Derrick there.

"Are you ready to go?" His piercing eyes took note of her pale cheeks and troubled eyes.

"Ready as I'll ever be." She placed her arms through the coat he held up for her.

"You look excited."

"What do I have to be excited about?" She pulled away from him, angry that he could read her so easily.

"Nothing yet," he paused suggestively. "But soon."

She gasped. "Are you ready?"

He smiled. "More than ready."

He placed an arm around her slender waist as they walked down the hall. When they reached the top of the spiral staircase, she saw that the single women had gathered at the bottom of the staircase. Alesha turned her back to them and threw the bouquet down. Laughter and shouts of glee reached her as Angela came up with the bouquet, minus a few flowers that had been snatched out along the way as many hands had tried to grab it. Alesha threw a kiss to her best friend, who smiled and held up the bouquet as if she didn't know what to do with it.

She turned toward Derrick, who was smiling wickedly. He slowly slid his hand under the hem of her skirt, raising it slightly to reveal her upper thigh and the pale blue garter that rested there. She braced herself so as not to melt as his hand splayed warmly against her sensitive skin before his fingers began to remove the garter from her thigh. Ever so slowly he pulled the elastic down before finally straightening, eyes gleaming with merriment as he stared into her flushed, embarrassed face. He placed a kiss on her luscious lips before turning and throwing the garter down into the howling men below, right into Cam's outstretched fingers.

"Way to go, Cam!" Derrick's shout caused everyone to burst out in laughter.

"Thanks, bro." Cam's dry tone prompted more laughter from the gathered crowd.

Cam and Angela turned to stare at each other, smiling slightly. He walked over to her slowly, and amid more laughter and wolf calls, placed the garter on her thigh.

"I guess we're next." He smiled into Angela's good-natured eyes.

"That is the tradition." She returned his smile. They both turned to stare as Derrick and Alesha made their way down the stairs.

"I've never been one for traditions, but I think I could make an exception in this case," Cam whispered in her ear.

"Maybe I could, too," she softly responded with her back still toward him, not daring to turn around to face him.

All too quickly, Derrick and Alesha were off amid flying birdseed and well wishes. She caught a glimpse of her mother and brother and blew them both a kiss. Her mother looked ecstatic, while her brother's expression was a mask of melancholy.

They exited the door and ran hand in hand to Derrick's black Jaguar. Once tucked inside, Alesha tried unsuccessfully to quell the nervousness mounting within her. Derrick started the car and it moved smoothly and speedily down the road. She stared out the window until the reception hall was a tiny blur in the distance. Lord help her, she had done it. She was on her way to her new life—a life that, if she was honest with herself, didn't terrify her nearly as much as she had thought it would.

They had been driving for a little over an hour, saying little, each engrossed in their own thoughts. She placed a hand on her nervously churning stomach and closed her eyes, resting her head on the soft leather headrest. She tried to calm her nerves. She wouldn't think about anything for a few minutes. She would just relax and listen to the soft music wafting from the speakers.

Derrick glanced at Alesha's silent profile. Her eyes were closed and she looked tenser than he had ever seen her. He knew she was nervous, but he didn't know what he could do to alleviate that. He had tried to talk and she had been unresponsive. Maybe once they arrived at the house, she would relax, although he silently admitted she would probably get even more tense. He knew she was worried about being alone with him.

He reminded himself again that she had known exactly what she was letting herself in for. He hadn't lied to her or tried to deceive her in any way. He had told her what he had expected, and she had agreed to his terms. Now she would just have to learn to live with her decision.

"Well, here we are."

She jumped nervously at his voice. Opening her eyes, she glanced out the frosty window at the lovely two-story house (which he had called a cottage) as he stopped the car. She remained inside until he walked around and opened the door for her. Taking her hand, he helped her out before leading her inside.

"It's beautiful." She glanced around her apprehensively.

"Thanks." He took her coat and hat, placing them onto a chair in the hallway.

He went back out into the cold night air and returned moments later with their bags, which he sat down in front of the stairs. "Would you like to go to our bedroom and change for dinner?"

Our bedroom, she silently echoed. Oh, the visions those little words fired off in her head. "Yes, thank you."

He nodded and, picking up their bags, started up the stairs. "Follow me."

He ushered her into a spacious room with a huge cherry-oak, king-size bed covered with a black-satin comforter and shams. Much to her relief and dismay, he quickly excused himself after showing her where the bathroom was.

She walked over to the bed and sat down nervously. She fingered the soft comforter, her eyes lingering on the huge bed she and Derrick would be sharing shortly. Visions of the two of them lying there naked, entangled in the soft sheets, tortured and teased her mind. What would his skin feel like against hers? What would it be like to…? She refused to complete that thought, quickly jumped up and almost ran into the bathroom, hoping a hot shower would ease the confusion and maddening sense of anticipation coursing through her veins.

Chapter 7

Approximately forty minutes later, she descended the stairs, wearing an emerald-green, long-sleeved silk dress. Her hair was swept away from her face, though she had left it loose.

Following soft strands of romantic music, she entered the study. Derrick was standing in front of a floor-to-ceiling window, but turned to stare appreciatively at her as she entered.

He was dressed in tan slacks and a burgundy sweater. He had shaven, and seeing his slightly damp hair, she realized that he had showered, too. At least he had not barged in on her. She conceded he was trying to be considerate—for that she was grateful.

At her puzzled gaze, he said, "I used the guest bedroom to change." He slightly stressed the word *change,* making her aware that he would not be using it later when it came time for bed.

She forced herself to walk over to where he stood, stopping inches in front of him. She would have spoken to break the uneasy silence, but she didn't know what to say.

"Did you find everything you needed?" With great difficulty, he resisted the need to touch her.

"Yes." She linked her hands together nervously.

"Dinner is ready, if you are."

"I'm ready." She paused before quickly elaborating, "I'm ready for dinner."

He smiled broadly at her words, but made no further response, ushering her into the dining room where a romantic, candlelit table for two was set. A magnum of champagne was beside the table, and a bouquet of red roses lay beside her plate. She almost laughed out loud as her eyes surveyed the romantic scene before her. If things were different, she would have been pleased—a big part of her was pleased, even now.

He held out her chair for her as she sat down before seating himself opposite her at the small table. He only had to reach his hand out to touch her face—that thought made her breath catch in her throat. To remove her eyes from the disturbing depths of his, she looked at the roses, fingering a soft petal lightly.

"These are beautiful."

"I'm glad you like them."

He wondered why he had an absurd impulse to say something corny, like she was the most beautiful woman he had ever known, or that he was glad she was his wife. "Would you like some champagne?"

"I'd love some." She gratefully accepted, raising her glass as he popped the cork before placing some of the foaming liquid into her glass.

She downed the contents in one gulp before the bubbles had subsided and offered her glass for more. Derrick raised an eyebrow at her actions, but refilled her glass nevertheless. She disposed of that in the same fashion and offered her glass for more. But he shook his head.

"Getting drunk is not going to help anything." He replaced the champagne in its holder.

"I'm not trying to get drunk."

She only wanted to relax—something that seemed impossible to do in his presence.

"Alesha, try to calm down. I'm not going to devour you."

Absurdly, she thought it might not be such a bad thing if he did. She wanted to unleash the passion that had been hinted at every time they had touched. She wanted him, but she was afraid—both of him and of herself.

She managed a half smile. "Derrick, I…"

Unexpectedly, he grabbed her hand, his fingers lightly caressing hers. "It's not as if this is your first time."

She blushed hotly and looked away. How did he expect her to discuss such intimate matters with him? If she told him that he was her first, he wouldn't believe her. He wouldn't believe her because she had led him to believe otherwise, she silently amended.

"Alesha." The soft yet firm way he called her name made her look at him. "I won't rush you."

"I know." Her voice was barely audible as tiny shivers of anticipation raced up her arm at his light, teasing touch.

"Do you?" He spoke so softly she thought she had imagined it.

"Yes." She took a deep breath and then released it slowly. "Maybe if I had a few days to…"

"No, Alesha, there will be no days, weeks or months," he quickly yet gently interrupted, fingers stilling their seduction of her wrist. "I mean to make love to you tonight."

She snatched her hand away from his. "Do you have to talk so bluntly?"

He sat back in his chair and poured himself a glass of

champagne. Taking a sip he reminded, "We are husband and wife."

"I know, but it's so…new…" Her voice trailed off. She suddenly longed for some more champagne—a lot more.

"You want me, don't you?"

His question made her eyes grow to twice their normal size. She was glad she didn't have any champagne in her glass to drink. She would have choked on it.

"How can you ask me such a thing?" She brought a hand to her suddenly constricted throat.

"It's obvious." He smiled slightly at her distress. "That bothers you, doesn't it?"

"What do you expect? Ours is not exactly a normal marriage, is it?" She didn't deny or confirm his words. "Can't you try to be more patient?"

"I am, and I have been." His response was calm. "I could have already taken you while we were engaged. However, I gave you time to adjust."

"Don't say that!" She fidgeted uncomfortably in her seat as red stained her cheeks.

"Say what?" He smiled slightly, knowing to what she alluded.

"You know what." She ran her tongue across her dry lips and his eyes watched her every movement. "It sounds so, so…animalistic." He laughed heartily at her words, and that was her undoing. "Damn you. Don't be amused by me!"

"It's hard not to be." He wiped the tears of merriment from his eyes. *"Animalistic?"* he echoed, still smiling. Then, seriously, he said, "You don't know what animalistic is…" He paused for emphasis before adding, "yet."

She stood abruptly, food forgotten. "I'm really not very hungry. I'd like to…" She stopped herself, eyes widening in shock at what she had been about to say.

He also stood. "You'd like to what?" He smiled wickedly.

"Go to bed?" He'd correctly interpreted what she had been about to say.

"No, I wasn't going to say that, I…" Her voice trailed off as her heart leaped in her throat.

"Let's both go to bed." He took her hand and nearly dragged her up the stairs, not stopping until they reached their bedroom.

Once inside, he started to pull her into his arms. "Wait!" She placed hands on his chest to ward him off. Things were moving too fast—much too fast. "I—I have to change."

"Why? You won't wear it for long." He pulled her body closer again.

"Please, please, Derrick." Her hands on his chest warded him off.

He looked at the nervous expression on her face and he knew she needed a little more time. "All right, but don't take too long."

"I won't." She picked up her overnight case before almost running to the bathroom, shutting the door behind her and locking it.

She leaned weakly against the door. She tried to quiet the frantic thudding of her heart as she opened her overnight bag. She should be angry and appalled that in a few minutes she would be expected to make love to Derrick, but she wasn't. If she were honest with herself, she was expectant. She was also nervous, excited and confused.

Damn Derrick's undeniable effect on her and damn Robert, too, for getting her into this mess! With a sigh of resignation, she glanced into her overnight bag and saw a white silky negligee with matching robe, which left nothing to the imagination.

"Oh, Mother!"

How could her mom have done this to her? She must have taken out her flannel gown and replaced it with this one. She couldn't go out there wearing this! She rummaged further into her luggage and saw other negligees, all just as revealing. Carefully inspecting the diaphanous, flimsy creation in her hands, she admitted it was a knockout. The long gown was made of several layers of the sheerest chiffon she had ever seen, and the bodice and waist consisted of lace, which would allow tantalizing glimpses of her skin to peek out. The single-layer chiffon robe might as well be nonexistent for all that it covered. Well, it was either wear this sexy creation or nothing, so she quickly donned the ensemble and almost fainted when she saw how little it actually hid.

After several minutes of deep breathing, which did nothing to calm her nerves, Alesha went to the door and grabbed the doorknob. She willed herself to calm down. She was married now, and on the other side of the door, her husband waited for her. Though their marriage was the result of a distasteful arrangement, she silently admitted that their mutual desire for each other was very real—as real as real could get. Soon she would know the culmination of the scandalous kisses they had shared. At that thought, she trembled visibly and, gathering the folds of the robe closer to her in one hand, she opened the door with the other and slowly exited the bathroom.

The only light in the bedroom came from candles beside the bed, which had been turned down. Derrick stood on the opposite side of the room, though he faced her as she entered. He was dressed in a black robe.

Alesha stopped just outside the bathroom. He couldn't believe the tremendous surge of hunger he felt just staring at her luscious body in that sexy gown. In fact, he couldn't believe she had packed such a piece of lingerie, but he was glad she had.

She was the most beautiful woman he had ever seen. He wanted her as he had wanted no other. He couldn't believe that finally she was going to be completely his. Slowly, purposefully, he walked toward her, expecting her to flee at any moment. Yet she remained rooted to the spot, nervous, expectant eyes making tentative contact with his. The pulse at the base of her neck was beating rapidly and he longed to place his lips there. He stopped mere inches away.

"*Beautiful* is too mild a word to describe how you look."

He reached out his hands and lightly cupped her warm cheeks. A shudder passed through her at his touch. He took her breath away for he was staring at her as if she were the most important person in the world. If she didn't know any better, she would think he was madly in love with her.

"Alesha, we've waited a long time for this."

She shook her head in agreement. "I know, but…" She paused, unable and unwilling to try to verbalize her topsy-turvy feelings as far as he was concerned.

"But what?" His hands dropped to her shoulders, lightly massaging her tense flesh.

"I—I don't know…" Her voice trailed off again.

"You don't have to know anything." His strong hands made soothing circles on her overheated skin. "Except that I want you."

"Do you?" His sincere words helped quiet some of the butterflies intent on making mincemeat out of her stomach lining.

"Yes, I do. Very much." The ease of his confession left little doubt as to its veracity. "Do you believe me?" He had always wanted her, and finally she was going to be his.

"Yes." She sighed the word.

"And you want me."

She gasped lightly as his fingers drew the robe from her shoulders and let it fall in a soft heap at her feet. His eyes mesmerized her.

"I…" She couldn't bring herself to admit that, too.

"It's all right. I know."

That voice of his was turning her bones to mush. His hands slid down her bare, silky arms and back up again several times, causing her breathing to increase expectantly.

"All right."

The arms on her shoulders drew her closer until their bodies were touching lightly. His eyes never left hers. Though she made no effort to move out of his arms, he knew she was still apprehensive. He wanted to replace her anxiety with passion and longing—emotions he knew were smoldering just beneath the surface.

He slowly lowered his lips to hers, and placed a light kiss on her quivering mouth. His lips then trailed down her cheek to her earlobe, where he gently bit into her flesh before moving to the side of her neck, his teeth and tongue lingering there, reverently tasting her silky, delicately perfumed skin.

Something strange was happening to her as he continued his pleasing caresses. She felt a little breathless as overpowering feelings began building within her body. After several long, pleasing minutes, his mouth trailed down her shoulder, his hands sliding the thin straps of her gown out of the way, down her arms, as his lips explored her tremulous skin. She closed her eyes, allowing herself to enjoy the extraordinary sensations engulfing her body at his every touch.

His lips moved to her other shoulder, teeth gently scraping across her skin, sending shivers of delight up and down her spine. The hands that had been resting on his muscled arms tightened slightly as he trailed his hot tongue from her neck to her cheek, slowly outlining her tender lower lip. Her eyes were half closed as wonderful tremors coursed through her.

His hands moved from her shoulders to her lower back, to rest intimately on her buttocks, pulling her closer to his masculine physique. She was suddenly aware of every muscle in his body as she was molded to his hard frame. The ache in the pit of her stomach increased almost unbearably.

His lips played lightly with hers, rubbing, nipping softly and then pulling away again, but refusing to end the sweet torture he was subjecting her to. She unashamedly longed to feel his mouth close warmly and decisively over her own. What was he doing to her? This question ran through her dazed mind while she could still think, before, finally, she received what she wanted when his strong mouth hotly engulfed hers.

Like a starving man feasting, his lips hungrily wandered over hers, his marauding tongue sliding beneath the quickly conquered barrier of her white teeth to find and engage in a slow, thorough dance of rising passion with hers. She felt light-headed, overwhelmed with sensation and completely wanted and desired. They had shared many kisses since their engagement, but this was different because she knew, this time, there would be no stopping, interruptions or turning back, and she was absurdly pleased about that. After an eternity of waiting, she was about to fully experience Derrick's lovemaking, and she wanted that more than she had ever wanted anything.

Her arms on his shoulders encircled his neck of their own will. Her fingers tentatively massaged his nape. At her response, his mouth hardened, crushing her lips beneath the pressure his exerted as he intimately deepened the kiss, voraciously ravaging her sweet mouth.

She moaned in pleasure, on fire and wanting—what, she didn't know. Vaguely, she felt him slide the gown from her overheated body and realized she was standing naked in his arms, but she didn't care. All that mattered was that he not stop kissing her—ever. She clung to him unashamedly as he thirstily drank again and again from her luscious lips.

As he lifted her easily, she then felt the cool, satiny softness of the sheets beneath her back. She vaguely realized they were both lying on the bed. Derrick still wore his robe and the textured material brushed against her overly sensitive flesh.

He reluctantly released her enticing lips and withdrew from her slightly to stare at her face. She was so beautiful, and he wanted her so much, yet he couldn't rush her or himself. After years of waiting, he was determined that she would enjoy this as much as he was going to. She stared at him through half-closed, aroused eyes, a thousand questions in her expression.

He smiled slightly and, propping himself up on one elbow, trailed one hand from her collarbone to the tip of a firm, ripe breast, slowly drawing circles around her chocolate nipple. He smiled as she audibly gasped in pleasure. His smile deepened and his traveling fingers became more ardent as he continued his masterful manipulations of her willing flesh.

When his thumb and forefinger encircled her hard nipple, she moaned aloud, unable and unwilling to stop herself. His mouth slowly lowered to taste the flesh his hand had just caressed. She waited for what seemed like hours until his hot, warm, rough tongue licked across her nipple and she groaned louder, closing her eyes against the sweet pain rapidly invading her body.

His hand trailed down her flat, trembling stomach, his palm rubbing against her skin as his mouth enclosed her breast. He pulled at her skin, softly at first, but then with increasing intensity. She felt as if she would die at any second from the exquisite torture he was inflicting on her.

Her hands drifted to the back of his head, holding him closer to her flesh. When he bit into her skin, she simultaneously bit her lip to hold back the scream that wanted so desperately to escape from her mouth, while her hands held him closer still. After several agonizingly wonderful seconds, his hot roving mouth moved to repeat the process on her other breast. She stopped trying to hide her pleasure at his touch and passionate moans of pleasure escaped from her lips.

Her fingers ran up and down his head, holding him closer still, and the hand on her stomach moved to trail across one of her silky inner thighs, before moving to touch her more intimately than anyone ever had, and she was suddenly lost in a savage, merciless storm.

Raising his head, he watched the play of emotions that crossed her face as he did things to her she had only dreamed of. Her body shuddered uncontrollably and her hoarse screams of pleasure filled the room as he continued his mind-shattering stroking of her pliant body. He wanted her to forget every other man she had ever been with. His would be the face she saw, his the name she uttered. She would cling to his body and give herself to him completely.

He fought the urge to plunge into her. She was so wet, so warm, so inviting. His teeth bit into her nipple again and she arched against him, her hips moving rhythmically against his skillful fingers as he continued to assail her with passion.

Why hadn't someone warned her that she would feel this way as his expert hands stroked her novice body? She had never imagined that anything could feel so marvelous! It couldn't get any better than this, could it? Her question was answered emphatically yes with each subsequent devastating caress Derrick bestowed on her. She clung to him weakly, unabashedly begging for release of the sweet tension coiling inside her. She didn't think she could take much more, but each touch proved her wrong.

Derrick shrugged out of his robe and immediately cov-

ered her soft, welcoming body with his own. She gasped at
the intimate contact, feeling every hard, masculine inch of
him against her. His lips covered hers again and again. Her
arms entwined around his neck before moving to slide down
his powerful shoulders and his muscled back, enjoying the
rough texture of his flesh against the satiny softness of her
own. Her body begged him to end the wonderful torment
he had stirred up within her.

He tore his mouth away from hers to bury it in the soft
hollow of her neck as he rasped her name over and over
again before lifting his head to stare at her face—highly
aroused, yet somewhat troubled. She opened her eyes
slightly within a few seconds and stared at him question-
ingly. He wanted to bury himself in her, he wanted to lose
himself in her, and he was going to do just that and more.

His eyes burned her with their intensity, his body lighting
an answering inferno within her own as one of his muscled
legs slipped between her satiny thighs. She gasped at the
intimacy and her heavy eyelids began to droop.

"Alesha, just enjoy it—enjoy us," he urged. "Just feel,"
he added as he devastated her in a kiss that seared her to her
very being.

His limbs entangled closely with hers. Intent on savoring
each second, he slowly, inch by inch, merged their bodies
into one. She felt engulfed by heat and slight pain as he
slowly filled her—he was hot, hard and throbbing. He then
glanced down at her, shock evident in his expression.

"Alesha?"

He couldn't comprehend what his mind and her body was
telling him. She was a virgin! How could she be a virgin?
He continued to stare into her shimmering eyes. He started
to withdraw, but she was so soft, so warm and fluid that he
couldn't bring himself to leave her, so he pressed deeper.
He lay motionless for a few moments, and when she began

to whimper against his hot mouth, and the hands on his back began to caress him, only then did he begin to move—slowly at first, yet urgently.

Her body shuddered beneath his as momentary pain quickly gave way to immense pleasure. Hot molten lava flowing through her veins at his every erotic, pleasurable touch. Sensations she hadn't dared to imagine erupted from the core of her being as Derrick opened her eyes to a wondrous desire whose existence she had never suspected.

His powerful body continued to move frantically against hers. She instinctively arched to get closer to him. He groaned at her actions and his hands moved down her sides to rest on her hips, pressing her closer still, wrapping one of her slender legs around his waist as their passion rose higher and higher still, threatening to consume them both with its ferocious intensity.

Many times, she had dreamed of this moment—what it would feel like to make love to Derrick completely and totally—yet this surpassed all her expectations. Forgotten was the fact that she had once driven him away, as was the fact that she had married him only to save her brother. Now, right now, he was the only person who could give her the release she so desperately craved. He was the only one who could bring her dormant body to glorious, vibrant life.

They floated high, higher still on tenuous waves of life-affirming passion. When the moment of culmination came, she cried out into his mouth and he into hers. Her eyes, filled with wonder, flew open to stare into the blazing depths of his. Their bodies began to shake uncontrollably as the throes of their passion blinded them to everything except the unparalleled bliss they experienced in each other's arms as they drifted slowly into a miraculous abyss of complete and total fulfillment.

Some time later, he marshaled enough energy to remove

his body from hers. They lay breast to breast on their sides, his hand resting on her waist.

"Did I hurt you?" His warm breath vibrated against her ear.

"No." Her single-word response was muffled as she hid her face in his hair-covered chest, inhaling the heady male scent of him, which intoxicated her.

On the contrary, she silently amended. He had made her feel wonderful, vibrant and alive. She had wantonly enjoyed his thorough possession of her, as she had never enjoyed anything else in her life. She had clung to him, whimpering, begging for his kisses and caresses. She had found rapture in his arms beyond belief. Had he known? Of course, he must have. Why didn't that bother her? She had responded shamelessly to him and her body felt completely fulfilled against his, as if this was where she was meant to be.

Out of duty to some absurd unwritten rule, she tried to roll away from him, but was glad when he wouldn't let her go. His strong arms held her close to his masculine form, a body that had moments before given her the greatest gratification she had ever imagined. She stayed where she was, where she wanted to be, close to her husband.

Derrick knew she wanted some time to rationalize what had just happened between them, and he knew that no matter how hard she tried, she wouldn't be able to. She would never be able to discount what they had just shared—neither would he. She felt so good lying in his arms, her soft body yielding against his.

She was so inexperienced, but she had aroused him as no other woman ever had. He was her first lover, the first one to awaken her to the desires of her own sumptuous body. Given what had happened two years ago, he didn't understand how that could be. However, it was undeniably true—Alesha had been a virgin. Why had she lied to him about that?

Slowly, he ran his hands down her slender, silky back, pressing her closer, feeling her shudder against him. He wanted her again and again. Yet he resisted temptation for the moment—they needed to talk. He needed some long-overdue answers. He lowered his head to look at her and she tried to bury her face into his chest. His hand moved under her chin, forcing her to meet his gaze.

"Look at me."

When she complied, he placed a lingering kiss on her tempting lips, but pulled away before things got out of hand. Her beautiful face was marred with uneasiness and he knew she was aware of the questions swirling through his mind.

"Derrick…"

"Alesha, why didn't you tell me you were a virgin?"

He asked the question she dreaded but expected. How in the world should she respond?

"I don't want to talk about it." She lowered her head onto his chest to escape his piercing gaze.

"We have to talk about it." A firm hand under her chin lifted her eyes to meet his darkening ones. "Why did you lie to me two years ago?"

"Derrick, please. I can't talk about this now—not now." Her eyes begged him to understand what he couldn't possibly.

"I don't know what game you're playing…" His voice was understandably upset.

"It's not a game," she quickly contradicted. It hurt her to have him think of her as deceptive when she was merely confused.

"Then, what?" He studied her with simmering anger evident in his expression. "Why the pretense?"

She longed to tell him everything, but what had once seemed so clear and logical now seemed silly and juvenile. She could no longer justify to herself her reasons for hurting him two years ago and for denying them the bliss they had just shared. How could she justify it to him?

All she wanted was to snuggle in his arms, close her eyes and enjoy being with him, but she couldn't. She felt too ashamed and too confused to do that, and she couldn't face any more of his justifiable anger and questions, either.

"Please, just leave me alone."

Avoiding his eyes, she turned away from him again. This time, he allowed her to break free from his embrace. She immediately missed his warm hard body and felt completely bereft.

He looked at her bare back oddly and started to touch her, but stopped himself. Damn her, she owed him an explanation, and he wanted one! He reached out a hand to turn her around to face his righteous anger, but stopped himself. He needed to calm down. If they spoke now, he would say things out of anger he would regret later. Unable to help himself, he swore out loud and she jumped at the sound, though she made no move to face him again. He lay back against the pillows and placed a hand on his head in disbelief. Given the sweet rapture they had just shared, how ludicrous that they were now acting like complete strangers. Damn her, and damn himself for still wanting her with every breath he took!

She pulled the satin sheet closer about her and her body tingled as the soft material brushed against her flesh, made overly sensitive by Derrick's hands, mouth and body. Even now, she unabashedly wanted him. Her body ached for his, but did he still want her?

Chapter 8

Hours later, she was still lying with her back to him as far to her side of the bed as possible—not wanting any incidental contact of their bodies to spark any smoldering flames in either of them. She had never been so uncomfortable in her life, afraid almost to breathe for fear that he would know she was awake and once again ask questions she didn't know how to answer.

She wanted him as desperately as she had hours ago. She longed to feel his strong arms around her, but she couldn't face the anger or the questions that she knew would still be reflected in his eyes when he looked at her. What was she going to do now? How was she going to continue in this marriage and face his inquiries about her past behavior on a daily basis?

What she silently feared and longed for occurred when he shifted suddenly, placing a strong arm around her waist, pulling her back against his warm, hard body. The fingers of one of his hands splayed across her stomach as his lips caressed the side of her neck and shoulder.

The hand on her stomach moved up slowly, massaging her pliant flesh to cup a full breast. He stroked her skin as his warm lips explored the soft skin of her neck, shoulder and back.

She closed her eyes as familiar sensations began to overwhelm her. When one of his legs slid between hers, she moaned with pleasure. His wandering fingers slid languidly back down her quaking body to her stomach and lower, moving to gently explore her pulsing depths, pushing deeply inside her again and again, eliciting ecstasy within her.

"Oh, God," she whispered as he continued his devastating caresses.

She felt him smile against her shoulder and his teeth bit gently into her flesh. She arched back against him and one of her hands covered his as his fingers drove her crazy with longing.

His hands slowly turned her until she was lying on her back and his mouth captured hers in a singeing, greedy kiss, which stole her labored breath away. His body covered hers, his hands entangling themselves in her hair as he pulled her mouth closer to his. Her hands clung weakly to his shoulders before urgently moving down his back to rest on his hips as his mouth continued to ravage hers again and again. She wanted him so much it hurt.

He never said a word, yet his body spoke volumes. She didn't doubt he was still angry at her, but he also still wanted her. Perhaps that would be enough for now.

Her body melted against his. She willingly lifted her hips as he plunged forcefully into her waiting void—filling her completely. She closed her eyes and traveled with him to that wonderful place he had carried her to before, where nothing mattered except the two of them and their passion for each other.

He manipulated her, controlled her, sent her into such a fever pitch, she thought she would literally burst from the mind-bending pleasure she felt. She didn't, though, but rather yearned for more. His lips slid from hers to rest in the hollow of her neck, opening moistly over the pulse beating erratically there, his teeth scraping over her skin. His body continued to masterfully caress hers.

Hoarse moans of pleasure escaped from her lips. Her eyes were tightly shut as her body began to shudder, softly at first, but with increasing intensity, as did his. Her fingers stroked his rippling back as she pressed closer to the man who was now her husband and her lover. His body pressed hers into the soft mattress as they soared higher and higher on waves of desire. Once again, she obtained a glimpse of heaven in her husband's arms.

She slowly awakened the next morning, stretching languidly against the unfamiliar feel of satin on her naked skin. Her hair covered her eyes, and she pushed it away with an impatient hand.

She glanced around the unfamiliar room. Why was her body so sore? Where was she? These and many other questions tumbled through her dazed mind, until she suddenly remembered. Slowly, she turned to look toward the side of the bed on which Derrick had lain last night but, to her relief—and dismay—he was gone.

She slowly brought a trembling hand to her mouth as she remembered him turning to her again in the night. More importantly, she remembered her response to him. She had to admit that he had been a wonderful, considerate and passionate lover. In fact, he had been everything she had ever fantasized about and more.

Sighing, she slid out of bed, taking the sheet with her. She walked by her robe and gown, which Derrick had strewn carelessly on the floor. As she bent to pick them up before placing them on a chair, her mind again drifted toward last night and the wonderful discovery it had held.

She entered the bathroom and dropped the sheet. Her mouth dropped open as she caught a glimpse of herself in the full mirror and stopped in shock. Was this her? Her face looked different, maturer. Her lips were slightly swollen from the numerous ardent kisses Derrick had placed there. Her breasts looked full and tender from his hands and mouth. Hot color flooded her cheeks as she beheld the evidence of Derrick's conquest of her body. She was a woman now—she was Derrick's woman. Derrick, her husband, a man who baffled and inflamed her mind, body and soul.

Turning away from the disturbing picture she presented, she walked over and turned the shower on full blast. Stepping under the steaming spray, she grabbed a bar of soap and slowly foamed her still-tingling body. Where was Derrick? What would she say to him when she saw him? She still had no satisfactory answers to his questions.

Long minutes later, she stepped out of the shower, her skin squeaky-clean. She wrapped a towel, sarong-style, around her wet hair and grabbed a bath sheet to place over her body. Before she could accomplish that task, however, the door burst opened and Derrick appeared casually dressed in jeans and a white sweater—looking very handsome and desirable.

She gasped at his intrusion and tried to pull the towel in front of her. However, his strong hands stopped her. Taking the plush material from her fingers, he slowly proceeded to thoroughly dry every inch of her.

He slid the towel slowly down her shoulders and arms. Then he drew the material across her collarbone and sen-

suously across her swollen breasts, which hardened at the
contact of his toweled hands. A soft sigh escaped from her
lips as she waited for him to go further.

His eyes moved from her aroused face to follow the path
of his hands as they continued their descent down her satiny
skin, moving to brush across her flat stomach, shapely hips,
thighs and feet before he slowly walked behind her and dried
her back, buttocks and legs.

Returning to stand in front her, he dropped to his knees,
his toweled hands moving to her inner thighs with increasing urgency, staying there longer than was necessary before
he totally discarded the towel and replaced it with his fingers. Her knees went weak, and she swayed until her back
gratefully encountered a nearby wall.

Her breathing was ragged and her fingers flexed on his
broad shoulders to steady herself as his fingers continued
their manipulation of her fevered body. When his mouth
replaced his fingers, she cried out at the multitude of new,
wonderful feelings that assaulted her tremulous body.

His hot tongue delved deeply into her moist, pulsing recesses, darting, twisting, turning, retracting and seeking
again and again—first slowly, then faster and faster. He
drove her to the brink of ecstasy and back. All the while,
she longed for more, much more.

Her body shook convulsively. She closed her eyes tightly
and her head rolled from side to side as he continued his devastating exploration of her all-too-willing flesh. A thousand
tiny, brilliant stars exploded behind her closed eyes as his
mouth and lips slowly trailed back up her body to stare at
her face, clouded by passion, silently pleading with him for
a release only he could give. He removed the towel from her
wet hair, fingers sliding through the damp tresses.

She was trembling as he reverently stared at her naked
form, his eyes burning her with their intensity. She almost

pleaded with him to make love to her. She didn't have to verbalize her desire—he knew what she wanted, and he wanted the same thing.

He reached out and lightly brushed her nipple, which hardened automatically at his now-familiar touch. He smiled slightly as he drew her into his arms and placed a passionate, all-consuming kiss onto her quivering lips. Despite her resolve not to, she welcomed his erotic kisses as much as she had his intimate caresses.

His hands pulled her slightly away from the wall to roam down her bare back, pressing her closer. He suggestively rubbed his hips against hers and she whimpered against his mouth. Her arms encircled his neck and she ardently returned his kisses. Feelings—similar to those that had surfaced last night, yet somehow stronger—began to overwhelm her, nearly crippling her. God help her, she wanted him with every painful breath she took.

His mouth plundered hers for several wonderful minutes. She began to moan against his lips, opening her mouth wider beneath his, wishing he would stop this sweet, sweet torture and satisfy them both.

She was quivering uncontrollably as his lips slid from hers and he slowly took a full breast into his hot mouth. His hands moved to her round buttocks, holding her closer against his intense need as he continued to taste her overheated skin.

He hadn't meant for this to happen. He had wanted to catch her off guard and demand answers to questions she had evaded last night. However, one look at her luscious body and all rational thought had fled—just as it had last night. He didn't know why, despite her obvious deceit, but she excited him and made him feel more alive than he ever had.

Her fingers held his head closer to her and his teeth bit

into her nipple, causing her to gasp out aloud. His hands lightly caressed her sides before moving to her back as he lifted his head to again ravage her mouth, simultaneously sliding his hands up to rest on her lower back. Her fingers held his head fast as their wild, unexpected, intensely satisfying encounter proceeded.

Suddenly, he pulled his mouth away from the intoxicating depths of hers and, disengaging her hands from his head, placed them on his chest instead. She opened passion-glazed eyes to stare longingly at him, not wanting him to stop— ever.

"Undress me."

His soft, urgent command made its way through the foggy recesses of her mind. She gasped audibly, but her fingers moved to obey, sliding beneath the sweater he wore, lightly touching his muscled, hairy chest, making him suck in his breath sharply. Her fingers lightly stroked his chest before she pulled the garment up and over his head, throwing it in a careless heap on the floor. Fascinated eyes watched as her fingers slowly smoothed over his powerful shoulders to his arms, enjoying every nuance of the journey.

"Now my pants." His words were whispered against her mouth, his tongue urgently reaching between her lips to touch hers.

His hands guided her to the snap of his jeans, helping her unfasten it. Her hands would have moved away, and he knew it. So his own hand captured one of hers, slipping it beneath the material to encounter his burning flesh.

She gasped, her eyes staring into his hypnotic gaze. She saw the blatant desire written in his eyes and knew it mirrored her own. At his insistence, she touched him fleetingly before his fingers urged her to engulf him totally.

Her breathing was now ragged, as was his. She wanted to move her hand away, yet wanted to continue her forbidden exploration of his marvelous masculine form. He filled her hand as she longed for him to fill her body. Again his lips closed over hers hotly, eyes blazing bright before hers closed against the intense brilliance.

Somehow, his jeans were discarded and he grabbed her buttocks, lifting her slightly before he entered her easily. Her legs automatically wrapped themselves around his waist as he pressed her against the cool, white-tile wall with his body, frantically.

She clung to him wildly, her mouth mating recklessly with his. As she raked her nails down his rippling back, she vaguely wondered who this ravenous stranger was. It couldn't be her! Just as soon as the thought entered her mind, it left, as Derrick's masterful body continued to bombard hers, driving all rational reasoning from her mind. Agonizing pleasure built inside her until she thought she would explode from the force rapidly mounting to near bursting.

"You're so sweet—so sweet," he murmured against her mouth, his breath erotically intermingling with hers before engulfing her lips once again.

Her hands moved up and down his muscled back, her nails digging into his rippling flesh. The legs around his waist tightened, pulling him closer to her as his writhing body continued to both soothe and excite hers. After several long, agonizing moments, she hoarsely screamed into his mouth as he fulfilled her totally. His mouth took her screams, cries and whimpers as their bodies fiercely gave and took from each other.

She suddenly opened her eyes, staring into the fiery depths of his as their passion reached the wonderful moment of gratification. In that instant, she knew, as she was sure he did also, that her body belonged to him. There was no way she could deny that. However, she must take special care to ensure that her heart didn't follow suit. Yet she silently admitted it was already much too late for that.

Later, about 2:00 p.m., they walked side by side dressed alike in jeans, sweaters and leather jackets. Despite herself, Alesha had to admit she was having a good time with her husband. It was a cloudy, cold November day with the temperature in the forties. She sniffed appreciatively as different pleasant fragrances assailed her overactive senses.

Much to her surprise, Derrick made no attempt to question her about the revelations of last night, but rather showed her particular points of interest, and what she had seen of the grounds on which his house sat was lovely. They stopped to sit on a cobblestone bench in front of a babbling brook.

She unexpectedly asked, "Why have you never married?"

Did she imagine it or did a shadow fall over his face at her query? She didn't know what had made her ask that question, or why she waited with baited breath for his response.

He stood and walked to stare into the water with his back to her. She waited for him to speak.

"I'm sorry if that was too personal."

He threw a rock into the pond and turned to face her. "I was married briefly after we broke up."

Her mouth dropped open in shock. She couldn't help it, nor could she seem to force it to close again. She waited silently for him to continue, his demeanor telling her there was much more to the story.

"Nothing to say?"

His voice was bitter, and though he still had his back to her, she imagined his eyes matched his suddenly dark mood.

"I—I don't know what to say."

He smiled slightly without humor. "No questions?"

She had a thousand, but she didn't dare ask any of them. Who had he married? Had he loved her? How soon after their breakup had he married her? When and why had they divorced? Did they keep in touch? Did she live in Washington?

"Do you want to tell me about it?"

She stood and walked over to him. She watched, intrigued, as a multitude of emotions, none of which she could name, crossed his face. He treated her to a piercing, unnerving stare.

"There's nothing to tell. To make a short story even shorter, after too much liquor, I married her in Vegas on the spur of the moment—it was the worst mistake of my life. We didn't know each other, but it soon became apparent that we wanted different things out of life, so we quickly divorced." He succinctly, coldly summed up the worst period of his life.

"I'm sorry." Even to her own ears, her apology sounded pathetic.

"Why are you sorry, Alesha?" He walked closer to her. "Because you know your actions drove me to it?"

"No." She shook her head and stood abruptly. "I didn't know."

"Oh, but you did." He grabbed her arm and pulled her close. "How does that make you feel? Strong? Elated? Happy?"

"No!" She tried to pull her arm free, but he wouldn't release her.

"Why? Why did you do it?" He grabbed her other arm and pulled her closer.

"I don't know what you mean."

"The hell you don't!" His grip tightened on her.

"I don't want to talk about this." Her heart was pounding frantically—surely he must hear it.

"Well, I do!" His fingers tightened on her flesh to the point of bruising. "Tell me!"

"I don't know." She shook her head slowly, trying unsuccessfully to free herself.

"Don't give me that, Alesha. Dammit, you owe me the truth!"

She had never seen him this angry, and she hoped she never would again.

"I don't..." The pure rage in his eyes halted her words.

"Tell me!" He shook her slightly.

"You frightened me!" she blurted out and almost fell as he suddenly released her.

"Frightened you?" He stood and looked as if she had struck him.

"Yes." She rubbed her throbbing arms.

"How?" That one word was spoken tightly and contained a multitude of anger and pain.

She moistened her lips and met his incredulous gaze. "We had only known each other for a short time, yet what I felt for you, what I sensed you felt for me, was so intense. You consumed my every waking and sleeping thought. I was saturated with you. I—I just couldn't handle it anymore."

"So you let me believe you had just been passing time with me, playing with my emotions while your lover was out of town?" He shook his head disbelievingly.

"I never meant to do that." Her eyes and voice pleaded with him to believe her.

"But that's what you did!"

"I didn't have a choice."

"You didn't have a choice?" He stared at her as he tried to comprehend her statement.

"You wouldn't leave me alone," she said softly, resuming her seat on the bench. "When you came to my apartment that morning and found Kevin there, one look in your eyes and I knew what you were thinking and I let you think we were lovers because it meant I wouldn't see you again." With difficulty, she recounted the event that had sealed their fate.

"And that's what you wanted?"

It wasn't the chilliness of the day that sent a shiver down her spine, but rather his frigid eyes as he tried to comprehend what she was saying. No, it wasn't what she had wanted at all, but at the time she had thought it was the only option available to her—now she wasn't so sure.

"That's what I needed."

"What you did to both our lives is a crime." His voice was angry, tired and sad.

"I didn't have a choice," she miserably whispered.

"Yes, you did. But for whatever reason, you made the wrong one."

His voice was colder than she had ever heard it and, unfortunately, it was directed toward her. Her actions had made perfect sense to her two years ago, but right now she agreed with his assertion.

"I did what I had to do."

Even as she said the words, she didn't believe them. She deliberately didn't tell him the rest of the story. Why, she didn't know—perhaps because she now doubted her fateful choices, as well.

He opened his mouth to ask one of the thousand questions that he still had, yet closed it again. He turned away as if the sight of her disgusted him and lifted his eyes heavenward. She wanted to say something—anything—but there was nothing she could say, so she remained silent. After long minutes, he turned and gazed at her again.

"Do you know what your rejection taught me?" His voice held an eerie aloofness, which his eyes now echoed.

"What?" She was not sure she really wanted to hear his response.

"That love doesn't exist. It's just a pretty word people

use to get others to do what they want." He smiled without humor.

"You don't mean that."

Her heart contracted at his cold assertion. She had seen a soft and passionate side to him only a few hours ago. The man she knew he was didn't at all fit with the callous picture he was painting for her now.

"I assure you I do."

He stared at her as if he didn't know her, and it was the loneliest she had ever felt in his presence. She forced herself to remain expressionless, but his words hurt—more than she would have thought possible. She understood his feelings and agreed with them. Honestly, she didn't understand her actions herself, anymore—how in the world could she expect him to?

She stood up suddenly. "I'm ready to go back now."

He looked at her strangely before following her as she retraced their steps back to the house. Both were silent as they walked side by side, neither looking at the other, but rather glancing straight ahead contemplatively. When they entered the house, the phone was ringing. Derrick answered it angrily and she stood in the hallway, waiting for him to finish. As he hung up the headset, he told her he had to drive into the city to meet with Cam.

"Do you have to go?"

She should be happy for a respite from his anger, but she wasn't. She hated leaving things as they were between them, even though she had no idea how to repair the damage her lies had inflicted.

"Politics never sleeps." He glanced at her oddly before shrugging and promising, "Don't worry, I'll be back tonight."

"Will you?" Her question was spoken so softly, he thought he had imagined hearing it.

Though he was still upset with her, unable to resist, he placed a hand under her chin and lifted her mouth to his. He kissed her and she returned the kiss, her hands tentatively resting on his shoulders. Though their mouths ate voraciously, he purposefully kept their bodies apart, because if they touched intimately, both knew they wouldn't stop with just a kiss. After long, fulfilling moments, his mouth slowly released hers and he walked to the door.

"I'll see you later."

She sighed heavily. He might hate her for what she had done in the past, but clearly he still wanted her. That was something, wasn't it? Perhaps they could rebuild some semblance of a civil relationship on that. She hoped so, just as she prayed one day he wouldn't look at her with veiled anger and disappointment in his eyes.

Chapter 9

After Derrick left, she wandered around the study before choosing a lengthy murder mystery to read. Before she knew it, she had finished the novel and it was after 6:30 p.m.

She fixed herself a snack then returned to the study, turned on the television and found to her delight that *Casablanca* was on. It was one of her favorite movies. Shortly thereafter, a loud clap of thunder rattled overhead. She walked to the window and opened the blinds. To her amazement, ominous clouds loomed in the sky and streaks of lightning could be seen in the horizon.

The out-of-season storm had blown in without warning. She didn't mind, though—there was nothing she liked better than a good movie and a thunderstorm. Walking back to the television, she turned up the volume to drown out the thunder and sat down again with her feet curled under her. Some minutes later, lightning lit up the room, there was a particularly violent clap of thunder and the TV went black, as did the lamp on the table beside her.

"Oh, no," she moaned, getting up and trying the light switch on the wall, which also refused to illuminate the dark room. "Great! So much for television."

It was almost impossible to see, but she felt her way back to the kitchen and, after searching through several drawers, she found some candles and a box of matches. Lighting several, she walked into the hallway and peered out at the ghostly reflections made by the barren tree limbs when the lightning briefly illuminated the dark. After several seconds, she decided she might as well go upstairs.

Once there, she tried the light switch, just in case, but the room remained in darkness. Placing one candle beside the bed, she lit the other candles Derrick had placed there last night, before taking one with her into the bathroom.

She turned on the water and began to draw a hot bath for herself—hoping the soothing water would help alleviate the jitters, which had suddenly crept up on her.

Once the tub was full, she undressed and sank into the sudsy, steaming water. As she slowly ran her hands over her body, she remembered other hands that had explored her flesh the night before and this morning—Derrick's hands—strong, sensual and pleasing.

Try as she might, and Lord knew she had tried, she could not deny that she wanted him with a single-minded passion that overwhelmed, frightened and yet empowered her. Last night and this morning, she had longed for him to somehow defy the laws of physics and merge their bodies into one. At several points, she had felt as if he had done just that.

Vivid memories of crying out in his arms, clinging to him, and the feel of his naked flesh against hers tormented her. Against her will, her eyes were drawn across the room to one of the white-tile walls. Hot color flooded her cheeks as she remembered how she had shamelessly clung to Derrick this morning as they had made love in this very bathroom.

She grudgingly admitted that he was a fantastic lover— better than all the heroes in the romance novels she had read and in all the love stories she had watched on television or at the movies. With one look from those expressive eyes of his, he could inflame her soul. The slightest touch of his fingers turned her into a mass of putty that begged to be shaped by him. Yes, she was inexperienced, but she somehow knew that no one would ever compare to him.

She sighed audibly as she closed her eyes again, trying without success to make sense out of her ambivalent feelings as far as her husband was concerned. Would he still be angry at her when he returned? No doubt, he would. He had every reason to be. She wondered if she should tell him the rest of the story. Would it make her more sympathetic in his eyes, or more pitiful?

She opened her eyes and slowly stood. Her thoughts wouldn't allow her to relax as she had hoped when she had sunk into the tub. All she seemed capable of doing was thinking of Derrick—wondering where he was, what he was thinking and feeling—and both dreading and looking forward to his return.

Her fingers grabbed a huge black bath sheet and began to dry her body. Automatically, memories of this morning rushed to her mind. She dreamily remembered how his mouth had caressed hers and how his body had… Damn! She forcefully ended that train of thought, angrily threw the towel down and picked up another seductive negligee. This one was black satin and clung to her every curve. In spite of herself, she smiled slightly as she mentally pictured her mother shopping for the revealing nightgowns she had placed into Alesha's luggage.

She shivered as she reentered the bedroom and walked

over to switch on the gas-powered heat before climbing beneath the soft satin sheets and comforter, pulling the cover up to her chin. In a few seconds, she felt completely warm. Her limbs relaxed and her mind was quiet.

All that was missing was… No! She would not say his name again. The rain now mixed with something that sounded like sleet and pelted against the window. She snuggled down against the fluffy pillows beneath her head and began to drift off into sleep. Despite herself, the last thought she had was of Derrick as she wished for his safe return.

Derrick listened impatiently as Cam outlined the remainder of his campaign strategy. Although he hated to admit it, his mind was not on this meeting, but rather on his wife. It was a little after 8:30 p.m. He had been gone longer than he had expected. The snow mixed with sleet worried him, and he hoped she was all right. He had tried to phone her about an hour ago, but the phone lines were down.

"Cam, how much longer are we going to be?" He tapped his fingers against the mahogany tabletop.

"Not much longer, why?"

"Because I'm tired and I want to get back home before the roads get too bad." He sprang off the sofa like a caged tiger and went to stare out the frosty window.

Cam walked over to stand by his friend. "It's not the road conditions that are prompting your sudden lack of interest in your campaign."

Derrick turned to face him, wishing Cam couldn't read him so well. "I am not unconcerned—I'm just tired."

"You're worried about Alesha, aren't you?"

He sighed in annoyance. "Come on, man. Don't start speculating on my relationship with Alesha. We have a business arrangement—that's all!" he insisted with more force than was necessary.

Truthfully, after what had transpired between them last night and this morning, he wasn't sure where they stood, or what he wanted to happen between them. Despite her unexplained lies, all he knew for certain was that he couldn't get her out of his mind, out from under his skin or, he grudgingly admitted, out of his heart.

"If that's true, why are you so worried about her?"

"She's alone in an unfamiliar place with no transportation or phone, and a snowstorm is raging outside. Isn't that enough reason for anyone to be concerned?" Derrick's reasoning was flawless, but he knew it wouldn't fool his best friend.

"Yes."

"But?" Derrick knew he was not going to leave it at that.

"But I think there's more to it than that. I think that, despite yourself, you care for Alesha—that you really see her as your wife, not just as a means to an end."

Hearing his feelings articulated so brilliantly by his friend was unnerving and frustrating. Frustration oozed from every pore.

"Look, Cam, we both know that I tried that once, and I'm not going to make that mistake again."

"Please! As for your first wife, if you want to call her that, she was never right for you. I tried to tell you that. Alesha, however, is another story. But then, you know that, don't you?"

"I'm using her—that's where it begins and ends!" His forceful insistence was more for his own benefit than for Cam's.

"If you say so, Derrick." Cam smiled.

Derrick rolled his eyes. "You believe what you want—you will, anyway. I'm going home." He picked up his jacket and walked to the door.

"Derrick?"

"What?" He turned around impatiently.

"Give Alesha a kiss for me."

"Good night, Cameron," he said, sighing heavily before opening the door.

"Good night, bro." Cam smiled. "Drive carefully."

Derrick made his way home as fast as the lousy weather would permit, which was at a slow crawl, giving him too much time to meditate on Cam's words. Was he beginning to care for Alesha, despite his resolve not to? He knew the answer was yes—he had known that from the moment he had seen her again. He had been strongly attracted to her when they had first met two years ago. He had wanted her since their first touch and had burned for her since their first kiss. Now, after finally making love to her, he couldn't deny that he still cared about her very much.

Why had she lied to him two years ago? He could understand her feelings for him scaring her—hell, he had felt the same way—but why had she allowed him to believe she was involved with someone else? Why not just tell him she felt overwhelmed? It didn't make any sense. There had to be more to it than she was admitting, but what?

He sighed loudly. Why did her motivations matter to him one way or another? He was only using her, wasn't he? As he had told Cam, once he had won the Senate seat, he would let her go and he wouldn't think twice about it. He promised himself that he would. However, he knew he was lying, because the thought of life without Alesha left him chilled to the bone.

Alesha was up nervously pacing the floor when she heard a car drive up around 11:00 p.m. She carefully peered out of the bedroom window and was relieved to see Derrick. She absently noted that the ground was covered with a layer of snow. She ran to the door and prepared to open it, but stopped herself abruptly. What was she doing? She couldn't let him know she had been waiting up for him!

Changing course, she ran over and jumped into the bed, pulling the covers over herself before turning onto her side. Closing her eyes, she began to breathe heavily and evenly as if in a deep sleep. Seconds later, the bedroom door opened and Derrick came in. She felt him peer down at her and forced her breathing to remain even.

He smiled slightly as she pretended to be asleep. He had seen her silhouette at the window, and knew instinctively she had been worried about him; that pleased him immensely. He picked up a candle, humming as he walked into the bathroom, leaving the door partially open. Seconds later, Alesha heard the shower running and Derrick singing.

"Inconsiderate oaf." She sat up slightly. "What if I really was asleep? He could wake up the dead with all of that noise."

When he shut the water off some long minutes later, she quickly resumed her previous position, once again feigning sleep. She heard him walk through the door and, seconds later, the bed shifted beneath his weight as he slid underneath the covers, naked beside her.

She held her breath as he rolled closer to her, placing his arm around her waist, before turning her on her back. She continued to feign sleep, hoping he would take the hint that she didn't want to talk about the past anymore.

"I know you're not asleep. Stop pretending," he said softly, leaning over her.

Knowing it was useless, she slowly opened her eyes to stare at him—his face was only inches away from hers. She resisted the sudden urge to trace the rugged outline of his face with her fingers, followed by her lips. Thankfully, he didn't seem angry, just tired. She prayed he wouldn't bombard her with more questions she had no idea how to answer.

"Do you want to talk?" she asked in spite of herself.

"No. No, I don't want to talk."

He lowered his head to hers and she stared at him, mesmerized by his hungry eyes as his lips ever-so-slowly neared hers and touched her mouth. He caressed her lips with butterfly kisses until she was trembling with need. It was all she could do to refrain from begging him to stop this sweet torture and make love to her, and she knew that he knew it, too.

"Cam asked me to give you something."

"What?" Why in the world was he talking about Cam at a time like this?

"This."

His hands threaded themselves into her thick hair and lifted her head slightly off the pillows, forging his lips with hers. He kissed her in a way that should have been illegal and probably was. There was no way she could fail to respond to the sensual assault, and she offered no resistance. Rather, she capitulated without thought or question.

Her lips melted against the incinerating heat of his, her tongue responding to the insistent pressure of his. He laid her head back on the pillows and his body half covered hers as he continued to devastate her with his mouth.

His hands moved to her shoulders, easing the thin straps of her gown down as his fingers explored her creamy, burning flesh. His lips slid from her mouth to her chin, gently biting into her burning skin before moving down her silky throat to rest in the valley between her full breasts.

Her breathing increased rapidly at his touch, and a familiar ache began slowly spreading through her abdomen at his increasingly ardent caresses. He pulled the gown down to reveal her breasts and blew his warm breath onto one of her nipples, which stiffened in response. She moaned as he pulled her swollen flesh into his mouth—his tongue and teeth ravaging her softly scented skin.

His wandering hands moved to pull the gown farther down her quivering body, from her stomach to her hips, as he continued to devour her with increasingly ardent caresses. Her hands moved to his shoulders, pressing closer to his body as he continued to ignite her with his fiery touch.

She began to moan, wantonly craving his total possession. She clung to him openly, her own hands exploring his rippling back, pressing him tightly against her throbbing body. At times his caresses hurt, at others they soothed—yet, always they pleased and inflamed.

He raised his head to lightly touch his lips to hers, and she dazedly realized that she no longer wore her gown. Their bare, heated bodies now touched intimately. She waited for his kiss, and when it didn't materialize, she opened her glowing eyes to encounter the smiling yet darkly excited depths of his as he stared down at her.

"Do you want me to leave you alone?"

His question was whispered against her lips as his mouth touched hers again and again—refusing to satisfy her by thoroughly claiming what she so readily offered. Why did he have to make her verbalize what was so evident by her actions? Her body arched against his convulsively as his hands trailed down her sides to rest on her firm buttocks, pressing her feverish body closer still to his own hard length, making her wholly aware of his need for her.

"Do you?" He persisted when she remained silent, running his tongue along the outline of her lips.

Aching pleasurably all over, she still held back admitting what he already knew. He sought her complete capitulation—mentally and physically—and she didn't have the strength to resist him.

"Why do you have to make me say it?" Her desire-laden voice was barely above a whisper.

"Because I need to hear it, and you need to admit it."

He took her lower lip between his teeth, pulling at her flesh slightly as his strong hands slowly slid up her body to rest at her waist. She moaned aloud, her fingers moving to the back of his head, pressing him closer.

As she pulled his lips to hers, she hissed into his mouth, "No—God help me— I don't want you to leave me alone."

At her admission, his smile deepened before her eyes closed and his lips claimed hers in a scorching kiss. She couldn't think or breathe—all she could do was feel. He sent the blood coursing through her veins boiling out of control with every touch. There wasn't a part of her that didn't belong to him and she was unashamedly glad about that.

She decided then and there to accept their mutual desire and try to make the best of their complicated relationship—while it lasted. She would focus on his being a man, her being a woman and on their sharing the basic needs, even though she reluctantly conceded that she wanted much more than that from him. But did he want more from her?

He rolled onto his back suddenly, taking her with him so that she was lying on top of him. His hands intertwined in her hair, withdrawing her clinging lips from his reluctantly. He smiled at her dazed, questioning expression.

"Touch me." At his soft command, he sensed rather than saw the rush of color that flooded her cheeks as she lowered her eyes demurely. "Alesha." His insistent calling of her name made her to look at him again. "Touch me."

As if spellbound by his tone and his request, she brought her hand up and ran her fingers lightly over his cheek. It was not long before she had memorized every curve, every line of his handsome face. She lowered her head and her lips and tongue slowly followed the path her fingers had left behind. She inhaled deeply at his neck, intoxicated by the clean smell of his flesh. She couldn't believe she was doing this—wanting and needing to do this. It was as if she were outside her body, watching someone else. She was unable to stop her investigation of his body, though, because what she was doing felt too good to end.

Her fingers lightly touched his chest before threading themselves in the short hair she found there, tugging lightly. His quick intake of breath told her she must be doing something right. She raked her long nails down the length of his chest before bringing them back up again. Then she lowered her head, tasting his salty flesh, slowly covering his chest and abdomen with wet kisses—thoroughly enjoying herself. Her tongue licked his lower stomach, sliding in and out of his belly button, but she was still too inhibited to explore any further, and though he longed for her to, he refrained from demanding more than she was able to give.

After several moments longer, she raised her head and lowered her lips toward his. As they touched, he started to take control of the kiss, but resisted the urge. He wanted her to realize she could arouse him and initiate intimacy instead of just responding to his advances. As her eyes stared deeply into his, her mouth continued its descent until their lips touched. Her hair fell over her face and his as she opened her mouth over his, kissing him amorously. His hands cupped her face, holding her closer as she continued to kiss him with mounting passion.

Her hands moved to cover his as they rested on her face, moving them to her breasts before moving her own to frame his face as they continued to kiss. He groaned at her initiative, his hands moving from her breasts to her hips, lifting her slightly before bringing her back down to engulf him totally.

She gasped and straightened to stare at him with passion-glazed eyes. His hands showed her how to please him and herself—for several long wonderful minutes she was in control of their passion and she reveled in it.

Suddenly, unable to bear her sweet torture another second, he reared up and rolled until she was beneath his hard, throbbing body and he took control of their passionate dance.

"You feel so good," he breathed into her mouth as his body bombarded hers.

She wanted to tell him he felt good, too, but coherent words eluded her. So, she just moaned in agreement. Incredible pleasure began to fill and overflow from her burning body once again. Trembling hands moved to his back, holding him tight. She pressed against him and draped one of her legs over his in order to bring him deeper into her as she pulsed around him, intensifying the pleasure with his every thrust. Nothing else mattered except the wonderful wildfire racing through her veins and the sound of Derrick's ragged, hoarse breath intermingling with hers. Nothing was important except the strong beating of his heart next to hers—nothing, except the rapture she experienced once again with him.

The next morning, she awakened with a heavy weight on her chest, which she soon realized was Derrick's head. One of his arms was draped casually across her waist, his eyes were closed and his breathing was even and steady, evidence that he was still asleep.

Her heart skipped several beats at the intimacy of their positions. She was tempted to awaken him, but stopped herself suddenly. Why would she choose a course of action she knew would lead to another passionate bout of lovemaking between them? As she gingerly smoothed a few tendrils of hair away from her eyes, she admitted that, even now, her body craved his. She should be exhausted, but she wasn't. She was becoming an addict, and his body was the drug she now needed more than anything else in the world. And, like all addicts, she didn't think she would be able to give him up until he nearly destroyed her.

Softly, her fingers moved to trace the outline of his sleeping face, remembering the sweet love they had made together last night. There had been a blending, a sharing of emotions that each of them was powerless to stop. Once she would have been troubled by that. Instead, the knowledge now made her happy and hopeful. Her heart somersaulted as she fought the impulse to slide down level with his face, kiss him awake and once again experience a bit of heaven in his arms.

She closed her eyes and sighed contentedly, enjoying the feel of him against her. She could lie here with him this close to her all day and never need to move. Her body had never felt so relaxed or so alive, nor had her soul. As her fingers lightly moved across his lips, she remembered the intense delight they had given her last night. She again fought against waking him so that she could experience the mind-boggling enjoyment she found only when they were pressed close as one. Despite her resolve not to, she silently admitted that she had lost a huge piece of her heart to him last night.

Quickly, she reopened her eyes, fingers stilling their exploration of his handsome outline. God, what was she doing? How had she allowed herself to reach this point? She hadn't meant to become emotionally involved with him again, and yet, against her better judgment, she had. It had been so easy and, what was more terrifying, she wasn't the least bit sorry that she had.

He was a good man and she was tired of fighting the fact that she needed and wanted him in her life. The real question was this: did he feel the same way about her? Once, she had been certain he had, but now, she didn't know how he felt about her. He wanted her, but what did he think about them being together permanently? She finally knew what she wanted without a doubt, but what did Derrick want?

Very slowly, she inched herself away from her husband's warm, inviting body. He stirred several times before rolling away from her onto his side of the bed. She waited a few moments and then carefully got up so as not to awaken him and donned a thin robe over her naked form. Immediately, she missed the heat of his body as the coldness of the room engulfed her.

Tiptoeing over to the thermostat, she adjusted it higher before walking quickly and quietly to the bathroom, softly closing the door behind her. Once there, she leaned against the door and let out a sigh, partly thankful that she had made it without waking him, and partly disappointed because she hadn't. She then flipped the light switch and was glad to see that the power had returned overnight.

Derrick lifted his head from the pillow and sat up in the bed. His fingers slowly retraced the spot on his face that Alesha had just caressed. He tamped down the urge to join her in the bathroom, realizing she needed some space and so did he.

Even as his body longed for hers, he resisted fulfilling the desire that was never far from his mind when he thought of his wife. Even though they had just been married a few days and had some important issues to resolve between them, she felt much more like his wife than the woman who had held the title before her. There were questions he still needed answers to—answers only she could give him—and he would get those answers soon. He had to, because his feelings for her were growing astronomically. He didn't know how to contain them. Did he even want to try?

* * *

An hour later, Alesha placed a glass of orange juice next to the plate of steaming pancakes she had just prepared for herself and Derrick. She shivered as she looked out at the snow-covered terrain beyond the window, and walked out of the kitchen to the foot of the stairs.

"Derrick, breakfast is ready," she yelled.

"I'll be right down."

She turned, went back into the kitchen and sat down. She had just taken a sip of her juice when he came through the door dressed casually in a Washington Redskins sweat suit. He stopped by her chair to kiss her cheek, nearly causing her to spill her juice before sitting down opposite her.

"Good morning." He smiled and looked out at the snowy day. "It's a good thing we don't have to go out today."

"Yes, it is." She watched him as he cut into a pancake and placed a large piece in his mouth—a mouth that had given her the most gratification she had ever known.

"Mmm, this is delicious," he said, breaking into her disturbing thoughts.

"Thank you."

There was welcome silence as he continued to eat and she pretended to do so. She felt so odd, as if they were really a married couple enjoying a leisurely breakfast together. Of course, they were, but this was hardly an ordinary relationship, she firmly reminded herself. However, she wished it was. Suddenly, she wanted to talk to him about little things, to have him smile at her without mockery, to freely touch him and to feel...

"Alesha?"

"I'm sorry, what?" She reluctantly roused herself from her disquieting contemplation.

He smiled then, that smile she hated—the one that said he knew exactly what she was thinking. Why did he seem to know her so well, at times even better than she knew herself?

"I said you're an excellent cook," he slowly reiterated, razor-sharp eyes studying her flushed features.

"Thanks." She smiled slightly, a little embarrassed.

"I missed you when I woke up."

His seemingly innocent sentence caught her off guard, making her drop her fork noisily onto the plate in front of her. She swallowed the lump in her throat and glanced up from her plate.

She stared into his eyes as warm color began to flood her cheeks and stammered, "I—I, um, well, you were out so late and I wanted to let you sleep in."

He smiled that shrewd smile before replying, "I know what you wanted."

Her pupils dilated to twice their normal size. Had he been awake when she had caressed his face? Had he known she had almost awakened him with kisses and an invitation not for food, but for herself? At that thought, her discomfiture increased almost unbearably.

"Would you like some more coffee?" She stood up, seeking an escape from his presence.

"Alesha, don't be afraid of me," he said, grabbing her hand as she prepared to walk past him, halting her progress.

"I'm not," she whispered without looking at him.

"Yes, you are," he softly contradicted, pulling on her hand until she was sitting in the chair next to his, forcing her to meet his intense gaze. "You're also afraid of yourself and of us," he correctly surmised.

"This is all so new to me." She didn't bother to deny his observation.

"It's new to me, too," he assured her.

"You were married before," she reminded him, daring to glance into his understanding face.

"Not like this," he said quickly, surprising himself and pleasing her.

"No?" Why did her heart skip a beat at his admission?

"No," he reiterated, refusing to elaborate. "It doesn't have to be an unpleasant experience."

"It's not," she replied before she could stop herself, waiting for a sarcastic response that never came. Instead, he smiled at her more gently than he ever had. In doing so, he melted her heart.

"And that's what bothers you."

"Yes," she replied truthfully, unable to look away from his irresistible eyes.

His free hand moved to lightly touch her warm cheek as he suggested, "Stop berating yourself for what you feel as far as we're concerned."

"I don't know if I can."

She couldn't believe they were having a serious soul-searching conversation. It was a novel, yet welcome, experience.

"Maybe it will help if you know that I feel the same way, too," he admitted.

"Do you?" Surprised eyes stared deeply into his warm ones.

"Yes, I do." He brought her hand to his lips. "We both know why we married, but what we have together is real—as real as it can get. There's no shame in admitting that."

He was being so kind to her—she didn't know what to say. This was the last thing she had expected when she had bared her soul. It added just one more layer of confusion to her already troubled heart.

"It feels real." She sighed softly.

"It is real." He traced the outline of her lower lip with his fingers. "We're the only two people who will ever know what we feel when we're together. I promise I won't ever use that knowledge against you, or make you sorry for wanting me."

"You're shattering all my evil illusions about you, Derrick Chandler." Her voice was husky with emotion as she fought back tears his compassionate words evoked.

"Good. You should have none when it comes to people. You should make up your own mind."

The smile he gave her was tender and, dare she think it, loving. She felt her heart melt even further at the look he gave her, and knew she was very rapidly losing her battle not to become any more emotionally involved with him.

"You're right."

"Let's take it one day at a time," he suggested.

He continued to smile, not the smile she hated, but one she knew she could definitely learn to love.

"One day at a time." She raised her glass of juice and lightly touched it with his before taking a sip.

Their eyes locked and held. She felt raw and wonderfully alive. She suddenly knew she was fighting a losing battle as far as he was concerned. In such a short time, he had completely insinuated himself into her life and, more importantly, her heart. She doubted she would ever be able to totally extricate herself again and wondered if she even wanted to try.

Chapter 10

They had returned from Derrick's country house a month ago and their life had switched into high gear. Their days were full with campaigning, and their nights were full of unbelievable passion. Derrick smiled as he contemplated being alone with his wife tonight. Thoughts of her caused the days to linger interminably and being with her made the nights go by much too quickly.

His smile was replaced by a frown as he riffled through a ton of mail that had accumulated since yesterday. He was grateful to be interrupted by the buzz of the intercom.

"Yes, Dorothy, what is it?"

"Sir, Mrs. Chandler is here."

He frowned at his assistant's strange tone. "Send her in."

"Yes, sir."

He stood and walked from behind his desk. When the door opened, the smile that had been plastered on his face changed into a shocked frown as a tall, slender woman sauntered into his office.

"Hello, Derrick."

"Diana. This is a…"

She smiled brightly. "Pleasure?"

"Surprise."

She kissed his stiff cheek. "A good one, I hope."

He reclined against his desk. "What are you doing here?"

"You know I've been out of the country."

"No—" he shook his head "—I didn't."

"I just got back to the States and imagine my surprise when I saw my husband's picture plastered all over the news."

He raised an eyebrow. "Ex-husband."

"Anyway—" she walked closer "—I just had to see you."

"Why?"

"To congratulate you on your senatorial run. The polls say your chances are excellent."

"A phone call would have sufficed."

"I know." She placed a hand on his thigh. "But I like the personal touch."

"What's with calling yourself Mrs. Chandler?" He pointedly removed her hand. "You didn't use my name when we were together."

"I wanted to make sure you would see me."

"I would have seen you."

She smiled. "That's good to know."

"There's something else you should know."

She leaned toward him. "What?"

"There is a new Mrs. Chandler in my life."

"Yes." She ran fingers through her short hair. "I've heard you remarried."

"I did." He stood, walked around his desk and sat down.

"So, how's married life treating you the second time around?"

"Great."

"Really?" She sat on the edge of his desk and crossed her long legs.

He smiled. "Really."

"I can't wait to meet her."

"Why?"

She shrugged. "I'm just curious."

"Don't be." He picked up an envelope from his desk. "If you'll excuse me, I have a lot of work to do."

"I thought we could catch up."

He shook his head. "We don't have anything to catch up on."

She smiled at his bent head and stood. "All right. I'll be seeing you around, Derrick."

"I doubt it." He glanced at her briefly. "We run in different circles."

"You never know." She blew him a kiss and left.

Once he was alone, he slammed the folder shut and glared at the closed door. This unexpected, unpleasant turn of events was the last thing he needed.

"Damn!"

Alesha took a glass of champagne from a passing waiter. She made her way onto the covered and heated balcony while Derrick and Cam talked with a donor inside the ballroom. Tonight, they were attending another in a long line of political fundraisers.

"Hello, Alesha."

She turned and smiled at the woman who touched her arm. She was tall with short hair and smooth brown skin, and she wore a red figure-hugging, low-cut sequined gown that made Alesha's long-sleeved black dress seem dowdy by comparison.

"Hello, do I know you?"

"We haven't been formally introduced." The woman smiled. "Nice party, isn't it?"

Alesha returned her smile. "Very."

"I prefer quieter, more intimate settings, myself."

"So do I, but this is the political life," Alesha said, laughing. "Are you here alone?"

"Mmm." She sipped her drink. "Yes, I wanted to hear Derrick speak in person."

Alesha's eyebrow rose at the woman's familiar use of her husband's name. "Do you know Derrick?"

"You could say that," the woman said, smiling secretively. "I'm sorry. Allow me to introduce myself." She paused for maximal effect before revealing, "I'm Diana Chandler."

Alesha choked on her drink. "Who?"

"Diana Chandler." She smiled at her discomfiture. "I guess I should say Diana Davis-Chandler."

Her eyes widened. "You're Derrick's ex-wife?"

"Yes. I'm sorry if I shocked you."

Alesha knew she wasn't sorry at all. Diana had deliberately sought her out to announce herself. The question was, why hadn't Derrick told her?

"Didn't Derrick tell you I was back in town?"

"No." Alesha shook her head. "No, he didn't."

"Well—" she shrugged dismissively "—I'm sure it just slipped his mind."

"It must have."

She placed a hand on her hip. "So you're the new Mrs."

"Yes, I am."

"We must trade stories some time."

"I don't think so." Alesha placed her half-empty glass on a passing waiter's tray. "Excuse me."

"Surely. It was nice to meet you."

She didn't return Diana's sentiments as she walked away quickly. Why hadn't Derrick told her his ex was in town?

Had he been meeting secretly with her? What did she want? As she reentered the ballroom, her arm was grabbed by a familiar hand.

"Alesha, where have you been?"

"On the patio."

Derrick glanced at her distraught face. "What's wrong?"

"Nothing." She shook her head.

"Come on, Alesha. What is it?"

"I just met Diana."

He frowned. "She's here?"

"Yes." She stared at him. "Why didn't you tell me she was in town?"

"There was no reason to."

She glared at him. "No reason to?"

"No." He studied her closely. "What did she say to you?"

"Nothing."

"Alesha…"

"I need to get out of here, Derrick. Now!" She pulled her arm free and ran from the room.

Diana watched the scene from across the room gleefully. Derrick encountered her smiling eyes and shot her an angry glare before following his wife out.

They entered their house and Alesha angrily threw her purse and coat down on the hall table before stalking into the living room. Derrick sighed and followed her slowly.

"How long am I going to get the silent treatment?"

She turned from the window to glare at him. "You want to talk?" At his positive nod, she obliged him. "Fine! Why didn't you tell me Diana was in town?"

He sighed. "Her comings and goings don't have anything to do with me or, more importantly, us."

"Derrick." She walked closer. "I deserved to know!"

"Why?"

"Why?" She spread her hands wide. "Oh, I don't know. Maybe so I would be prepared for a woman accosting me at a fundraiser claiming to be Mrs. Chandler!"

He scowled. "She didn't."

"She did!"

Anger darkened his eyes. "Damn that woman!"

"Damn you both!"

"Alesha." He deliberately kept his voice measured. "I didn't know she was going to be there tonight."

"But you knew she was in town!"

"I only found out today."

"That was long enough to tell me, Derrick!"

"Dammit, I didn't see a reason to tell you!" His frustration was evident. "As far as I was concerned, I didn't expect to see her again."

She eyed him suspiciously. "Of course you didn't."

He frowned. "What is that supposed to mean?"

"I'm sure you can figure it out."

"Will you stop behaving so irrationally?"

"I'm sorry that I'm not cold and sophisticated enough for you."

"What are you talking about? I didn't say that."

"You implied it." She was angry and hurt, and she didn't want to be reasonable. "If my company displeases you so much, why don't you go and find Diana? I'm sure she'll accommodate you any way she can."

She pushed past him, but he grabbed her arm, halting her retreat. Her eyes sparkled furiously.

"Don't be an idiot!" he said.

She gasped. "So now I'm an idiot?"

She tried to pull her arm free. He refused to release her, pulling her closer instead.

"You are if you think I want anything to do with Diana."

"You married her."

He had married Diana voluntarily—it hadn't been an antiseptic arrangement, like their marriage.

"I also divorced her—quickly."

"Do you regret that decision?"

Damn, he thought they were beyond nonsense like this. He had hoped they were building something special and permanent over the past months. They had been before Diana's sudden reappearance in his life.

She held her breath and waited for his response. A response she dreaded yet needed to hear. His prolonged silence sent fingers of fear dancing up her spine.

"Where are these absurd questions coming from?"

"Answer me!"

He squared his shoulders. "No, I don't think I will."

They stubbornly stared at each other for a few pregnant seconds before she pulled her arm from his and stalked from the room. He followed.

"Where are you going?"

"To bed." She paused before pointedly adding, "Alone!"

"Alesha…"

"I don't want to talk to you anymore tonight!"

"That's fine with me!" He grabbed his keys from the table.

She paused on the stairs. "Where are you going?"

"Do you care?"

"No, I don't care at all." She continued up the stairs.

"Good!" He stormed out, slamming the door behind him.

Early the next morning, Alesha was sitting on the sofa in her robe, drinking her second cup of coffee when she heard the front door open. Seconds later, Derrick walked into the room, disheveled, still dressed in his tuxedo from the night before. He looked exhausted. He barely glanced at her as he walked over and poured himself a cup of black coffee.

"Where were you last night?"

"Why?" His voice was terse.

Her lips thinned. "Were you with her?"

He made contact eye contact with her. "With whom?"

"With Diana."

"You sound like you're jealous." He watched her closely. "But that's impossible, isn't it?"

She lowered her eyes. "Of course it is."

"Yeah, it would be since our marriage isn't real, is it?"

His observation cut her to the quick. To her, their marriage was very real—she had thought he felt the same way. With superhuman effort, she turned to him with a frosty expression.

"You know the answer to that."

His eyes burned. "We're just playing house, aren't we?"

"Yes." She picked up her juice and resisted an urge to throw it in his face.

"Then why do you care where I was?" He nearly shouted the question, angered by her response.

"I don't." She smiled coldly. "You can stay with Diana, for all I care."

"I wasn't with Diana!" He slammed his cup down hard, sloshing liquid onto the table.

"Is that right?"

"Yes, that's right!" At her disbelieving stare he swore savagely, "Dammit, nothing is going on between us and if you don't believe me, then that's your problem!"

Before she could respond, she watched Derrick turn and angrily walk up the stairs, two at a time. Was he telling the truth? She wanted to believe him with every breath she took, but could she trust him? She had before Diana's arrival. Should she now?

* * *

Cam watched as Derrick continued pacing angrily in front of his desk.

"What's the matter with you?"

"Nothing!"

"Really?" An eyebrow rose in disbelief. "Is that why you look like you're contemplating murder?"

"Maybe I am."

"Who's the target?"

Derrick leaned against his desk. "Diana."

Cam frowned. "Diana who?"

"Davis."

"What?" Cam stood to face his angry friend. "Is she in town?"

"Unfortunately."

"What has she done?"

"She was at the fundraiser last night and accosted Alesha."

"Oh, no." Cam rolled his eyes. "Tell me all about it."

"She introduced herself to Alesha as Mrs. Chandler!"

"That woman!" Cam shook his head in exasperation.

"Alesha and I had a fight last night. She's angry because I didn't tell her Diana was in town."

"When did you find out?"

"Yesterday afternoon. She came by my office."

"Why didn't you tell Alesha?"

"I had hoped she would just go away."

Cam sighed. "Wishful thinking."

"I should find her and wring her neck!"

"No." Cam placed a hand on Derrick's shoulder. "Just stay away from her. She's nothing but trouble."

He sighed. "You're right."

"Nice to hear you admit it for once."

Derrick continued to frown. His friend's attempt at humor was completely lost on him.

"What does she want, Cam?"

He shrugged. "Running for office is just like winning the lottery—people come out from the woodwork, trying to latch onto your coattails."

"I suppose, but she's not going to ruin my marriage."

"Your marriage of convenience?"

Derrick silently cursed his slip of the tongue. He had enough trouble right now without getting into a philosophical discussion with his friend about the status of his marriage.

"I'm not going to let her screw up my election chances."

Cam smiled. "No, you had it right the first time."

"Cameron…"

He laughed. "Save your protestations for someone else."

Derrick rubbed his tired eyes. "How did everything get so out of control?"

"It's called life, my friend." He patted Derrick's shoulder comfortingly.

Derrick reopened determined eyes. "I'm not going to let Diana demolish what I've worked so hard to build."

"I hope not." He couldn't resist adding, "What you and Alesha have is special, but then, I don't have to tell you that, do I?"

Derrick sighed heavily. "This has nothing to do with Alesha."

"Oh, man, why don't you stop lying to yourself?" Cam shook his head in remonstration. "You care about your wife very much and if you won't admit it to me, at least admit it to yourself."

Derrick made eye contact with his friend, but remained silent. There was no need to say a word because they both knew he was right. The question was, what was he going to do about it?

That afternoon Alesha smiled wistfully as she listened to the antics of her onetime colleague, related as only Angela could. She hadn't seen Angela since the wedding and had missed her terribly, but she wasn't miserable in her new life as she had thought she would be—that is, not until Diana had shown up.

"So, how's married life?"

"Great." She forced a smile.

"I should be so lucky to find a guy like Derrick." Angela took a sip of her water.

"There are other fish in the ocean. What about Cam?"

"Derrick's friend?"

"Yes, the man who took great care placing my garter on your thigh at my wedding."

"Oh, yeah. I remember him." Angela smiled secretively. "He's very cute."

"I noticed."

"Really? What else did you notice?" Alesha leaned forward.

"Nothing."

"So did you two talk?"

"We exchanged a few words."

"And?"

"And nothing. You've already taken the top prize."

"And I intend to keep him." Her teasing smile faltered slightly when she realized how much she meant the words she had so easily spoken.

"I didn't doubt that for a moment." Angela's smile turned to a frown. "Hey, what's wrong?"

Alesha blinked rapidly. She had been trying with all her might to appear carefree and happy, and had thought she was doing an admirable job until Angela's question.

"Nothing's wrong." She sipped her drink. "Why would you think that?"

"Something's bothering you." She frowned. "What is it?"

"It's…"

"Don't you dare say 'nothing'!" Angela touched her hand. "Tell me."

She remained silent as she contemplated answering her friend's question. The truth was, she needed to talk to someone and Angela was her confidante. She would keep her secret. Besides, she could use some wise advice right about now.

"Derrick and I went to a fundraiser last night."

"And?"

"His ex-wife was there."

Angela's mouth dropped open in shock. "He was married before?"

"Briefly, two years ago."

"Did you know?"

"Of course," she said.

Angela frowned suspiciously. "What did she do to you?"

She sighed. "She introduced herself as Diana Chandler."

Angela gawked. "No, that hussy didn't!"

Alesha chuckled at her choice of words. "She did."

"The nerve of her!"

Alesha sipped her drink. "Oh, she has plenty of that."

"What did Derrick do?"

"He wasn't around when we met."

"Well, you don't have anything to worry about."

"I don't?"

"Of course not. Anyone seeing you and Derrick together can see you're meant to be."

"We are?"

"Definitely. His ex is just jealous that you have what she couldn't hold on to."

"I suppose you're right." Alesha prayed she was right.

"You're not worried about her, are you?"

"No."

"No?"

She sighed. "Maybe a little bit."

"Did you talk to Derrick?" After Alesha nodded, Angela said, "What did he say?"

She left out all the colorful language and shouting and succinctly responded, "That he's not interested in her."

"Of course he's not. I rest my case." She frowned at her friend. "You do believe him, don't you?"

"Of course. It was just unnerving meeting her out of the blue."

"I'm sure it was, but, girl, Derrick is so hung up on you he's not going to let anyone come between you, especially not his ex-wife." She paused. "And *ex* is the operative word."

"I know." She smiled. "You're right."

"Of course I'm right. Diana is just trying to stir up trouble where none exists. Don't give her the satisfaction. You're Mrs. Chandler now—not her."

"Yes, I am," she said, smilingly.

"And don't you forget it," Angela ordered.

"I won't," Alesha promised, and that was one promise she intended to keep.

Alesha returned home a little after 7:00 p.m. after making several appearances at different functions and giving a speech at a women's club—all after her much-needed lunch with Angela. She was exhausted.

She kicked off her black high-heel pumps and walked into the living room. There, she threw her purse and keys onto the tabletop and limply fell onto the plush black-leather sofa, closing her eyes contentedly as she let out her breath on a deep, grateful sigh. Thankfully, Derrick wasn't home—she didn't have the strength to fight with him again.

They needed to talk about Diana, but she promised herself that when they did, they would do it civilly. She grimaced at the thought of the woman who had upset the tenuous balance of their world. What did Diana want? She silently reprimanded herself. It was obvious that she wanted Derrick. The question was, did he want her? A queasy feeling invaded her stomach as she considered the last question. He said he didn't. He gave no indication that he did. She wanted to believe him, but should she?

"Rough day?"

She opened her eyes to stare into Derrick's, not realizing she had briefly dozed off. He was smiling down at her with a bouquet of red roses and thankfully appeared to be in a better mood than he had been that morning. Frankly, so was she after her lunch with Angela. Maybe Cam had calmed him down. She hoped so.

She sat up and tucked her legs beneath her. "Are those for me?"

"Yes." He handed her the flowers. "They're a peace offering.

"Thank you." She smiled. "Derrick, about last night and this morning…"

"Alesha." He sat down on the coffee table in front of her. "I don't want to argue with you again."

"Neither do I." She sighed in relief. "I'm sorry."

"Me, too." He paused before admitting, "I should have told you about Diana."

She watched him closely. "Why didn't you?"

"I honestly didn't think I would see her again, or that you two would ever meet."

"Why is she here, Derrick?"

"I don't know and I don't care, but it has nothing to do with me or us."

She fingered a soft petal. "Doesn't it?"

"Not as far as I'm concerned." He touched her hand and serious eyes bore into hers. "I'm not interested in Diana. Do you believe me?"

She nodded slowly. "Yes, I do."

He smiled in relief. "Good." He kissed her briefly before standing and going to the bar.

"Does it really matter to you what I think?"

"Yes, it does." He turned to stare at her. "For the record, I spent the night in my car, which is why I was in such a foul mood this morning."

His words were like music to her ears. She had suffered last night and today, envisioning him with that witch, Diana.

"Why did you do that?"

He smiled sheepishly. "To teach you a lesson."

She laughed. "I think I got the better end of the stick—I slept in our nice, comfy bed."

His eyes darkened. "I'll join you tonight."

She blushed before changing the subject. "Um, I saw Angela today."

"How is she?" He noisily dropped a few pieces of ice in a glass.

"She's Angela." She chuckled and he joined her.

"Can I get you something?"

"No, thanks." All she wanted to do was to stay where she was and continue their polite conversation.

"We'll have to invite her to dinner soon."

"That would be nice. Maybe we can invite Cam, too."

"Matchmaking?" He sipped his drink and walked back toward her. A whimsical smile tilted the corners of his mouth.

"No, not really."

"No?"

"Well, maybe a little," she confessed.

He sat down beside her on the sofa, placed his drink on the side table and pulled her legs across his lap, forcing her to lean back, and softly began massaging her weary feet and legs. She started to protest, but what he was doing felt so wonderful. She sank into the cushions and watched him through half-closed eyes.

"Oh!" She moaned gratefully, instantly forgetting what they had been talking about. "That feels wonderful."

He smiled at her and continued in silence. His strong fingers kneaded her tired flesh until it was putty in his hands. His fingers slid up and down the soles of her aching feet before moving to her ankles, making soothing little circles on her silky skin.

"How was your day?" She fully opened her eyes to stare at his handsome profile.

"Very profitable."

He glanced at her shortly before returning his eyes to her legs. His magical fingers continued massaging her calves.

"Perhaps you're in the wrong line of business." She sighed dreamily.

He frowned at that and turned to stare at her. "Why do you say that?"

"You should be a masseur."

He laughed out loud, a pleasing sound she never tired of hearing. "You think so?" He ran his hands forcefully up and down her tingling calves.

"Oh, yes." She nearly purred the words.

His hands moved up to her thighs underneath the wool skirt she wore, suddenly causing a different kind of sensation—a familiar pain began growing in the pit of her stomach. His warm, strong hands caressed her inner thighs.

She stared longingly into the darkening intensity of his eyes and knew he was thinking the same thing she was. She realized how this encounter was going to end, and she welcomed it. She silently admitted she had been secretly waiting for this moment all day long.

Suddenly, there was a knock at the door followed by the entrance of their housekeeper. "Excuse me, sir, ma'am.

There's a call for you, Mr. Chandler." She handed Derrick the phone before soundlessly leaving.

Derrick absently continued to rub her legs, and she watched him unobtrusively. She bet he could charm a snake out of its skin without even trying. She half listened to his conversation and realized that he was talking to Cam. She prayed they would not have to go out for the evening—she just didn't have the strength.

"Yes, Cam, everything is fine." He smiled at her. "Thanks, but we're looking forward to an evening alone."

She could have kissed him for refusing Cam's invitation.

"Alesha's had a rough day and I'm tired, too," he explained and then drily laughed. "Yes, Cameron."

He hung up and stared at her. His hands reached out and grabbed hers, pulling her until she was sitting upright. Her legs were still draped over his thighs. Her face was inches away from his. They stared at each other intensely. Whenever he was near, she completely forgot everything, except for the wonderful way he made her feel. She held her breath, waiting and longing for him to kiss her. Just the slightest movement on her part and their lips would touch. However, neither of them moved to initiate it.

"Cam says hello." He traced her cheek with his thumb, setting off little eruptions within her.

"Oh."

"Hmm." His fingers moved to her burgundy lips, taking extreme care to outline every curve. "What do you want to do tonight?"

"Let's stay in."

"And do what?"

Enigmatic eyes stared into her aroused ones. His voice was low and sexy. It touched her in all the right places.

"Let's make some popcorn and watch a good movie," she said.

He smiled. "That sounds like a good start."

"Yes."

He stood, took her hand and pulled her up with him. "But after the movie, I get to decide what we do next."

Her pupils dilated and she leaned toward him. "Deal."

They smiled at each other, both glad the unpleasantness of last night was behind them. He placed a quick kiss on her lips before leading her out into the hallway.

Chapter 11

They sat side by side on a soft black-leather sofa, watching a horror movie. The lights were off and the atmosphere in the room was both eerie and romantic. At a particularly scary part, Alesha screamed and automatically sought out the comfort of Derrick's chest, hiding her face there. He laughed at her, but his arm went around her shoulders as he pulled her closer.

"It's all right."

She felt him smile against her hair. Suddenly realizing the intimacy of their positions, she prepared to move away. His arm, however, tightened around her shoulders, pulling her closer.

"Don't move."

She didn't want to move from his comforting presence. So she did as he indicated and stayed right where she was. Tucking her legs underneath her, she turned her head until her cheek was resting on his warm chest and she continued to watch the movie.

She felt and heard the strong thudding of his heart. That wonderfully woodsy-smelling cologne he wore drifted up to tickle her nose, almost tempting her to unbutton his shirt and bury her face in his muscular chest until she was absorbed by his intoxicating smell.

His hand absently massaged her shoulder before moving to lightly play with her hair. Early in their relationship, she had realized that he liked to do that, just as much as she liked for him to. She inhaled deeply, again assaulting her senses with his scent. Suddenly, even though she was enjoying the film, the last thing she wanted was to finish watching it. Before she gave in to an irrepressible urge to pull his mouth down to hers, she abruptly stood, taking them both by surprise.

"I'm going to get some more tea." She answered his questioning gaze.

He grabbed her hand as he, too, stood. He noted the slight flush to her face and the pulse beating erratically at her neck. He longed to place his lips on that spot. He instinctively knew that she wanted him to do that, too—that and much more.

"No, you don't want any tea." His arms pulled her close.

His lips found and enclosed hers. She didn't even pretend to resist, sighing in pleasure against his mouth. Her hands drifted upward to rest on his chest. She felt herself sinking to the floor and her hands trailed up to his sturdy shoulders as they continued to engage in a thoroughly enjoyable embrace.

Against her will, he removed his lips from hers and firmly responded, "You want this—you want me."

She was unable to respond as his sizzling mouth covered hers again. He had to be the most fabulous kisser in the world, she thought. She felt herself leaving her body. His touch inflamed her soul, making her feel as if she were the most important person in his life. As her arms encircled his neck, she silently prayed that assumption was correct. Her eyes closed against the blazing heat emanating from his gaze.

"Yes, I do want you," she unashamedly admitted. "I want you very much."

They both lay close together on the softly carpeted floor. His lips fused against hers, their tongues engaged in a heated dance of rising passion. Her mouth caressed his. Once again she felt consumed by him and longed to feel only as he could make her feel. They savored the tastes and textures of each other's mouths.

His hands moved down her back to her softly rounded bottom, to the back of her thigh, intimately draping one of her legs over his, pressing her firmly against his solid length, making her fully aware of the hardening bulge in his groin. His body telegraphed a wild need for hers, a need that matched hers for him.

His roving hands moved to unbutton the front of her blouse with expert ease, slipping beneath to explore her breasts. His lips placed tender kisses down her cheek to her neck before his teeth bit into a pebble-hard nipple through the sheer lacy fabric of her bra. She closed her eyes tighter as mounting pleasure built unbearably within her tingling body.

Her fingers flexed on his shoulders before moving under his T-shirt to caress his chest before exploring his muscular back, her nails raking across his taut skin as her hunger for him surged. His hot mouth teased her flesh until she thought she would explode.

She moaned aloud, clinging to him, begging him with her body to make love to her. In response, his mouth blazed a trail of fire up her trembling body to capture her lips once again, plundering her. One of his legs eased intimately between hers and he rolled until he was half lying on top of her, crushing her body into the floor as he ravaged her mouth. She wanted him so much that it physically hurt and it was a heady feeling knowing that he wanted her just as much.

Her body molded against his perfectly. She clung to him, moaning. His caresses grew more ardent, more insistent. His hands slid down to her hips and then moved to the front of her jeans, slipping under the waistband to stroke the smooth flesh he found there.

His mouth bruised hers, but she didn't care. All she wanted was him—always him and only him. She sighed as her naked chest and abdomen moved against his. She longed to feel his naked body imprinting itself on hers. Her hands moved to his firm bottom, pressing closer to his rock-hard length, silently pleading with him to give them both what they so desperately wanted and needed.

She felt him smile slightly at her actions and she didn't care if he knew how much she wanted him. Nothing mattered except the completeness she felt every time his body claimed hers.

Neither of them heard the doorbell ring, or the door open and close, because they were so engrossed with each other. Neither of them saw the man who entered and stood staring down at them in total shock. Neither of them heard his swiftly indrawn breath. Not until he spoke did they realize they were no longer alone.

"Excuse me!"

Simultaneously they turned passion-glazed eyes to stare reluctantly at Robert. He glanced away, but not until he encountered their intimately entwined limbs and his sister's unbuttoned blouse. Her arms were holding the man who had blackmailed her into marriage and his were around her.

It was Derrick who spoke first, the expression on his face

turning from passionate to annoyed, and then to amused. He sat up and faced Alesha's brother. This was going to be interesting.

"Robert, what are you doing here?" He almost laughed at the look of distaste on the other man's face.

Alesha was mortified! She sat up and shakily rebuttoned her blouse, grateful that Derrick was sitting in front of her, shielding her from her brother's gaze. Her head was lowered and she smoothed her hair, which had seconds before been disarrayed by Derrick's fingers. She couldn't bring herself to look at either man. Derrick grasped her hands once she had finished buttoning her blouse, and they both stood to face her brother.

"What's going on here?"

"What does it look like?" Derrick's disdain was evident. "I was about to make love to my wife," he told Robert.

Robert's eyes darkened in fury and he lunged for Derrick, snarling, "Why you son of a…"

Alesha quickly positioned her small frame between them, and exclaimed with her back to Derrick, "Stop it!"

Derrick's hands automatically moved to her waist, encircling it, making Robert aware that she was his wife—a wife whom he could touch anytime he pleased.

Alesha didn't move away, seeking to forestall any further scene between them. Instead, she asked her brother, "Robert, why are you here?"

"To see how you're doing." His eyes narrowed as they darted to Derrick's hands still encircling her waist, his flat palm resting on her stomach possessively.

"As you can see, we were doing fine before we were interrupted." Derrick's hand possessively pulled her back against him.

"Derrick, please." She turned to stare at him. "Let me speak with Robert alone."

"You don't have to ask his permission!"

"Nor does she have to explain anything to you." Derrick smiled at Robert's indignation. "Whatever predicament Alesha finds herself in is not her fault—it's yours."

"Why, you…" Robert began moving toward Derrick again.

"Derrick, Robert, stop it!" Alesha placed a hand on each one's chest, trying to keep them apart.

"Alesha, I need to speak with you—alone," Robert said pointedly, his eyes spitting darts at her husband, who smiled at his expression, infuriating the other man more.

"Derrick, please leave us alone." She turned to look at him imploringly, both of her hands now on his chest.

He looked as if he were about to refuse, but something in her eyes made him relent. She could automatically sense this. It was remarkable how she had learned to read him—when he wanted her to, she amended. She lowered her hands from his chest, knowing he was about to acquiesce to her request.

"I'll be upstairs in *our bedroom*." Then, for Robert's benefit and his own pleasure, he bent and kissed her on the mouth before leaving.

Without preamble, Robert began, "What on earth are you doing?"

"What do you mean?"

"You're sleeping with him!"

She defiantly shot back, "Of course I am—I'm his wife. What did you expect?"

"I thought he would have some scruples!" Robert didn't bother to lower his voice.

"Oh, Robert, for heaven's sake!" She raked shaky fingers through her mussed hair. "Derrick's running for office. He can't be seen around town with other women when he's married to me. So I have to perform my wifely duties." She resented having to explain her relationship with her husband to him.

"I can't believe what I'm hearing! You're defending him? What happened to my little sister?"

"She grew up."

"How can you allow him to touch you?" Robert refused to comprehend her behavior.

One word quickly sprang to her mind to answer her brother's question—*easily.* It was no hardship experiencing Derrick's touch, just as it wasn't repugnant living with him as his wife and his lover.

"How could I stop him?" She wished he would leave.

"Do you mean he forces himself…"

"No." She shook her head.

"Then what?" He motioned with his hands, begging for understanding.

She closed her eyes and then opened them again to stare at her brother. "Robert, I'm his wife." She prayed he would leave it at that. He didn't.

"So? You're not his possession." He grabbed her shoulders and shook her slightly.

She pulled out of his grasp. "What do you want from me?"

"I want you to come with me. We have to get you out of here." He grabbed her hand.

"No!"

She wrenched her hand from him. His suggestion was repulsive to her. She didn't stop to consider why.

"Why not?"

"Have you forgotten why I married him?"

"It doesn't matter any longer."

"It does matter!" she responded hotly. "I won't have Mom find out what either of us has done. It would kill her."

"Sis, you've got to listen…"

"No, you listen." Her voice was deadly serious, though quiet. "I am not going to leave Derrick."

"Why not?"

She evaded his eyes. "Because I'm not."

"That's not an answer, Alesha." He watched her closely and illumination widened his eyes. "Do you want to stay here? Is that it?"

That was exactly it, but how could she admit that to him? Would he understand that the man she had married to cover up her brother's theft was a man she never wanted to be parted from?

"Robert, I'm not going to discuss my marriage with you."

"Alesha…"

"Robert, I love you." Her voice lost much of its sting. "But I don't want to hear another word from you about this—okay?" At his reluctant nod, she kissed his cheek. "Good. I'll talk to you later."

She turned and walked up the stairs, leaving him staring after her. He wouldn't have believed it had he not witnessed it—she cared for Derrick and, from the scene he had interrupted, Derrick felt something for her, too. He smiled slightly before walking to the front door. Damned if he had expected this turn of events. And he doubted that either of them had.

As she slowly entered the bedroom, she found Derrick sitting on the sofa by the window, papers strewn around him. He looked up.

"How did it go?" He walked over to her.

"All right." She walked away from him to sit at her vanity table.

He frowned. "Just all right?"

"Do you want a blow by blow?" She didn't want to talk about Robert. She needed to think.

"I want to know if I should expect another visit from your brother."

"Don't worry. I don't think Robert will be back without an invitation."

"Good." His response was brief and cool.

He watched her. As usual, when he was around his wife, strange emotions began to surface in him. Why did he have an almost overwhelming urge to simply hold her and tell her everything would be all right?

Without thinking, he reached out and placed a hand lightly on her shoulder. She jumped from the unexpected contact and he immediately removed his fingers, the kind words he had been about to utter vanishing just as suddenly as they had appeared.

"Don't worry. I'm not going to try to finish what we started downstairs."

He turned and walked toward the door, stopping to pick up his papers from the sofa. He was obviously angry. She glanced up and encountered his cool eyes in the mirror.

"Where are you going?"

"To the study to finish my speech for tomorrow night." He turned away. Something made him turn and face her again. "Unless you want me to stay."

She hesitated shortly before responding. What she really wanted was for him to hold her close and make her forget everything except him. However, she couldn't admit that. Or, more to the point, she wouldn't.

"You go ahead. I think I'll turn in." She lowered her eyes so that he wouldn't glimpse the misery behind them.

"Good night, then."

When she raised her eyes again, he was gone. She lowered her aching head into her hand, trying to make sense out of the situation. Her feelings were so jumbled, so mixed-up. If anyone asked her what day it was, she didn't think she would be able to correctly tell them. Just when she had come to some sort of inner peace about her relationship with Derrick, it seemed that life was throwing up obstacle after obstacle to undermine her tenuous hold on happiness.

She slowly stood and walked over to the bed before sitting down heavily on it. She stared at the door through which Derrick had exited moments earlier. She wanted to ask him what she meant to him. Where did he see their marriage going, if anywhere? Was she more to him than just a means to get elected? She wanted to ask all those things, but she couldn't—not until she was ready to impart a few truths of her own. She wanted to bare her soul to him, but she was afraid of being rejected. She knew he desired her, but did his feelings go any deeper than that?

Things had been going so well on their honeymoon, but ever since they had returned, the fragile happiness and peace they had attained had been sorely tested by outside forces, namely Diana and now Robert. Her feelings for Derrick placed her in enough inner turmoil—she didn't need anything or anyone adding to her already confused state.

One monumental certainty pierced through the fog of her mind—she wanted to remain Mrs. Chandler. Derrick wanted her physically, but did he want a life with her forever? The answer to that single question held the key to her future happiness.

Derrick stared blankly at the pages in front of him. His mind continued to stray to Alesha. Her demeanor a short while ago had baffled and angered him. She was so damn frustrating! Didn't she realize how much he wanted her?

"Dammit!" He hit the top of his desk in frustration. Last night it had been Diana and tonight Robert who had caused unnecessary friction between him and his wife. He seriously entertained the thought of whisking her away from everything and everyone. They seemed to get along so much better when they were all alone. Since they had returned to civilization, all they seemed to do was fight, and he hated that.

At that thought, he tried reminding himself that he was using Alesha as a means to an end—that was all. But he knew he was lying. He could no more stop caring about her than he could stop breathing. He had thought of little else for the years they had been separated. Now that they were together again, she had easily and quickly become an essential part of his life.

He looked forward to coming home to her and talking with her. He loved the fresh way she made everything seem to him. Most of all, he delighted in the way she made him feel. When they made love, there was an undeniable blending of hearts and minds. When they touched on purpose or accidentally, something dormant in him sprang to life—instinctively, he knew it was the same way for her. He needed her. She was crucial to his well-being and his happiness.

God, when had he lost control? What was he going to do to get it back? He sighed as he admitted he had never had any control as far as Alesha was concerned. There was no use in lying to himself anymore about that.

He glanced at his watch and his eyes wandered to the papers strewn carelessly on his desk. He hadn't gotten a thing done. All he had accomplished in the past two and a half hours was to think about Alesha. Sighing once again, he stood and rubbed his tired eyes. All he wanted to do was go to bed, lie down next to his wife and feel complete and whole as only she could make him feel.

She heard the bedroom door opening as Derrick came in. She was lying in bed on her back, pretending to be asleep. She heard him stop beside her before going into the bathroom, closing the door behind him. Seconds later, she heard the shower running.

She lay there, wanting to tell him how miserable she was feeling and have him comfort her. She longed to have him lie down beside her and tell her he could no longer envision his life without her, because that was definitely the way she felt about him.

Derrick emerged from the bathroom a few minutes later, switched off the light and slipped into bed. She forced herself to remain still, her back turned toward him. The heat from his body radiated toward hers and she wished for it to enclose her, dispelling the arctic chill that had encased her heart and flesh.

Suddenly, he rolled over until her back touched his chest and stomach. She nearly purred because it felt so good to be close to him, especially when a warm, strong arm encircled her waist and held her soothingly.

"Alesha?" he said, his warm breath sending shivers of desire down her spine. He softly kissed her ear. "Relax. I have no intention of trying to force myself on you."

His statement was unnecessary. They both knew he wouldn't be forcing her. She would give herself to him willingly, as she always had.

"Derrick…" She paused, not knowing what to say, or rather how to articulate what she desperately wanted from him. So she remained silent.

He pulled her closer still. "I know the confrontation with your brother was hard for you. Let me help. Let me hold you."

She couldn't believe her ears. Why was it she never knew what he was going to do next? His sincere, kind words affected her more than she would have thought possible. If only he would go a few steps further and confess his feelings.

She allowed herself to completely relax, and her hand moved slowly to rest on his as he pulled her near. She closed her eyes and he kissed her neck before resting his head by hers on the pillow. Neither made any further attempt to speak, and before she knew it, her eyes began to droop, but not before the fierce cold that had invaded her body was replaced by comforting warmth, safety and security, unlike any she had ever experienced. Soon her troubled thoughts began to dissipate, making way for restful, much-needed sleep in her husband's tender embrace.

Derrick continued to hold her. He felt the even rise and fall of her chest, indicating that she was fast asleep. Her soft form melted perfectly against his. Her fingers were entwined with his as they rested on her stomach.

Thoughts he had squelched earlier resurfaced, and again he wondered why he felt an overwhelming sense of protectiveness toward her. He pulled her nearer. She shifted slightly and then stilled. He inhaled deeply the wonderful fragrance of her hair, and he acknowledged that he truly thought of her as his wife—not just as a tool to get him elected or as an enemy to punish. He cared about her deeply—why else did the thought of her leaving him on the day their arrangement ended suddenly cause an uneasy feeling in the pit of his stomach that felt much like agony?

He shifted slowly so as not to disturb her, removing his arm from her waist to lie on his back, one hand behind his head. He stared at the ceiling. In a few short months, she had insinuated herself into his life so much that he couldn't even remember what it had been like without her or, more importantly, he didn't want to remember what it had been like without her. Before seeing her again, he had thought he was content; yet, he now knew that had been a lie. She had brought happiness and meaning into his life, which was something he admitted he had been sorely lacking for a long,

long time—since he had last been with her. She made him whole. God, she made him happy.

Alesha suddenly turned until she was lying with her head on his chest. Her arm rested across his waist, and one of her legs sprawled lazily across his.

"Derrick," she whispered contentedly before stilling.

He immediately noted how good she felt against him, as if that was where she had always belonged. Here in his arms was where he always wanted her to be. He tenderly stroked her soft hair before moving to massage her shoulder and back. She sighed comfortably and snuggled deeper into his chest. Her arm moved up to rest in the base of his neck before stilling again.

His arms pulled her closer and he smiled self-mockingly. He had been emotionally snared in a trap of his own making—one he didn't at all want to escape from. He just prayed Alesha felt the same way.

The next morning, Alesha stretched languidly in bed. She could not remember when she had experienced such a peaceful sleep. She reached out her hand in Derrick's direction, but found him gone, much to her disappointment.

She glanced at the crystal clock on the nightstand and saw it was a little after nine. He was probably long gone for the office. Rolling onto her back, she lazily pushed strands of tousled hair away from her eyes as wonderful memories of last night engulfed her.

Her husband had held and comforted her all night long. He had given of his strength unselfishly, and had demanded nothing in return from her. She would never forget how wonderful he had been to her.

She gently touched the place on her pillow where his head had lain. A smile appeared across her face. A very tangible soft spot had formed in her heart for Derrick, and there was nothing she could do to keep it from growing. Her mind tried to convince her that she was in grave danger, yet, remarkably, her heart didn't feel that way at all. She felt totally comfortable with where her relationship with Derrick was heading. She wouldn't allow anything or anyone to spoil the happiness she now felt. She laughed aloud. She was happy— Derrick made her happy and, in her heart, she knew he felt the same way about being married to her.

She lounged around in bed a few seconds longer, contemplating their future before donning a flimsy robe over her silky black gown and going downstairs. For once she would allow herself the luxury of having an unhurried breakfast— remarkably, the entire day was hers to do with as she wished. She had no political functions to attend, until tonight, and no speeches to make. She planned to have a long visit with her mother later and just indulge herself by doing absolutely nothing.

The house was quiet, confirming her suspicions that Derrick had already left. As she passed his study door, though, she heard a voice. Her heart leaped in gladness with the realization that he was still home. Without thinking, she opened the door and went in.

"Derrick, I thought you…" She stopped in midsentence as she found him sitting behind his desk, phone poised in one hand.

She was about to exit when he motioned for her to enter. She only had to wait several seconds before he wrapped up his phone conversation and stood. As he walked over to her, he noticed with satisfaction her relaxed fresh appearance and felt good that he had helped contribute to it.

"Good morning." He smiled tenderly at her.

"Good morning." Her response was given a little shyly.

"How are you feeling?" He eyed her closely.

"Much better." She paused before adding, "Thank you, Derrick."

"You're welcome, Alesha." He stared at her as if he couldn't bear to tear his eyes away.

She returned his intense gaze, wanting to say something, but not knowing what. His expressive eyes roamed over her curvaceous body through the thin negligee she wore before returning to engage hypnotically with hers. Every nerve ending in her body tingled—feeling as if he had reached out and physically explored the path that his eyes had traveled. They began to speak without saying a word, and it was very strange, very powerful and completely entrancing.

Come closer, his eyes seemed to say, and she did.

I want to touch you, her eyes responded.

Then, do it, his invited.

Her hand rose slowly, obeying her desire and his unspoken command. She trailed her fingers down his brow to his cheekbone to the side of his mouth before stopping there. Eyes that had followed the progress of her fingertips gazed into his. She moved closer, or did he? Neither really knew nor cared; it was as if they were one, yet separate, longing to be joined.

Kiss me, she spoke aloud or in her mind—she didn't know which.

I am, she heard his unspoken response as clearly as her own ragged breathing.

Her lips parted the instant his captured hers and she both fell and was drawn into his waiting embrace. Her arms were entwined tightly around his neck. His fingers raked through her tresses, pressing her lips closer to the bruising, yet caressing, force of his.

She closed her eyes and moaned in ecstasy as his strong hands roamed down her shoulders to her midback, pressing her closer. She yearned to feel his naked flesh against hers and shamelessly wished her gown and robe and his spotless charcoal-gray suit would magically disappear. She wanted him so much, and at this moment nothing else mattered, except the need they both shared for each other.

His lips devastated hers again and again. She consumed him. He didn't understand how he could want or need anyone as much as he did her. He knew if the world suddenly ended, he would be all right as long she remained right where she was, in his arms.

They both eagerly anticipated the way this passionate embrace would end, and they welcomed it. However, soon they were interrupted by a very loud cough.

It took several seconds before the sound registered in either of their minds. Reluctantly, his lips departed from hers and his eyes turned in the direction of the intrusion.

Alesha was slower to respond, first wondering why Derrick had stopped kissing her. When she opened her passion-clouded eyes and followed the direction of his gaze, she saw Cam standing in the doorway, smiling broadly. She knew the reason for Derrick's withdrawal.

"I'm sorry to interrupt. I thought you were alone, Derrick." Cam continued, smiling brightly, "Where are my manners? Good morning, Alesha."

She wished he hadn't singled her out. Pulling the folds of her flimsy robe tightly together with one hand and smoothing her tangled hair with the other, she forced herself to meet his gaze.

"Hello." Her voice was a soft whisper as she quickly lowered her embarrassed eyes.

"Is it time to leave yet?"

Derrick easily addressed his friend, and she envied his cool composure. She herself was a mass of quivering jelly.

"Just about." Cam continued grinning at them both.

"Would you two excuse me?" Alesha shot Derrick a quick

glance before she nearly ran from the room and up the stairs to the safety of their bedroom.

"Well, well, well." Cam sat on the side of Derrick's desk.

"Don't start, Cameron." Derrick's eyes darted regretfully to Alesha's hastily retreating back.

"Have you told Alesha how you feel?"

"Not that it's any of your business, but no."

"Why not?"

"Cam, our relationship is complicated."

"Made so by the both of you." He treated Derrick to an exaggerated wink before standing. "Derrick, just tell her! From what I saw, she feels the same way about you."

"You think so?" He walked from behind his desk and scratched his chin.

"Oh, yeah, I think so." He patted his shoulder. "Make it work, man, or you'll regret it."

"Let's go." Derrick picked up his briefcase and preceded him out without answering, though his expression was very thoughtful.

Chapter 12

Alone in their bedroom, Alesha sat on the bed, smiling secretively to herself while replaying the last kiss Derrick and she had shared, fantasizing about the different ending both had wanted before Cam had interrupted them. She gingerly touched her lips and jumped when the phone rang. Sighing, she leaned over to pick up the handset.

"Hello."

"Hi, it's Derrick."

She nearly dropped the phone upon hearing his warm, husky voice. Had he somehow known she was thinking about him? Her insides warmed to know he had been thinking of her.

"Derrick."

There was an uncomfortable pause, each waiting for the other to speak. She had so much she wanted to say, yet she didn't know where to begin.

"What do you have planned for the day?" He asked the question just to hear her voice.

"Well, for a change, my schedule is free." She laughed a little nervously. "I'm probably going to visit Mom."

"That's good. She'll be glad to see you. Give her my best."

"I will."

After a few seconds, he added, "I called to remind you about dinner tonight."

"Thanks, I remember." She chewed on her lower lip thoughtfully.

"Could you make sure my tux is back from the cleaners?"

"Of course, I'll be happy to." She smiled, closing her eyes and picturing his handsome face. "Did you finish your speech?" That was her roundabout way of bringing the conversation back to last night.

"No, but I will at the office." He paused. "I'm sorry Cam walked in on us." He came to the real purpose for his call.

She opened her eyes and was suddenly glad he couldn't see her. Was he apologizing for her embarrassment, or because they had been unable to finish what they had started?

"So was I," she said, realizing how her voice sounded. She quickly added, "What I mean is…"

"I know what you meant."

She could hear the smile in his voice and embarrassment kept her from responding. She wished he was with her now so that they could… She shook her head forcefully, forestalling completion of that thought.

"Well, I'll see you tonight around six."

"Derrick?" She stalled, realizing he was about to hang up.

"Yes?" He waited.

"I—I'll see you tonight. Have a good day." She didn't have anything else to say—she simply didn't want to let him go.

"Tonight," he echoed before ending the call.

She slowly replaced the phone in its cradle. Smiling brightly, she entered the bathroom to prepare for her day.

A short while later, Alesha was still smiling when she sat down beside her mom on the sofa. "How have you been?"

"I've been fine, but I want to hear about you and Derrick. How are the two of you doing?" She smiled.

"Wonderfully, though we're both very busy. I was lucky to have today free." Alesha placed an affectionate kiss on her mother's cheek.

"I'm glad you did." Barbara smiled, adding approvingly, "Derrick is a very nice man. I'm glad you found him."

"Yes, so am I." Her admission came out breathless.

"I've enjoyed our talks."

"Your talks?" Alesha frowned.

"Yes, dear. He calls several times a week and stops by at least once a week."

Her mother's words floored her. Did Derrick really keep in such close contact with her? If so, why?

"He does?"

"Of course. Didn't you know?"

"He didn't mention it. I suppose it slipped his mind."

"You're probably right." Her mother nodded in agreement. "I've told him not to try to fit me into his busy schedule, but he doesn't listen."

"That's Derrick for you." Alesha silently pondered her mother's words.

"A mother couldn't ask for a better son-in-law or husband for her only daughter. He's such a good man."

"Yes, he is, Mom." Alesha smiled contemplatively.

"When are you two going to make me a Big Momma?"

"Momma!" A hand flew to her mouth in shock.

"What?" Barbara laughed at her. "You're not getting any younger and neither am I."

"We've only been married a few months."

She winked conspiratorially. "That's all it takes."

"I know, but let us get used to being married first, okay?"

"What's there to get used to?" Barbara persisted. "That's what's wrong with young people these days—you think you have all the time in the world. Believe me, time waits for no one."

"I know that, but—" she paused as an unnerving thought formed in her mind "—you haven't talked to Derrick about this, have you?"

"Of course not, dear. I was saving my pleading for you."

"Good."

Alesha visibly relaxed. She would have been mortified if her mother and husband had been discussing something so intimate.

"Well?"

"Momma, let me enjoy being a newlywed for a while."

Barbara sighed. "Oh, all right. As long as you remember what I said about running out of time."

"I'll remember."

"Good." Barbara beamed. "I can't wait."

Alesha smiled at her mother indulgently, but wisely remained silent as, for the first time, she fantasized about having Derrick's baby. At the thought of her husband, her heart began to flutter erratically.

She had become so accustomed to being his wife in every sense of the word, even before he had slipped the wedding ring on her finger. And now her mother had planted the idea of having his child, a thought that filled her with joy. How would he react? she wondered.

He cared for her. If she had any doubt about that, last night had erased it. The evolution of their marriage had been natural and inevitable. She had wanted him since that first kiss in his office months ago. She had wanted him every day for the past two years, though she had fought like hell against acknowledging that truth. She smiled at her mother. Life was funny and surprising. She only prayed it would give her what she wanted most—Derrick's heart.

That night, Alesha was dressed in a black, figure-hugging, sleeveless slip dress with a slight train at the back. She wore opera-length black satin gloves. A double-strand pearl-and-diamond bracelet rested on her left gloved wrist, and teardrop pearl-and-diamond earrings dangled from her ears. Her hair was swept loosely up with curls escaping, caressing her neck. A few loose tendrils were flung carelessly over her right eye.

She had told Derrick she was wearing her hair as a compromise—wanting to wear it up, but knowing he preferred it loose. He had laughed at her words, though she had known her explanation had pleased him.

Derrick was dressed in a crisp-white dinner jacket and shirt, and black slacks. He walked out of his dressing room attempting to fasten his tie. Alesha laughed at his predicament and brushed his fingers away.

"Here, let me do it." She picked up the material and tied it perfectly.

She raised her eyes and found him staring at her with the strangest expression. Impulsively, he placed a feathery kiss on her lips, but moved away suddenly to inspect her handiwork in the mirror.

"Thanks."

"You're welcome." She smiled slightly, wishing their kiss had not been so brief or so unsatisfying.

"You look exquisite."

She blushed as his piercing eyes swept over her. It was amazing how a mere look from Derrick could suck the air from her lungs.

"Thank you." After studying his appearance, she added, "You look pretty good yourself."

He smiled at her words and unexpectedly asked, "How did your visit go with your mother?"

"Fine." She walked past him to freshen up her lipstick.

"I'm glad." He smiled as he walked over to stand beside her, searching the dresser top for his cuff links.

She picked up a bottle of perfume and lightly sprayed her bare neck. Derrick inhaled the sensuous scent deeply and their eyes met again in the mirror. Her chest rose rapidly and his eyes darted to her neck. She felt breathless, as if his hands were caressing her, silently wishing they were. She lowered the perfume with one hand and picked up a double-strand pearl-and-diamond necklace with the other, her eyes never leaving his in the mirror.

He took the necklace from her fingers and placed it around her neck before fastening it. His fingers lingered unnecessarily long on her soft flesh. There was no denying what they both wanted.

To remove temptation, he turned and walked over to the bed and sat down. He put on his black shoes. She watched him through the mirror, wondering why he hadn't given in to an impulse she knew they both had shared. He raised his head and caught her questioning gaze before she quickly looked away.

"Mom asked about you." She spoke primarily to have something to say.

"That was nice of her." He stood and placed a handkerchief inside the pocket of his dinner jacket.

"She said something that surprised me." She walked over to where he stood, placing her hand on his strong arm while she slipped into her black pumps.

"What was that?" He looked at her curiously as she straightened to face him.

"That you keep in regular contact with her." She watched him closely.

"So?" He wondered where this was leading.

"So, why haven't you ever mentioned it to me?"

His eyebrows arched slightly and he stepped away to grab his keys off the nightstand. "I wasn't aware I had to. I happen to like Barbara and I care about how she's doing. Do you have a problem with that?"

"No, not at all." She was warmed by his words. "I was just surprised you hadn't said anything about it to me."

He stared at her strangely. "We'd better get going." He picked up her faux-mink black stole and helped her into it.

"I need to put the finishing touches on my makeup. Why don't you bring the car around?"

"You look beautiful." He kissed her cheek before opening the door. "But go ahead and finish your war paint and I'll meet you downstairs."

"Okay."

He quickly descended the stairs and opened the front door, finding Diana loitering there. He didn't bother to hide his displeasure. Damn, what now?

"Diana, what are you doing here?"

"May I come in?"

"No. Alesha and I are on our way out."

"I need to speak with you, darling."

She walked past him into the foyer. He reluctantly closed the door and turned to face her.

"First of all, I'm not your darling and, second, I don't have time to waste on you—now or ever."

"Can we go into your study?"

"No."

Alesha's footsteps faltered and stopped at the top of the stairs as Derrick's voice and a female one she recognized as Diana's wafted up to her. What was she doing here?

"What do you want?"

"I want you to take me back."

"Have you lost your mind?" He looked at her as if she had. "I'm married."

"You don't love her," Diana scoffed.

"And I suppose you think I love you?" At her silence he continued, "Diana, why would I want you back and, more importantly, why would you want me? I never loved you—I made no pretense about that."

Her smile faltered. "That's not true."

"Still delusional, I see." He laughed. "You didn't want a husband. You wanted a puppy dog to follow you around while you embellished your career—something I was never going to be. I wasn't ambitious enough for you then, but now that I have a shot at being a U.S. Senator, I look better in your eyes, is that it?"

"I've realized we want the same things, Derrick. I could help you become the best senator and you could help my lobbying firm once you get in office."

He chuckled as her motives were finally revealed. "Is that what this is all about—the powerful, influential people I will meet once I'm in the Senate? People you think can further your career?"

"Our careers, Derrick." Her eyes pleaded with his. "I can help you in ways she never could!"

"I doubt that."

"Derrick." Her red nails dug into his arm. "Don't be a fool!"

"I was once." His eyes narrowed as he removed her hand. "But never again."

"I'll go to the press."

He raised an eyebrow. "With what? A lame exposé of how I married you on the rebound, quickly realized my mistake and happily remedied it, but not before I felt soiled by you?"

At the top of the stairs, Alesha watched and listened to the exchange with keen interest. She learned more as an observer than she ever could have from questioning Derrick about his ex. This woman had nerve and a half! Angela was right—she was a hussy! Having heard enough, she walked down the stairs, ready for battle.

"You know it's sisters like you who give other sisters a bad name."

"Amen!" Derrick shook his head in agreement.

"Is that right?" Diana turned hateful eyes in her direction as Alesha walked over to stand by Derrick.

"Yes, that's right," Alesha said, placing a possessive hand on her husband's arm. "I was threatened by you, but now I see how silly I was."

"Really?" Diana scowled.

"Yes." Alesha laughed. "You're pathetic."

"Listen, you little…"

"I'm Mrs. Derrick Chandler." She slowly enunciated every word and smiled at Derrick when he placed his arm supportively around her waist. "That's something you'll never be again."

"She certainly won't," Derrick vowed.

"I'll be the one by Derrick's side when he takes his place in congress, not you. You had your chance and you blew it. He doesn't want you. How many ways does he have to say that before it sinks in?"

She'd had her fill of this insufferable woman! Despite the way their marriage had begun, she and Derrick were married. He was hers and she had no intention of giving him up, especially not to the likes of this woman!

"Diana, I don't know what story you think you have to sell to the press, but go ahead and sell it to the highest bidder."

"You don't mean that."

"Don't I?" He pulled Alesha closer. "I have what I want and need right here in my arms and there's nothing you can do to take it away."

"Nothing at all," Alesha firmly chimed in.

"If you want to ruin your own career by spreading malicious lies about our brief, unpleasant dalliance, then go ahead. But knowing how ambitious you are, I don't think you will."

"Now that you've embarrassed yourself beyond compare, will you do us the pleasure of leaving our home and never returning?" Alesha smiled brightly.

"Gladly." Diana's eyes shot daggers at them both. "You two deserve each other!"

"See, darling? I think she finally got the message."

To twist the knife further, Alesha turned into his arms and kissed Derrick. They heard heels clicking and a door slamming, and when they pulled apart, she was gone.

"Good riddance!" Derrick vowed. "The audacity of that woman!"

"She is a brassy one." Alesha laughed, wiping lipstick from his mouth with her fingers. "What did you ever see in her?"

He joined her laughter. "I don't know. She caught me at a low point and I foolishly thought she could help me forget."

"Me?"

"Yes. What an idiot I was." He laughed at himself. "She's nothing like you, which, I guess, was her appeal."

She sobered at his admission. "Derrick, I'm sorry."

"You don't have anything to be sorry about."

"Yes, I do." She closed her eyes briefly and came to a decision. "I want to tell you why I pushed you away two years ago. Everything."

"Now?" He brushed a stray strand of hair out of her troubled eyes.

"Yes, it's about time. Don't you think?"

She was tired of keeping secrets from him, of all people. She needed to be completely honest with him. He deserved it.

"It can wait."

"No. I've held this in long enough. You have been so wonderful to me. You deserve the truth, if you still want to hear it." She placed her palms on his chest and waited for his response.

"I do." He covered one of her hands with his.

She took a deep breath and then released it. "First of all, what I said at your country house after the wedding about my feelings for you frightening me was true."

"I felt the same way." His admission made it easier for her to proceed.

"Do you remember when we were dating before and you wanted me to meet Cam?" She focused her attention on a pearl-white button on his shirtfront.

"Of course. We were going to have dinner, but you had to cancel."

"I was there at the restaurant." She tilted her head until her eyes meet his.

"You were?"

"Yes. I was coming out of the ladies' room. You and Cam had your backs to me and I overheard you telling him that you were so happy to be in a relationship with someone who didn't want anything from you. Someone who wasn't carrying around a lot of excess baggage, or who had a mountain of problems she expected you to miraculously fix." She related his words verbatim.

"Alesha, I didn't mean…" Her fingers on his lips silenced him.

"No, it's all right." She removed her fingers from his mouth to rest on his jaw. "I had just learned that morning that Momma had a life-threatening heart condition—one that was going to require surgery and long rehabilitation."

"Oh, God!" He finally had the missing piece of the puzzle. "She seems so healthy."

"She's been doing great since her surgeries."

"Thank God for that."

"Robert and I wanted her to have the best doctors."

"Of course you did."

"I ended up emptying my savings and other bank accounts and selling what good jewelry I had and my car. Robert did the same and got a second job, but it still wasn't enough. Even after insurance and taking out loans, it left us with huge bills, but about six months ago, she had a slight relapse and her doctor wanted her to see a specialist—one who wouldn't consult on her case unless we came up with our share of the money upfront, and that's why Robert took your money."

He paused before asking, "Why didn't you tell me?"

She shrugged. "I was going to the day we met again, but…"

He sighed. "But I said I didn't care."

"Yes."

"I lied. I did and I do care."

"Thank you for saying that."

"I mean it. Barbara is a special lady."

"She's everything to Bobby and me."

"I know. I'll apologize to him."

"You don't have to do that."

"Yes, I do." His eyes grew intense. "Who is Kevin? Obviously, he wasn't your lover as you led me to believe."

"No." She shook her head. "He's the brother of a friend. He came up to see his sister for the weekend, but she was out of town, so I let him sleep on my sofa. He's like a brother to me."

"Why did you let me think something else?"

"Because I had tried everything to get you to accept my decision to end things between us, and you wouldn't do it. I didn't plan for you to see me and Kevin the way you did—me dressed in a robe and him only in shorts, both obviously fresh out of the shower. The opportunity just presented itself and I shamelessly took advantage of it." She paused. "I knew what it looked like, I knew what you thought and I let you believe we were lovers because I knew that would end things between us once and for all. It hurt too much to keep seeing you and speaking to you on the phone—telling you I didn't want a relationship with you when the truth was that was all I did want, but couldn't have at that time."

"Why didn't you come to me once things were somewhat resolved?"

"How could I after the horrible way we parted?" She shrugged helplessly. "I honestly didn't think you would want to see me again and I didn't want to face your contempt."

Her eyes implored him to understand her actions and the reasons behind them. His thumbs lightly stroked her cheeks and he smiled at her tenderly. His mind sorted through dozens of questions that suddenly seemed meaningless. He had just received the answers to the most important questions.

"Oh, Alesha." He sighed her name. "So there never was anyone else?"

"Never." She shook her head. "I was just so overwhelmed, but now my reasons for pushing you away seem so trivial and stupid."

"You always wanted me?" He skipped to the heart of the matter—the only question he needed answered.

"Always," she agreed without hesitation.

Neither of them spoke for a long time. They simply stared

into each other's eyes, silently telegraphing secret messages of regret, sorrow—and hope.

"It's in the past. Let's leave it there and go forward," he finally suggested.

"That sounds good."

His thumb brushed away a tear that escaped from the corner of her eye. He smiled slightly and kissed her—the gentlest, softest kiss she had ever experienced—and it melted her soul and her heart. He was such an enigma to her. She never knew what he was going to do or say, yet he always seemed to do and say the right thing.

"It hurt me more than I thought anything could when you suddenly and completely shut me out of your life." He tenderly fingered her hair. "It infuriated me that you never gave us a fighting chance."

"I couldn't. You sucked up all the oxygen until I didn't have anything left. Bottom line—my mother needed me and I didn't have the time, inclination or strength to be in a relationship with you, no matter how much I wanted to."

"Did you want to?"

"Yes. In the short time we dated, I felt alive as I never had before."

"Your rejection sent me headlong into a disastrous relationship with a woman I should never have given the time of day."

"Your marriage to Diana."

"Legally." He smiled ruefully. "But what I had with her was never a marriage."

"I was so jealous when you told me about her."

"Why?"

She took a deep breath before admitting, "Because she was your wife, a wife you *wanted* to marry."

"We were married, Alesha, but she was never my wife—not like you."

"I'm just a means to an end."

He frowned. "Do you honestly believe that, still?"

"I don't want to."

"You're my wife, Alesha." His hands framed her face. "That's how I think of you."

"And you're my husband." She paused before asking, "Do you want to stay married to me, Derrick?"

"Do you?"

They smiled at each other tenderly, without answering verbally. She suddenly knew she could never live without him—just as she knew she had fallen helplessly, irrevocably in love with him twice. After all the years of soul-searching she had done, that revelation came as naturally and effortlessly to her as breathing did. For a moment, she thought that she had spoken her feelings out loud, because Derrick's expression shifted to one of total gentleness and understanding. Did she imagine it, or was there a reciprocal wonderment in his eyes as if he, too, had come to the same conclusion?

Chapter 13

At the party, both Derrick and Alesha tried to put the unpleasant scene with Diana out of their minds. They were on the dance floor. Her head lay on Derrick's shoulder, eyes closed. One hand rested on his opposite shoulder, while the other was clasped in his warm hand, close to her face as they swayed to the soft music. His head rested against her hair as he held her close.

"Are you okay?" Derrick's question forced Alesha to lift her head.

"Yes, I'm fine." She stared at him adoringly. More than anything, she wanted to feel his lips on hers.

His eyes shifted to her moist lips, reading her mind, and then moved back to her beautiful face. "We can leave if you want to."

"This is important to you—we can stay." Then at his continued look of concern, she added, "Really, I'm fine."

He gave in to temptation then and grazed her lips with his. He allowed himself to lightly caress her mouth for a few seconds, before he pulled away—knowing if he didn't, things would get embarrassing.

She replaced her head on his shoulder, instinctively knowing why he had ended their brief kiss. Disentangling her hand from his, she slid her hand up his shoulder until both her arms encircled his neck. His hands moved from her waist to her lower back, holding her closer still as they continued to dance.

She closed her eyes again, allowing herself to escape. It felt so good to be in his arms. She didn't want to be anywhere else, except where she was, and she knew that neither did he. This was where she was meant to be—forever.

He wished he had her home right now, because he would make passionate love to her—he would make her forget all the pain she had experienced. He was determined to erase the past hurts and dissolve the years they had spent without each other. In his arms, he would make her feel nothing except complete ecstasy.

Unfortunately, the song ended too quickly, and they reluctantly left each other's arms and walked off the dance floor hand in hand, only to find Cam curiously watching them both. As they approached, Derrick's eyes silently warned him not to make any flippant comments.

"Senator Hatcher wants to speak with you, Derrick," Cam informed him as they reached his side.

"Do you want me to come with you?"

Alesha placed her hand on his arm as she stared at him lovingly. The look she gave him almost took his breath away.

"No, I'll be back shortly. Stay here and try to keep Cam out of trouble, will you?" His eyes darted to his friend.

"I'll try." She smiled. He kissed her softly before walking away.

"Where's Mary?" she asked, referring to Cam's date.

"Oh, she's in the ladies room or somewhere." Cam

seemed to have little interest in his date's whereabouts. "Are you enjoying yourself tonight?"

"I am."

"I know these functions can be very boring, but..."

"They're a necessary evil." She completed the sentence for him with a knowing wink.

"I see you've heard that from time to time."

"Once or twice." She smiled.

Cam laughed. "Derrick can be a workhorse when it comes to his career, but he's also very kind and giving. Of course, you know that, don't you?"

"He's a very complex man." She cautiously eyed him over the rim of her glass.

"Not really, not once you understand his motivations. I hope you'll try to."

"Why is that so important to you?"

"He's my friend—my best friend. I want him to be happy, and you make him happy."

"What about Diana?"

He grimaced. "Please! She wouldn't know how to think about someone else if her life depended on it!"

"Have you seen her since she returned to town?"

"No, and God willing I will be spared that unpleasantness."

She laughed. "You don't like her very much, do you?"

"Nope." He shook his head emphatically. "And I never did."

"Why?"

"Because she is, was and always will be a user."

"You're right about that."

He frowned. "What is she trying to pull?"

"Oh, nothing." Alesha shook her head. "She doesn't matter."

"I'm glad to hear you say that."

"Why?"

"Because I know she came back into town to try to cause trouble for you and Derrick."

"She did, but she can't." Alesha smiled. "We won't let her."

"I think Diana has met her match."

She smiled secretively. "I think she knows that now."

"Derrick would have my hide if he knew I was saying this to you." Cam glanced away briefly to make sure his friend was nowhere to be seen.

"But?"

"But I'm going to say it anyway. You're good for him. As I told him this morning, I don't understand why the two of you won't admit your marriage is real."

"You told him that?" Her face registered surprise and gratitude.

"I did."

"What was his response?"

"What's yours?" he quickly countered.

"Well, I…" She was interrupted by Derrick as he joined them, placing a possessive arm around her waist.

"What were you two so engrossed in?" He eyed them both closely.

"Your campaign. What else?" Cam smiled.

Alesha shot him a grateful look. Derrick noted the quick exchange between them and made a mental note to find out what mischief Cam had been up to in his absence.

Hours later when they entered their bedroom, Derrick helped her off with her stole, placing it on a nearby chair. He reached for the light, but Alesha's hand prevented him from flipping the switch on. Her hand traveled up his muscled arm to his shoulder, coming to rest behind his head as she moved closer to him. She pulled his face toward hers as she placed a lingering kiss on his lips.

She kissed him slowly, enjoying every second, every movement of their lips against each other's. His hands caressed her waist as she continued to astonish and delight him with her forwardness. When she slowly withdrew her lips from his, he stared at her expectantly, yet made no move toward her—leaving the outcome in her hands.

Her fingers deftly unfastened his tie before moving to unbutton his shirt, sliding it and the jacket simultaneously from his broad shoulders. As her fingers lightly touched the hair on his chest, he sucked in his breath quickly, as if the contact burned him. She moved closer to his hard body and her hands splayed across his muscled back as her lips captured his once again.

He couldn't believe this was happening. Alesha was initiating intimacy between them. He had longed for this moment for what seemed like forever. He knew tonight was going to be special beyond compare.

"Will you undo my necklace?" Her question was posed softly.

His lips captured hers briefly, promising a much more satisfying union, before he walked behind her. She raised her hair out of the way as his fingers quickly unclasped her necklace. He kissed her neck, and she reached her gloved hand up behind her to caress the side of his face before moving to his nape, holding him closer. Then she turned around in his arms. He unclasped the bracelet on her wrist. Her hand still held his face—she reluctantly released him to remove one glove and then the other, before placing her hands on his chest.

"Unzip my dress."

He smiled at her words, and readily did as she gently commanded, sliding his hands beneath the material at her back, pulling her closer as the dress fell to the floor. Their lips played with each other's, nipping, caressing briefly and moving away, his fingers unclasped her hair, freeing the silky tresses, running his fingers slowly through it.

"You've wanted to do that all night, haven't you?" she asked.

He returned her smile tenderly before admitting, "Yes. Just as I've wanted to do this." His lips attacked hers with such ferocity she felt as if she were being eaten alive. The passionate mating of their lips caused an answering response in their bodies as they pressed closer.

Her hands clutched at his shoulders, arching against his hard, unbending frame. His hands roamed down her bare back to her hips, pressing her tighter against him as he greedily took what she so freely offered. Soon, however, they knew this was not enough—they needed more, much more.

"Derrick, make love to me. I need you. How I want you."

She was going for broke tonight—she was tired of hiding her feelings. One way or another, she would find out what she meant to him and she would tell him what he meant to her.

He bent and scooped her up in his arms. Walking over to the bed, he laid her down on it before following her with his own body. They kissed passionately as her hands trailed down his flat, hard stomach to his belt buckle, urgently undoing it before unzipping his pants. She touched his skin, softly at first and then more fervently. He was on fire and becoming more inflamed with her every caress.

She watched the expressions race across his face at her ardent manipulations. She squeezed him intimately until his hand covered hers, ending her sweet torture. She tried unsuccessfully to elude his grasp and when he refused to release her, she turned questioning eyes to the fiery depths of his.

"Don't you want me to touch you?" She bit his chin softly.

He closed his eyes shortly before opening them again and hissing, "Yes!"

"Then why are you stopping me?" Her lips traced his jaw-line, her hand escaping from his, continuing her tantalizing exploration.

"Because if you don't stop, I'm going to go insane." His promise was growled as his lips ardently nipped at hers.

"Good." She sighed between caresses. "I don't want you to be in control. I want you to lose yourself in me as I am in you."

His eyes grew dark at her words as his hands slid down her throat to her smooth shoulders. His lips replaced his hands, trailing across her satiny skin, igniting a fire within that she knew would soon consume them both.

"Make me yours, Derrick. Travel with me to that special place in the universe only we two can occupy together."

She didn't need to ask twice. His mouth devastated hers and she participated eagerly in their passionate, all-consuming kisses. When his lips lifted from hers, their now-naked limbs pressed closely together.

He rasped, "I will. Right now."

"I want you so much that it hurts," she groaned without hesitation.

"Alesha!" He nearly exploded as her wandering hand enfolded and caressed him.

"Do you want me?"

"Yes, more than you know."

"Then take me, darling. Make me yours forever." She arched against his hard body.

His fingers caressed her hair, roughly pulling her lips back to his. She was here in his arms, saying things he had longed to hear her say, responding to him unashamedly, feeling free to touch him.

His hands descended her sides to her hips, pressing her closer as he joined his body to hers without further hesitation. They melted together perfectly—proof that they had been made for each other. She shivered uncontrollably against his throbbing body. She had said she wanted no control and she received none. He claimed her body and heart and she willingly gave him everything she had, and received all in return.

His lips left hers and she bit into his strong shoulder, simultaneously raking her nails down his torso. His body continued to scorch hers. They belonged to each other—nothing was held back by either of them. Their bodies made rapturous music, and after several long, passion-filled hours, the unique love song they had created neared its inevitable, unforgettable conclusion.

They soared higher on wings of pure, unselfish love. He moaned hoarsely and she groaned in ecstasy as waves of intense pleasure cascaded through their souls. It was a total union of hearts and souls—this time, they truly did break the barrier of their bodies as they combined themselves into one life force. He loved her, and she loved him totally without reserve. All pretense of anything else was stripped away. They both knew nothing had ever been, or would ever be, so right again.

Much later, she was nearly sleeping, head resting on Derrick's chest. Her fingers were entwined with his. She sighed in contentment—everything was perfect. Finally, she knew she had all she would ever need—right here in Derrick's arms.

He had never felt as close to anyone as he did now. He belonged to her with every fiber of his being, with all that he possessed. God, he adored her. He finally admitted to himself what he had long felt. How could he possibly deny it?

"You know, Cam has told me on more than one occasion that we should try to make our marriage work." His fingers trailed up and down the satiny skin of her back.

"He told me the same thing tonight." She lifted her head to stare at him lovingly.

"What did you tell him?"

"Nothing, you interrupted us." She smiled.

"Do you want our marriage to work?" He held his breath as he waited for her answer—the most important answer he would ever receive in his life.

"Our marriage does work." She kissed his chest before raising her eyes to meet his again. "We work. I'm your wife and you're my husband. There's nothing false about that, or the fact that I love you more than I thought I could ever love anyone." She finally admitted what had been in her heart for a long time.

He smiled at her as tenderly as she had ever seen and let out a breath that she realized he had been holding expectantly. "I love you, too, very much."

"Really?" She kissed his lips lightly.

"Yes. Didn't you know?" He ran fingers through her tousled hair.

"I hoped."

"So did I." He pulled her head down to his to engage in a passionate, loving kiss. "Alesha…" he whispered against her lips.

"Hmm?" She tried to bring his mouth back to hers, but when he resisted, she opened dreamy eyes to stare into the serious depths of his. "What's wrong?"

"I'm sorry." His solemn words startled her.

"For what?" She traced his furrowed brow with her fingers.

"For forcing you into this marriage." He painfully articulated the guilt that had plagued him for months.

"Derrick, you didn't force me—I always had a choice."

"Yes, but I took advantage..." Her fingers on his lips forestalled his words.

"Shh. I'm where I want to be —I don't care how I got here. I only care that I did get here—that we got here together, finally."

"Really?" He searched her eyes.

"Really." She nodded, allowing every ounce of love she felt for him to shine in her eyes, for him to see. "Why didn't you tell me you loved me sooner?"

He smiled sheepishly. "I was waiting for you to say it."

"Oh, yeah." She laughed softly. "Well, I guess I can't blame you for that."

"I love you so much." He made up for lost time. "I have from the first moment I saw you."

"I love you, too. With all my heart."

Loving fingers caressed her face. His mouth captured hers, ending any response she had been about to make. She wiggled on top of him and stretched her soft body out the length of his. Their legs entangled intimately.

After reluctantly releasing her lips, he groaned, "You have sapped all my energy, but I want you again and again."

"Then take me, darling, as many times as you want me. I'm yours."

"Mine?" His hands roamed down her bare back.

"Completely." She smiled. "Forever."

Their mouths fused together, sealing their promise of eternal love with an endless kiss.

A week later, they were at her mother's, enjoying the unseasonably warm weather with an impromptu backyard barbecue.

"Hey, you guys, is it done yet?"

"In a minute." Derrick laughed at his wife. "You sure have been eating a lot lately."

"Love does wonders for my appetite."

"Mine, too." He bobbed his eyes at her.

"Derrick!"

He and Robert laughed before turning back to the grill. In Barbara's honor, they were having a heart-healthy meal consisting of grilled salmon and vegetables.

Barbara glanced toward the two men. "I'm so glad Robert is warming up to Derrick."

Alesha smiled. "So am I."

"He was having trouble letting his little sister go, but now he knows you're in good hands."

"I definitely am."

"You're happy," her mother responded.

"Deliriously." She reached across the table and squeezed her hand. "Can something so wonderful possibly last?"

"It did with your father and me until the day he died."

"That's what I want with Derrick."

"Then that's what you'll have," Barbara promised. "You two are perfect together."

Robert and Derrick laughed as they fought back flames and quickly removed food from the grill.

"I don't think I've ever seen Alesha happier and I have you to thank for that."

Derrick smiled. "I should be thanking you."

"Why?"

"You brought us back together again and I will forever be in your debt. I know what my life was without her and I never want to experience that pain again."

"You love her." Robert nodded in approval.

"With all my heart."

"I'm happy for you both, Derrick."

"Thanks, Robert. That means a lot coming from you."

"Just keep her happy."

"Always."

"Derrick," he slowly began. "I'm sorry I embezzled from your campaign. I'll pay you back."

"No." He shook his head. "Thank you for your apology, but I don't want your money."

Robert frowned. "Why not?"

"Alesha told me why you took it. I'm a part of this family now and I love Barbara, too."

"Thanks." Robert smiled. "Welcome to the family."

Derrick returned his smile. "Thank you."

They were laughing when they carried the food over to the table. Derrick bent down and kissed his wife briefly before sitting down next to Barbara.

"Here you are." Robert placed a platter of grilled corn on the cob next to the salmon.

"Mmm..." Alesha's eyes sparkled. "It smells and looks wonderful!"

Barbara eyed the healthy feast cautiously. "It does look good, but what I wouldn't give for a plate of ribs!"

"When you taste this, you'll forget all about greasy ribs," Derrick promised, kissing her cheek.

"If you say so, dear." She patted his hand.

"Momma, behave yourself," Alesha chided.

"Mom, you know how bossy she is," Robert said sympathetically.

"She's perfect," Derrick said, coming to his wife's defense.

"Thank you, darling." She blew him a kiss. "I love you."

"And I love you."

Barbara smiled approvingly. "Aren't they cute, Robert?"

He chuckled. "Adorable."

"Just you wait—your turn will come." Alesha wagged her finger at him.

"Let's eat." Robert wisely avoided responding to her prediction.

Everyone laughed and all set about filling their plates. Above the laughter and good-natured banter, Derrick and Alesha's eyes met and held. They smiled at each other secretively. There was no need for words. She loved and needed him—how wonderful to know that he felt the same way about her. All her life, she had searched for this and now it was finally hers. She was so glad to know that her mother was right—they were perfect for each other.

Epilogue

It was the middle of November and Derrick and Alesha would be celebrating their one-year anniversary in two weeks. She reclined against the soft back of the sofa, remote in her hand as she again proudly watched her husband giving his senatorial victory speech. A fire crackled comfortingly as Derrick sat beside her, his ear and hands pressed to her huge stomach, anticipating some sign of activity from their unborn child.

"Sweetheart," he said, leaning against her stomach. "Aren't you tired of watching this?"

"No, and you're not, either."

"I can't believe a year has passed. I'm a senator and you're about to give birth to our first child." He repositioned his ear on her stomach.

"I know what you mean." She smiled down at him.

He lifted his head to stare at her adoringly. He looked just like a kid on Christmas Day. She laughed out loud at the anxious expression in his eyes.

"What?"

"You look so cute!" Her smile widened at his scowl.

He sat up, hands still placed gingerly on her huge stomach and indignantly replied, "Cute? I am not cute."

"Oh, yes, you are, darling." She laughed, kissing his nose softly. "Did you feel that?" She beamed as the baby kicked.

"Yes, yes, I did."

He moved his fingers around to see if he could capture that amazing evidence of life growing within her. Her hands covered his as both waited, and another and yet another kick came.

"Our son or daughter is certainly active tonight."

"Yes, he or she is." His fingers lightly caressed her swollen stomach. "Are you in any pain?"

"No."

"Do you think we should get going to the hospital?" He sat up and watched her anxiously.

"No, sweetheart. I haven't had a contraction for a while. I think we still have time." She tried unsuccessfully to soothe his frayed nerves.

"I think we should go now— just in case."

"Derrick, I'll know when it's time to go." She stroked his furrowed brow.

"Well, if you're sure…"

"I am." Trying to get his mind off her impending labor, she replied, "Life is so funny."

"In what way?"

"Well, look at us—two people who were sworn enemies a short time ago, who are now totally in love with each other and anticipating the birth of our child."

"I never considered you an enemy." His hands still wandered over her huge stomach.

"But, darling, I considered you mine." She smiled.

"Really?"

She laughed. "Well, maybe for all of a second."

"I am crushed!"

"No, you're not." Her hand caressed his jaw.

"No, I'm not." He moved closer to her. "But I'm not your adversary anymore, am I?" His lips gravitated to within mere inches of hers.

"Of course not. You're my best friend, the love of my life. In fact, I love you more than life itself." She sighed before his lips closed over hers in a warm kiss. "I'm so happy."

"I'm going to make sure you stay that way." He kissed her again, lingering on her lips this time.

"I will as long as I have you." She snuggled contentedly, placing his head in the crook of her neck.

"You have me forever." They were silent for a while before he spoke again. "Sweetheart, do you ever think of returning to nursing?"

"No. Why?" She wondered where that question had come from.

"I just want you to be content, and I know how much your career means to you." He turned his head to stare at her profile intensely.

"*Meant* to me," she quickly corrected. "I have all I want and need right here in this room."

"Are you sure?"

"Definitely, but I love you for asking." She smiled.

"I'd do anything to make you happy."

"You have and you do."

He repositioned his head in her neck, taking love bites out of her soft flesh. "Gimme a kiss."

"My pleasure." She turned her head ever so lightly, bringing her lips into contact with his. Before their kiss could deepen, though, she winced in pain. "Ouch!"

Immediately his head lifted from her shoulder, concern

and apprehension emanating from every aspect of his being. "Another contraction?"

"Yes." She began to pant slightly. "How long has it been since the last one?"

"About fifteen minutes." He nervously glanced at his watch.

They both looked at each other, and she could tell he was quickly beginning to panic. "Derrick, calm down. Women have babies every day."

"Not my wife!" He jumped up and anxiously began pacing to and fro, unable to decide what to do first. "Can you walk? Do I need to carry you?"

Between the pain and panting breaths, she began to laugh hysterically, unable to stop herself. He was so funny!

"Derrick! Derrick, relax, baby," she pleaded through giggles.

He finally decided on a course of action, running to grab her already packed suitcase. Then he picked up both of their coats and his car keys before rushing back to the sofa where she sat doubled over in pain and laughter.

"It's not nice to laugh at your newest senator." He held out his hands to help her to her feet.

"If your constituents could see you now." She kissed his cheek gently as he pulled her upright. "Don't forget to call Momma and Robert."

"I'll call from the car."

He placed her coat around her shoulders before leading her slowly, yet urgently, to the door. She fought against another bout of laughter as she glanced at his tense, terrified expression.

"I love you." She suddenly stopped, smiled and kissed his lips thoroughly and, she hoped, comfortingly.

"I love you, too."

When she once again winced in pain, he bent down to

scoop her up into his strong arms, tossing the suitcase and his coat carelessly onto the floor.

"We'd better get out of here before this baby is born, because there's no way I'm going to deliver him or her." His face and tone were so serious that she couldn't contain another outbreak of hysterical laughter.

"Let's go have our baby," she agreed between chuckles.

"I'm with you." He smiled before nearly running out of the door with his panting, giggling wife.

* * * * *

HIS INNOCENT'S PASSIONATE AWAKENING

MELANIE MILBURNE

Dedicated to Rachel Bailey –
a fellow dog-lover, romance writer, and
awesome brainstorming partner!
Thanks for being such a wonderful friend. xxxxx
Licks and cuddles from Polly and Lily too.

CHAPTER ONE

Artemisia Bellante stared at her father's lawyer in abject horror. 'But there must be some mistake. How can Castello Mireille be...be *mortgaged?* It's been in my father's family for generations. Papa never mentioned anything about owing money to a bank.'

'He didn't owe it to a bank.' The lawyer, Bruno Rossi, pushed a sheaf of papers across the desk towards Artie, his expression grave. 'Have you heard of Luca Ferrantelli? He runs his late father's global property developing company. He's also a wine and olive producer with a keen interest in rare grape varieties, some of which are on the Castello Mireille estate.'

Artie lowered her gaze to the papers in front of her, a light shiver racing down her spine like a stray current of electricity. 'I've vaguely heard of him...' She might have spent years living in isolation on her family's ancient estate but even she had heard of the handsome billionaire playboy. And seen pictures. And swooned just like any other woman between the ages of fifteen and fifty.

She raised her gaze back to the lawyer's. 'But how did this happen? I know Papa had to let some of the gardeners go to keep costs down and insisted we cut back on housekeeping expenses, but he didn't mention anything about borrowing money from anyone. I don't understand how Signor Ferrantelli now owns most, if not all, my family's home. Why didn't Papa tell me before he died?'

To find out like this was beyond embarrassing. And deeply hurtful. Was this her father's way of forcing his shut-in daughter out of the nest by pushing her to the verge of bankruptcy?

Where would she find the sort of money to dig herself out of this catastrophic mess?

Bruno shifted his glasses further up the bridge of his Roman nose. 'Apparently your father and Luca's father had some sort of business connection in the past. He contacted Luca for financial help when the storm damage hit the *castello* late last year. His insurance policy had lapsed and he knew he would have no choice but to sell if someone didn't bail him out.'

Artie rapid-blinked. 'The insurance lapsed? But why didn't he tell me? I'm his only child. The only family he had left. Surely he should have trusted me enough to tell me the truth about our finances.'

Bruno Rossi made a shrugging movement with one shoulder. 'Pride. Embarrassment. Shame. The usual suspects in cases like this. He had to mortgage the estate to pay for the repairs. Luca Ferrantelli seemed the best option—the only option, considering your father's poor state of health. But the repayment plan didn't go according to schedule, which leaves you in an awkward position.'

Artie wrinkled her brow, a tension headache stabbing at the backs of her eyes like scorching hot needles. Was this a nightmare? Would she suddenly wake up and find this was nothing but a terrifying dream?

Please let this not be real.

'Surely Papa knew he would have to eventually pay back the money he borrowed from Signor Ferrantelli? How could he have let it get to this? And wouldn't Luca Ferrantelli have done due diligence and realised Papa wouldn't be able to pay it back? Or was that Ferrantelli's intention all along—to take the *castello* off us?'

Bruno leaned forward in his chair with a sigh. 'Your father was a good man, Artie, but he wasn't good at managing finances, especially since the accident. There have been a lot of expenses, as you know, with running the estate since he came home from hospital. Your mother was the one with the financial clout to keep things in the black, but of course, after she died in the accident, it naturally fell to him. Unfortunately, he didn't always listen to advice from his accountants and financial advisors.'

He gave a rueful movement of his lips and continued.

'I'm sure I wouldn't be the first person to tell you how much the accident changed him. He fired his last three accountants because they told him things had to change. Luca Ferrantelli's offer of financial help has meant you could nurse your father here until he passed away, but now of course, unless you can find the money to pay off the mortgage, it will remain in Luca's possession.'

Over her dead body, it would. No way was she handing over her family's home without a fight, even if it would be a David and Goliath mismatch. Artie would find some way of winning.

She *had* to.

Artie did her best to ignore the beads of sweat forming between her shoulder blades. The drumbeat of panic in her chest. The hammering needles behind her eyeballs. The sense of the floor beneath her feet pitching like a paper boat riding a tsunami. 'When and where did Papa meet with Signor Ferrantelli? I've been Papa's full-time carer for the last ten years and don't recall Signor Ferrantelli ever coming here to see him.'

'Maybe he came one day while you were out.'

Out? Artie didn't go *out*.

She wasn't like other people, who could walk out of their homes and meet up with friends. It was impossible for her to be around more than one or two people at a time. Three was very definitely a crowd.

'Maybe...' Artie looked down at the papers again, conscious of warmth filling her cheeks. Her social anxiety was far more effective than a maximum-security prison. She hadn't been outside the *castello* walls since she was fifteen.

Ten years.

A decade.

Two fifths of her life.

As far as she knew, it wasn't common knowledge that she suffered from social anxiety. Her father's dependence on her had made it easy to disguise her fear of crowds. She had relished the role of looking after him. It had given her life a purpose, a focus. She had mostly avoided meeting people when they came to the *castello* to visit her father. She stayed in the background until they left. But barely anyone but her father's doctor and physical therapists had come during the last year or two of his life. Compassion fatigue had worn out his so-called friends. And now that the money had run dry, she could see why they had drifted away, one by one. There wasn't anyone she could turn to. Having been home schooled since her mid-teens, she had lost contact with her school friends. Friends wanted you to socialise with them and that she could never do, so they, too, had drifted away.

She had no friends of her own other than Rosa, the housekeeper.

Artie took a deep breath and blinked to clear her clouded vision. The words in front of her confirmed her worst fears. Her home was mortgaged to the hilt. There was no way a bank would lend her enough funds to get the *castello* out of Luca Ferrantelli's hands. The only job she had ever had was as her father's carer. From fifteen to twenty-five she had taken care of his every need. She had no formal qualifications, no skills other than her embroidery hobby.

She swallowed and pushed the papers back across the desk. 'What about my mother's trust fund? Isn't there enough left for me to pay off the mortgage?'

'There's enough for you to live on for the short-term but not enough to cover the money owed.'

Artie's heart began to beat like a wounded frog. 'How long have I got?' It sounded like a terminal diagnosis, which in some ways it was. She couldn't imagine her life without Castello Mireille. It was her home. Her base. Her anchor.

Her entire world.

Bruno Rossi shuffled the papers back into a neat pile. 'A year or two. But even if you were by some chance to raise finance to keep the estate, the place needs considerable maintenance. Costly maintenance. The storm damage last year showed how vulnerable the *castello* is. The north wing's roof still needs some work, not to mention the conservatory. It will cost millions of euros to—'

'Yes, yes, I know.' Artie pushed back her chair and smoothed her damp palms down her thighs. The *castello* was crumbling around her—she saw evidence of it every single day. But moving out of her home was unthinkable. Impossible.

She literally *couldn't* do it.

Panic tiptoed over her skin like thousands of tiny ants wearing stilettoes. Pressure built in her chest—a crushing weight pushing against her lungs so she couldn't take another breath. She wrapped her arms around her middle, fighting to hold off a full-blown panic attack. She hadn't had one for a while but the threat was always lurking in the murky shadows of her consciousness. It had followed her like a malevolent ghost ever since she came home from hospital from the accident that killed her mother and left her father in a wheelchair.

An accident that wouldn't have occurred if it hadn't been for *her*.

The lawyer cleared his throat. 'There's something else…' The formal quality of his tone changed and another shiver skittered down Artie's spine.

She straightened her shoulders and cupped her elbows with her hands, hoping for a cool and dignified stance but falling way too short. 'W-what?'

'Signor Ferrantelli has proposed a plan for you to

repay him. If you fulfil his terms, you will regain full ownership of the *castello* within six months.'

Artie's eyebrows shot up along with her heart rate. And her anxiety grew razorblade wings and flapped frantically against her stomach lining like frenzied bats. How could she ever repay those mortgage payments in such a short space of time? What on earth did he require her to do? 'A plan? What sort of plan?' Her voice came out high and strained like an overused squeaky toy.

'He didn't authorise me to discuss it with you. He insists on speaking to you in person first.' Bruno pushed back his chair, further demonstrating his unwillingness to reveal anything else. 'Signor Ferrantelli has requested a meeting with you in his Milan office nine a.m. sharp, on Monday, to discuss your options.'

Options? What possible options could there be? None she wanted to think about in any detail. Ice-cold dread slithered into her belly. What nefarious motives could Luca Ferrantelli have towards her? A woman he had never met? And what was with his drill sergeant commands?

Nine a.m. Sharp. In his office. In Milan.

Luca Ferrantelli sounded like a man who issued orders and expected them to be obeyed without question. But there was no way she could go to Milan. Not on Monday. Not any day. She couldn't get as far as the front gate without triggering crippling, stomach-emptying, mind-scattering panic.

Artie released her arms from around her body and gripped the back of the nearest chair. Her heart was racing like it was preparing for the Olympics. 'Tell him to meet me here. It's not convenient for me to go to Milan.

I don't drive and, from what you've just told me, I can't afford a taxi or even an Uber.'

'Signor Ferrantelli is a busy man. He expressly told me to tell you he—'

Artie stiffened her spine and raised her chin and ground her teeth behind her cool smile. 'Tell him to meet me here, nine a.m. sharp, on Monday. Or not meet with me at all.'

Luca Ferrantelli drove his Maserati through the rusty entrance gates of Castello Mireille on Monday morning. The *castello* was like something out of a Grimm brothers' fairy tale. The centuries-old ivy-clad stone building was surrounded by gardens that looked like they hadn't been tended for years, with overgrown hedges, unpruned roses, weed-covered pathways and ancient trees that stood like gnarly sentries. The *castello* had loads of potential—years of running his late father's property development company had taught him how to spot a diamond in the rough.

And speaking of diamonds...

He glanced at the velvet box on the seat next to him containing his late grandmother's engagement ring, and inwardly smiled. Artemisia Bellante would make the perfect temporary bride. Her father, Franco, had emailed Luca a photo of his daughter shortly before he died, asking Luca to make sure she was looked after once he was gone. The photo had planted a seed in Luca's mind—a seed that had taken root and sprouted and blossomed until all he could think about was meeting her—to offer her a way out of her present circumstances. Young, innocent, sheltered—she was exactly the sort of young woman his conservative grandfather would deem suitable as a Ferrantelli bride.

Time was rapidly running out on convincing his grandfather to accept the chemo he so desperately needed. Luca had a small window of opportunity to get Nonno to change his mind. Luca would do anything—even marry a poverty-stricken heiress—to make sure his elderly and frail *nonno* could live a few more precious years. After all, it was his fault his grandfather had lost the will to live. Didn't he owe Nonno some measure of comfort, given how Luca had torn apart the Ferrantelli family?

A vision of Luca's father, Flavio, and older brother, Angelo, drifted into his mind. Their lifeless bodies pulled from the surf due to his reckless behaviour as a teenager. His reckless behaviour and their love for him—a lethal, deadly combination. Two lives cut short because of him. Two lives and their potential wasted, and his mother and grandparents' happiness permanently, irrevocably destroyed. No one had been the same since that terrible day. No one.

Luca blinked to clear away the vision and gripped the steering wheel with white-knuckled force. He couldn't bring his father and brother back. He couldn't undo the damage he had caused to his mother and Nonna and Nonno. His grandmother had died a year ago and since then, his grandfather had lost the will to live. Nonno was refusing treatment for his very treatable cancer, and if he didn't receive chemotherapy soon he would die. So far, no amount of talking, lecturing, cajoling or bribing or begging on Luca's part had helped changed his grandfather's mind.

But Luca had a plan and he intended to carry it out no matter what. He would bring home a fresh-faced young bride to give hope to his grandfather that the Ferrantelli family line would continue well into the future.

Even if that was nothing but a fairy tale.

Artie watched Luca Ferrantelli's showroom-perfect deep blue Maserati come through the *castello* gates like a prowling lion. The low purr of the engine was audible even here in the formal sitting room. The car's tinted windows made it impossible for her to get a proper glimpse of his face, but the car's sleek profile and throaty growls seemed like a representation of his forthright personality.

Didn't they say a person's choice of car told you a lot about them?

Artie already knew as much as she wanted to know. *More* than she wanted to know. That would teach her for spending the weekend trawling over the internet for any mention of him. Her research had revealed him as a flagrant playboy who brokered property deals and broke female hearts all over the globe. Barely a week went past without a gossip page featuring Luca Ferrantelli with a star-struck sylph-like blonde draped on his arm.

The powerful sports car came to a halt at the front of the *castello*. Artie sucked in a breath as the driver's door opened, her heart giving a sudden kick, her eyes widening as a vision of potent, athletic maleness unfolded from behind the wheel. The internet photos hadn't done him justice. How could it be possible to be so spectacularly attractive? Her pulse fluttered as if someone had injected her veins with thousands of butterflies.

The good-looks fairy godmother had certainly excelled herself when it came to Luca Ferrantelli. Six foot four, lean and athletic, with wavy black hair that was casually styled in a just-out-of-bed or just-combed-with-his-fingers manner, he was the epitome of heart-stopping handsome. Even though she was looking at him from a distance, Artie's heart was stopping and starting like a spluttering engine. How was she going to be when he was in the same room as her? Breathing the same air? Within touching distance?

As if Luca Ferrantelli sensed her gaze on him, he took off his aviator-style sunglasses and locked gazes with her. Something sprang open in her chest and she suddenly couldn't breathe. She quickly stepped away from the window and leaned back against the adjacent wall, clutching a hand to her pulsing throat, heat pouring into her cheeks. She had to get a grip. And fast. The last thing she wanted to do was appear gauche and unsophisticated, but, given she had been out of society for so long, she was at a distinct disadvantage. He was the poster boy for living in the fast lane. She was a wallflower who hadn't been seen in public for a decade.

It was some minutes before the housekeeper, Rosa, led Luca Ferrantelli to where Artie was waiting to receive him, but even so, her pulse was still leaping when the sitting room door opened. What if she became tongue-tied? What if she blushed? What if she broke out in a sweat and couldn't breathe? What if—?

'Signor Ferrantelli to see you,' Rosa announced with a formal nod in Luca's direction, before going out of the room and closing the door behind her with a click.

The first thing Artie noticed was his hair wasn't

completely black. There were several strands of steel-grey sprinkled around his temples, which gave him a distinguished, wise-beyond-his-years air. His eyes were framed by prominent eyebrows and were an unusual hazel—a mix of brown and green flecks, fringed by thick, ink-black lashes. His amazing eyes were a kaleidoscope of colours one would normally find in a deeply shadowed forest. His jaw was cleanly shaven but the faint shadow of regrowth around his nose and mouth hinted at the potent male hormones working vigorously behind the scenes.

The atmosphere of the room changed with his presence, as if every stick of furniture, every fibre of carpet and curtains, every portrait frame and the faces of her ancestors contained within them took a collective breath. Stunned by his looks, his commanding presence, his take-charge energy.

'*Buongiorno*, Signorina Bellante.' Luca Ferrante's voice was like the sound of his car—low and deep, with a sexy rumble that did something strange to the base of her spine. So, too, did seeing his lips move when shaping and pronouncing her name. His lower lip was full and sensual, the top lip only marginally less so, and he had a well-defined philtrum ridge beneath his nose and a shallow cleft in his chin.

Artie slipped her hand into his outstretched one and a zap of electricity shot from her fingers to her core like a lightning bolt. His grip was strong and yet strangely gentle, his fingers long and tanned with a light dusting of dark masculine hair that ran over the backs of his hands and disappeared beneath the cuffs of his business shirt and jacket. Armani, at a guess. And his aftershave an equally intoxicating blend of citrus and spice and sophistication that teased her senses into a stupor.

'*Buongiorno*, Signor Ferrantelli.'

Artie aimed for cool politeness but sounded more like a star-struck teen in front of a Hollywood celebrity. She could feel warm colour blooming in her cheeks. Could feel her heart thumping like it was having some sort of medical crisis. Could feel her female hormones responding to his male ones with little tingles and pulses deep within her body.

Let go of his hand!

Her brain gave the command but her hand was trapped in some kind of weird stasis. It was as if her hand had a mind of its own and was enjoying being held by his warm, dry one, thank you very much. Enjoying it so much, she could feel every whorl of his skin as if it were being engraved, branded into hers.

Luca removed his hand from hers but his gaze kept hers tethered. She couldn't look away if she tried. Magnetic. Enthralling. Mesmerising. His eyes seemed to draw secrets from within her while concealing his own.

'Firstly, allow me to offer my condolences on the recent passing of your father.'

'*Grazie.*'

She stepped back and waved her still-tingling hand in the direction of the sofa. 'Would you like to sit down? I'll call Rosa to bring in coffee. How do you take it?'

'Black and strong.'

Of course you do.

Artie pressed the intercom pad and summoned Rosa, surreptitiously eyeing him while she requested coffee from the housekeeper. Everything about Luca Ferrantelli was strong. Strong, determined jaw. Strong, intelligent eyes. A strong and muscled body that hinted at a man who wasn't afraid of pushing himself to the limits of endurance. A man who set goals and didn't let anyone or anything stop him from achieving them.

Artie ended the intercom conversation with Rosa and sat on the nearest sofa, and only then did Luca take the seat opposite. He laid one arm along the back of the sofa in a casually relaxed pose she privately envied. She had to place her hands on the tops of her thighs to stop her knees from trembling. Not from fear but from a strange sense of fizzing excitement. She tried not to stare at his powerfully muscled thighs, his well-formed biceps, the flat plane of his stomach, but her gaze kept drifting over him of its own volition. Drinking in the planes and contours of his face, wondering what was going on behind the screen of his gaze, wondering if his firm lips would soften when he kissed…

Artie blinked and sat up straighter on the sofa, crossing her legs to try and control the wayward urges going on in her lower body. What was wrong with her? He had barely exchanged more than half a dozen words with her and she was undressing him with her eyes. She curled her hands into balls on her lap and fixed a smile on her lips. 'So, how was your drive from Milan? I hope it didn't inconvenience you too much to come here?' Who said she couldn't do small talk?

Luca's half-smile and his glittering forest floor eyes made something slip sideways in her stomach. 'It didn't inconvenience me at all. But we both know that was your intention, was it not?'

Artie forced herself to hold his penetrating gaze. 'Signor Ferrantelli, I am not the sort of woman to jump when a man says jump.'

The dark gleam in his eyes intensified and a hot trickle of something liquid spilled deep in her core. 'You may have no choice, given I now own nine tenths of Castello Mireille, unless you can buy me out within the next twenty-four hours.' There was a don't-mess-with-me warning in his tone that made her want to mess with him to see what would happen.

Artie disguised a swallow, her heart picking up its pace. 'My father's lawyer informed me of the unusual financial arrangement you made with my father. One wonders why you didn't buy all of it off him while you had the chance.'

His gaze was unwavering. 'He was a dying man who deserved some dignity in the last months of his life.'

Artie gave a cynical smile while her blood boiled in her veins and roaring anger bubbled in her chest. 'Do you expect me to believe you felt some measure of compassion for him? Even while you were systematically taking his home away from him ancient stone by ancient stone?'

Luca didn't change his casual posture on the sofa but a ripple of tension passed across his features, tightening his jaw, flaring his nose, hardening his eyes. 'Your father approached me late last year for help. I gave it to him. It was a straightforward business deal. And now I have come to collect on my investment.'

Artie shot up from the sofa as if someone had pressed an ejector switch. She glared at him with the full force of her fury, chest heaving like she had just completed a marathon without training first. 'You can't take my home off me. I won't allow it.'

Luca Ferrantelli's gaze was diamond-hard. 'My intention is to give the *castello* back to you—after a time. And for a price.'

Something heavy landed on the floor of her belly. 'What price? You must know I can't possibly raise the necessary funds to pay out the mortgage?'

He held her gaze in a lock that made the backs of her knees tingle. 'I will erase the debt and give the deeds of the *castello* back if you agree to be my wife for six months.'

CHAPTER TWO

ARTIE STARED AT HIM in open-mouthed shock, her heart pounding like it was going to punch its way out of her chest. Had she heard him correctly? Was her imagination playing tricks on her? Putting words in his mouth he couldn't possibly have said? Had he said *wife? W.I.F.E?* The woman a man chose to spend the rest of his life with in a contract of love and commitment?

'Your…*what?*'

He hooked one ankle over his bent knee, his finger idly flicking the zipper toggle on his Italian leather boot. *Flick. Flick. Flick.* So relaxed. So casual. So confident and in control it was maddening.

'You heard—I need a wife for six months. On paper.' The note of self-assurance in his voice made her dislike of him go up another notch.

On paper? Her eyes widened while her feminine ego shrank. She might not be a social butterfly or model material, but as far as she knew she hadn't broken any mirrors lately. 'You mean a marriage of convenience?'

'But of course.'

Why 'but of course'? It was ridiculous to be affronted

by his unusual proposal, but what woman wanted to be dismissed outright as a potential lover?

But why would he want you? the voice of her conscience sneered. *Who would want you? You killed your mother, you maimed your father—all for the sake of going to a stupid party.*

Rosa, the housekeeper, came in at that moment carrying a tray with cups and saucers and a steaming percolator of freshly brewed coffee. Rosa handed Luca a cup before turning to give one to Artie. But as soon as Rosa left the room Artie put her coffee on a side table, not trusting her shaking hands to bring the cup safely to her tombstone-dry mouth. Her conscience was right. Why would he want to marry *her?* Why would anyone?

Luca lowered his crossed ankle to the floor and, reaching for his cup, took a sip of his coffee as if this was a regular old coffee morning. Not one in which he had delivered a bombshell proposal to a virtual stranger.

'May I ask, why me?' Artie inserted into the silence. 'You surely have no shortage of far more suitable candidates for the role.' Socialites. Supermodels. Not a shut-in like her.

Luca put his cup back in its saucer with unnerving and methodical precision. It hinted at the man he was—self-assured, focused, confident he could get anything he set his mind to. 'Your father was the one who planted the idea in my—'

'My *father?*' Artie choked over the words.

'He was concerned about your future, given how badly his financial situation had become and how it would impact on you long-term. He wanted you well provided for, so I devised a plan to make sure we both got what we wanted. You get to keep the *castello*. I get a temporary wife.'

Artie clasped her hands together, trying to keep control of her galloping pulse. Her legs were threatening to give way beneath her but she was reluctant to sit back down, because it would bring her closer to him than she wanted to be. 'But why would you want me to be your...your wife?' Saying the word felt strange on her lips and yet her mind ran with the image it evoked. Images popped into her head of her wearing a white dress and standing next to Luca at an altar. His arms going around her, drawing him closer to his muscled body. His mouth slowly coming down to seal hers in a kiss...

'You're exactly the sort of woman my grandfather would approve of as my bride,' Luca said, his gaze drifting to her mouth as if he was having the same thoughts as her. About kissing, touching, needing, wanting.

Artie arched her eyebrows. 'Oh, really? Why is that?'

His lips curved in a satirical smile. 'You're the sweet, homespun type— or so your father led me to believe.'

What else had her father told him about her? She had made him promise not to tell anyone about her social anxiety. Had he broken that promise? She was pretty sure he hadn't told Bruno Rossi, the lawyer, otherwise he would have mentioned it yesterday. It was her shameful little secret. Her father's dependence on her since the accident had made it easy for her to hide it from others, but with him no longer here...

Artie kept her expression neutral but on the inside, she was seething. How dared her father set her up for auction to this incorrigible man? It was positively feudal. And why did Luca Ferrantelli want to please his grandfather? What was at stake if he didn't? 'Look, Signor Ferrantelli, I think there's been some sort of misunderstanding between you and my father. I can't think of a single set of circumstances in which I would ever consider marrying you.'

Luca's mocking smile broadened. 'Perhaps not as sweet and biddable as your father said.' His tone was musing, the lazy sweep of his gaze assessing. 'But, no matter. You will do.'

She straightened her shoulders and sent him a look so frosty icicles could have formed on her eyelashes. 'Please leave. We have nothing left to discuss.'

Luca remained seated on the sofa, still in that annoyingly relaxed pose. But his eyes contained a glint of intractability that made her wonder if she was wise to lock horns with him. She had no experience in dealing with powerful men. She had no experience, period. Any fight between them would be like Tinkerbell trying to take down a Titan.

'The way I see it, you don't have any choice. You will lose the *castello* if you don't agree to marry me.'

Artie ground her teeth and clenched her fists, anger flicking along her nerve endings like a power surge of electricity. It was all she could do not to slap him. She pictured herself doing it—landing her palm against his lean and chiselled jaw with a resounding slap. Imagining how his rougher skin would feel under the soft skin of her palm. Imagining how he might grasp her by the wrist and haul her closer and slam his mouth down on hers in a passionate kiss…

Eek! She shouldn't have watched *Gone with the Wind* so many times.

She stretched out one arm and pointed her index finger towards the door. 'Get. Out.'

Luca raised his long, lean, athletic frame from the sofa with leonine grace and came to stand in front of her. She fought not to step back, determined to show he didn't intimidate her with his commanding, disturbing presence. Even though he did. Big time. She had to crane her neck to maintain eye-contact, and give her traitorous body a stern talking-to for reacting to his closeness with a hitch of her breath and an excited leap of her pulse.

'I'll give you twenty-four hours to consider my proposal.'

Artie raised her chin to a defiant height. 'I've already considered it and flatly turned it down. I'll give you the same answer tomorrow, so don't waste your time or mine by coming back.'

His lazy smile ignited a light behind his eyes as if her refusal had thrilled rather than disappointed him. 'You have a lot to lose, Signorina Bellante.' He swung his gaze around the room before bringing it back to meet hers. 'Are you sure you want to throw all this away for the sake of your pride?'

'Pride has nothing to do with my decision. If and when I marry, it will be for love.'

The loud cackling of her conscience rang in Artie's ears like clanging bells.

Marry for love? You? Who's going to love you?

His eyes flicked to her mouth and lingered there for a heart-stopping moment. 'You love this place, do you not? Your family's home for how many centuries? If that's not marrying for love, I don't know what is.' The deep, mellifluous tone of his voice had a mesmerising effect on her. She had to fight to stay focused on resisting him. It would be so easy to say yes. To have all her problems solved by agreeing to his plan—even if by doing so it threw up new ones. Dangerous ones. Exciting ones.

Artie pressed her lips together. 'Of course I love it. It's the only home I've ever known.'

The only home I can ever know.

His eyes meshed with hers. Dark, mysterious, unknowable. 'If you don't marry me, you will lose it. And I won't lose a wink of sleep about taking it off you. Business is business. I don't let emotions cloud the issue. Think about it, hmm?'

She tried to ignore the cynical gleam in his eyes. Tried to ignore the slippery eels of panic writhing in her belly. Tried not to think about her home being lost for ever. Of it being made into a plush hotel with strangers walking through every room, occupying every private space, every special corner made into a flashy showpiece instead of a private sanctuary where her most precious memories were housed. 'You can't force me out of my home. I have some rights, surely?'

'Your father signed those over to me when he begged for my help.'

Artie raised her chin, summoning every bit of willpower she possessed to stand up to his monumental ego. 'You came here expecting me to say yes, didn't you? Does anyone ever say no to you?'

'Not often.' He reached inside his jacket pocket and took a velvet box and held it out to her in the middle of his palm. 'This might help you come to a decision.'

Artie reared back from the box like it was a cockroach. 'You think you can bribe me with diamonds?'

'Not just diamonds.' He flicked open the velvet box with his thumb and a glittering sapphire and diamond engagement ring winked at her. 'Take it. Try it on for size.'

Artie brought her gaze back to his, her mouth tightly compressed. 'No, thank you.'

There was a beat or two of silence.

Luca snapped the lid of the ring box closed and placed it on the coffee table. If she had offended him with her point-blank refusal then he didn't show it in his expression.

'I'll be back for your decision tomorrow. *Ciao.*'

He gave a mock bow, and without another word he walked out of the salon, closing the door on his exit.

Artie let out a scalding breath, her body sagging with the aftershocks of too much cortisol racing through her system. She sat back on the sofa before she fell down, her legs shaking, her hands trembling, her mind whirling.

How could this be happening? It was like something out of a period drama. She was being blackmailed into marrying a man she didn't know in order to save her home. What had her father been thinking to plant such a ridiculous idea in Luca Ferrantelli's head? This was nothing but a business deal to Luca but it was her home that was on the line. And not just her home—her security. Her future. She would have nothing to fall back on if she didn't have the *castello.*

It was her heritage.

Her birthright.

Her safety.

How dared Luca Ferrantelli dangle it before her like a plump, juicy carrot in front of a dumb donkey?

She was *not* going to be a pawn in his game. If he thought she was so desperate for a husband she would say yes to the first man who asked her, then he had better think again.

Rosa came back into the salon to collect the coffee cups. 'Your guest left, then. What did he want?' Her eyes went to the ring box on the coffee table. 'Ooh, what's this?'

Artie got up from the sofa and speared her fingers through her hair. 'You wouldn't believe me if I told you. *Grr.* I don't know how I stopped myself from slapping him. He's the most detestable man I've ever met.'

Rosa's look was wry. 'Like you've met heaps of men. Just saying…' She prised open the lid of the ring box and whistled through her teeth. '*Mamma mia.* That is what I call an engagement ring.'

Artie snatched the box off her and snapped it shut and clutched it tightly in her hand. 'If he's representative of the men outside the *castello* walls, then I'm glad I haven't met heaps of them. Do you know what he said? He wants to marry me. For six months. A paper marriage or some such nonsense. And do you know what's worse? Papa put the idea in his head. Luca Ferrantelli will only give me back the *castello*, debt-free, if I marry him.'

'And you said?'

Artie frowned. 'What do you think I said? I said an emphatic, don't-ask-me-again *no.*'

Rosa loaded the coffee percolator onto the tray with

implacable calm. 'Would you say yes if the marriage wasn't on paper?'

'No, of course not.'

'Then what's the problem? Don't you trust him to keep his word?'

Artie put her hands on her hips. She could feel the ring box digging into the soft skin of her palm but did her best to ignore it. She would *not* look at it again. She would not look at those sparkling diamonds and that impossibly blue sapphire and imagine a life free of financial stress.

She would not think of being Luca Ferrantelli's bride. She. Would. Not.

'Are you seriously telling me I should accept his crazy proposal? Are you out of your mind?' Artie narrowed her gaze and added, 'Wait—do you know something about this? Did Papa talk to you about his scheme to marry me off to a stranger to settle his debts?'

Rosa picked up the coffee tray and held it in front of her body, her expression set in her customary pragmatic lines. 'Your father was worried about you in the weeks before he died—about what would happen to you once he was gone. You gave up your life for him these last few years. He shouldn't have asked it of you and nor should he have run the estate the way he did, but he was never the same after the accident. But you have a chance now to turn things around. To reclaim your life and your inheritance. And Luca Ferrantelli can't be much of a stranger to your father, otherwise he wouldn't have gone to him for help. Why would he have asked Luca if he didn't trust him to do the right thing by you? Six months isn't long. And as long as everything is legally sound, you've got nothing to lose and everything to gain.'

Artie tossed the ring box on the sofa. 'I can't believe you think I should marry that odious man.'

'You can't stay locked away here for ever, Artie. It's not healthy. Your father desperately wanted you to move on with your—'

Artie blew out a breath of exasperation. 'I *can't* leave. I thought you of all people understood. You've seen me at my worst. I feel paralysed with anxiety as soon as I get to the front gates. It's not as if I want to be like this. I can't help it.'

Nothing had helped. Medication. Home visits by a psychologist. Meditation and mindfulness. Nothing had freed her from the curse of her phobia. She had resigned herself to a lifetime of living in isolation.

What else could she do but accept her lot in life?

Rosa shifted her lips from side to side, her dark brown eyes serious. 'You'll have no choice but to leave if the *castello* is sold out from under you.'

The thought of leaving her home, having it taken it away from her by force, made her skin pepper with goosebumps and her heart pound with dread. She had tried so many times to imagine a life outside of Castello Mireille. But it was like a pipedream that never could be realised. It was completely and utterly out of her reach.

Artie glanced at the ring box on the sofa, her heart giving a funny little hopscotch. 'Luca Ferrantelli is an international playboy. He changes lovers every week. What sort of husband is he going to be?'

'You'll never know if you don't marry him, *sì*?' Rosa said. 'Convince him to marry you here at the *castello*—

you won't have to leave at all. It's a marriage in name only so there won't be a honeymoon. In six months, you'll have full ownership again. Plus, a gorgeous ring to keep. Problem solved.'

Eek! She hadn't even thought about a honeymoon. Luca wanted a bride but not *that* sort of bride…or did he? Her lower body tingled at the thought of his hands touching her. His mouth pressing against hers. His body doing things to hers she had only fantasised about and never experienced.

Artie pressed her fingers against her temples once Rosa had left the room. What crazy parallel universe had she stumbled into that even the housekeeper thought she should marry Luca Ferrantelli? She let out a ragged breath and looked around the salon. The black velvet ring box on the white sofa seemed to signify the either/ or choice she had to make. The sofa cushions still contained the impression of Luca's tall athletic body. The air still smelt faintly of his citrus and spice aftershave. Her heartrate was still not quite back to normal.

Would it ever be again?

Meeting Luca Ferrantelli had jolted her into an intense awareness of her femininity. Her body felt alive— tinglingly alive in a way it never had before. Her mind might have decided Luca was the most obnoxious man she'd ever met but her body hadn't got the memo. It was operating off script, responding to him in ways she had never thought possible. Every appraising look he cast her way, every smouldering twinkle in his hazel eyes, every lazy smile, had heated her blood and upped her pulse and fried her brain until even *she* was thinking about accepting his proposal.

Artie walked back to the sofa and picked up the ring box. She curled her fingers around it, telling herself she would put it in the safe until Luca came back tomorrow. But suddenly her fingers were prising open the lid. The ring glinted at her as if to say, *Put me on*.

It was the most beautiful ring she had ever seen. She might not be able to window shop like other people but she did plenty of shopping and browsing online. She ran her fingertip over the top of the arabesque setting, stunned by the ring's exquisite design and breathtaking quality. Money was no object to filthy rich men like Luca Ferrantelli. He thought he could dangle a ridiculously expensive diamond in front of her nose and she would accept his stupid proposal without question.

She stared at the ring some more, turning the box this way so she could see how the diamonds picked up the light coming in from the windows. It was probably too big for her anyway. Artie pulled her lower lip inside her mouth. What would it hurt to try it on just the once? No one had to know. She hadn't been in a bricks-and-mortar jewellery shop since she was a teenager, when her mother bought her a pair of earrings. This was her chance to do what others took for granted.

She took the ring out of the box and set the box down on the table again. She slipped the ring on her left ring finger, pushing it past her second knuckle. It was kind of weird that it was a perfect fit. She couldn't stop staring at it. The sheer brilliance of the diamonds and the deep blue of the sapphire stole her breath clean away.

'Don't get too comfortable there,' Artie addressed the ring. 'I'm not keeping you.'

The ring glinted back at her as if to say, *Are you sure about that?*

Artie took off the ring, placed it back in its velvet box and closed the lid with a definitive snap. She held the box in the middle of her palm, glaring at it like it contained a lethal insect. 'I'm not looking at you again, do you hear me?' She left the box on the coffee table and went to where Rosa was working in the kitchen.

Rosa looked up from where she was preparing vegetables for soup. 'Did the ring fit?'

Artie pursed her lips. 'What makes you think I tried it on?'

Rosa gave a knowing smile. 'It's not every day a girl gets to try on a ring as stunning as that.'

Artie frowned. 'I thought you'd be on my side. Aren't you the least bit concerned about my situation?'

'I'm deeply concerned you're going to lose everything if you don't do what Luca Ferrantelli says,' Rosa said. 'You could do a lot worse than him for a husband. He's handsome and rich and will no doubt spoil you, if that ring is any indication.'

'What if I don't want to be spoilt?'

Rosa picked up an onion and held it in her palm. 'See this? Men like Luca Ferrantelli are like this onion. You're only looking at the surface of him—the façade he shows the world. Peel back the layers and you'll see the man behind the mask. You never know—you might be pleasantly surprised at what you find.'

'And how will I know if peeling back his layers reduces me to tears like that onion will?'

'That's a risk we all take when we get close to someone.' Rosa sliced into the onion with a knife. 'And God knows, you're never going to get close to anyone living on your own here. This is a lifeline and you'd be a fool not to take it.'

Maybe Rosa was right, because, if Artie didn't marry Luca Ferrantelli she would have to leave the *castello*. Permanently.

She couldn't allow that to happen.

No matter what.

But how could she work this to her advantage? What could Luca do for her in return? Apart from buying her a stunningly beautiful engagement ring that just begged to come out of that box and sit proudly on her finger. Artie went back to the salon and picked up the velvet box. She told herself she was going to put it in the safe until Luca returned the following day. But before she could stop herself, she opened the box and took the ring out and placed it back on her finger. She promised herself she would only wear it for a couple of hours, just for the heck of it. Then, once she got tired of it, she would put it back in the box and hand it back to Luca tomorrow with a firm, *Thanks, but no, thanks*.

She couldn't possibly marry him...*could she?*

Later that evening, Artie was doing her embroidery when she suddenly realised the ring wasn't on her finger. She jumped off the sofa and searched around the scatter cushions, her heart racing. Where was it? Had it fallen off somewhere? Oh, God. Oh, God. Oh, God. The ring was worth a fortune. Luca would be furious if she lost his blasted ring. He had no right to buy her such an expensive ring. Her stomach pitched. Would he want her to replace it? Yes, he would.

Rosa came in at that point. 'Look, I know things are

bad financially but surely you don't have to search the back of the sofa for loose change?'

Artie swung around to face her, eyes wide in panic. 'I can't find Luca's wretched engagement ring!'

Rosa frowned. 'Didn't you put it in the safe?'

'No, I stupidly put it on for a couple of hours.' Artie tossed all the scatter cushions on the floor and began lifting off the sofa cushions to no avail. 'What am I going to do?'

Rosa joined in the search. 'You'll have to retrace your steps. Where have you been in the last few hours? Did you go outside to the garden?'

'No, I've only been indoors.'

Artie emptied her embroidery basket onto the floor—thimbles, reels of thread, needles going everywhere. The disorder on the floor in front of her was the same as inside her mind. Chaos. Tangled thoughts. Prickling conscience.

'It must be here somewhere. Oh, God, how could I lose it?'

She stuffed the embroidery items haphazardly back in the basket, pricking her finger with one of her needles.

'Ouch.' She stuck her finger in her mouth and sucked up the droplets of blood. She removed her finger from her mouth and gave Rosa a baleful look. 'He had no right to give me such an expensive ring. I'll have to marry him now.'

But deep down you want to, don't you? Marriage to Luca Ferrantelli just might give you some control over your life. The control you've been seeking for a long time. Money. Freedom. Not to mention a wickedly handsome 'paper' husband...

Rosa bent down and carefully sorted through Artie's basket for a moment. 'Ah, here it is.' She handed Artie the engagement ring. 'You'd better put it back on and leave it on until you give it back to Signor Ferrantelli.'

Give it back?

Lose her one chance of taking back control of her life?

Lose her home?

Artie slipped the ring back on her finger, her thoughts finally untangling. 'I'm not giving it back. Maybe you're right. This is my chance—maybe my only chance—to take control of my life. I'm going to make this work for me. On my terms. It's only for six months—what have I got to lose?'

Rosa raised one brow. 'Your heart?'

Artie set her mouth in a determined line. 'Not going to happen. This is a business deal. If Luca Ferrantelli can keep his emotions out of this, then so can I.'

Luca could not remember looking forward to a meeting more than returning to the Castello Mireille the following day to see Artemisia Bellante. Something about her intrigued him in a way few people did. He'd expected her to be biddable and submissive and instead found her spirited defiance a refreshing change from all the sycophants who surrounded him, pandering to his every whim. He'd found it so hard to take his eyes off her—slim, but with generous curves in all the right places, flashing brown eyes, wild, curly dark brown hair and a ski-slope nose, a stubborn chin and a cherry-red mouth—he'd almost offered her a real marriage. Only joking. No real marriages for him. Ever. He neither wanted nor needed love from a partner. Love was a reckless emotion that had the potential to cause immeasurable harm. He'd had a ringside seat to see just how much harm.

But a six-month hands-off arrangement to give his grandfather the motivation to get chemo was definitely doable. He hadn't been able to save his father or brother but he could save his grandfather. And marrying Artemisia Bellante was the way to do it. The only way.

In all their phone and email conversations, Franco Bellante had told him Artemisia was shy around men. Luca hadn't seen too much shyness. He'd seen sass and spirit and a damped down sensuality that was irresistibly attractive. He'd seen her surreptitious glances at his mouth and felt the supercharged energy in the air when their gazes collided. Did that mean she would be interested in tweaking the terms of their paper marriage?

Don't even think about it.

Luca knew how to control his impulses. He had learned the hard way not to rush into things without careful consideration first. Artemisia Bellante might be the most alluring young woman he'd met in a long time but a deal was a deal and his word was his word. Their paper marriage would last six months and no longer. Nonno's doctors had given him no more than a year to live if he didn't start treatment soon. The clock was ticking on the old man's life and Luca was determined to present him with the perfect choice of bride.

The housekeeper led him to the same salon as yesterday, where Artemisia was waiting for him standing by the windows. Her hands were clasped behind her back, her posture guarded. She looked regal and elegant even though she was wearing casual clothes—blue jeans and a white shirt with a patterned scarf draped artfully around her neck. The jeans highlighted the shapely curves of her hips and the white shirt brought out the creamy tone of her skin. Her chin was at a proud height, her deep brown eyes shining with unmistakable dislike.

Hot and heavy desire tingled in his groin. Her dislike of him was a bigger turn-on than he'd expected. Dating had become a little too easy for him lately—a little too boring and predictable. But nothing about Artemisia Bellante was boring or predictable.

Rein it in, buddy. You're not going there, remember?

Luca gave a sweeping bow. '*Buongiorno*, Artemisia. Have you made your decision?'

Her indrawn breath was like the hiss of a cornered cat. 'I have.'

'And?' Luca was only conscious of holding his breath when his lungs began to tighten. He wanted her as his bride. No one else was going to do. He *had* to have *her*. He couldn't explain his intractable stance other than that something about her ticked all the boxes.

She held his gaze with her icy one, her jaw set, her colour high. 'I will marry you.'

The relief that swept through him momentarily caught him off guard. It wasn't that he'd expected her to say no but somehow he hadn't realised until now how *much* he'd wanted her to say yes. 'Good. I'm glad you see the sense in doing so.'

Her eyebrows rose ever so slightly above her glittering eyes. 'However, I have some conditions on my acceptance of your offer.'

Luca was not one to allow people to push him around

but something about her expression made him make an exception. She stirred him in a way he had never been stirred before. His blood heated with a backbeat of desire, his nostrils flaring to take in the flowery scent of her perfume. 'Go on.'

She unfolded her arms and smoothed her hands down the front of her thighs. He ran his gaze down the slim length of her legs and her neat calves. She was wearing light brown suede ankle boots that gave her an inch or two more height. But even with the benefit of heels, she still wouldn't make it to the top of his shoulder. But that wasn't the only thing she was wearing—his grandmother's engagement ring winked proudly, almost defiantly, on her left hand. The arabesque design chosen so lovingly by his *nonno* to give to the love of his life— Luca's grandmother—suited Artemisia's hand as if designed especially for her. A faint alarm bell sounded at the back of his mind. He would have to be extra careful to keep his emotions out of this arrangement. Their relationship was a business deal and nothing more. There was no point feeling a little sentimental about seeing his grandmother's ring on Artie's hand. There was nothing sentimental about his choice of engagement ring. Sure, he could have bought any other ring but he had deliberately used his *nonna*'s ring knowing it would add authenticity to his committed relationship status in the eyes of his grandfather.

It was his grandfather who was sentimental.

Not him.

'Won't you sit down?' Artie's tone was all cool politeness but her eyes were hard with bitterness.

Luca gestured to the sofa nearest her. 'Ladies first.'

Artie drew in another sharp breath and sat on the sofa, her hands clasped around her crossed knee, her plump mouth tightly set. 'So, I've decided to accept your offer on the proviso we're married here at the *castello*. A quiet wedding, minimal guests.'

It intrigued him why she wanted a low-key wedding. Didn't most young women want to be a princess for the day? He could think of at least half a dozen of his ex-lovers who had dropped enormous hints about their dream wedding. It had killed his interest in them stone-dead. 'Is there any particular reason why you want to be married here and not at one of the local churches?'

Her gaze didn't quite meet his but aimed for the top of his left shoulder. 'My father's funeral was held here, so too was my mother's. It's where many of my ancestors are buried.'

'*Sì*, but a funeral is a little different from a wedding, is it not?'

Her clear brown gaze collided with his. 'Not from my perspective. This isn't a real marriage. I would be uncomfortable desecrating a church by saying vows neither of us intends to keep. It would be disrespectful. Nor do I want a big, flashy wedding with people I don't know and have nothing in common with attending. It would be a waste of money and effort.'

Luca didn't care where they were married as long as they were married. He only hoped Nonno would be well enough to be able to travel from his home in Tuscany, but, since Umbria was a neighbouring region, it wasn't a long journey—just over two hours' drive.

'Fine. We'll marry here. Leave the arrangements to me. I've already applied for a licence so we don't have to wait the six weeks normally required. Your father sent me a copy of your birth certificate and passport before he died. I took the liberty of getting things on the move.'

Her eyes widened and her mouth fell open. 'You were so sure I would accept? But you hadn't even met me in person until yesterday.'

He shrugged one shoulder. 'Your father showed me a photo and he talked about you a lot. I was satisfied you would be suitable.'

She uncrossed her legs and sprang off the sofa, moving some distance away. 'I would have thought a man in your position wouldn't have to resort to finding a mail-order bride.' Scorn underlined every word she spoke. 'What if I'd said no?'

Luca gave a slow smile. 'I would have found some way to change your mind.'

Her chin came up and her eyes flashed. 'I can't believe my father encouraged you in this ridiculous mission to acquire a wife. When did you meet with him? I've never seen you come here before yesterday and I barely left my father's side.'

'I visited your father when he was in hospital with pneumonia late last year. He talked you up so much it intrigued me. I was disappointed not to see you on one of my visits but he said you weren't keen on hospitals since the accident. We emailed or phoned after that.'

She bit her lip and looked away. 'Did he say anything else about me?'

'Just that you were shy and not much of a party girl.'

She gave a snort of humourless laughter. 'Yes, well, that's certainly true.'

Luca rose from the sofa and walked over to a row of

picture frames on a sideboard. He picked up a photo taken when Artie was a child, sitting on her mother's knee. 'Your mother was very beautiful. She was English, *sì*?'

'Y-yes…' There was a slight catch in her voice.

Luca put the photo back on the sideboard and turned to face her. 'It's hard to lose a parent in your teens, especially the same sex parent.' Harder still when you were the cause of their death. And the death of your only brother. The guilt never left him. It sat on his shoulder. It followed him. It prodded him. It never let him forget. It kept him awake at night. His own personal stalker, torturing him with the what-ifs and the if-onlys.

Her brown eyes met his. 'You lost your father and older brother when you were a teenager, didn't you?'

Luca knew there was still stuff about his father and brother's death online. Not so easy to come across these days but it was still there if you did a thorough enough search. It had been a big news story at the time due to his father's high profile in business circles.

He could still see the headlines now—*Property developer CEO and son and heir lost in heavy surf in Argentina.*

There had been nothing about Luca's role in their drowning and he only found out years later it was because his *nonno* had pulled some strings in order to protect him.

Another reason his marriage to Artie had to go ahead and soon. He owed his *nonno* peace in this last stage of his life.

'Yes. When I was thirteen.' He stripped his voice of all emotion—he could have been discussing the stock exchange instead of the worst day of his life.

'I'm sorry.' Artie waited a beat and added, 'Is your mother still alive?'

'Yes. She lives in New York now.'

'Has she remarried?'

'No.'

There was a silence.

Luca could have filled it with all the reasons why his mother no longer lived in Italy. Her unrelenting grief. His strained relationship with her that nothing he said or did could fix. The constant triggers being around him caused her. The empty hole in her life that nothing could fill. The hole he had created by his actions on that fateful day. He hadn't just lost his father and brother on that day—he'd lost his entire family as he'd known it. Even his grandparents—as caring and supportive as they tried to be—had been sideswiped by grief and became shadows of their former selves. His extended family—aunts, uncles, cousins—all of them had been affected by his actions that day.

'So, what changed your mind about marrying me?' Luca decided it was safer to stay on the topic of their upcoming marriage rather than drift into territory he wanted left well alone. 'Let me guess. Was it the engagement ring?'

She swallowed, her cheeks blooming with colour. 'In a way, yes.'

Luca hadn't taken her for a gold-digger but it was a damn fine ring. His eyes flicked to her left hand. 'It looks good on you. But I hope you don't mind it being second hand. It belonged to my grandmother. She left it to me in her will.'

Her eyes widened to the size of dinner plates. 'Your

grandmother's? Oh, my goodness. Just as well I—' She bit her lip and shifted her gaze a fraction, the colour in her cheeks deepening.

'Just as well you…?' Luca prompted, intrigued by her cagey expression.

Her slim throat rose and fell over a swallow and her gaze slipped out of reach of his. 'I—I misplaced it for a couple of hours. But it's your fault for giving me such a ridiculously valuable ring. A priceless heirloom, for pity's sake. What on earth were you thinking? Of course, I'll give it back to you once the six months is up.'

'I don't want it back. It's a gift.'

Her gaze flicked back to his, shock written all over her features. 'I couldn't possibly keep it. It's worth a small fortune, not to mention the sentimental value.'

Luca shrugged. 'It's no skin off my nose what you do with it once our marriage is over. It's just a ring. I will have no further use for it after this. It means nothing to me.'

Her mouth tightened. 'Is there anything that means something to you other than making disgusting amounts of money?'

Luca slanted his mouth into a cynical smile. 'There isn't a law against being successful in business. Money opens a lot of doors.'

'I would imagine it closes others. How would you know if people liked you for you or for your wealth?'

'I'm a good judge of character. I soon weed out the timewasters and hangers-on.'

Her top lip curled and her eyes shone with loathing. 'Well, bully for you.'

CHAPTER THREE

ARTIE WOULDN'T HAVE admitted it even under torture, but she was getting off on sparring with Luca Ferrantelli. Every time they exchanged words, little bubbles of excitement trickled into her bloodstream. He was intelligent and quick-witted and charming and she had to keep on her toes to keep up with him.

She couldn't understand why he had given her his grandmother's engagement ring. *Eek!* Just as well she hadn't lost it. But he didn't seem all that attached to the stunning piece of jewellery, and yet she had fallen in love with it at first sight. Surely he had at least one sentimental bone in his body, or was everything just another business deal?

Luca's brief mention of his father and brother intrigued her. Mostly because he seemed reluctant to dwell on the subject. His expression had given little away, his flat, emotionless tone even less. But still, she sensed there was pain beneath the surface—deep pain that made him distance himself from it whenever he could.

Maybe Rosa was right—Luca Ferrantelli had more than a few layers to his personality that begged to be explored.

But Artie knew all too well about deep emotional pain. Talking about her mother, thinking about the accident and its aftermath sent her into a spiral of despair. Guilt was her constant companion. Wasn't it her fault her father had lost control of his finances? He hadn't been the same after the accident. Losing Artie's mother, and losing the use of his legs as well as an acquired brain injury, had meant he was not the same man—nor ever could be—and she was entirely to blame. Nothing Artie could do would ever change that. It was only fitting that she wed Luca Ferrantelli and reclaim her family's heritage.

It was her penance. The price she must pay. But she would make the best out of the situation by owning her choice to marry Luca rather than feel he had forced her hand.

'We need to discuss the honeymoon.' Luca's expression was inscrutable. 'Do you have somewhere you'd like to go?'

Honeymoon?

Artie widened her eyes so far she thought they might pop right out of her head. She clasped her hand to her throat where her heart now seemed to be lodged. 'A…a honeymoon? Whatever for? You said it's going to be a marriage in name only. Why would we need to go on a honeymoon?' Even saying the word 'honeymoon' made her body go all tingly and her heart race and her blood heat. Heat that stormed into her cheeks and simmered in other more secret places.

One of his dark eyebrows lifted at her stuttering protest, a satirical glint shining in his gaze. 'I'm fine with a quiet wedding here at the *castello* but I insist on a honeymoon. It will give our marriage more credibility if we are seen to go away together for a short break.'

Seen? In public? Be in wide open spaces? Rushing crowds. Traffic. Noise. Busyness. Artie stumbled backwards, her arms wrapping around her body, her breathing tight and laboured. 'No. I can't do that. I don't want to go. There's no need. It's not a proper marriage and it's wrong of you to insist on it.'

Breathe. Breathe. Breathe.

Luca frowned. 'Are you worried I'll take advantage of you? Please be assured that is not going to happen. I gave you my word.'

'I don't want to go anywhere with you,' Artie said. 'How could you think I would? I don't even like you.'

His eyes dipped to her mouth then back to her gaze. 'Artemisia, we need to be seen together in public. It's not going to work unless we present as a normal couple. We'll have to live together most, if not all, of the time.'

Her stomach turned over. 'L-live together?'

'But of course. Isn't that what husbands and wives do?'

Artie gulped. Her skin prickled, her legs trembled, her mind raced. Live with Luca Ferrantelli? What would that entail? She couldn't even leave her own home. How on earth would she move into his? Should she tell him about her social phobia? Would he understand? No. Not likely. Few people did. Even the professionals who had visited her at the *castello* had more or less given up on her.

Her gaze moved out of reach of his and she fiddled with the sleeve of her shirt for something to do with her hands. 'I'm sorry, but couldn't you move in here?

I mean, this place is huge and you can have your own suite of rooms and we'd hardly have to see each other and no one would ever know we're not—'

'No.' His tone was so adamant the word could have been underlined in thick black ink.

Artie swung away from him, trying to get her breathing back under control. She was light-headed and nauseous, her stomach churning fast enough to make butter. She was going to faint… No, she wasn't. She was going to fight it. Fight *him*. She took a deep breath and turned around to face him. 'I will *not* leave my home. Not for you. A marriage of convenience is supposed to be convenient for both parties. It's not convenient for me to move right now. I've only just buried my father. I'd like more time to…to spend grieving out of the view of the public.' It wasn't completely a lie. She missed her father, not because they were particularly close but because looking after him had given structure and purpose to her life.

Luca studied her for a long moment, his expression giving nothing away. She tried not to squirm under his unnerving scrutiny but it was a mammoth effort and only added to her light-headedness. 'All right. We'll delay the honeymoon.'

Relief swept through her and she brushed back her hair from her face, her hand not quite as steady as she would have liked. 'Thank you.'

She hadn't been in a car since coming home from hospital after the accident. She hadn't been in a plane or train or bus since she was fifteen. She hadn't been around more than two or three people in a decade. Her life was contained within these four ancient stone walls and she couldn't see it changing any time soon.

Luca closed the distance between them and held her gaze for another beat or two. 'I realise your father's financial situation has come as a shock to you. And I understand how resistant you are to my plan to turn things to your advantage. But I want my grandfather to see us married and living as a couple.'

'Why is that so important to you?'

'He's got cancer but he won't agree to treatment.'

'Oh... I'm sorry.'

Luca ran a hand down his face, the sound of his palm scraping over his regrowth loud in the silence. 'Unless he has treatment soon, he will die within a year. His dream has always been to see me settled down with a nice young woman. He disapproves of my casual approach to relationships and has been at pains to let me know at every opportunity. I want him to find a reason to live, knowing I've found a suitable bride.'

A suitable bride.

If only Luca knew how unsuitable she really was. Would he still want to marry her if he knew the truth about her? 'Will your grandfather be well enough to come here for the wedding?'

'I hope so.'

Artie bit her lip. She was conflicted about keeping her social anxiety from Luca but neither could she risk losing her home if he decided to withdraw his offer of marriage. She didn't know him well enough to trust he would make allowances for her. He'd already told her he was a ruthless businessman who didn't allow emotion to cloud his judgement. How could she hope he might be understanding and compassionate about her mental health issues? 'But you only know me as my father presented me. I might be the worst person in the world.'

A lazy smile tilted his mouth and his eyes darkened. 'I like what I've seen so far.'

Artie could feel colour pouring into her cheeks. Could feel a faint hollow ache building, beating between her thighs. Could feel a light tingling in her breasts. His gaze went to her mouth and she couldn't stop herself from sweeping them with the tip of her tongue. His eyes followed the movement of her tongue and liquid warmth spread through her core like warmed treacle. What invisible chemistry was doing this to her? What potent force did Luca Ferrantelli have over her? She had never been so aware of another person. Never so aware of her own body. Her senses were on high alert, her pulse racing.

Suddenly he wasn't standing a metre away but was close enough for her to smell the sharp, clean citrus notes of his aftershave. Had he moved or had she?

She looked into the depths of his gaze and her heart skipped a beat. And another. And another, until it felt like tiny racing footsteps were pounding against the membrane surrounding her heart.

He lifted his hand to her face, trailing his index finger down the slope of her cheek from just above her ear down to the base of her chin. Every nerve in her skin exploded with sensation. Every pore acutely sensitive to his faintest touch.

'You are much more beautiful in person than in the photo your father showed me.' Luca's tone was a bone-melting blend of rough and smooth. Honey and gravel. Temptation and danger.

Artie couldn't take her eyes off his mouth, drawn by a force as old as time. Male and female desire meeting. Wanting. Needing. Tempting. 'I don't get called Artemisia…most people call me Artie.'

Oh, for pity's sake. Couldn't you think of something a little more sophisticated to say?

Luca gave a crooked smile and something warm spread through her chest. 'Artie. It's cute. I like it. Artemisia, Queen of Halicarnassus. She was an ally of the Persian King Xerces in 430 BCE and reputedly brave in battle.'

That's me—brave. Not.

'My mother chose it. She loved Greek history.'

His gaze became hooded and he glanced at her mouth again. 'There will be times when we'll be expected to show affection towards one another. Are you going to be okay with that?'

'W-what sort of affection?'

'Kissing. Holding hands. Touching.'

Her lower body began to throb with a strange kind of ache. She couldn't stop herself thinking about places he might touch her—places that were already tingling in anticipation. How would she cope with a casual brush of his hand? His strong arm around her waist? His mouth pressed to hers? No one had ever touched her with a lover's touch. No one had ever kissed her. The desire to be touched by him was overwhelming. Her body craved it like a drug.

'Okay.'

Okay? Are you out of your mind?

Artie *was* out of her mind—with lust. She had never felt so out of control of her body. It was acting of its own volition, responding to him in ways she had never expected. She didn't even like him. He was arrogant and confident in a way she found irritating. It was as if he expected her to throw herself at him just like any other woman he had encountered. How was she going to resist him if he kissed her? How would it feel to have that firm mouth moving against hers?

Luca continued to look at her with a heart-stopping intensity. 'If you don't want me to kiss you then you need to tell me, because right now I can think of nothing I want to do more.' His voice lowered to a deep bass that sent another wave of heat coursing through her body.

'What makes you think I want you to kiss me now? What would be the point? There's no one here but us.' Artie was proud of her calm and collected tone when inside her body was steaming, simmering, smouldering.

His thumb pressed lightly on the middle of her bottom lip, sending tingles down the length of her spine. 'The way you're looking at me.'

'How am I looking at you?'

Eek. Was that her voice? She had to do something about her voice. None of that whispery, husky rubbish. She had to be brusque and matter-of-fact.

'You must be imagining it.'

He cupped one side of her face with his hand, the slight roughness of his palm making her insides coil and tighten with lust. 'Maybe.' He gave a quick on-off smile and dropped his hand from her face. 'So, the wedding. How does this weekend sound?'

Artie only just managed to suppress a gasp. '*This* weekend? What's the rush?'

'I'm not a fan of long engagements.'

'Funny. But how am I going to find a dress in time? Or are you expecting me to turn up naked?'

Argh. Why did you say that?

A dark glint came into his eyes. 'Now, there's an idea.'

Artie pursed her lips, hoping her cheeks were not glowing as hot as they felt. 'I can safely say I will never, ever be naked in front of you.'

He glided a lazy finger down her burning cheek, a smile in his eyes. 'Have you been naked in front of anyone?'

Artie stepped back, annoyed with herself for not doing so earlier. She *had* to keep her distance. It was dangerous to stand so close to him. She had so little immunity to his sensual power. She had to remember he was a powerful magnet and she was a tiny iron filing.

'I'm not going to discuss my private life with you. It's none of your damn business.'

'We have to know a few things about each other otherwise no one will accept our marriage as the real thing.'

Artie frowned. 'What? Are you going to pretend you're in love with me or something? Who's going to believe it? We're total opposites.'

'Ah, but don't they say opposites attract?' His smile melted her bones—she could feel her legs trembling to keep her upright.

Artie compressed her lips and iced her gaze. 'This may come as a surprise to a man with an ego the size of yours but I'm not attracted to you.'

He gave a deep chuckle. 'Then you're going to have to call on every bit of acting power you possess to convince my grandfather otherwise. Think you can do that, *cara mia*?'

The Italian endearment almost made her swoon. She hoisted her chin. 'Do you, Mr Hardened Cynical Playboy, think *you* can act like a man passionately in love with his bride?'

His gaze held hers in a smouldering lock that made the backs of her knees tingle. 'That will be the easy part.'

CHAPTER FOUR

ARTIE STOOD IN FRONT of the cheval mirror in her bedroom and checked her appearance. She had decided against wearing her mother's wedding dress and chosen a cream satin ballgown of her mother's instead. It was a classic design with a tulle underskirt that emphasised her neat waist, and a close-fitting bodice that hinted at the shape of her breasts without revealing too much cleavage. She hadn't wanted to taint her mother's beautiful wedding gown with her charade of a marriage. Her parents had married for love and lived happily together until Artie insisted on going to a birthday party against their wishes when she was fifteen.

She bit down on her lip until it hurt. Why had she been so adamant about going to that stupid party? Where were those supposed friends of hers now? Only a handful came to visit her in hospital. None had come to the *castello* once she had been released. None had come to her mother's funeral. She had stood beside her father's wheelchair as her mother was lowered into the family plot at the *castello* with her heart in pieces, guilt raining down on her heavier than what was coming from the dismal sky above. How could one teenage decision have so many unforeseen consequences?

Artie plucked at the skirt of her dress, her stomach an ants' nest of nerves. Today was her wedding day. The day she married Luca Ferrantelli in a paper marriage to save her family home. Would this be another decision she would later regret? Or would the consolation of getting the *castello* back into her possession wipe out any misgivings? She glanced at the engagement ring on her hand. The longer she wore it, the more she loved it. She felt strangely connected to Luca's grandmother by wearing her ring. But would the old lady spin in her grave to know Artie was entering into a loveless union with her grandson?

Rosa came in carrying a bouquet of flowers she had picked from the garden. 'You look beautiful, Artie.' She handed her the simple but fragrant bouquet. 'You're not wearing a veil?'

Artie brought the flowers up to her nose and breathed in the heady scent of roses and orange blossom. 'This isn't a proper wedding.'

Rosa frowned. 'But it's still a legal one. You might as well look like a proper bride. And make that handsome groom of yours sit up and take notice.' She went to the large wardrobe and pulled out the long cardboard box where Artie's mother's wedding dress and veil were stored on the top shelf. She placed the box on the bed and lifted the lid and removed the tissue-wrapped heirloom hand-embroidered veil that had been worn by both Artie's mother and grandmother. Rosa shook out the veil and then brought it over to Artie. 'Come on. Indulge me.'

Artie rolled her eyes but gave in, allowing Rosa to fasten the veil on her head, securing it with hair pins. Rosa draped the veil over Artie's face and then stepped back to inspect her handiwork. 'You will knock Luca Ferrantelli's socks off, *si*?'

Artie turned back to look at her reflection. She did indeed look like a proper bride. She glanced at Rosa. 'Tell me I'm not making the biggest mistake of my life. My second biggest, I mean.'

Rosa grasped one of Artie's hands, her eyes shimmering with tears. 'You have already lost so much. You can't lose the *castello* as well. Sometimes we have to do whatever it takes to make the best of things.' She released Artie's hand and brushed at her eyes and gave a rueful smile. 'Weddings always make me emotional. Just as well I didn't get married myself.'

'Would you have liked to?' Artie was surprised she hadn't thought to ask before now. Rosa was in her sixties and had been a part of the *castello* household for as long as Artie could remember. They had talked about many things over the years but not about the housekeeper's love life or lack thereof.

Rosa made a business of fussing over the arrangement of the skirt of Artie's gown. 'I fell in love once a long time ago. It didn't work out.'

'What happened?'

Rosa bent down lower to pick a fallen rose petal off the floor. She scrunched it in her hand and gave a thin-lipped smile. 'He married someone else. I never found anyone else who measured up.'

'Oh, that's so sad.'

Rosa laughed but it sounded tinny. 'I saved myself a

lot of heartache. Apparently, he's been divorced three times since then.' Her expression suddenly sobered. 'Your parents were lucky to have found each other. I know they didn't have as long together as they would have liked but it's better to have five years with the right one than fifty with the wrong one.'

But what about six months with a man who had only met her a matter of days ago? A man who was so dangerously attractive, her blood raced every time he looked at her?

Luca stood in the *castello*'s chapel, waiting for Artie to appear. His grandfather had been too unwell to travel, but Luca planned to take his new bride to meet him as soon as their marriage was official. Luca had organised for a priest to officiate rather than a celebrant, because he knew it would please his grandfather, who was a deeply religious man—hence his disapproval of Luca's life in the fast lane.

As much as he wanted his grandfather to meet Artie as soon as possible, he was quite glad he would have her to himself for a day or two. They would hardly be convincing as a newly married couple if they didn't look comfortable and at ease with each other.

She was a challenge he was tempted to take on. Her resistance to his charm was potently attractive. Not because he didn't respect and honour the word no when a woman said it. He could take rejection and take it well. He was never so emotionally invested in a relationship that he was particularly cut up when it ended.

But he sensed Artie's interest in him. Sensed the chemistry that swirled in the atmosphere when they were together. Would it be risky to explore that chemistry? She was young and unworldly. What if she didn't accept the terms of the deal and wanted more than he was prepared to give? He couldn't allow that to happen. If she fell in love with him it would change everything.

And if he fell in love with her...

He sidestepped the thought like someone avoiding a sinkhole. Loving her would indeed be a pitfall. For her and for him. Love was a dangerous emotion. Whenever he thought of the possibility of loving someone, his heart would shy away like a horse refusing a jump. Too dangerous. Too risky. Too painful.

The back of Luca's neck started to tingle and he turned to see Artie standing in the portal. He suppressed a gasp, his eyes drinking in the vision of her dressed in a stunning cream ballgown and off-white heirloom veil. The bright golden sunlight backlit her slim frame, making her look like an angel. As she walked towards him carrying a small bouquet of flowers he had to remind himself to breathe. The closer she got, the more his heart pounded, the more his blood thundered. And a strange sensation flowed into his chest. Warmth spreading over something hard and frozen, melting, reshaping, softening.

He gave himself a mental slap. No emotions allowed. This was a business deal. Nothing else. So what if she looked as beautiful as an angel? So what if his body roared with lust at the thought of touching her? This wasn't about him—it was about his grandfather. Giving him the will to live long enough to have treatment that could cure him or at least give him a few more precious years of life.

Artie came to stand beside him, her face behind the veil composed, and yet twin circles of pink glowed in her cheeks. Her make-up highlighted the flawless, creamy texture of her skin, the deep brown of her eyes and the thick ink-black lashes that surrounded them. Her lips shone with a hint of lip gloss, making him ache to press his mouth to hers to see if it tasted as sweet and luscious as it looked. He could smell her perfume, an intoxicating blend of fresh flowers that reminded him of the sweet hope of spring after a long, bleak winter.

'You look breathtaking,' Luca said, taking her hands in his. Her small fingers moved within the embrace of his and a lightning rod of lust almost knocked him off his feet. Maybe he shouldn't have suggested a paper marriage. Maybe he should have insisted on the real deal. The thought of consummating their marriage sent a wave of heat through his body. But his conscience slammed on the brakes. No. No. No. It wouldn't be fair. He wasn't the settling-down type and she had fairy-tale romance written all over her. Which, ironically, was why she was perfect for the role of his temporary bride. No one else would satisfy his grandfather. It *had* to be her.

'I—I'm nervous...' Her voice trembled and her teeth sank into the plush softness of her bottom lip.

Luca gently squeezed her fingers. 'Don't be.' His voice was so deep and rough it sounded like it had come from the centre of the earth. He didn't like admitting it, but he was nervous too. Not about repeating the vows and signing the register—those were formalities he could easily compartmentalise in his brain. He was worried his promise to keep their relationship on paper was going to be the real kicker. He gave her hand another light squeeze and smiled. 'Let's do this.'

And they turned to face the priest and the service began...

'I, Artemisia Elisabetta, take you, Luca Benedetto, to be my husband...' Artie repeated her vows with a slight quaver in her voice. 'I promise to be true to you in good times and bad, in sickness and in health.' She swallowed and continued, conscious of Luca's dark gaze holding hers, 'I will love and honour you all the days of my life.'

She wasn't a particularly religious person but saying words she didn't mean made her wonder if she was in danger of a lightning strike. The only lightning strike she had suffered so far had been the tingling zap coursing through her body when Luca first took her hand. Every cell of her body was aware of him. Dressed in a mid-blue morning suit, he looked like he had just stepped off a billboard advertisement for designer menswear. She could smell the lemon and lime of his aftershave—it teased her nostrils, sending her senses into a tailspin. How could a man smell so damn delicious?

Eek! How could a man look so damn attractive?

Double eek! How could she be marrying him?

Luca's hand took her left one and slipped on the wedding ring as he repeated his vows. 'I, Luca Benedetto, take you, Artemisia Elisabetta, to be my wife. I promise to be true to you in good times and bad, in sickness and in health.' He paused for a beat and continued with a rough edge to his voice, 'I will love and honour you all the days of my life.'

Artie blinked back moisture gathering in her eyes.

He sounded so convincing. He even looked convincing with his gaze so focused on her, his mouth smiling at her as if she was the most amazing woman who had ever walked upon the face of the earth.

It's an act. Don't be fooled by it. None of this means anything to him and neither should it mean anything to you.

'You may kiss the bride.'

The priest's words startled Artie out of her reverie and she only had time to snatch in a breath before Luca's hands settled on her hips and drew her closer, his mouth descending inexorably towards hers. The first warm, firm press of his lips sent a jolt of electricity through her body. A jolt that travelled all the way down her spine and fizzed like a sparkler deep in her core. He lifted his lips off hers for an infinitesimal moment as if time had suddenly paused. Then he brought his mouth back to hers and sensations rippled through her as his lips moved against hers with increasing pressure, his hands on her hips bringing her even closer to the hard heat of his stirring body.

One of his hands left her hip to cradle one side of her face, his touch gentle, almost reverent, and yet his mouth was pure sin. Tempting, teasing, tantalising. She opened to him and his tongue touched hers and her insides quaked and throbbed with longing. She pressed closer, her arms going around his neck, her senses reeling as his tongue invited hers in an erotic dance. Every nerve in her lips and mouth awakened to his kiss, flowering open like soft petals to strong sunshine. She became aware of her body in a way she never had before—its needs, urges, flagrantly responding to the dark primal call of his.

Luca angled his head to change position, his tongue stroking against hers, a low, deep groan sounding in his throat. It thrilled her to know he was as undone by their kiss as she was. Thrilled and excited her to realise her own sensual power. Power she hadn't known she possessed until now.

The priest cleared his throat and Luca pulled back from her with a dazed look on his face. Artie suspected she was looking just as shell-shocked as him. Her mouth felt swollen, her feminine core agitated with a roaring hunger he alone had awakened.

Luca blinked a couple of times as if to reset his equilibrium. 'Well, hello there, Signora Ferrantelli.' His voice was rusty, his gaze drifting to her mouth as if he couldn't quite believe what had happened between them moments before.

Artie licked her lips and tasted the salty sexiness of his. 'Hello...'

Luca spoke briefly to the priest, thanking him for his services, and then led Artie to where Rosa had set up refreshments in the garden. She sensed him pulling up a drawbridge, a pulling back into himself. He stood without touching her, his expression inscrutable.

'Right. Time to celebrate. And then tomorrow we'll go and visit my grandfather.'

A wave of ice-cold dread washed over her. 'But can't we leave it a while? I mean, wouldn't he expect us to be on our honeymoon and—?'

'I can't afford to leave it too long before I introduce

you to him,' Luca said, frowning. 'He's in a vulnerable state of health.'

Artie chewed at her lip and lowered her gaze. 'I understand all that but I need more time to get used to being your…wife. I'm worried I'll do or say something that will make your grandfather suspicious.'

Luca gave her a smouldering look. 'If you kiss me like you did just then, any doubts he has will disappear.'

Artie could feel her cheeks firing up. 'I was only following your lead. I haven't been kissed before, so—'

'Really?' His eyebrows shot up in surprise.

She pulled away from him and hugged her arms around her body. 'Go on, mock me for being a twenty-five-year-old virgin. I must seem like a pariah to someone like you who changes lovers daily.'

Her conscience rolled its eyes. *I can't believe you just told him you're a virgin.*

He scraped a hand through his hair, making it tousled. 'Look, I kind of figured from your father that you were lacking in experience but I didn't realise you've never had a boyfriend, even as a teenager. Did your father forbid you from going out or something?'

Artie averted her gaze. 'No. I was busy looking after him after the accident that killed my mother and seriously injured him. There wasn't time for dating.'

His deep frown brought his dark eyebrows together. 'Why were you the one looking after him? Why didn't he employ a nurse or carer?'

Artie turned slightly so she was facing the view over the estate. Luca's penetrating gaze was too unsettling, too unnerving. How could she explain her reasons for taking care of her father? How could she explain the guilt that had chained her to his side? The guilt that still plagued her and had led her to marry Luca in order to save her family's home? The home that was the only thing she had left of her family. 'It was my choice to look after him. I was happy to do it.'

Luca came up behind her and placed his hands on the tops of her shoulders and turned her to face him. He expression was still etched in a frown, his hazel eyes gentle with concern. 'You were just a child when the accident occurred. It was unfair of your father to allow you to sacrifice yourself in such a way. But what about school? Surely you would have had plenty of opportunity to mix with people your own age?'

Artie pressed her lips together for a moment. 'I finished my education online. I was given special permission. I didn't want to leave my father to the care of strangers. He was stricken with grief after losing my mother. We both were. It was my choice to take care of him—no one forced me to do it.'

His hands began a gentle massaging movement that made the tense muscles in her neck and shoulders melt like snow under warm sunshine. 'I think what you did for your father was admirable and yet I can't help feeling he exploited you. You should've had more time to yourself doing all the things teenagers and young adults do.'

Artie stepped out of his hold and interlaced her fingers in front of her body. She glanced to where Rosa was hovering with a bottle of champagne. 'Shouldn't we be mingling with Father Pasquale and our two other guests?' She didn't wait for him to answer and turned and walked towards the housekeeper standing with the priest and the other witness, who worked part-time on the Castello Mireille estate.

Luca watched Artie pick up a glass of champagne from the silver tray the housekeeper was holding. Her expression was now coolly composed but he sensed he had pressed on a nerve when discussing her role of caring for her father. He'd already suspected she was a virgin—her father had intimated as such—but no way had he suspected she had zero experience when it came to dating.

No one had kissed her before him.

She had never had a boyfriend, not even during her teens. How had her father allowed that to happen? Surely he must have realised his daughter was missing out on socialising with people her age?

Luca ran his tongue over his lips and tasted the sweet, fruity residue of her lip gloss. He could still feel the soft imprint of her lips on his, could still feel the throb of desire kissing her had evoked in his body, the deep pulses in his groin, the tingles in his thighs and lower spine.

He had kissed many women, too many to recall in any detail, but he knew he would never forget his first kiss with Artie. It was embedded in his memory. He could recall every contour of her soft mouth, every brush and glide of her tongue, her sweet vanilla and wild-strawberry taste.

But he would have to find some way to forget, for theirs was to be a paper marriage. A six-month time frame to achieve his goal of setting his grandfather's mind at peace. Knowing Artie had so little experience was an even bigger reason to stick to his plan of a hands-off arrangement. It wouldn't be fair to explore the physical chemistry between them, because it might raise her expectations on their relationship.

He didn't *do* relationships. And certainly not *that* type of relationship.

Long-term relationships required commitment and responsibility for the health and safety of your partner. His track record on keeping those he loved safe was appalling. It was easier not to love. Easier to keep his emotions in check, to freeze them so deep inside himself they could never be thawed. To imagine oneself falling in love just because of a bit of scorching hot chemistry was a foolish and reckless thing to do. He no longer did anything reckless and foolish.

Luca glanced at Artie and something pinched in his chest. She was standing next to the ancient stone fountain, the tinkling of water and the sound of birds chirping in the shrubbery a perfect backdrop for her old-world beauty. The sunlight brought out the glossy sheen of her dark brown hair, the light breeze playing with a curl that had worked its way loose from her elegant up-do. She was looking into the distance, a small frown on her forehead, and every now and again the tip of her tongue came out and swept across her lips where his had recently pressed. She turned her head and caught him staring at her, and her cheeks pooled with a delicate shade of pink.

Had he made a mistake in choosing her to be his temporary bride? She was so innocent, so untouched and other-worldly, like she had been transported from another time in history or straight out of a classic fairy tale. And yet he'd felt a connection with her from the moment he met her. A powerful connection that no amount of logic and rationality could dismiss. His brain said *Don't go there* and yet his body roared with primal hunger.

But he would have to get his self-control back in shape, and fast, because falling for his sweet and innocent bride would be the most reckless and foolish thing of all.

CHAPTER FIVE

ARTIE WAS AWARE of Luca's gaze resting on her every time she glanced his way. Aware of the way her body responded to his lightest touch. The merest brush of his fingers set off spot fires in her flesh, sending heat travelling to every secret place in her body. Smouldering there like hot coals just waiting for a breath of oxygen to fan them into vibrant life.

His kiss...

Best not to think too much about his kiss. They were supposed to be keeping their relationship platonic, but nothing about Luca's kiss was platonic. It was sensory overload and she wondered if she would ever recover. Or stop wanting him to kiss her again. And why stop at kisses? He had woken something in her, something hungry and needy that begged to be assuaged. The idea of asking Luca to tweak the rules of their marriage slipped into her mind like an uninvited guest. It would be an ideal opportunity for her to get some experience on board. A six-month marriage where she could indulge in the delights of the flesh. What was there to lose other than her virginity?

Your pride? her conscience piped up. *He can have*

anyone. You're not even his type. How do you think
you could ever satisfy him for six minutes, let alone
six months?

Luca took a glass of champagne off Rosa and came
over to where Artie was standing near the fountain. He
glanced towards the priest and then back to her. 'Father Pasquale is having a good time indulging in Rosa's
food. How long has she been working here?'

'Since I was a baby,' Artie said. 'This is her home
as much as it is mine.'

'So, what would she do if you were to sell up and
move away?'

Artie raised her chin. 'I would never sell the *castello*.
And I don't want to live anywhere but here.'

I can't live anywhere but here.

Luca held her gaze for a long moment. 'How will you
maintain the estate? It needs a lot of work, and sooner
rather than later.'

She drained her champagne glass and sent him a
narrowed glance. 'Is this the right time to discuss this?
It's our wedding day.'

His brows drew together in a frown. 'Do I have to
remind you of the terms of our marriage?'

'No.' She flashed him a pointed look. 'Do *you* need
reminding? That kiss was a little enthusiastic for someone who insisted on keeping things on paper.'

His gaze went to her mouth, and the atmosphere
throbbed with heightened intensity. 'Maybe, but it wasn't
a one-way kiss, was it, *cara*? You were with me all the
way.' His tone was so deep and rough it sent a tingle
down her spine. And his eyes contained a glint that made
something warm and liquid spill between her thighs.

Artie went to swing away from him but his hand came down on her arm. A shiver coursed through her body at the feel of his long, strong, tanned fingers encircling her wrist. She looked down at his hand on her flesh and the warm, liquid sensation in her lower body spread like fire throughout her pelvis. She lifted her gaze to his and raised her eyebrows in a haughty manner. 'W-what are you doing?' Her tone was breathless rather than offended.

His broad thumb began a slow caress over the pulse point on her wrist, the fast-paced throb of her blood betraying her even further. She breathed in the scent of him—the exotic mix of citrus and clean, warm male, her senses reeling from his closeness.

'We're married, *cara*. People will expect us to touch each other.'

Her heart skipped like it was trying to break some sort of record. 'I'm not used to people touching me.'

Luca brushed his bent knuckles against the curve of her cheek, his gaze holding hers in a sensual lock that made her insides quake with desire. 'But you like it when I touch you, *si*?' His thumb moved from her pulse point and stroked along her lower lip. 'You like it very much.'

Artie wanted to deny it but she had hardly helped her case by kissing him back the way she had earlier. Nor was she helping it now by not pulling away from his loose hold. Her willpower had completely deserted her—she wanted his touch, craved it like an addict craved a forbidden substance. She couldn't take her eyes off his mouth, couldn't stop thinking about the warm, sensual pleasure of it moving against hers. Couldn't stop thinking about the stroke and glide of his tongue and how it had sent torrents of need racing through her body.

She drew in a ragged breath and forced her gaze back to his. 'I'm sorry if I keep giving you mixed messages. It wasn't my intention at all.'

He brought her hand up to his mouth and pressed a barely-there kiss to her bent knuckles, his gaze unwavering on hers. 'You're not the only one sending mixed messages.' He dropped her hand and gave a rueful smile. 'I'm not going to change the terms of our marriage. It wouldn't be fair to you.'

Not fair? What was fair about denying her body the fulfilment it craved? 'Are you worried I might fall in love with you?' The question popped out before she could stop it.

His dark eyes dipped to her mouth for a moment, his forehead creasing in a frown as if he was quietly considering the possibility of her developing feelings for him. When his gaze came back to hers it was shuttered. Screened with secret thoughts. 'It would be very foolish of you to do so.' His voice contained a note of gravity that made the hairs on the back of her neck tingle.

'Have you ever been in love with anyone?'

'No.' His answer was fast and flat.

Artie twirled the empty champagne glass in her hand. 'I didn't realise it was possible to prevent oneself from falling in love. From what I've heard it just happens and there's nothing you can do to stop it. Maybe you haven't met the right person yet.'

'I have no doubt such feelings exist between other people but I have no interest in feeling that way about someone.'

'Why?'

Luca shrugged one broad shoulder, his gaze still inscrutable. 'It seems to me an impossible task to be someone's soulmate. To be everything they need and want you to be. I know I can't be that person. I'm too selfish.'

Artie wondered if that was entirely true. He was prepared to marry a virtual stranger to keep his grandfather alive for a few more years. How was that selfish? And he was prepared to hand her back the *castello* at the end of six months instead of keeping his nine-tenths ownership. Hardly the actions of a self-serving man, surely?

Rosa approached at that moment carrying a tray with fresh glasses of champagne. 'Another quick one before the official photos are taken?' she asked with a smile. 'The photographer is setting up near the rose garden.'

Artie put her used glass on the tray and took a new one. *'Grazie.'*

'And you, Signor Ferrantelli?' Rosa turned to Luca, offering him a fresh glass off the tray.

He shook his head. 'Not for me, thanks. One is enough. And please call me Luca.' He took Artie's free hand and nodded in the direction of the photographer. 'Shall we?'

Once a small set of photos were taken, Artie helped Rosa tidy away the refreshments after the priest and photographer had left. But when the housekeeper announced she was going to have an early night, Artie was left at a loose end. She hadn't seen Luca since the photo session—he'd said he wanted to check a few things out on the estate and hadn't yet returned. She'd thought about what he'd said back at the fountain and his reasons for saying it. The more she got to know him, the more she wanted to know. Why was he so adamant about keeping his emotions in check? What was so threatening about loving someone that made him so unwilling to experience it for himself? She might not have any experience when it came to falling in love, but she knew enough from her parents and books and movies it was a real and powerful emotion that was impossible to block once it happened. But since the accident, she had given up on the hope of one day finding true love. Any love she felt would be one-sided, for how could anyone return her love once they knew the destruction she had caused?

Luca had warned her about falling in love with him—'It would be very foolish of you to do so.' But how could she stop something that was so beyond her control? She was already aware of her vulnerability where he was concerned. He was so suave and sophisticated, and occupied a world she hadn't been party to her entire adult life. Hadn't his passionate, heart-stopping kiss shown her how at risk she was to developing feelings towards him?

Artie circled her wrist where his fingers had held her. A shiver shimmied down her spine as she recalled the tensile strength in his hand, the springy black masculine hairs that peppered his skin, the way his touch spoke to her flesh, awakening it, enlivening it, enticing it. He was temptation personified and she would be a fool indeed to allow her feelings to get the better of her. He had been clear about the terms of their relationship.

Why, then, did she ache for more of his touch? Why, then, did she want to feel his mouth on hers again?

Artie sat in the main salon with her embroidery on her lap, when Luca came in. His hair looked tousled from the wind or the passage of his fingers or both. And he had changed out of his morning suit into jeans and a white cotton shirt, the sleeves rolled back to reveal his strong wrists and forearms. The white shirt highlighted his olive-toned tan, the blue jeans the muscled length of his legs. He brought in with him the fresh smell of outdoors and something else…something that made her female hormones sit up straighter and her senses to go on high alert.

She put the sampler she was working on to one side and crossed one leg over the other, working hard to keep her features neutral. 'I wasn't sure of your plans, so I got Rosa to make up one of the guest rooms for you. It's on the second floor—the green suite overlooking the vineyard.'

His gaze held hers with a watchful intensity. 'So, she knows our marriage is a hands-off affair?'

Artie moistened her lips, conscious of the slow crawl of heat in her cheeks. 'Yes, well, I thought it best. I'm not the best actor when it comes to playing charades, and she's known me a long time and would sense any hint of inauthenticity.'

'I would prefer you not to tell anyone else about the terms of our relationship.' His tone was firm. 'I don't want any idle gossip getting back to my grandfather.'

'Rosa is the soul of discretion. She would never betray a confidence.' It was the one thing Artie could rely on—the housekeeper was loyal and trustworthy to a fault. Rosa had never revealed Artie's struggles to anyone and had always been as supportive as possible.

Luca came over to the sofa where she was sitting and leaned down and picked up the sampler she'd been working on. He ran his fingers over the tiny flower buds and leaves she had embroidered. 'This is exquisite work. Have you been doing it long?' he asked.

Artie shrugged off the compliment but inside she was glowing from his praise. No one apart from her father and Rosa had ever seen her work. 'It's just a hobby. I started doing embroidery after I got out of hospital. I'm self-taught, which you can probably tell.'

He turned the sampler over and inspected the other side, where the stitches were almost as neat and precise as on the front. 'You undersell yourself, *cara*. You could start a small business doing this sort of thing. Bespoke embroidery. There's a big swing away from factory-produced or sweatshop items. What people want these days is the personal touch.'

'Yes, well, I'm not sure I'm ready for that.' Artie took the sampler out of his hand and folded it and put it inside her embroidery basket, then closed the lid with a definitive movement.

'What's stopping you?'

I'm stopping me.

Her fear of the big, wide world outside the *castello* was stopping her from reaching her potential. She knew it but didn't know how she could do anything to change it. How could she run a business locked away here? She met his probing gaze for a moment before looking away again. The thought of revealing her phobia to him made her blood run cold. What would he think of her? She had effectively married him under false pretences. 'I'm happy leaving it as a hobby, that's all. I don't want to put myself under pressure of deadlines.'

'Speaking of deadlines...' Luca rubbed a hand down his face, the raspy sound of his palm against his light stubble making her recall how it had felt against her skin when he'd kissed her. 'I'd like to make an early start in the morning. My grandfather gets tired easily, so the first part of the day is better for him to receive visitors.'

Artie blinked. Blinked again. Her pulse began to quicken. Her breathing to shorten. Her skin to tighten. She rose from the sofa on unsteady legs and moved to the bank of windows on the other side of the room. She turned her back to the room and grasped the windowsill with white-knuckled force. 'Maybe you should go alone. I need more time before I—'

'There isn't time to waste.' The intransigent edge to his tone was a chilling reminder of his forceful, goal-directed personality.

Artie swallowed a tight lump in her throat and gripped the windowsill even harder. 'I... I can't go with you.'

There was a beat or two of intense silence. A silence so thick it seemed to be pressing in on her from all four walls and even the ceiling. A silence that echoed in her head and roared in her ears and reminded her she was way out of her depth.

'What do you mean, you can't? We made an agreement, Artie. I expect you to adhere to it.' His voice throbbed with frustration. 'Be ready at seven thirty. I'm not taking no for an answer.'

Artie released her grip on the windowsill and turned

to face him. Her stomach was roiling, her skin damp with perspiration, her mind reeling at the thought of going beyond the *castello* gates. 'Luca, please don't do this.' Her voice came out sandpaper-hoarse.

He gave a savage frown. 'Don't do what? All I'm asking is for you to uphold your side of our agreement. Which, I might remind you, is a legal one. You signed the papers my lawyer prepared—remember?'

Artie steepled her hands against her nose and mouth, trying to control her breathing. Her heart was doing cartwheels and star jumps and back flips and her pulse was off the charts. 'It's not that I don't want to go...'

'Then what is it?'

She lowered her hands from her face and pressed her lips together to stop them from trembling. She clasped her hands in front of her body, her fingers tightly inter-laced to the point of discomfort. She couldn't bring her gaze up to meet his, so instead aimed it at the carpet near his feet. 'There's something I haven't told you... something important.'

Luca crossed the room until he was standing in front of her. He lifted her chin with the end of his finger and meshed his gaze with hers. His frown was still in place but was more concerned now than angry. 'What?' His tone was disarmingly gentle and his touch on her chin light but strangely soothing. 'Tell me what's going on. I want the truth, *cara*.'

Artie bit the inside of her mouth, trying to find the words to describe her condition. Her weakness. Her shame. 'I... I haven't been outside the *castello* grounds since I was fifteen years old. It's not that I don't want to leave it—I can't.'

His hand fell away from her face, his forehead creased in lines of puzzlement. 'Why can't you? What's stopping you?'

She gave a hollow, self-deprecating laugh and pointed a finger at her chest. '*I'm* stopping me.' She stepped back from him and wrapped her arms around her body. 'I have crippling social anxiety. I can't cope with crowds and busy, bustling places. I literally freeze or have a meltdown—a full-blown panic attack.'

He opened and closed his mouth as if trying to think of something to say.

'I'm sorry,' Artie said. 'I should have told you before now but I was too embarrassed and—'

'Please. Don't apologise.' His voice was husky, his expression etched with concern. He shook his head like he was trying to get his muddled thoughts in some sort of order. 'Why didn't your father say something to me? He led me to believe you were—'

'Normal?' She raised her brows in an arch manner. 'Is that the word you were looking for? I'm hardly that, am I?'

Luca made a rough sound at the back of his throat. '*Cara*, please don't run yourself down like that. Have you seen a health professional about it?'

'Four.'

'And?'

Artie spread her hands outwards. 'And nothing. I couldn't cope with the side effects of medication. Meditation and mindfulness helped initially but not enough to get me outside the *castello* grounds. Talk therapy helped too at first but it was expensive and I didn't have the time with my caring responsibilities with Papa to keep going with it.' She gave a sigh and added, 'I found it exhausting, to be honest. Talking about stuff I didn't really want to talk about.'

'The accident?'

Artie nodded, her gaze slipping out of reach of his. 'So, there you have it. My life in a nutshell—no pun intended.'

Luca brushed a finger down her cheek. 'Look at me, *cara*.' It was a command but so gently delivered it made something move inside her chest like the slow flow of warm honey.

Artie raised her eyes back to his, the tip of her tongue sneaking out to sweep over her lips. 'I'm sorry for misleading you. You probably wouldn't have married me if you'd known. But I was so desperate to keep the *castello*. I don't know what I'd do without it. It's the only home I've ever known and if I'm forced to leave...' She bit her lip until she winced. 'I can't leave. I just can't.'

He touched her lip with the pad of his thumb. 'Stop doing that. You'll make it bleed.' His tone was gruff and gently reproving, his gaze surprisingly tender. 'We'll find a way to manage this.'

'How? If your grandfather is too ill to travel, then how will I ever get to meet him?'

'Technology to the rescue.' He gave a quick smile and patted his jeans pocket, where his phone was housed. 'We can set up a video call. Nonno's eyesight isn't great and he's not keen on mobile phones but it will be better than nothing.'

Artie moved a step or two away, her arms crossing over her body, her hands rubbing up and down her upper arms as if warding off a chill. 'You're being very understanding about this… I wouldn't blame you if you tore up the agreement and took full possession of the *castello*.'

Please God, don't let him do that. Please. Please. Please.

Luca came up behind her and placed his hands on her shoulders. 'That's not going to happen.' She suppressed a shiver as the movement of air when he spoke disturbed the loose strands of her hair around her neck. 'We'll work together to solve this.'

Artie turned to face him with a frown. 'Why are you being so generous? You said earlier today you're a selfish man, but I'm not seeing it.'

His smile was lopsided and his hands gently squeezed the tops of her shoulders. 'I can be extremely selfish when it comes to getting what I want.' His gaze drifted to her mouth and her heart skipped a beat. After a moment, his eyes came back to hers. Dark. Lustrous. Intense. The air suddenly vibrating with crackling energy as if all the oxygen particles had been disturbed.

'Luca?' Her voice was barely audible, whisper-soft. Her hand crept up to touch his lean jaw, her fingers trailing over the light prickle of his stubble. She sent her index finger around the firm contours of his mouth, the top lip and then the slightly fuller lower one. He drew in a sharp breath as if her touch excited him, thrilled him, tempted him.

His hand came up and his fingers wrapped around her slim wrist as if to pull her hand from his face. But then he made a low, deep sound at the back of his throat and his head came down and his mouth set fire to hers.

CHAPTER SIX

LUCA KNEW HE should stop the kiss before it got out of control. Knew he shouldn't draw her closer to his body where his blood was swelling him fit to burst. Knew he was forty times a fool to be tempted to change the rules on their paper marriage. But right then, all he could do was explore her soft mouth and let his senses run wild with the sweet, tempting taste of her lips. She opened to him on a breathless sigh and the base of his spine tingled when her tongue met his—shy and yet playful, innocent and yet daring. Need drove him to kiss her more deeply, to hold her more closely, to forget about the restrictions he'd placed on their relationship. Call him reckless, call him foolish, but right now he would die without the sweet temptation of her mouth responding to his.

Artie pressed herself against him, her arms winding around his neck, her young, slim body fitting against him as if fashioned specially for him. He ached to explore the soft perfection of her breasts, to glide his hands over her skin, to breathe in the scent of her, to taste her in the most intimate way possible.

His hands settled on her hips, holding her to the aching throb in his pelvis, his conscience at war with his body. He finally managed to find the willpower to drag his mouth off hers, but he couldn't quite bring himself to let her go.

'You know this can't happen.' His voice was so rough it sounded like he'd swallowed ground glass.

She looked up at him with eyes bright and shining with arousal. 'Why can't it? We're both consenting adults.'

Luca placed his hands around her wrists and pulled her arms from around his neck, but he still didn't release her. His fingers circled her wrists in a loose hold, his desire for her chomping at the bit like a bolting thoroughbred stallion. 'You know why.'

Her mouth tightened, her cheeks pooling with twin circles of pink. 'Because I'm a virgin? Is that it?'

Luca released her wrists and stepped away, dragging a hand through his hair in an effort to get his pulse rate to go back to somewhere near normal. 'It's not just about that.'

'Are you saying you don't find me attractive? Not desirable?' Self-doubt quavered in her tone.

Luca let out a gusty sigh. 'I find you extremely attractive and desirable but that's not why I married you. It's not part of the deal. It will make things too complicated when we end it.'

'How do you know that? People have flings all the time without falling in love with each other. Why not us?'

Luca put some distance between their bodies, but even a metre or so away he could still feel the magnetic pull of hers. 'You're young, Artie. Not just in chronological years but in experience. You said it yourself—you haven't been outside the *castello* for ten years. Those were ten valuable growing-up years.'

Her expression soured and hurt coloured her tone. 'You think I'm immature. A child in an adult's body? Is that what you're saying?'

Luca pressed his lips together, fighting to keep his self-control in check. Her adult body was temptation personified but he had to keep his hands off her. It wouldn't be fair to take things to another level, not now he knew how limited her experience. He was the first man to kiss her, to touch her, to expose her to male desire. She was like a teenager experiencing her first crush. A physical crush that had to stop before it got started. 'I'm saying I'm not the right man for you.'

'Consider my offer withdrawn.' She folded her arms around her body and sent him a sideways glance. 'Sorry if I offended you by being so brazen. Believe me, I surprised myself. I don't know what came over me.'

Luca fought back a wry smile. 'We should keep kissing to the absolute minimum.'

Artie gave an indifferent shrug but her eyes displayed her disappointment. 'Fine by me.'

The silence throbbed with a dangerous energy. An energy Luca could feel in every cell of his body. Humming, thrumming sensual energy, awakened, stirred, unsatisfied.

It would be so easy to take back everything he had said and gather her in his arms, to assuage the longing that burned in his body with hot, flicking tongues of flame, to teach her the wonder of sexual compatibility—for he was sure they would be compatible.

He had not felt such electrifying chemistry from kissing someone before. He had not felt such a rush of lust from holding someone close to his body. He had not felt so dangerously tempted to throw caution to the wind and sink his body into the soft silk of another's.

Artie released her arms from around her middle and absently toyed with her wedding ring. 'If you don't mind, I think I'll go to bed.' Her cheeks reddened and she hastily added, 'Alone, I mean. I wasn't suggesting you join—'

'Goodnight, *cara.*'

Artie bolted up the stairs as if she were being chased by a ghost. *Eek.* How could she have been so gauche as to practically beg Luca to make love to her? She couldn't understand why she had been so wanton in her behaviour. Was there something wrong with her? Had her lack of socialising with people her own age affected her development? Her body had woken from a long sleep the moment he kissed her at the wedding. His mouth had sent shivers of longing to every pore of her skin, made her aware of her female needs and desires, made her hungry for a deeper, more powerful connection. A physical connection that would ease the tight, dragging ache in her core.

She closed her bedroom door behind her, letting out a ragged breath. *Fool. Fool. Fool.* He had laid down the rules—a paper marriage with no emotional attachment. A business contract that was convenient and for both parties. But what was convenient about the way she felt about Luca? The heat and fire of his touch made her greedy for more. She had felt his physical response to her, so why was he denying them both the pleasure they both craved?

Because he doesn't want you to fall in love with him.

Artie walked over to her bed and sank onto the mattress with another sigh. Luca thought her too young and innocent for him, too inexperienced in the ways of the world for their relationship to be on an equal footing. But the way her body responded to him made her feel more than his equal. It made her feel alive and feminine and powerful in a way she had never imagined she could feel.

She looked down at the engagement and wedding rings on her left hand, the symbol of their union as a married couple. She was tied to him by law but not by love. And she was fine with that. Mostly. What she wanted was to be tied to him in desire, to explore the electrifying chemistry between them, to indulge herself in the world of heady sensuality.

Artie bounced off the bed and went to her bathroom, staring at her reflection in the mirror above the marble basin. Her eyes were overly bright, her lips still pink and swollen from Luca's passionate kiss. She touched her lower lip with her fingers, amazed at how sensitive it was, as if his kiss had released every one of her nerve endings from a deep freeze.

Artie touched a hand to the ache in the middle of her chest. So, this was what rejection felt like. The humiliation of wanting someone who didn't want you back.

Why am I so unlucky in the lottery of life?

Luca wasn't a drinker, but right then he wanted to down a bottle of Scotch and throw the empty bottle at the wall.

He wanted to stride upstairs to Artie's bedroom and take her in his arms and show her how much he wanted her. He wanted to breathe in the scent of her skin, taste the sweet nectar of her lips, glide his hands over her beautiful body and take them both to paradise. But the hard lessons learned from his father's and brother's death had made him super-cautious when it came to doing things that couldn't be undone.

Making love with Artie would change everything about their relationship. It would change the dynamic between them, pitching them into new territory, dangerous territory that clashed with his six-month time limit.

He had thought himself a good judge of character, someone who didn't miss important details. And yet he hadn't picked up on Artie's social phobia, but it all made perfect sense now. Why she hadn't been at the hospital when he'd visited her father. Why she'd insisted on the wedding being held at the *castello* instead of at one of the local churches. Why she had such a guarded air about her, closed off almost, as if she was uncomfortable around people she didn't know. He still couldn't get his head around the fact that she had spent ten years living almost in isolation. Ten years! It was unthinkable to someone like him, who was rarely in the same city two nights in a row. He lived out of hotels rather than at his villa in Tuscany. He lived in the fast lane because slowing down made him think too much, ruminate too much, hurt too much.

It was easier to block it out with work.

Work was his panacea for all ills. He had built his father's business into a behemoth of success. He had brokered deals all over the world and cashed in on every one of them. Big time. He had more money than he knew what to do with. It didn't buy him happiness but it did buy him freedom. Freedom from the ties that bound others into dead-end jobs, going-nowhere relationships and the drudgery of duty-bound responsibilities.

Luca walked over to the windows of his suite at the *castello*. The moon was full and cast the *castello* grounds in an ethereal light. The centuries-old trees, the gnarled vines, the rambling roses were testament to how many generations of Artie's family had lived and loved here.

Love. The trickiest of emotions. The one he avoided, because loving people and then letting them down was soul destroying. The stuff of nightmares, a living torture he could do without.

Luca watched as a barn owl flew past the window on silent wings. Nature going about its business under the cloak of moonlight. The *castello* could be restored into a showcase of antiquity. The gardens tended to and nurtured back into their former glory, the ancient vines grafted and replanted to produce award-winning wine. It would cost money…lots of money—money Artie clearly didn't have. But it would be his gift to her for the time she had given up to be married to him.

Six months, and day one was just about over. A day when he had discovered his bride was an introverted social phobic who had never been kissed until his mouth touched hers. A young woman who had not socialised with her peers outside the walls of the *castello*. A young woman who was still a virgin at the age of twenty-five. A modern-day Sleeping Beauty who had yet to be woken to the pleasures of sex.

Stop thinking about sex.

But how could he when the taste of her mouth was still on his lips? The feel of her body pressed against him was branded on his flesh. The ache of desire still hot and tight and heavy in his groin.

The *castello* was huge, and Artie's bedroom was a long, wide corridor away from his, but his awareness of her had never been more heightened and his self-control never more tested. What was it about her that made him so tempted to throw his rules to one side? Her unworldly youth? Her innocence? Her sensual allure? It was all those things and more besides. Things he couldn't quite name but he was aware of them all the same. He felt it in his body when he kissed her. A sense of rightness, as if every kiss he'd experienced before had been erased from his memory so that her mouth could be the new benchmark of what a kiss should be. He felt it when he touched her face and the creamy perfection of her skin made his fingers tingle in a way they had never done when touching anyone else. He felt it when he held her close to his body, the sense that her body was a perfect match for his.

Luca turned away from the window with a sigh of frustration. He needed his laptop so he could immerse himself in work but he'd left it in the car. He knew there wouldn't be too many bridegrooms tapping away on their laptops on their wedding night, but he was not a normal bridegroom.

And he needed to keep reminding his body of that too.

When Artie came downstairs the following morning, Rosa was laying out breakfast in the morning room, but not with her usual energy and vigour. Her face was pale and there were lines of tiredness around her eyes.

'Are you okay?' Artie asked, going to her.

Rosa put a hand to her forehead and winced. 'I have the most dreadful headache.'

'Then you must go straight back to bed. I'll call the doctor and—'

'No, I'll be fine. It's just a headache. I've had them before.'

Artie frowned at the housekeeper's pallor and blood-shot eyes. 'You don't look at all well. I insist you go upstairs to bed. I'll manage things down here. It's about time you had some time to yourself. You've been going non-stop since Papa died. And well before that too.' Artie didn't like admitting how dependent she had become on the housekeeper but she wouldn't have been able to cope without Rosa running errands for her.

Rosa began to untie her apron, her expression etched with uncertainty. 'Are you sure?'

Artie took the apron from the housekeeper and tossed it to one side. 'Upstairs. Now. I'll check on you in a couple of hours. And if you're not feeling better by then, I'm calling the doctor.'

'*Sì, sì*, Signora Ferrantelli.' Rosa mock-saluted Artie and then she left the room.

Artie released a sigh and pulled out a chair to sit down at the breakfast table but her appetite had completely deserted her. What *would* she do without Rosa? The housekeeper was her link to the outside world. Her only true friend. If anything happened to Rosa she would be even more isolated.

Stranded.

But you have a husband now...

The sound of firm footsteps approaching sent a tingle down Artie's spine. She swivelled in her chair to see Luca enter the breakfast room. His hair was still damp from a shower, his face cleanly shaven, the sharp tang of his citrus-based aftershave teasing her nostrils. He was wearing blue jeans and a white T-shirt that lovingly hugged his muscular chest and ridged abdomen.

'Good morning.' Her tone was betrayingly breathless and her cheeks grew warm. 'Did you sleep well?'

'Morning.' He pulled out the chair opposite, sat down and spread his napkin over his lap. 'I ran into Rosa when I was coming down. She didn't look well.'

Artie picked up the jug of fresh orange juice and poured some into her glass. 'I've sent her back to bed. She's got a bad headache. She gets them occasionally.' She offered him the juice but he shook his head and reached for the coffee pot. The rich aroma of freshly brewed coffee filled the air.

Luca picked up his cup, glancing at her over the rim. 'Has she got plans to retire? This is a big place to take care of. Does anyone come in to help her?'

Artie chewed at the side of her mouth. 'They used to but we had to cut back the staff a while back. I help her. I enjoy it, actually. It's a way of thanking her for helping me all these years.'

'And how does she help you?' His gaze was unwavering, almost interrogating in its intensity.

Artie lowered her gaze and stared at the beads of condensation on her glass of orange juice. 'Rosa runs errands for me. She picks up shopping for me, the stuff

I can't get online, I mean. She's been with my family for a long time. This is her home. Here, with me.'

Luca put down his cup with a clatter on the saucer. 'She can't stay here for ever, Artie. And neither can you.' His tone was gentle but firm, speaking a truth she recognised but didn't want to face.

She pushed back her chair and tossed her napkin on the table. 'Will you excuse me? I want to check on Rosa.'

'Sit down, *cara*.' There was a thread of steel underlining each word. The same steel glinting in his eyes and in the uncompromising line of his jaw.

Artie toyed with the idea of defying him, a secret thrill shooting through her at the thought of what he might do to stop her flouncing out of the room. Grasp her by the wrists? Hold her to his tempting body? Bring that firm mouth down on hers in another toe-curlingly passionate kiss? She held his gaze for a heart-stopping moment, her pulse picking up its pace, the backs of her knees fizzing. But then she sat heavily in the chair, whipped her napkin across her lap and threw him a look so sour it could have curdled the milk in the jug. 'I hope you're not going to make a habit of ordering me about like I'm some sort of submissive slave.'

His eyes continued to hold hers in a battle of wills. 'I want to talk to you about your relationship with Rosa. I get that she's been supportive for a long time and you see her as a friend you can rely on, but what if she's actually holding you back from developing more autonomy?'

Artie curled her lip. 'I didn't know you had a psychology degree amongst your other impressive achievements.'

'I don't need a psychology degree to see what's happening here.' He picked up a teaspoon and stirred his coffee even though he didn't take sugar or milk. He put the teaspoon down again and continued. 'I know it's hard for you but—'

'How do you know anything of what it's like for me?' She banged her hand on the table, rattling the cups and saucers. 'You're not me. You don't live in my mind, in my body. I'm the only one who knows what this is like for me.' Her chest was tightening, her breathing becoming laboured, her skin breaking out in a sweat. She could feel the pressure building. The fear climbing up her spine. The dread roiling in her stomach. The hammering of her heart. The panic spreading, growing, expanding, threatening to explode inside her head.

Luca rose from his seat and came around to her side of the table and crouched down beside her chair. He took one of her hands in his, enclosing it within the warm shelter of his. 'Breathe, *cara*. Take a slow, deep breath and let it out on the count of three. One. Two. Three. And again. That's it. Nice and slow.'

Artie concentrated on her breathing, holding tightly to the solid anchor of his hand, drawing comfort from his deep and calming tone. The panic gradually subsided, retreating like a wild beast that had been temporarily subdued by a much bigger, stronger opponent. After a long moment, she let out a rattling sigh. 'I'm okay now... I think...' She tried to remove her hand but he kept a firm but gentle hold on her, stroking the back of her hand with his thumb in slow, soothing strokes that made every overwrought cell in her body quieten.

'Take your time, *mia piccola*.'

Artie chanced a glance at his concerned gaze. 'I suppose you think I'm crazy. A mad person who can't walk out of her own front gate.'

Luca placed his other hand beneath her chin and locked her gaze on his. His eyes were darkened by his wide pupils, the green and brown flecks in his irises reminding her of a nature-themed mosaic. 'I don't think any such thing.' He gave a rueful twist of his mouth and continued. 'When my father and brother drowned, I didn't leave the house for a month after their funeral.' A shadow passed across his face like scudding grey clouds. 'I couldn't face the real world without them in it. It was a terrible time.' His tone was weighted with gravitas, his expression drawn in lines of deep sadness.

Artie squeezed his hand. 'It must have been so tragic for you and your mother. How did you survive such awful loss?'

One side of his mouth came up in a smile that wasn't quite a smile. 'There are different types of survival, *si*? I chose to concentrate on forging my way through the morass of grief by studying hard, acing my exams and taking over my father's company. I taught myself not to think about my father and brother. Nothing could bring them back, but I figured I could make my father proud by taking up the reins of his business even though it was never my aspiration to do so. That was my brother's dream.' His half-smile faded and the shadow was back in his gaze.

Artie ached for what he had been through, knowing first-hand how such tragic loss impacted on a person. The way it hit you at odd moments like a sudden stab, doubling you over with unbearable pain. The ongoing reminders—birthdays, anniversaries, Christmas, Mother's Day. So many days of the year when it was impossible to forget. And then there was the guilt that never went away. It hovered over her every single day of her life. 'How did your mother cope with her grief?'

Luca released her hand and straightened to his full height. Artie could sense him withdrawing into himself as if the mention of his mother pained him more than he wanted to admit. 'Enough miserable talk for now. Finish your breakfast, *cara*. And after that, we will call my grandfather and I'll introduce you to him.'

Her stomach fluttered with nerves. 'What if he doesn't accept me? What if he doesn't like me or think I'm suitable?'

Luca stroked his hand over the top of her head, his expression inscrutable. 'Don't worry. He will adore you the minute he meets you.'

CHAPTER SEVEN

LUCA CALLED HIS GRANDFATHER on his phone a short time later and selected the video-call option. He sat with Artie on the sofa in the salon and draped an arm around her waist to keep her in the range of the camera. The fragrance of her perfume wafted around his nostrils, her curly hair tickling his jaw when she leaned closer. His grandfather's image came up on the screen and Luca felt Artie tense beside him. He gave her a gentle squeeze and smiled at her before turning back to face his grandfather.

'Nonno, allow me to introduce you to my beautiful wife Artemisia—Artie for short. We were married yesterday.'

The old man frowned. 'Your wife? *Pah!* You think I'm a doddering old fool or something? You said you were never getting married and now you present me with a wife? Why didn't you bring her here to meet me in person?'

'We're on our honeymoon, Nonno,' Luca said, wishing, not for the first time, it was true. 'But soon, *sì*?'

'*Buongiorno*, Signor Ferrantelli,' Artie said. 'I'm sorry you've been ill. It must be so frustrating for you.'

'I'll tell you what's frustrating—having my only

grandson gadding about all these years as a free-dom-loving playboy, when all I want is to see a great-grandchild before I leave this world. It's his duty, his responsibility to carry on the proud family name by producing a new generation.'

Luca gave a light laugh. 'We've only just got mar-ried, Nonno. Give us time.' He suddenly realised he didn't want to share Artie with anyone. He wanted to spend time alone with her, getting to know her better. He wanted her with an ache that wouldn't go away. Ever since he'd kissed her it had smouldered like hot coals in-side him. The need to explore her body, to awaken her to the explosive pleasure he knew they would experience together. But he refused to even think about the cosy domestic future his grandfather hoped for him. Babies? A new generation of Ferrantellis? Not going to happen.

'You've wasted so much time already,' Nonno said, scowling. 'Your father was married to your mother and had Angelo and you well before your age.'

'*Sì*, I know.' Luca tried to ignore the dart of pain in his chest at the mention of his father and brother. And his mother, of course. He could barely think of his mother without feeling a tsunami of guilt for how his actions had destroyed her life. Grandchildren might soften the blow for his mother, but how could he allow himself to think about providing them? Family life was something he had never envisaged for himself. How could he when he had effectively destroyed his own family of origin?

'Luca is everything I ever dreamed of in a husband,' Artie piped up in a proud little voice that made some-thing in his chest ping. 'He's definitely worth waiting for.'

Nonno gave a grunt, his frown still in place. 'Did you give her your grandmother's engagement ring?' he asked Luca.

'*Sì,*' Luca said.

Artie lifted her hand to the camera. 'I love it. It's the most gorgeous ring I've ever seen. I feel incredibly honoured to be wearing it. I wish I could have met your wife. You must miss her terribly.'

'Every day.' Nonno shifted his mouth from side to side, his frown softening its grip on his weathered features. 'Don't leave it too long before you come and see me in person, Artie. I haven't got all the time in the world.'

'You'd have more time if you follow your doctor's advice,' Luca said.

'I'd love to meet you,' Artie said. 'Luca's told me so much about you.'

'Yes, well, he's told me virtually nothing about you,' Nonno said, disapproval ripe in his tone. 'How did you meet?'

'I met Artie through her father,' Luca said. 'I knew she was the one for me as soon as I laid eyes on her.' It wasn't a lie. He had known straight up that Artie was the only young woman his grandfather would approve of as his bride.

Nonno gave another grunt. 'Let's hope you can handle him, Artie. He's a Ferrantelli. We are not easy to live with but if you love him it will certainly help.'

'I think he's the most amazing man I've ever met,' Artie said, softly. 'Take care of yourself, Signor Ferrantelli. I hope to meet you in person soon.'

The most amazing man she'd ever met? Luca mentally laughed off the compliment. Artie had met so few men it wasn't hard to impress her. What he wanted to do was help her get over her phobia. Not just because he wanted her to meet his grandfather but because he knew it would open up opportunities and experiences for her that had been denied her for way too long. But would she trust him enough to guide her through what would no doubt be a difficult and frightening journey for her?

Artie turned to face Luca once the call had ended. His arm was still around her waist and every nerve beneath her skin was acutely aware of its solid warm presence. 'I'm not so sure we convinced him. Are you?'

Luca's expression was etched in frowning lines. 'Who knows?' His features relaxed slightly and he added, 'You did well. That was a nice touch about me being your dream husband. It's kind of scary how convincing you sounded.' He brushed a stray strand of hair away from her face, his gaze darkening.

Artie disguised a swallow, her heart giving a little kick when his eyes drifted to her mouth. 'Yes, well, I surprised myself, actually.' She frowned and glanced down at the engagement and wedding rings on her hand and then lifted her gaze back to his. 'I feel like I'm letting you down by not being able to leave the *castello*. If we'd gone in person to see him, or even better, married somewhere closer so your grandfather could have attended...'

'You're not letting me down at all,' Luca said. 'But what if I tried to help you? We could start small and see how it goes—baby steps.'

'I've had help before and it hasn't worked.'

'But you haven't had my help.' He smiled and took her hand, running his thumb over the back of it in gentle strokes. 'It's worth a try, surely?'

Panic crawled up her spine and sent icicles tiptoeing across her scalp. 'What, now?'

'No time like the present.'

Artie compressed her lips, trying to control her breathing. 'I don't know...'

He raised her chin with the end of his finger. 'Trust me, *cara*. I won't push you further than you can manage. We will take it one step at a time.'

Artie swallowed and then let out a long, ragged breath. 'Okay. I'll try but don't be mad at me if I don't get very far.'

He leaned down and pressed a light kiss to the middle of her forehead. 'I won't get mad at you, *mia piccola*. I'm a very patient man.'

A few minutes later, Artie stood with Luca on the front steps of the *castello*, her gaze focussed on the long walk to the brass gates in the distance. Her heart was beating so fast she could feel its echo in her ears. Her skin was already damp with perspiration, and her legs trembling like a newborn foal's. She desperately wanted to conquer her fear, now more than ever. She wanted to meet Luca's grandfather, to uphold her side of their marriage deal but what if she failed yet again? She had failed every single time she had tried to leave the *castello*. It was like a thick glass wall was blocking her exit. She could see the other side to freedom but couldn't bring herself to step over the boundary lines. The *castello* was safe. She was safe here. Other people on the outside were safe from *her*.

What would happen if she went past her self-imposed boundary?

Luca took her hand and smiled down at her. 'Ready? One step at a time. Take all the time you need.'

Artie sucked in a deep breath and went down the steps to the footpath. So far, so good. 'I've done this before, heaps of times, and I always fail.'

'Don't talk yourself into failure, *cara*.' His tone was gently reproving. 'Believe you can do something and you'll do it.'

'Easy for you to say.' Artie flicked him a glance. 'You're confident and run a successful business. You've got runs on the board. What do I have? A big fat nothing.'

Luca stopped and turned her so she was facing him, his hands holding her by the upper arms. 'You have cared for your father for a decade. You quite likely extended his life by doing so. Plus, you're a gifted embroiderer. I have never seen such detailed and beautiful work. You have to start believing in yourself, *cara*. I believe in you.'

Artie glanced past his broad shoulder to the front gates, fear curdling her insides. She let out another stuttering breath and met his gaze once more. 'Okay, let's keep going. I have to do this. I *can* do this.'

'That's my girl,' Luca said, smiling and taking her by the hand again. 'I'm with you every step of the way.'

Artie took two steps, then three, four, five until she lost count. The gates loomed closer and closer, the outside world and freedom beckoning. But just as she got to about two-thirds of the way down the path a bird suddenly flew up out of the nearby shrubbery and Artie was so startled she lost her footing and would have tripped if Luca hadn't been holding her hand. 'Oh!' she gasped.

'You're okay, it was just a bird.'

Artie glanced at the front gates, her heart still banging against her breastbone. 'I think I'm done for one day.'

He frowned. 'You don't want to try a little more? We're almost there. Just a few more steps.'

She turned back to face the safety of the *castello*, breathing hard. 'I'm sorry but I can't do any more. I'll try again tomorrow.'

And I'll fail just like every other time.

Luca stroked his hand over the back of her head. 'You did well, *mia piccola*.'

Artie gave him a rueful look. 'I failed.'

He stroked her cheek with a lazy finger, his gaze unwavering. 'Failure is when you give up trying.' He took her hand again with another smile. 'Come on. It's thirsty work wrestling demons, *sì*?'

Once they were back inside the *castello* in the salon, Artie let out a sigh. 'It's not that I don't want to go outside...'

He handed her a glass of mineral water. 'What are you most frightened of?'

She took the glass from him and set it on the table next to her, carefully avoiding his gaze. 'I'm frightened of hurting people.'

'Why do you think you'll hurt someone?'

Artie lifted her eyes to his. 'It was my fault we had the accident.'

Luca frowned and came over to sit beside her, taking her hands in his. 'But you weren't driving, surely? You were only fifteen, *si*?'

She looked down at their joined hands, her chest feeling so leaden it was almost impossible to take in another breath. 'I wanted to go to a party. My parents didn't want me to go but like teenagers do, I wouldn't take no for an answer. They relented and I went to the party, which wasn't as much fun as I'd hoped. And when my parents picked me up that night...well, my father was tired because it was late and he didn't see the car drifting into his lane in time to take evasive action. I woke up in hospital after being in a coma for a month to find my mother had died instantly and my father was in a wheelchair.'

Luca put his arms around Artie and held her close. 'I'm sorry. I know there are no words to take away the guilt and sadness but you were just a kid.'

Artie eased back to look up at him through blurry vision. 'I haven't ever met anyone else who truly understood.' She twisted her mouth wryly, 'Not that I've met a lot of people in the last ten years.' She lifted her hand to his face and stroked his lean jaw and added. 'But I think you do understand.'

A shadow passed through his gaze and he pulled her hand down from his face. 'You don't know me, *cara*. You don't know what I'm capable of.' His voice contained a note of self-loathing that made the back of her neck prickle.

'Why do you say that?'

He sprang off the sofa in an agitated fashion. 'I haven't told you everything about the day my father and brother died.'

She swallowed tightly. 'Do you want to tell me now?' Her voice came out whisper-soft.

Luca pulled at one side of his mouth with his straight white teeth, his hands planted on his slim hips. Then he released a ragged breath. 'It was my fault they drowned. We were on holiday in Argentina. We had gone to an isolated beach because I'd heard the waves were best there. I wanted to go back in for another surf even though the conditions had changed. I didn't listen to my father. I just raced back in and soon got into trouble.' He winced as if recalling that day caused him immeasurable pain. 'My father came in after me and then my brother. The rip took them both out to sea. I somehow survived. I can never forgive myself for my role in their deaths. I was selfish and reckless, and in trying to save me, they both lost their lives.'

Artie went to him and grasped him by both hands. 'Oh, Luca, you were only a child. Kids do stuff like that all the time, especially teenage boys. You mustn't blame yourself. But I understand how you do…you see, I blame myself for my mother's death and my dad's disability.'

'I do understand.' His eyes were full of pain. 'There were times when I wished I had been the one to die. I'm sure you wished the same. But that doesn't help anyone, does it?'

'No…' She leaned her head against the solid wall of his chest, slipping her arms back around his waist. 'Thank you.'

'For?' The deep, low rumble of his voice reverberated next to her ear.

Artie looked back up at him. 'For listening. For understanding. For not judging.' She took a little hitching breath and added, 'For wanting me when I thought no one ever could.'

Luca brushed his thumb over the fullness of her lower lip, setting off a firestorm in her flesh. 'I want you. I've tried ignoring it, denying it, resisting it, but it won't go away.' His voice dropped to a lower pitch, tortured almost, as if he was fighting a battle within himself between what he should do and what he shouldn't.

Artie licked her lips and encountered the saltiness of his thumb. 'I want you too.' She touched his firm jaw with her hand. 'I don't see why we have to stick to the rules. We are attracted to each other physically. Why not enjoy the opportunity? How else am I going to gain experience? I'm hardly going to meet anyone whilst living here, and we're married anyway, so why not?' She could hardly believe how brave she was being, speaking her needs out loud. But something about Luca made her feel brave and courageous. His desire for her spoke to her on a cellular level, making her aware of her body and its needs in a way she hadn't thought possible.

Luca cupped one side of her face in his hand, his thumb stroking over her cheek in slow, measured strokes. A frown settled between his brows, his eyes darker than she had ever seen them. 'Is that really want you want? A physical relationship, knowing it will end after six months?'

Maybe it won't end.

Artie didn't say it out loud—she was shocked enough at hearing it inside her head.

Since the accident, she had denied herself any dreams of one day finding love, of marrying and having a family. She had destroyed her family, so why should she have one of her own? But now she had met Luca, she realised what she was missing out on. The thrill of being attracted to someone and knowing they desired you back. The perfectly normal needs within her body she had ignored for so long were fully awake and wanting, begging to be assuaged. 'I want to know what it is like to make love with a man,' Artie said. 'I want that man to be you. I trust you to take care of me. To treat me with respect.'

He stroked her hair back from her forehead, his eyes dark and lustrous. 'I can't think of a time when I wanted someone more. But I told myself I wasn't going to take advantage of the situation—of you. I don't think it would be fair to give you false hope that this could lead to anything…more permanent.'

She leaned closer, winding her arms around his neck. 'Stop overthinking it. Do what your heart is telling you, not your head. Make love to me, Luca.'

Luca placed his hands on her hips and bent his head down so their lips were within touching distance. 'Are you sure? There's still time to change your mind.'

Artie pressed her lips against his, once, twice, three times. 'I'm not changing my mind. I want this. I want you.'

He stood and drew her to her feet, dropping a warm, firm kiss to her lips. 'Not here. Upstairs. I want everything to be perfect for you.'

A short time later, they were in Luca's bedroom. He closed the door softly behind them and ran his gaze over Artie. She had expected to feel shy, self-conscious about her body, but as soon as he began to undo the buttons on her top, she shivered with longing, desperate to be naked with him, to feel his skin against her own.

He kissed her lingeringly, taking his time nudging and nibbling her lips, teasing her with his tongue, tantalising her senses with his taste and his touch. His mouth moved down to just below her ear and she shivered as his lips touched her sensitive skin. One of his hands slipped beneath her unbuttoned top, gliding along the skin of her ribcage to cup one of her breasts. His touch was gentle and yet it created a tumultuous storm in her flesh. Her nipple tightened, her breast tingled, her legs weakened as desire shot through her like a missile strike.

'I want to touch you all over.' His tone had a sexy rough edge that made her senses whirl.

'I want to touch you too.' Artie tugged his T-shirt out of his jeans and slid her hands under the fabric to stroke his muscular chest. His warm, hard flesh felt foreign, exotically foreign, unlike anything she had touched before. She explored the hard planes and ridged contours of his hair-roughened chest, marvelling at the difference between their bodies. A difference that excited her, made her crazy with longing, eager to discover more.

Luca unclipped her bra and gazed at her breasts for a long moment, his eyes dark and shining with unmistakable desire. 'So beautiful.' His thumbs rolled over each of her nipples, his gaze intent, as if he found her breasts the most fascinating things he'd ever seen. Before this moment Artie had more or less ignored her breasts other than to do her monthly breast check. But now she was aware of the thousands of nerve-endings that were responding to Luca's touch. Aware of the way her tender flesh tingled and tautened under his touch. Aware of the primal need it triggered in her feminine core—of the ache that longed to feel the hard male presence of his body.

Artie gasped as Luca brought his mouth to her breasts, her hands gripping him by the waist, not trusting her legs to keep her upright as the sensations washed through her. His tongue teased her nipple into a tight point, and then he circled it with a slow sweep of his tongue.

The slight roughness of his tongue against her softer skin evoked another breathless and shuddering gasp from her. 'Oh... *Oh...*'

Luca lifted his mouth off her breast and smiled a bone-melting smile. 'You like that?'

Artie leaned closer, the feel of her naked breasts pressing against his muscular chest sending another riot of tingling sensations through her body. 'I love it when you touch me. I can't get enough of it.'

He slid his hands down to the waistband of her jeans, his fingers warm against her belly as he undid the snap button. Who knew such an action could cause such a torrent of heat in her body? Artie could barely stop her legs from shaking in anticipation. He held her gaze in a sensual lock that made her heart skip and trip. He slid his hand beneath the loosened waistband, cupping her mound through the thin, lacy barrier of her knickers. Her body responded with humid heat, slickening, moistening with the dew of desire.

'I can't seem to get enough of you either,' he said. 'But I don't want to rush you. I want to go slowly to make it good for you.'

Artie placed her hands on the waistband of his jeans. 'Can I?'

His eyes gleamed. 'Go for it.'

She held her breath and undid the fastening and slid down the zipper. She peeled back his underwear and drank in the potent sight of him engorged with blood, thickened with longing. Longing for *her*.

Luca drew in a sharp breath as her fingers skated over his erection. He removed her hand and returned his mouth to hers in a spine-tingling kiss that spoke of the primal need pulsing through his body. The flicker of his tongue against hers, the increasing urgency and pressure of his mouth drew from her a fevered response she hadn't thought possible.

Within a few breathless moments they were both naked and lying on the bed together, Luca's eyes roving over her body in glinting hunger. He placed a hand on her hip, turning her towards him, his expression becoming sober. 'There's something we need to discuss. Protection. We can't let any accidents happen, especially given the terms of our relationship.'

Artie knew he was being reasonable and responsible but a secret part of her flinched at his adamant stance on the six-month time frame. An accidental pregnancy would change everything. It would tie them together for the next eighteen years...possibly for ever. 'I understand. I wouldn't want any...accidents either.' She had not allowed herself to think of one day having a baby but now a vision popped into her head of a gorgeous, dark-haired baby... Luca's baby.

Don't get any ideas. You know the terms. Six months and six months only.

Her conscience had an annoying habit of reminding her of the deal she had made with Luca. A deal she hoped she wouldn't end up regretting in the end.

Luca stroked his hand down the flank of her thigh, his gaze centred on hers. 'It's important to me that you enjoy our lovemaking. I want you to feel comfortable, so please tell me if something isn't working for you or you want to stop at any point.'

Artie traced the shape of his lower lip with her finger. 'I've liked everything so far. I thought I'd be nervous about being naked with someone but this feels completely natural, as if we've done this before in another lifetime. Does that make sense?'

He smiled and captured her hand and pressed a kiss to each of her fingertips, his eyes holding hers. 'In a strange way, yes, although I have to say I've never made love to a virgin before.'

'Are *you* nervous?'

His mouth twisted into a rueful grimace. 'A bit.'

'Don't be.' She pressed her lips to his in a soft kiss. 'I want you to make love to me. I feel like I've been waiting all my life for this moment.'

Luca brought his mouth back to hers in a kiss that drugged her senses and ramped up her desire for him until she was arching her back and whimpering. His hands explored her breasts in soft strokes, his lips and tongue caressing her until she was breathless with longing. The ache between her legs intensified, a hot, throbbing ache that travelled through her pelvis like the spread of fire.

He moved down her body with a series of kisses from her breasts to her belly and then to the heart of her femininity. Artie drew in a breath, tense with excitement as his fingers spread her, his lips and tongue exploring her, teasing a response from her that shook her body into a cataclysmic orgasm. It swept her up in its rolling waves, the pulsations carrying her into a place beyond the reach of thought or even full consciousness. Blissful sensations washed over her, peace flooding her being—the quiet after the storm.

'I had no idea it could be like...like *that*...' Artie could barely get her voice to work and a sudden shyness swept over her.

Luca moved back up her body to plant a kiss to her lips. She could taste herself on his lips and it added a whole new layer of disturbing but delightful intimacy. 'It will only get better.' He brushed his knuckles over her warm cheeks. 'Don't be shy, *cara*.'

Artie bit her lip. 'Easy for you to say. You've probably done this a hundred times, possibly more. I'm a complete novice.'

He smoothed her hair back from her face, his expression suddenly serious. 'The press makes a big thing out of my lifestyle but I haven't been as profligate as they make out. Unfortunately, my grandfather believes what he reads in the press.' His mouth twisted ruefully. 'I've had relationships—fleeting ones that were entirely transactional. And I've always tried not to deliberately hurt anyone. But of course, it still does happen occasionally.'

I hope I don't get hurt.

The potential to get hurt once their relationship came to its inevitable end was a real and present worry, but even so, Artie couldn't bring herself to stop things before they got any more complicated. He had revealed things about himself that made her hungry to learn more about him. His workaholism, his carefully guarded heart, his history of short-term, going-nowhere relationships. He was imprisoned by his lifestyle in the same way she was imprisoned by the *castello*. Would he go back to his playboy existence once they parted?

Artie lifted her hand and stroked his stubbly jaw. 'I want you to make love to me. I want you to experience pleasure too.'

Luca's eyes were dark and hooded as he gazed at her mouth. 'Everything about you brings me pleasure, *cara*. Absolutely everything.' And his mouth came down and sealed hers.

The kiss was long and intense and Artie could feel the tension rising in his body as well as her own. His legs were entangled with hers, his aroused body pressing urgently against her, his breathing as ragged as hers. His mouth moved down to her breasts, subjecting them to a passionate exploration that left her squirming and whimpering with need. She slid her hand down from his chest to his taut abdomen, desperate to explore the hard contours of his body. He drew in a quick breath when her hand encountered his erection and it made her all the bolder in her caresses. He was velvet-wrapped steel, so exotically, erotically different from her, and she couldn't wait to experience those differences inside her body.

Luca eased back and reached for a condom, swiftly applying it before coming back to her, his gaze meshing with hers. 'I'll go slowly but please tell me if you want to stop at any point. I don't want to hurt you.'

Artie brushed his hair back from his forehead, her

lower body so aware of his thick male presence at her entrance. 'You won't hurt me.' Her tone was breathless with anticipation, her body aching for his possession.

He gently nudged apart her feminine folds, allowing her time to get used to him as he progressed. Slow, shallow, sensual. Her body welcomed him, wrapping around him without pain, without resistance.

'Are you okay?' he asked, pausing in his movements.

'More than okay.' Artie sighed with pure pleasure, her hands going to his taut buttocks to hold him to her.

He thrust a little deeper, still keeping his movements slow and measured. She arched her hips to take more of him in, her body tingling with darts and arrows of pleasure as his body moved within hers. His breathing rate changed, becoming more laboured as his pace increased. She was swept up into his rhythm, her senses reeling as the tension built to an exquisite crescendo. She was almost at the pinnacle, hovering in the infinitesimal moment before total fulfilment. Wanting, aching, needing to fly but not sure how to do it.

Luca reached down between their bodies and coaxed her swollen feminine flesh into an earth-shattering orgasm. Spirals of intense pleasure burst through her body, ripples and waves and darts of bliss, throwing her senses into a tailspin and her mind into disarray.

Luca reached his release soon after, an agonised groan escaping his lips as his body convulsed and spilled. Artie held him close, breathing in the scent of their lovemaking, thrilled to have brought him to a place of blissful satiation.

Artie lay with him in the peaceful aftermath, her thoughts drifting... The boundaries between the physical and the emotional were becoming increasingly blurred. She knew she would always remember this moment as a pivotal one in her life as a woman.

Luca Ferrantelli. Her husband. Her first lover.

The presence of his body, the desire that drew them together bonded her to him in a way that was beyond the physical. The chemistry between her and Luca was so powerful, so magical it had produced a cataclysmic reaction. An explosion of pleasure she could still feel reverberating throughout her body.

How could she have thought he was arrogant and unyielding? He had taken such respectful care of her every step of the way. He had held back his own release in order to make sure she was satisfied first. She couldn't have asked for a more considerate and generous lover.

But it didn't mean she was falling in love with him.

Artie knew the rules and had accepted them. She could be modern and hip about their arrangement. Sure she could. This was about a physical connection so intense, so rapturous she wanted to make the most of it.

Luca leaned up on one elbow and slowly withdrew from her body, carefully disposing of the condom. He rolled back to cradle one side of her face with his hand, his eyes searching hers. 'How do you feel?' His voice had a husky edge, his expression tender in a way she hadn't been expecting. Had he too been affected by her first time and their first time together?

'I'm fine.'

A frown pulled at his brow. 'I didn't hurt you?'

'Not at all.' She smoothed away his frown with her fingertip. 'Thanks for being so gentle with me.'

His hand brushed back the hair from her face in the

tenderest of movements. 'Your enjoyment is top priority for me. I don't want you to feel you ever have to service my needs above your own.'

Artie ran her fingertip over the fullness of his bottom lip, not quite able to meet his gaze. 'Was it good for you too?'

He tipped up her chin and smiled, and her chest felt like it was cracking open. 'Off the charts.' He leaned down to press a soft, lingering kiss to her lips. He lifted off again, his expression becoming thoughtful. 'I've never been a virgin trophy hunter. A woman's virginity is not something I consider a prize to be claimed or a conquest to be sought.' He captured a loose strand of her hair and tucked it back behind her ear. 'But I have to say I feel privileged to have made love with you.'

Artie wrapped her arms around his waist and leaned her cheek against the wall of his chest. 'I feel privileged too. You made it so special.'

There was a moment or two of silence.

Luca stroked his hand down between Artie's shoulder blades to the base of her spine. 'I should let you get up and get dressed.'

Artie lifted her head off his chest to smile at him. 'Is that what you really want me to do right now?'

He grinned and pressed her back down on the bed with his weight playfully pinning her. 'Not right now.' And he brought his mouth back down to hers.

CHAPTER EIGHT

LATER THAT MORNING, Luca had to convince himself to get out of bed with Artie. He couldn't remember a time when he had spent a morning more pleasurably. Making love with her for the first time had affected him in a way he hadn't been expecting. The mutual passion they had shared had been beyond anything he had experienced before. And that was deeply troubling.

Why was it so special? Because she was innocent and he so worldly and jaded that making love with her was something completely different from the shallow hook-ups he preferred? Or was it the exquisite feel of her skin next to his? Her mouth beneath his? Her touch, her sighs, her gasps and cries that made him feel more of a man than he ever had before?

The trust she had shown in him had touched him deeply. And he had honoured that trust by making sure she was completely satisfied, and yet his own satisfaction had risen to a whole new level of experience. It was as if his body had been asleep before now. Operating on a lower setting that didn't fully register all the nuances of mind-blowing sex. The glide of soft hands on his body, the velvet-soft press of lips on his heated skin, the delicious friction of female flesh against him. Every moment was imprinted on his brain, every kiss, every touch branded on his body.

And he wanted it to continue, which was the most troubling thought of all. He, who never stayed with a lover longer than a week or two. He, who never envisaged a future with anyone. He, who had locked down his emotions so long ago he didn't think he had the capacity to feel anything for anyone any more.

And yet...

Every time Artie looked at him with those big brown eyes, something tugged in his chest. Every time her pillow-soft lips met his, fire spread through his body, a raging fire of lust and longing unlike any he had felt before. Every time she smiled it was like encountering sunshine after a lifetime of darkness.

Luca swung his legs over the side of the bed before he was tempted to make love to her for the third time. He turned and held out a hand to her. 'Come on. Time for some more exposure therapy.'

Artie unfolded her limbs and stood in front of him, her hands going to his hips, sending his blood racing. Her eyes were bright and sparkling, her lips swollen from his kisses. 'Let's stay here instead. It'll be more fun.'

Luca gave her a stern look. Exposure therapy was well known to be the pits the first few times but it still had to be endured for results. '*Cara*, you're procrastinating. It's classic avoidance behaviour and it will only make things worse.'

Her gaze lost its playful spark and her mouth tightened. Her hands fell away from his hips and she turned and snatched up a loose bed sheet and covered her na-kedness, as if she was suddenly ashamed of her body. 'Last time I looked, you were my temporary husband and lover, not my therapist. I don't appreciate you try-ing to fix me.'

Luca suppressed a frustrated sigh. 'I'm not trying to fix you, *cara*. I'm trying to help you gain the cour-age to go a little further each day. I'll be with you all the time and I won't push you into doing anything you don't want to do. You can trust me, okay?'

Her teeth chewed at her lower lip, her gaze still guarded. 'Look, I know you mean well, but we tried it before and I failed.'

'That doesn't mean you'll fail today.'

There was a long moment of silence.

Artie released a long, shuddering breath. 'Okay... I'll give it another try.' She swallowed and glanced at him, her cheeks tinged with pink. 'Do you mind if I have a quick shower first?'

Luca waved his hand towards the bathroom. 'Go right ahead. I'll meet you downstairs in half an hour.' He needed to put some space between them before he was tempted to join her in the shower.

She walked to the door of the bathroom, then stopped and turned to look back at him with a frown between her eyes. 'Did you only make love to me to make me more amenable to going outside the *castello* grounds with you?'

'I made love with you because I wanted you and you wanted me.'

And I still want you. Badly.

Her teeth did another nibble of her lip, uncertainty

etched on her features. 'I hope I don't disappoint you this time…'

Luca came over to her and tipped up her chin and planted a soft kiss to her lips. 'You could never disappoint me.'

Artie showered and changed with her mind reeling at what Luca wanted her to do. She had failed so many times. Why should this time be any different? Panic flapped its wings in her brain and her belly, fear chilled her skin and sent a tremble through her legs. But she took comfort in the fact he promised to stay with her, to support her as she confronted her fear—a fear she had lived with so long it was a part of her identity. She literally didn't know who she was now without it. But making love with Luca had given her the confidence to step outside her comfort zone. Her skin still sang with the magic of his touch, the slightly tender muscles in her core reminding her of the power and potency of his body.

Luca was waiting for her downstairs and took her hand at the front door. 'Ready? Our goal is to go farther than we went yesterday—even if we don't make it outside the gates it will still be an improvement. That's the way to approach difficult tasks—break them up into smaller, achievable segments.'

Artie drew in a shaky breath, her chest feeling as if a flock of frightened finches were trapped inside. 'Sounds like a sensible plan. Okay, let's give it a go.'

The sun was shining and white fluffy clouds were scudding across the sky. A light breeze scented with old-world roses danced past Artie's face. Luca's fingers wrapped around hers, strong, warm, supportive, and she glanced up at him and gave a wobbly smile. 'Thanks for being so patient.'

He looped her arm through his, holding her close as they walked slowly but surely down the cobbled footpath to the wrought-iron front gates. 'I probably made you go too fast the first time. Let's slow it down a bit. We've got plenty of time to stop and smell the roses.'

Artie walked beside him and tried to concentrate on the spicy fragrance of the roses rather than the fear crawling over her skin. She was conscious of Luca's muscular arm linked with hers and the way he matched his stride to hers. She flicked him another self-conscious glance. 'You must think this is completely ridiculous. That *I'm* completely ridiculous.'

He gave her a light squeeze. 'I don't think that at all. Fear is a very powerful emotion. It can be paralysing. Fear of failure, fear of success, fear of—'

'Commitment,' Artie offered.

There was a slight pause before he answered. 'That too.'

'Fear of love.' She was on a roll, hardly noticing how many cobblestones there were to go to the front gate.

There was another silence, longer this time, punctured only by the sound of the whispering breeze and twittering birds in the overgrown shrubbery.

'Fear of not being capable of loving.' His tone contained a rueful note.

Artie stopped walking to look up at his mask-like expression. 'Why do you think you're not capable of loving someone? You love your grandfather, don't you?'

Luca gave a twisted smile that didn't quite reach

his eyes. 'Familial love is an entirely different sort of love. However, choosing to love someone for the rest of my life is not something I feel capable of doing. I would only end up hurting them by letting them down in the end.'

'But is loving someone a choice?' Artie asked. 'I mean, I haven't fallen in love myself but I've always understood it to be outside of one's control. It just happens.'

He captured a loose tendril of her hair and tucked it back behind her ear. His touch was light and yet electrifying, his gaze dark and inscrutable. 'A lucky few find love for a lifetime. But some lives are tragically cut short and then that same love becomes a torture for the one left behind.'

'Is that what happened to your mother?'

Luca's gaze drifted into the distance, his expression becoming shadowed. 'I will never forget the look of utter devastation on my mother's face when she was told my father and brother had drowned. She didn't come with us that day and when only I came home...' He swallowed tightly and continued in a tone rough and husky with banked-down emotion. 'For months, years, she couldn't look at me without crying. I found it easier to keep my distance. I hated seeing her like that, knowing I was responsible for what happened.'

Artie wrapped her arms around his waist and hugged him. 'Oh, Luca, you have to learn to forgive yourself. I'm sure your mother doesn't blame you. You were a young teenager. She was probably relieved you hadn't been taken as well. It could have happened. You could have all been drowned.'

He eased out of her hug and gave her a grim look. 'There were times in the early days when I wished I had been taken with them. But then I realised I owed it to my father and brother to live the best life I could to honour them.'

A life of hard work. A life with no love. No commitment. No emotional vulnerability. A life of isolation… not unlike her own.

A life of isolation she would go back to once their marriage was over.

Artie glanced at the front gates of the *castello* and drew in a shuddering breath. The verdigris-covered gates blurred in front of her into a grotesque vision of blue and green twisted metal. The sun disappeared behind a cloud and the birds suddenly went quiet as if disturbed by a menacing predator lurking in the shadows.

'Luca, I don't think I can go any further…'

He took her hand and looped her arm through his once more. 'You'll be fine. We're almost there. We've gone farther than yesterday. Just a few more steps and we'll be—'

'No.' Artie pulled out of his hold and took a few stumbling steps back towards the *castello*. 'I can't.'

Luca captured her by the wrist and brought her back to face him, his expression concerned. 'Whoa there. Slow down or you'll trip and twist your ankle.'

Her chest was so restricted she couldn't take a breath. Her stomach was churning, her knees shaking, her skin breaking out in a clammy sweat. She closed her eyes and a school of silverfish swam behind her eyelids. She opened her eyes but she couldn't see past the sting of tears. She tried to gulp in a breath but her throat wouldn't open enough for it to get through.

I'm going to die. I'm going to die. I'm going to die.

The words raced through her mind as if they were being chased by the formless fear that consumed her.

Luca gathered her close to his chest and stroked her stiff back and shoulders with slow, soothing strokes. 'Breathe, *cara*. Take a deep breath and let it out on the count of three. One. Two. Three. And again. One. Two. Three. Keep going, *mia piccola*. One. Two. Three.'

His gently chanted words and the stroke of his hands began to quieten the storm inside her body. The fog in Artie's brain slowly lifted, the fear gradually subsiding as the oxygen returned to her bloodstream.

She was aware of every point of contact with his body—her breasts pressed against his chest, the weight of his arm around her back, his other hand moving up and down between her shoulder blades in those wonderfully soothing strokes, his pelvis warm and unmistakably male against hers, his chin resting on the top of her head. She was aware of the steady *thud, thud, thud* of his heart against her chest, the intoxicating smell of his skin, the need awakening anew in her body. Pulses, contractions, flickers and tingles deep in her core.

Luca lifted his chin off her head and held her slightly aloft, his gaze tender. 'You did well—it's only our second try. Don't feel bad you didn't make it all the way. We'll try again tomorrow.'

Artie chewed her lip, ashamed she hadn't gone further. 'What if I'm never able to do it? What if I—?'

His finger pressed softly down on her lips to silence her self-destruction beliefs. 'Don't talk yourself into failure, *cara*. I know you can do it. You want to get better and that's half the battle, is it not?'

Artie gave a tremulous smile, heartened by his belief in her. Comforted by his commitment to helping her. Touched by his concern and patience and support. 'I do want to get better. I'm tired of living like this. I want to experience life outside the walls of the *castello*.'

He cupped one side of her face in his hand. 'And I can't wait to show you life outside these walls. There are so many things we can do together—dinner, dancing, sightseeing, skiing, trekking. I will enjoy showing you all my favourite places.'

Artie gave a self-deprecating smile. 'I have a lot of catching up to do. And only six months in which to do it.'

Luca's hand fell away from her face, his expression tightening as if her mentioning the time limit on their relationship was jarring to him. 'Of course, the most important thing we need to do is introduce you to my grandfather. I can't use the excuse of being on honeymoon for weeks or months on end.'

'Maybe he'll be well enough to come here soon.' It was a lame hope but she articulated it anyway.

His hand scraped back his hair in a distracted manner. 'There's no guarantee that's going to happen. Besides, I have work to see to. I can't stay here indefinitely.'

'I'm not stopping you from doing your work,' Artie said. 'You can leave any time you like.'

His gaze met hers. Strong. Determined. Intractable. 'I want you with me.'

A frisson scooted down her spine at the dark glint in

his eyes. The glint that spoke of the desire still smouldering inside him—the same desire smouldering inside her. She could feel the crackle of their chemistry in the air. Invisible currents of electricity that zapped and fizzed each time their eyes met and each time they touched. He stepped closer and slid his hand beneath the curtain of her hair, making her skin tingle and her blood race. His gaze lowered to her mouth, the sound of his breath hitching sending another shiver cascading down her spine.

'I didn't think it was possible that I could want someone so much.' His tone was rough around the edges.

Artie moved closer, her hands resting on the hard wall of his chest, her hips clamped to his, heat pooling in her core. 'I want you too.'

He rested his forehead on hers, their breath mingling in the space between their mouths. 'It's too soon for you. You'll be sore.' His voice was low, his hands resting on her hips.

Artie brought her mouth closer to his, pressing a soft kiss to his lips. 'I'm not sore at all. You were so gentle with me.'

He groaned and drew her closer, his mouth coming down on hers in a kiss that spoke of banked-down longing. She opened to the commanding thrust of his tongue, her senses whirling as he called her tongue into sensual play. Need fired through her body, hot streaks of need that left no part of her unaffected. Tingles shot down her spine and through her pelvis, heating her to boiling point. Her intimate muscles responded with flickers and fizzes of delight, her bones all but melting. One of his hands moved from her hip to cup her breast through her clothes, sending another fiery tingle through her body.

He deepened the kiss even further, his hand going beneath her top and bra to cup her skin on skin. The warmth of his palm and the possessive weight of his fingers sent her pulse soaring. He stroked her nipple into a tight bud of exquisite sensations, powerful sensations for such a small area of her body. He lifted his mouth off hers and lowered his lips to her breast, his tongue swirling over her engorged nipple, his teeth gently tugging and releasing in a passionate onslaught that made her gasp with delight.

The sound of Luca's phone ringing from inside his trouser pocket evoked a curt swear word from him as he lifted his mouth off her breast. 'I'd better get this. It's the ringtone I set up for Nonno's carer.' He pulled out his phone and took the call, a frown pulling at his forehead.

Artie rearranged her clothes and tried not to eavesdrop but it was impossible not to get the gist of the conversation. His grandfather had suffered a fall and was being taken to hospital with a suspected broken hip. Luca ended the call after reassuring his grandfather's carer he would leave for the hospital straight away.

He slipped the phone back in his pocket and gave Artie a grave look. 'You heard most of that?'

Artie placed her hand on his forearm. 'I'm so sorry. Is he going to be okay?'

He shrugged one shoulder, the almost casual action at odds with the dark shadows in his eyes. 'Who knows? Nonno is eighty-three. A broken hip is a big deal for someone of that age.' He released a breath and continued. 'I'm going to the hospital now. I want to speak to the orthopaedic surgeon. I want to make sure Nonno gets the very best of care.' He held her gaze for a moment. 'This might be your only chance to meet him.' His voice was husky with carefully contained emotion but she could sense the effort it took. His jaw was locked tight, his nostrils flaring as he fought to control his breathing.

Artie's throat tightened. 'I wish I could go with you, Luca. I really do.'

He gave a movement of his lips that wasn't quite a smile. He reached for her hand and gave it a gentle press. 'I'll be back as soon as I can.'

'Please send my best wishes for a speedy recovery.' Artie knew the words were little more than useless platitudes when all Luca wanted was her by his side. She was never more aware of letting down her side of the bargain. Letting *him* down. It pained her she was unable to harness her fear for his sake.

She watched as he drove away, her heart feeling as if it was torn in two. It felt wrong not to be with him— wrong in a way she hadn't expected to feel. As if part of her was missing now he was gone. The *castello* had never been more of a prison, her fear never more of a burden. Why couldn't she feel the fear and do it anyway? Was she to be imprisoned within these walls for the rest of her life? Luca needed her and she wasn't able to be with him, and yet she wanted nothing more than to be by his side.

She wanted to be with him because she loved him.

Artie could no longer suppress or deny her feelings about him. She had fallen in love with him in spite of his rules, in spite of her own efforts to keep her heart out of their arrangement. But her heart had been in it from the moment Luca kissed her. He had awoken her out of a psychological coma, inspiring her to live life in a full and vibrant way. How could she let him down now when he needed her? How could she not fight through her fears for him?

Rosa came out to join her, shading her eyes from the blinding sunshine. 'Do you know when he'll be back?'

Artie gave a despondent sigh. 'No. I feel so bad I wasn't able to go with him. What sort of wife am I that I can't even be by my husband's side when he needs me most?'

Rosa gave her a thoughtful look. 'I guess you have to measure up which thing is bigger—your fear of leaving here or your fear of not being there for him.'

Artie bit her lip, struggling to hold back a tumult of negative emotion. Her sense of failure, her lack of courage, her inability to overcome her phobia.

You're hopeless. A failure. An embarrassment.

Her harsh internal critic rained down abuse until she wanted to curl up into a tiny ball and hide away. But hiding never solved anything, did it? She had hidden here for ten years and nothing had changed.

And yet…something *had* changed. Luca had changed her. Awakening her to feelings and sensations she hadn't thought possible a few days ago. Feelings she could no longer hide from—feelings that were not part of Luca's rules but she felt them anyway. How could she not? He was the light to her darkness, the healing salve to her psychological wound, the promise of a life outside these cold stone walls. He was her gateway to the outside world, the world that had frightened and terrified her so much because she didn't trust it to keep her safe.

But she trusted Luca.

She had trusted him with her body, giving herself to him, responding to him with a powerful passion she could still feel in her most intimate flesh. Her love for him was bigger than her fear. Much bigger. That was what she would cling to as she stared down her demons. She had the will, she had the motivation, she had her love for him to empower her in a way nothing had been able to before. Luca was outside her prison walls, and the only way she could be with him in his hour of need was to leave the *castello*, propelled, empowered, galvanised by the love she felt for him.

Love was supposed to conquer all.

She would damn well prove it.

CHAPTER NINE

LUCA GOT TO the hospital in time to speak to his grandfather before he was taken for surgery. Nonno looked
ashen and there was a large purple and black bruise on
his face as well as his wrist and elbow where he had
tried to break his fall. Luca took the old man's papery
hand and tried to reassure him. 'I'll be here when you
come out of theatre. Try not to worry.'

Nonno grimaced in pain and his eyes watered. 'When
am I going to meet this new wife of yours? You'd better
hurry up and bring her to me before I fall off my perch.'

'Soon,' Luca said, hoping it was true. 'When you're
feeling better. You don't want to scare her off with all
those bruises, do you?'

A wry smile played with the corners of Nonno's
mouth. 'It's good that you've settled down, Luca. I've
been worried about you since...well, for a long time
now.'

'I know you have.' Luca patted his grandfather's
hand, his chest tightening as if it were in a vice. 'I was
waiting for the right one to come along. Just like you
did with Nonna.'

The strange thing was, Artie did feel right. Right

in so many ways. He couldn't imagine making love to anyone else, which was kind of weird, given there was a time limit on their relationship. A six-month time limit he insisted on because no way was he interested in being in for the long haul. Not with his track record of destroying people's lives.

'Your grandmother was a wonderful woman,' Nonno said, with a wistful look on his weathered features. 'I miss her every day.'

'I know you do, Nonno. I miss Nonna too.'

Another good reason not to love someone—the pain of losing them wrecked your life, leaving you alone and heartsore for years on end. If that wasn't a form of torture, what was? None Luca wanted any part of, not if he could help it.

He was already missing Artie, and he'd only been away from her the couple of hours it took to drive to the hospital. He'd wanted her to come with him to meet his grandfather but that wasn't the only reason. He genuinely enjoyed being with her, which was another new experience for him. The women he'd dated in the past were nice enough people, but no one had made him feel the way Artie did.

Making love with her had been like making love for the first time, discovering things about his body as well as hers. Being tuned in to his body in a totally different way, as if his response settings had been changed, ramped up, intensified, so he would want no one other than her. No one else could trigger the same need and drive. No one else would satisfy him the way she did. He ached for her now. What he would give to see her smile, to feel her hand slide into his and her body nestle against him.

His grandfather turned his head to lock gazes with Luca. 'I've been hard on you, Luca, over the years. I see it now when it's too late to do anything about it. I've expected a lot of you. You had to grow up too fast after your father and Angelo died.' He sighed and continued. 'You've worked hard, too hard really, but I know your father would be proud of your achievements. You've carried on his legacy and turned Ferrantelli Enterprises into a massive success.' He gave a tired smile. 'I've only ever wanted you to be happy. Success is good, but personal fulfilment is what life is really about.'

The hospital orderly arrived at that point to take Nonno down to the operating theatre.

Luca grasped his grandfather's hand and gave it a gentle squeeze. 'Try and get well again, Nonno. I'll be waiting here for you when you come back.'

Once his grandfather had been wheeled out of the room, Luca leaned back in the visitors' chair in his grandfather's private room and stretched out his legs and closed his eyes. Hospitals stirred emotions in him he didn't want to feel. It was a trigger response to tragedy. Being surrounded by death and disease and uncertainty caused an existential crisis in even the most level-headed of people. Being reminded of a loved one's mortality and your own. It would be a long wait until Nonno came out of theatre and then recovery but he wanted to be here when his grandfather came back. His gut churned and his heart squeezed and his breath caught.

If he came back...

* * *

Artie put her small overnight case in the back of Rosa's car and pressed the button to close the boot. She took a deep breath and mentally counted to three on releasing it. She came around to the passenger side and took another breath. 'Okay. I can do this.'

I have to do this. For Luca. For myself. For his grandfather.

She got in the car and pulled the seatbelt into place, her heart pounding, her skin prickling with beads of perspiration.

Rosa started the engine and shifted the gearstick into 'drive'. 'Are you sure about this?'

Artie nodded with grim determination. 'I'm sure. It won't be easy but I want to be with Luca. I need to be with him.'

Rosa drove towards the bronze gates, which opened automatically because of the sensors set on either side of the crushed limestone driveway. Artie concentrated on her breathing, trying to ignore the fear that was like thousands of sticky-footed ants crawling over her skin. Her chest was tight, her heart hammering like some sort of malfunctioning construction machinery, but she was okay...well, a little bit okay.

Rosa flicked a worried glance her way. 'How are you doing?'

Artie gripped the strap of the seatbelt that crossed her chest. Her stomach had ditched the butterflies and recruited bats instead. Frantically flapping bats. 'So far, so good. Keep going. We're nearly outside.'

They drove the rest of the way out of the gates and Artie held her breath, anticipating a crippling flood of panic. But instead of the silent screams of terror inside her head, she heard Luca's calm, deep voice, coaching her through the waves of dread.

'*Breathe,* cara. *One. Two. Three.*'

It wasn't the first time someone had taught her breath control—two of the therapists had done so with minimal results. But for some reason Luca's voice was the one she listened to now. It gave her the courage to go further than she had gone in over a decade. Out through the *castello* gates and into the outside world.

Artie looked at Rosa and laughed. 'I did it! I'm out!'

Rosa blinked away tears. '*Sì*, you're out.'

Artie wished she could say the rest of the journey was easy. It was not. They had to stop so many times for her to get control of her panic. The nausea at one stage was so bad she thought she was going to vomit. She distracted herself with the sights and sounds along the way. Looking at views she never thought she would see again—the rolling, verdant fields, the lush forests and the mountains, the vineyards and orchards and olive groves of Umbria. Scenes from her childhood, places she had travelled past with her parents. The memories were happy and sad, poignant and painful, and yet also gave her a sense of closure. It was time to move on. Luca had given her the tools and the motivation to change her thinking, to shift her focus. And the further away from the *castello* they got, the easier it became, because she knew she was getting closer to Luca.

But then they came to the hospital.

Artie had forgotten about the hospital. Hospitals. Busyness. Crowds. People rushing about. Patients, staff, cleaners, security personnel. The dead, the dying and the injured. A vision of her mother's lifeless, bruised and broken body flashed into her brain. A vision of her father in the Critical Care Spinal Unit, his shattered spine no longer able to keep him upright.

Her fault. Her fault. Her fault.

She had destroyed her family.

Artie gripped the edges of her seat, her heart threatening to pound its way out of her chest. 'I can't go in there. I can't.'

Rosa parked the car in the visitor's parking area and turned off the engine. 'You've come this far.'

'It was a mistake.' Artie closed her eyes so she didn't have to look at the front entrance. 'I can't do this. I'm not ready.'

I will never be ready.

'What if I call Luca to come out and get you?'

Artie opened her eyes and took a deep breath and slowly released it. Luca was inside that building. She was only a few metres away from him. She had come this far, further than she had in ten years. All she had to do was get to Luca. 'No. I'm not giving up now. I want to be with Luca more than anything. But I need to do this last bit on my own. You can go home and I'll talk to you in a few days once we know what's happening with Luca's grandfather.' She released her tight grip on the car seat and smoothed her damp palms down her thighs. 'I'm ready. I'm going in. Wish me luck?'

Rosa smiled and brushed some tears away from her eyes with the back of her hand. 'You've got this.'

Luca opened his eyes when he heard the door of his grandfather's room open, but instead of seeing a nurse come in he saw Artie. For a moment he thought he was dreaming. He blinked and blinked again then sprang out of the chair, taking her by the arms to make sure she was actually real and not a figment of his imagination. '*Cara?* How did you get here? I can barely believe my eyes.'

She smiled, her eyes bright, her cheeks flushed pink. 'Rosa brought me. I wanted to be with you. I forced myself to get here. I can't say it was easy. It was awful, actually. But I kept doing the slow breathing thing and somehow I made it.'

Luca gathered her close to his chest, breathing in the flowery scent of her hair where it tickled his chin. He was overcome with emotion, thinking about the effort it must have cost her to stare down her fears.

For him?

Fears she had lived with for ten years and she had pushed through them to get to his side. To be with him while he faced the very real possibility of losing his grandfather. He wasn't sure how it made him feel... awed, honoured, touched in a way he had rarely been touched. He was used to having entirely transactional relationships with people. He took what he wanted and they did too.

But Artie had given him something no one had ever done before—her complete trust.

'You were very brave, *mia piccola*. It's so good to have you here.' He held her apart from him to smile down at her, a locked space inside his chest flaring open. 'I still can't believe it.' He brushed his bent knuckles down her cheek. 'Nonno will be so pleased to meet you.'

Her forehead creased in concern. 'How is he? Did you get to speak to him before—?'

'Yes, he's in Theatre, or maybe in Recovery by now.' Luca took both of her hands in his. 'I've missed you.'

'I've missed you too.' Her voice whisper-soft, her gaze luminous.

He released her hands and gathered her close again, lowering his mouth to hers in a kiss that sent scorching streaks of heat shooting through his body. She pressed herself closer, her mouth opening to the probe of his tongue. Tingles went down the backs of his legs, blood thundered to his groin, rampant need pounding in his system. Her lips tasted of strawberries and milk with a touch of cinnamon, her little gasps of delight sweet music to his ears and fuel for his desire. A desire that burned and boiled and blistered with incendiary heat right throughout his body in pummelling waves. How could one kiss do so much damage? Light such a fire in his flesh?

Because it was *her* kiss.

Her mouth.

Her.

Luca lifted his mouth off hers to look down at her flushed features and shimmering eyes. 'If we weren't in my grandfather's hospital room, I would show you just how much I've missed you right here and now.'

Her cheeks went a delightful shade of pink. 'I've sent Rosa back home. It's okay for me to stay with you, isn't it?'

Luca smiled. 'I can think of nothing I'd like more. My villa is only half an hour from here.'

She stroked his face with her fingers, sending darts

of pleasure through his body. 'Thank you for helping me move past my fear. I know it's still early days, and I know I'll probably have lots of setbacks, but I feel like I'm finally moving in the right direction.'

Luca tucked a loose strand of her hair back behind her ear, feeling like someone had spilled warm honey into his chest cavity. 'I'm so proud of you right now. The first steps are always the hardest in any difficult journey.'

Artie toyed with the open collar of his shirt, her eyes not quite meeting his. 'I found it helped to shift my focus off myself and put it on you instead. I knew you wanted me with you and I wanted to be with you too. So, so much. That had to be a bigger driver than my fear of leaving the *castello*. And thankfully, it was.'

Luca framed her face in his hands, meshing his gaze with hers. 'Once Nonno is out of danger, I am going to introduce you to everything you've only dreamed of until now.'

She wound her arms around his neck and stepped up on tiptoe to plant a soft kiss to his mouth. 'I can hardly wait.'

A short time later, Luca's grandfather was wheeled back into the room. Artie held on to Luca's hand, feeling nervous at meeting the old man for the first time. She had met so few people over the last decade and had lost the art of making small talk. But she drew strength from having Luca by her side and basked in his pride in her for making it to the hospital. Something had shifted in their relationship, a subtle shift that gave her more confidence around him. He might not love her but he wanted her with him and that was more than enough for now.

It *had* to be enough.

Her love for him might seem sudden, but wasn't that how it happened for some people? An instant attraction, a chemistry that couldn't be denied, an unstoppable force. Luca didn't believe himself capable of loving someone, but then, she hadn't believed herself capable of being able to leave the *castello*. But she had left. She had found the courage within to do so. Would it not be the same for him? He would need to find the courage to love without fear.

Nonno groaned and cranked one eye open. 'Luca?'

Luca moved forward, taking Artie with him. He took his grandfather's hand in his. 'I'm here, Nonno. And so is Artie.'

The old man turned his head on the pillow and his sleepy gaze brightened. 'Ah, my dear girl. I'm so glad to meet you in person. I hope you'll be as happy with Luca as I was with my Marietta.'

Artie stepped closer. '*Buongiorno*, Signor Ferrantelli. It is so lovely to meet you face to face.'

The old man grasped her hand. 'Call me Nonno. You're family now, *si*?'

Family. If only Nonno knew how short a time she would be a part of the Ferrantelli family. Artie smiled and squeezed his hand back in a gesture of warm affection. 'Yes, Nonno. I'm family now.'

An hour or so later, Luca drove Artie to his sprawling estate in Tuscany a few kilometres from the town of San Gimignano, where fourteen of the once seventy-two medieval towers created an ancient skyline. The countryside outside the medieval town was filled with sloping hills and lush valleys interspersed with slopes of grapevines and olive groves and fields of bright red poppies. Tall pines stood like sentries overlooking the verdant fields and the lowering sun cast a golden glow over the landscape, the angle of light catching the edges of the cumulous clouds and sending shafts and bolts of gold down to the earth in a spectacular fashion.

Artie drank in the view, feeling overawed by the beauty to the point of tears. She brushed at her eyes and swallowed a lump in her throat. 'It's so beautiful... the colours, the light—everything. I can't believe I'm seeing it in real time instead of through a screen or the pages of a book or magazine.' She turned to him. 'Do you mind if we stop for a minute? I want to stand by the roadside and smell the air and listen to the sounds of nature.'

'Sure.' Luca stopped the car and came around to open her door. He took her hand and helped her out of the car, a smile playing at the corners of his mouth, creating attractive crinkles near his eyes. 'It's an amazing part of the country, isn't it?'

'It sure is.' Artie stood beside him on the roadside and lifted her face to feel the dance of the evening breeze. She breathed in the scent of wild grasses and sun-warmed pine trees. Listened to the twittering of birds, watched an osprey ride the warm currents of air as it searched for prey below. A swell of emotion filled Artie's chest that Luca had helped her leave the prison of her past. 'I never thought I'd be able to do things like this again.'

Luca put an arm around her waist and gathered her closer against his side. 'I'm proud of you. It can't have been easy, but look at you now.'

She glanced up at him and smiled. 'I don't know how to thank you.'

'I can think of a way.' His eyes darkened and his mouth came down to press a lingering kiss to hers. After a few breathless moments, he lifted his mouth from hers and smiled. 'We'd better get going before it gets dark.'

Once they were back in the car and on their way again, he placed her hand on the top of his thigh and her fingers tingled at the hard warmth of his toned muscles beneath her palm. 'Thank you for being so sweet to Nonno,' he went on. 'He already loves you. You remind him of my grandmother.'

Artie basked in the glow of his compliment. 'What was she like? Were you close to her?'

His expression was like the sky outside—shifting shadows as the light gradually faded. 'I was close to her in the early days, before my father and brother drowned. Their deaths hit her hard and she lost her spark and never quite got it back.' His hands tightened on the steering wheel, making his knuckles bulge to white knobs of tension. 'Like my mother, being around me reminded her too much of what she'd lost. I was always relieved when it was time to go back to boarding school and even more so when I moved away for university.'

Artie stroked his thigh in a comforting fashion, her heart contracting for the way he had suffered as a young teenager. She was all too familiar with how grief and guilt were a deadly combination. Destroying hope, suffocating any sense of happiness or fulfilment. 'I can only imagine how hard it was for all of you, navigating your way through so much grief. But what about your mother? You said she lives in New York now. Do you ever see her?'

'Occasionally, when I'm there for work.' His mouth twisted. 'It's…difficult being with her, as it is for her to be with me.'

'I don't find it hard to be with you.' The words were out of her mouth before she could stop them. She bit her lip and mentally cringed as heat flooded her cheeks. Next she would be blurting out how much she loved him. Words he clearly didn't want to hear. Love wasn't part of their six-month arrangement. Romantic love wasn't part of his life, period.

Luca glanced her way, a smile tilting the edges of his mouth and his eyes dark and warm. 'I don't find it hard to be with you either.' His voice was low and deep and husky and made her long to be back in his arms. To feel the sensual power of his body, the physical expression of his need, even if love wasn't part of why he desired her. But she realised now her desire was a physical manifestation of her love for him. A love that had awakened the first time his lips touched hers, waking her from a psychological coma. A coma where she had denied herself the right to fully engage in life and relationships. Locking herself away out of fear. But she was free now, freed by Luca's passion for her and hers for him.

'Will I get to meet your mother? I mean, is that something you'd like me to do?' Artie asked.

A frown formed a double crease between his eyes. 'I'm not sure it will achieve much.'

'But what if I'd like to?'

He flicked her a brief unreadable glance. 'Why do you want to?'

Artie sighed. 'I lost my mother when I was fifteen. It left such a hole in my life. I can barely watch a television show or commercials or movies with mothers in them because it makes me miss my mother all the more.'

'You have no need to be envious of my relationship with my mother,' Luca said in a weighted tone.

'At least you still have her.'

There was a protracted silence.

Luca released a heavy breath. 'Look, I know you are only trying to help but some family dynamics are best left alone. Nothing can be changed now.'

'But that's what I thought about my fear of leaving the *castello*,' Artie said. 'I lost years of my life by giving in to my fears, allowing them to control me instead of me controlling them. I never thought I could do it, but you helped me see that I could. Maybe it's the same with your relationship with your mother. You shouldn't give up on trying to improve the relationship just because it's been a little difficult so far. What you went through as a family was horrendously tragic. But you still have a family, Luca. You have your mother and your grandfather. I have no one now.'

Luca reached for her hand and brought it up to his mouth, pressing a soft kiss to her fingers. 'You have me, *cara*.' His voice had a note of tenderness that made her heart contract.

But for how long? Six months and no longer.
And then she would be alone again.

A short time later, Luca drove through the gates of his estate and pulled up in front of the imposing medieval villa.

Built like a fortress with four storeys, a central dome and several turrets, it was surrounded by landscaped gardens with a tinkling fountain at the front. 'Don't be put off by the grim façade,' he said, turning off the engine. 'I've done extensive renovations inside.'

'I try never to judge a book or a person by their cover,' Artie said. 'Not that I've met a lot of people lately, but still. Hopefully that's going to change.'

Luca's eyes glinted. 'I'm not sure I want to share you with anyone just yet. This is our honeymoon, *sì*?'

A shiver coursed down Artie's spine and a pool of liquid fire simmered in her core. She sent him a shy smile. 'So, we'll be alone here? Just you and me?'

He leaned closer across the gear shaft and, putting a hand to the back of her head, brought her closer to his descending mouth. 'Just you and me.'

CHAPTER TEN

ARTIE WOKE THE next morning to find her head tucked against Luca's chest and his arms around her and her legs tangled with his. One of his hands was moving up and down her spine in a slow stroking motion that made her pelvis start to tingle. His hand went lower, to the curve of her bottom, and every nerve in her skin did a happy dance. Her inner muscles woke to his touch, instantly recalling the magic of the night before and wanting more. Would she ever tire of feeling his hands on her body? His touch was gentle and yet created a storm in her flesh. A tumult of sensations that made her ache for closer, deeper, more intimate contact.

Luca turned her onto her back and leaned on one elbow to gaze down at her. He brushed some wayward strands of her hair back from her face, his eyes darkly hooded, a lazy smile tipping up one side of his mouth. 'Well, look who's been sleeping in my bed.' His voice had a sexy early-morning rasp to it that made something in her belly turn over.

Artie traced a straight line down his strong nose, a playful smile tilting her own mouth. 'I don't know that I did much sleeping.' Her finger began to circle his stubble-surrounded mouth and chin. 'Unless I was dreaming about you making love to me…how many times was it?'

His eyes darkened. 'Three.' He stroked her bottom lip with his thumb, a small frown settling between his brows. 'I would have gone for four or even five but I didn't want to make you sore. This is all so new to you and…'

Artie smoothed his frown away with her finger. 'New, but wonderful.' She looked deep into his eyes, holding her hand against his prickly jaw. 'I didn't think it would be so…so wonderful. Is it always like this?'

Luca held her gaze for a long moment, his eyes moving between each of hers before lowering to her mouth. He released a soft gust of air, his lopsided smile returning. 'No. It's not always as good as this.'

'Really? Are you just saying that to make me feel good?'

He picked up one of her hands and turned it over to plant a kiss to the middle of her palm, his eyes holding hers. 'I'm saying it because it's true. It feels…different with you.'

'In what way?'

He interlaced his fingers with hers, a contemplative frown interrupting his features. 'I can't explain it. It just feels different.'

Artie aimed her gaze at his mouth rather than meet his eyes. 'Is it because of my lack of experience? I must seem a bit of a novelty to someone like you who's had so many lovers.'

He tipped up her chin and his eyes met hers, and something shifted in the atmosphere. A new, electric energy, a background hum, as if each and every oxygen particle had paused to take a breath.

'I'm not going to dismiss any of my past lovers to faceless bodies who didn't leave a single impression on me, because it's simply not true.'

He stroked his thumb over her lower lip again—a slow-motion stroke that set her mouth buzzing.

'But with you…it feels like I'm discovering sex for the first time. Feeling things on a different level. A more intense level.'

Artie toyed with the hair at the back of his neck, her lower body tinglingly aware of the growing ridge of his erection. Aware of the potent energy that pulsed and throbbed between them. 'I couldn't have asked for a better first lover.'

His mouth came down and sealed hers in a mind-altering kiss that set her pulse racing. His fingers splayed through her hair, his tongue meeting hers in a playful dance with distinctive erotic overtones. Her lower body quaked with longing, her flesh recognising the primal call to connect in the most physically intimate way of all. Her legs tangled with his rougher ones, her breasts crushed against the firm wall of his chest, her nipples already tightening into pert buds.

One of Luca's hands cradled one of her breasts, his touch light, and yet it sent shockwaves of need coursing through her body. Molten heat was licking along her flesh…lightning-fast zaps and tingles that made her groan in pleasure. She moved closer, pressing her mound to his erection, opening her legs for him, desperate to have him inside her.

'Not so impatient, *cara*.' He gave a light laugh and

reached for protection, deftly applying it before coming back to her, his eyes gleaming with the fiery desire she could feel roaring through her own body.

Artie framed his head in her hands, her breathing erratic. 'I want you so much it's like pain.'

'I want you too. Badly.' He kissed her mouth in a kiss that spoke of his own thrumming desire, his lips firm, insistent, hungry.

He moved down her body, kissing her breasts, her belly, and to the secret heart of her womanhood. He separated her and anointed her with his lips and tongue, making her writhe and gasp with bone-melting pleasure. The wave broke over her in a rush, sending her spinning into a place of sheer physical bliss. The storm in her flesh slowly abated but then he created another one by moving up her body again, entering her with a slow, deep thrust that made every hair on her head tingle and tighten at the roots. Her back arched, her thighs trembled, her breath stalled and then came out in a rush of rapturous delight. Delicious sensations rippled through her as he continued to thrust, his breathing rate increasing along with his pace, his touch like fire where his hand was holding her hip, tilting her to him. The pressure built in her body, the primal need a drumbeat working its way up to a powerful crescendo. Blood pounded through her veins, a hot rush fuelled by the intense sensations activated by the erotic friction of his hard male body.

Artie lifted her hips to get him where she most wanted him but it was still not quite the pressure she needed. 'I'm so close…so damn close…'

'Relax, *mia piccola*. Don't fight it.' Luca slipped a

hand between their bodies and stroked the swollen heart of her flesh, sending her over the edge into a cataclysmic orgasm that surpassed everything she had enjoyed so far. Starlight burst behind her eyelids, fireworks exploded in her body, heat pouring like liquid flames all through her pelvis and down her legs to curl her toes.

'Oh, God. Oh, God. Oh, God,' she panted, like she had run a marathon, her heart pounding, her flesh tinglingly alive with mind-smashing ecstasy.

Luca's release followed hers and swept her up in its power and intensity. His entire body seemed to tighten as if he were poised on the edge of a vertiginous cliff. And then he gave an agonised groan and shuddered as if consumed with a rabid fever, his essence spilling, his body finally relaxing against hers.

Artie stroked her hands down his back where his firm flesh was still peppered with goosebumps. The in and out of his breath tickled the side of her neck but she didn't want to move in case it broke the magical spell washing over her, binding her to him in a way no words could possibly describe. There was a rightness about their union—a sense of belonging together for all time.

But you've only got six months, remember?

The prod of her conscience froze her breath and stopped her heart for a moment. It wasn't long enough. Six months was a joke. She wanted for ever. She wanted to be in his arms like this for the rest of her life. How could she ever move on from her relationship with him? Who would ever measure up? How could she love anyone else when he had stolen her heart from the first time he kissed her?

She didn't want to love anyone else. Her heart belonged to him and only him.

Luca must have sensed the subtle change in her mood, and quickly disposed of the condom, and then leaned up on one elbow to look at her, his hand idly brushing her wild hair out of her face. 'What's wrong?' His tone and gaze were gently probing.

Artie painted a smile on her lips. 'Nothing.'

His eyes moved between each of hers like a powerful searchlight looking for something hidden in the shadows. His thumb began to stroke the pillow of her lower lip in slow movements that sent hot tingles through every corridor of her flesh. 'I've been around long enough to know that "nothing" usually means "something". Talk to me, *cara*. Tell me what's worrying you.'

She aimed her gaze at his Adam's apple, her heart skipping rope in her chest. How could she be honest with him without relaying how she felt? He might call an end to their physical relationship and go back to the paper marriage he'd first insisted on. 'I'm just wondering how I will ever find another lover who makes me feel the way you do. I mean, in the future, when we're done.'

There was a beat or two of thick silence.

Then Luca's hand fell away from her face and he released a heavy sigh and rolled onto his back, one arm flung over the edge of the bed, the other coming up to cover his eyes. 'The last thing I want to think about right now is you with someone else.' There was a rough quality to his voice that hinted at a fine thread of anger running under the surface.

'But it's going to happen one day,' Artie said. 'We're

both going to move on with our lives. Isn't that what you planned? What you insisted on?'

He removed his arm from across his face and sat upright, the muscles of his abdomen rippling like coils of steel. He swung his legs over the edge of the bed, his hands resting on either side of his thighs, his back towards her, his head and shoulders hunched forward as if he was fighting to control his emotions.

There was another tight silence.

Artie swallowed, wondering if she had pushed him too far. 'Luca?' She reached out and stroked her hand down between his tense shoulder blades, and he flinched as if her touch burned him. 'What's wrong?'

'Nothing.' The word was bitten out. Hard. Blunt. *Keep-away* curt.

She had a strange desire to smile—her lips twitched as she tried to control it. What was sauce for the goose and all that. 'You know, someone told me recently that "nothing" usually means "something".'

Luca let out a gush of air and gave a deep, self-deprecating chuckle. He turned back to face her. 'Touché.' He took her nearest hand and brought it up to his mouth, locking his gaze with hers. He bit down gently on the end of her index finger and then drew it into his mouth, sucking on it erotically. She shivered and a wave of heat passed through her body, simmering, smouldering like hot coals in her core.

He released her finger from his mouth and returned to holding her hand in his. 'Sometimes I wonder if I need my head read for allowing this to go this far between us.' His thumb stroked over the fleshy part of her thumb, the back-and-forth motion making her stomach do a flip turn. 'But I can't seem to stop myself from wanting you.'

Artie leaned closer, placing her free hand on the rock-hard wall of his chest, her mouth just below his. 'Want me all you like.' She pressed her lips to his in a barely-there kiss, pulling back to gaze into his eyes. 'We've got six months.'

She kept her tone light. *I'm-totally-cool-with-having-a-time-limit-on-our-relationship* light.

He held her gaze for a long moment, shadows shifting in his eyes like filtered sunlight moving across a forest floor. Then his eyes lowered to her mouth, a muscle in his cheek pulsing as if something wasn't quite at peace within him. 'Then let's make the most of it,' he said and covered her mouth with his.

The following evening, after spending some time visiting Nonno, Luca took Artie out for dinner at a restaurant in San Gimignano with a spectacular view over the region. She sat opposite him at a table at the window at the front of the restaurant, feeling both nervous and excited about her first meal out at a restaurant since she was a teenager.

Artie took a sip of the crisp white wine Luca had ordered, and then surveyed the menu. 'So much to choose from…'

'Take your time.' His tone was indulgent, as if he sensed how overawed she was feeling.

Once their orders were taken by the waiter, Artie glanced up at Luca with a rueful expression. 'I'm frightened I might use the wrong cutlery or something. It's been so long since I've eaten in public. I'm glad the restaurant isn't busy tonight.'

He reached for her hand across the table, holding it gently in the cradle of his. 'I made sure it wasn't busy. I know the owner. I asked him to keep this part of the restaurant clear for us.'

Artie blinked at him in surprise. 'Really? But wouldn't that have incurred a considerable loss of income for him?'

Luca shrugged one broad shoulder. 'Don't worry. I've more than compensated him.'

She chewed at the side of her mouth, touched that Luca had gone to so much trouble and expense for her comfort. 'I guess I can hardly call myself a cheap date, now, can I?'

His fingers squeezed hers, a smile playing about his mouth. 'You're worth more than you realise, *cara*. My grandfather certainly thinks so—he was in much better spirits today. Meeting you has done him the power of good. He told me when you were using the bathroom earlier today that he's decided to go ahead with the chemo for his cancer. I have you to thank for his change in attitude. He wants to live now. You've given him a reason to.'

'I'm so glad,' Artie said. 'But I hope the chemo won't be too gruelling. He's not a young man.'

'No, but he's a tough old guy.' Luca stroked his thumb over the back of her hand and added in a heavy tone, 'It's something I've been dreading—losing him. He's the last link to my father and brother, apart from my mother, of course.'

Artie could sense the deep love he had for his grandfather and it gave her hope that he might one day learn to embrace other forms of love—romantic love. Love-for-a-lifetime love. *Her* love.

'Has your mother been to see Nonno recently?'

His mouth twisted, a shadow passing through his gaze. 'They talk on the phone now and again. My mother hates flying back to Italy. It reminds her too much of our flight back from Argentina with my father's and brother's bodies.' He released her hand and picked up his wine glass, staring at the golden liquid with a frowning expression.

Artie placed her hand on his other forearm where it was resting on the table. 'I can only imagine how devastated you both were on that trip home. I can relate to it with my own journey home from hospital after the accident. It felt surreal, like I was having a nightmare or something. I kept expecting my mother to be there when I got home, but of course she wasn't. And my father was a shell of himself. A broken shell. I blamed myself, just as you did and still do.'

Luca leaned forward and took both of her hands in his. 'We've both suffered terrible tragedies. Nothing is going to change the past. It's done and can't be undone. But it's important to live your own life.'

Artie looked down at their joined hands. 'At least I'm living my life now, thanks to you. I think I was asleep to myself for the last ten years.' She raised her gaze to his and continued, 'I didn't realise how much I'd let my fear control me. It kind of crept up on me until I was completely imprisoned by it. But somehow you got me to change my focus, to shift my thinking. How can I ever thank you for that?'

'You don't have to thank me. You did it all by yourself.' Luca idly stroked her hands with his thumbs. 'You're doing so well now. I can't tell you how shocked and delighted I was to see you appear at the hospital the other day. I thought I was dreaming.'

'I was sick with nerves,' Artie confessed. 'But knowing you were there at the end of my journey really helped. It gave me a clear goal to aim for.'

Luca smiled and released one of her hands, then took a flat rectangular jewellery box out of his jacket pocket. 'I have something for you.' He placed the box on the table between them. 'Open it.'

Artie prised open the lid to find a beautiful diamond and sapphire pendant and matching earrings. 'Oh, Luca, they're absolutely gorgeous!' She picked up one of the dangling earrings. 'But they're the same design as your grandmother's engagement ring. Does that mean they're—?'

'*Sì*, they were Nonna's. I want you to have the whole collection.'

'But they're priceless heirlooms. Why are you giving them to me?'

'Don't you think you're worth it?'

She put the earring back in the box, and ran her fingertip over the fine gold chain of the pendant. 'It's not that so much...' She glanced up at him. 'It's more that I feel uncomfortable with you being so generous to me when we're only going to be together for six months. I mean, I seem to be the biggest winner in this arrangement of ours. I get to keep the *castello* and all this amazing jewellery, and what do you get?'

His eyes held hers in a strange little lock that made

the hairs on the back of her neck tingle. 'I get some wonderful memories of our time together. Plus, my grandfather will hopefully recover now he's agreed to go ahead with the treatment.'

Artie frowned. 'But don't you want more than that?'

A screen came up in his gaze. 'What more could I want?'

Me. You could want me, for ever.

Artie couldn't bring herself to say it out loud but she wondered if he could hear her hopes in the ringing silence. 'Don't you want to keep your grandmother's jewellery in case one day you change your mind about marrying someone else?'

'Not going to happen.' He sat back in his chair, lifted his wine glass from the table and took a measured sip. 'I have no plans of that nature.'

Not going to happen.

The words taunted her for the rest of the meal.

Not going to happen.

He was so adamant about never falling in love.

Not going to happen.

How could he be so confident it wouldn't happen?

And how could she be so hopeful it would? That he would fall in love with her?

CHAPTER ELEVEN

ONCE DINNER WAS OVER, Luca led the way back to his car past a wine bar where live music was being played. The sweet strains of a well-known Italian love song filled the night air. He glanced down at Artie's wistful expression, and stopped in front of the entrance. 'Do you fancy going in for a bit?'

She shifted from foot to foot, looking like she was torn between running away and going in and letting her hair down. 'I haven't heard live music before. And I've never been to a wine bar. Or danced with anyone before.'

He took her hand and looped it through his arm. 'Come on, then. Let's dance.'

A short time later, Luca held Artie in his arms as they slow-waltzed to another old love song. Her head was resting against his chest, her hair tickling his chin, her flowery fragrance teasing his nostrils. Her body moved in perfect time with his, as if they had been dancing together for ever. The naturalness of their motion reminded him of the natural rhythm of their love-making. It was as if their bodies were in tune with each other, recognising the other as the perfect partner.

Perfect partner? You're hardly that.

The sharp prod of his conscience made him miss a step and he had to gather Artie closer to stop her from bumping into another couple on the small dance floor. 'Sorry,' he said. 'I lost my concentration.' Or maybe he'd momentarily lost his mind, thinking about the possibility of a future with her.

A future he couldn't offer her.

When he'd first offered her a six-month marriage it had seemed an inordinately long time to be tied to someone, and yet now it didn't seem long enough. He avoided thinking about their inevitable divorce. Avoided thinking about a time when she wouldn't be in his life. Avoided thinking about her with someone else. He felt sick to his guts at the thought of her making love with some other man. He'd never considered himself the jealous type but he couldn't stomach the thought of her with someone else. What if they didn't treat her with respect? What if they weren't patient with her struggles in public? What if they didn't understand how sensitive and caring she was?

Artie looked up at him with luminous eyes, her face wreathed in smiles. 'This is so much fun. Can we do this another night soon?'

Luca smiled and bent his head to kiss her. 'I can think of nothing I'd like more.'

The next couple of weeks passed in a whirlwind of activity where Artie's feet barely touched the ground. There were visits to the hospital to see Luca's grandfather, who was making good progress after his hip surgery. Then there were trips to various sightseeing spots, and picnics in the countryside overlooking the hills and valleys of the region. Luca taught her about the skill of wine-making and olive production and showed her the vines and groves on his estate. He took her for romantic dinners in award-winning restaurants as well as less famous ones, where the food was just as fabulous and the atmosphere intimate and cosy. Luca took her shopping and spoilt her with a completely new wardrobe of clothes, including a collection of swimsuits and gorgeous lingerie.

But it was the nights at home she enjoyed the most. Just being with him, sitting in the salon chatting, watching a movie or listening to music together, her head resting on his chest and his arms around her. It gave her a glimpse of what life could be like if they stayed together longer than the six months he'd stipulated. He was still driven by work and was often on the phone or answering emails, but she noticed he was more relaxed than before and seemed to smile and laugh more. Was it because his grandfather was on the mend and had decided to go ahead with his cancer treatment? Or was it because she had helped Luca to see there was more to life than work? That being in a romantic relationship could be positive rather than negative?

Artie had to bite her tongue so many times to stop herself from confessing how she felt about him but she let her actions do the talking instead. Every time she kissed him, she let her lips communicate her love. Every touch of her hands, every stroke of her fingers, every press of her body on his, love poured out of her. But she wanted to say it out loud. She needed to say it out loud. She needed him to hear the words—I love you.

They were sitting on the sofa watching the moon rise through the salon windows after a day of sightseeing. The moonlight cast a silver light over the surface of the infinity pool outside on the terrace overlooking the vineyard. Luca's arm was around her shoulders, her head resting on his shoulder, and soft music was playing through the sound system—cellos, violins and the sweetly lilting tones of a flute. A romantic ballad that tugged at her heartstrings and made her wish there wasn't a limit on their time together.

'Luca?'

'Mmm?' One of his hands began to play with her hair, sending shivers coursing down her spine.

Artie tilted her head to look at him. 'Luca, I want to talk to you about something. Something important.'

He brushed an imaginary hair away from her face, his eyes dark and serious. 'Go on.' His tone held a note of caution, unease, guardedness, but she refused to let it daunt her.

She swallowed a tight knot in her throat. 'There's so much I enjoy about being with you. You've spoilt me like a princess. You've treated me with so much patience and kindness and helped me build my confidence.'

He gave a half-smile, some of the wariness in his gaze fading. 'I like seeing you blossom, *cara*. You're a beautiful person who's been hiding away for too long.'

Artie touched his face with her fingers, her love for him taking up all the room in her chest so she could barely take a breath. 'I never thought I'd meet someone like you. And not just because I was locked away in the *castello*. But because I didn't think people as wonderful as you existed.'

Luca took her by the upper arms in a firm grip, his expression clouding. 'Look, don't go making me out to be a hero, Artie. I'm hardly that. You're confusing good chemistry with…other feelings.' Even the way he hesitated over the rest of his sentence showed how reluctant he was to the notion of love, but Artie pressed on regardless.

'Luca…' She took a deep breath and plunged in. 'I don't want our relationship to be temporary. I want more, and deep down I think you do too.'

His hands fell away from her arms and he sprang off the sofa to put some distance between them. 'You're wrong, Artie. That's not what I want. I've never wanted that. We made an agreement—'

Artie jumped off the sofa as well and stood in front of him. 'We made an agreement and then we changed it to what it is now—a physical relationship that works on every level but the one that means the most to me. I can't make love with you and keep my feelings to one side. They *are* the reason I want to make love with you. The only reason. I love you.'

Luca drew in a harsh-sounding breath and released it in a stuttered stream. He placed his hands on his hips, his shoulders hunched forward. 'You're young and inexperienced, of course, you're going to think the first person who makes love to you is the love of your life. But believe me, I am not that person.' His expression was like a walled fortress. Closed. Locked.

Keep out or face the consequences.

'You are that person.' Artie choked over the words as emotion welled in her throat. 'You've been that person from the moment we kissed at our wedding.

Something happened that day—I knew it on a cellular level. And—'

'Will you listen to yourself?' His tone had a cutting edge that sliced at her self-esteem like a switchblade. 'You're spouting forth a fairy-tale fantasy. It's not real, Artie. You've fashioned me into some sort of romantic hero who ticks all the boxes for you. You need more life experience. You need to date other men so you can gain more perspective. You'll thank me in the end. Tying yourself to me indefinitely would be a mistake. A mistake you'll regret for the rest of your life.' He turned away from her, drawing in another ragged breath, his tone softening. 'Let's leave this for now. I don't want to upset you.'

Artie swallowed a tight restriction in her throat, tears stinging at the backs of her eyes. 'But you've already upset me by not accepting that I love you. You've dismissed it as if I don't know my own mind. I know what I feel.' She banged her fist against her chest for emphasis. 'I can't deny my feelings or ignore them as you seem to do. They're here with me all the time.'

Luca turned back around and opened and closed his eyes in a slow, *God-give-me-strength* blink. 'Look, you're one of the nicest people I've ever met, *cara*. You have so much to offer and I want you to be happy. I really do. But I'm not the person to make you happy. It's not in my skill set. I don't want the same things as you.'

Artie pressed her lips together for a moment to stop them from trembling. 'I think you do want the same things but you don't feel you deserve them because of what happened to your father and brother. I understand that more than most people, because I've experienced the same guilt for the last ten years. It completely imprisoned me, kept me from having a life of my own. But meeting you changed that. You freed me from my prison of fear and showed me I could have more than I ever thought possible.' She came up to him and placed her hand on his forearm. 'I know you have deep feelings locked away inside you. I feel it every time you kiss me. I feel it every time you make love to me.'

Luca brushed off her arm as if it was soiling his sleeve, his gaze hard, his mouth tight, his firewall still up. 'You're mistaking good sex for something else. It's an easy mistake to make, especially when you're not very experienced. But in time, you'll gain experience and realise this is just a crush, an infatuation that can't last.'

'I don't have to be experienced to know how I feel,' Artie said. 'They're *my* feelings. I feel them. I own them.'

'And I know how I feel and it doesn't include the sort of love you're talking about.' He ran a hand over his face and continued, 'I care about you, of course. I enjoy being with you but that's all it is—companionship and mutual desire that has an end point, as per our agreement.'

Artie's heart gave a painful spasm, and for a moment she couldn't locate her voice. He cared about her and enjoyed being with her but that was all it was? How could she have got it so wrong? She was sure he was developing feelings for her—sure enough to reveal her own. He thought her young and gauche, a girl in the throes of her first crush. How could she get through to him? How could she prove she loved him? Or was it pointless? Was she fooling herself that he would one day change? Didn't so many deluded women fall for that fantasy? The vain hope that in time, enough love would change their difficult men to the man of their dreams?

But what if Luca never changed?

What if he was incapable of it?

'Luca, I took a huge risk in leaving the *castello* for you,' Artie said. 'Why can't you take a risk and allow yourself to feel what I know is in your heart? I know it's scary to admit how much you care about someone. And I know the last thing you want to do is be reckless and spontaneous but we've connected in a way people rarely do. Surely you can't deny it? We have so much in common, can't you see that? We're perfect for each other.'

Luca turned his back, drawing in a deep breath, his hands on his hips in a braced position. 'Stop it, Artie. This is a pointless discussion. You're making me out to be someone I can never be.'

Artie ran her tongue over her dry lips, tasting the metallic bitterness of disappointment. She clasped her hands together in front of her body, trying to contain the emotions rioting through her. 'You'll never be free of the prison of the past unless you learn to let go of control. To allow yourself to be reckless with your heart, to open it to the feelings I know you've buried there. I've let go of control. I've opened my heart to you. Why can't you do it for me? If you won't do it for me, then it wouldn't be fair to either of us to continue in a relationship that is so out of balance.'

'It's not out of balance.' Luca swung back around

to face her. 'I made it so we both get what we want. At the end of six months, you get to keep the *castello* and Nonno completes his chemo. It's a win-win.'

She shook her head at him. 'It's a lose-lose but you can't see it. I would choose love over a run-down old castle any day. And how are you going to explain the end of our marriage to your grandfather?'

He gave a dismissive shrug. 'Marriages break up all the time. It won't matter by then because he'll have finished the course of treatment. As I said—win-win.' His tone had a businesslike ring to it. No emotions. Ticking a box. Deal done.

Artie steepled her fingers around her nose and mouth, concentrating on keeping calm even though inside she was crumbling, the very foundations of her under assault as self-doubts rained down on her. She wasn't worthy of his love. She wasn't good enough. She was defective, damaged. He didn't love her. He would *never* love her. He had only married her as a means to an end, and yet she had fooled herself he was developing feelings for her. She was a fool for thinking he felt more for her than companionship and care.

Her old friend panic crept up behind her…lurking in the background.

You can't survive on your own. Stay with him. Put up and shut up.

Her skin prickled, fear slid into her stomach and coiled around her intestines, squeezing, tightening.

You'll lose the castello if you leave him now.

But Artie knew she couldn't lock herself in another prison. Staying with Luca in a loveless marriage for the next few months would be the same as locking herself in the *castello*. Shutting herself away from her hopes and dreams. From her potential.

From love.

She couldn't go back to being that frightened person now. She had to forge her way through with the strength and courage Luca had inspired in her. He had awakened her to what she most wanted in life and it would be wrong to go backwards, to silence the hopes and dreams she harboured. She owed it to herself to embrace life. To live life fully instead of living in negative solitude.

Artie lowered her hands from her face and straightened her shoulders, meeting his cold gaze with a sinking feeling in her stomach. 'I don't think there's any point in waiting out the six months. It will only make it harder for me. It's best if I leave now.'

A ripple of tension whipped over his face and his hands clenched into fists by his sides. 'Now? Are you crazy? You can't leave. We made an agreement.' There was a restricted quality to his voice. 'You'll lose everything if you leave now.'

Artie sighed. 'I can't be with you if you don't love me. It wouldn't be healthy for me. It would only reinforce the negative feelings I've had about myself in the past. That I'm not worthy, that I'm somehow the cause of everything bad that happens to me and those I care about. I need to leave that part of my life behind now. I need to embrace life as a fully awakened adult woman who knows what she wants and isn't afraid to ask for it.'

His hand scraped through his hair, leaving tracks in the thick black strands. He muttered a curse word in Italian, his mouth pulled so tight there were white tips at the corners. 'I can't stop you leaving but I should warn you there will be consequences. I'm not going to hand over a property with the potential of Castello Mireille just because you've pulled the plug on our agreement. I will keep it. I will develop it into a hotel and then I'll sell it.' His eyes flashed with green and brown sparks of anger. An anger so palpable it crackled in the air.

Artie ground her teeth, fighting to keep control of her own anger. 'Do what you need to do, Luca. I won't stand in your way. And I don't expect you to stand in mine.' She moved across to where she had left her phone. 'I'm going to call Rosa to come and get me.'

'Don't be ridiculous,' Luca said. 'It'll take her hours to get here.'

Artie faced him, phone in hand, eyebrows arched. 'Will you drive me?'

His top lip curled and his eyes turned to flint. 'You must be joking.'

Her chin came up. 'I'm not.'

He released a savage breath and muttered another curse. 'I'll organise a driver.' He took out his own phone and selected a number from his contacts.

Artie turned away as he told his employee to come and collect her for the journey back to Umbria. There was nothing in his tone to suggest he was shattered by her decision to leave him. He was angry, yes, but not devastated. Not as devastated as she was feeling. But how could he be? He didn't love her, so why would he feel anything but anger that she was pulling out of their agreement? His plans had been disrupted. His heart was unaffected.

Luca slipped the phone back in his pocket, his expression set in cold, emotionless lines. 'Done. Emilio will be here in five minutes.'

Artie moistened her parchment-dry lips again. Was this really happening? He was letting her go without a fight? It validated her decision to leave now, before she got even more invested in their relationship. But how much more invested could she be than what she was now? She loved him with her entire being and yet he felt nothing more for her than he would for a pet or a pot plant. He *cared* about her. That wasn't enough for her. It would never be enough. 'Thank you. I'd better go and pack a few things.' She turned for the door, waiting, hoping for him to call her back. She even slowed her steps, giving him plenty of time to do so. One step. Two steps. Three steps. Four...

'Artie.'

Her heart lifted like a helium balloon and she spun around. Had he changed his mind? Would he beg her to rethink her decision?

Oh, please, beg me to stay. Tell me you love me.

'Yes?'

His expression was mask-like but his throat rose and fell over a tight swallow. 'Keep safe.' His tone was gruff.

An ache pressed down on her chest, an avalanche of emotion that made it impossible for her to take a breath. Her eyes burned with unshed tears. She. Would. Not. Cry. Not now. She would not make herself look any more gauche and desperate. She would take a dignified stance. She would take a leaf from his relationship playbook—she would be cool and calm and collected, detached. Their business deal was over and she would move on. End of story. 'You too. And thanks for…everything.' She pulled the heirloom engagement ring off her finger as well as the wedding band and held them out to him. 'You'd better take the rings back. The earrings and pendant are upstairs. I'll leave them on the dressing table.'

'Keep them.'

'But they're family heirlooms—'

'I said, keep them.' The words were bitten out through a paper-thin slit between his lips, a savage frown pleating his brow.

Artie put the rings on one of the side tables and then turned and walked out of the room, closing the door softly but firmly behind her.

CHAPTER TWELVE

As soon as the car carrying her away disappeared from sight Luca sucked in a breath that tore at his throat like wolf claws. What did she expect him to do? Run after her and beg her to stay? He had told her the terms from the outset. He had made it clear where his boundaries were.

But you shifted the boundaries. You slept with her.

He dragged a hand down his face, his gut clenching with self-disgust. Yes, he had shifted the boundaries and he should have known better. Artie was so young and inexperienced, and sleeping with him had made things so much worse. It had fuelled her romantic fantasies about him, fantasies he could never live up to. But he hadn't been able to help himself. He'd wanted her the moment he met her, maybe even before that.

She was light and he was darkness.

She was naïve and trusting and he was ruthless and cynical.

She was in touch with her emotions and he had none…well, none that he wanted to acknowledge. Emotions were not his currency. It was a language he didn't speak and nor did he want any fluency in it.

Luca picked up the engagement and wedding rings from the side table, curling his fingers around them so he didn't have to look at the mocking, accusing eyes of the diamonds. He rattled them in his hand like dice and tossed them back on the table, turning away with an expletive.

He was not going to go after her. He. Was. Not. He was *not* going after her. His old self would have run up the stairs even before she packed and got down on bended knee and begged her to stay.

But he was not that reckless teenage boy any more. He was able to regulate his reactions, to think logically and carefully about his actions. He was able to weigh the checks and balances and act accordingly...except when it came to making love with her. That had been reckless and ill-advised and yet he had done it anyway. Done it and enjoyed every pulse-racing second of it. Artie had got to him in a way no one else ever had.

He *felt* different.

Something inside him had changed and he wasn't sure he could dial it back. But he was damn well going to try.

Artie spent the first month back at Castello Mireille vainly waiting for the phone to ring. She longed to hear Luca's voice, she longed to feel his touch, to be in his arms again. She was suffering terrible withdrawal symptoms, missing the stroke and glide of his body within hers, the passionate press of his lips on her mouth, her breasts and her body. She reached for him in the middle of the night, her heart sinking when she found the other side of the bed cold and empty.

She realised with a sickening jolt that this was what her father had gone through after the accident. He had grieved both physically and emotionally for her mother. The loss of an intimate partner was felt on so many levels, little stabs and arrows every time you were reminded of the person, every time a memory was triggered by sight, sound, taste, touch or hearing.

Losing Luca was like a death. He was gone from her life and she couldn't get him back, not unless she compromised herself in the process. And hadn't she compromised herself enough for the last decade? Denying herself any sort of life, any sort of enjoyment and happiness out of guilt?

She was no longer the girl in a psychological coma. She was awake to her potential, awake to what she wanted and no longer afraid to aim for it, even if it meant suffering heartbreak along the way. Luca was everything she wanted in a husband, but if he didn't love her, then how could she ever be happy settling for anything less than his whole heart?

Artie was working in the morning room on a christening gown for one of the villager's baby, waiting for Rosa to bring in morning tea. There was a certain sadness in working on babies' clothes when it was highly likely she would never have a baby now. How could she without Luca, the only man she wanted to have children with? The only man she could ever love? She placed another neat stitch in the christening gown, wondering what he was doing now. Working, no doubt. Visiting his grandfather. Taking a new lover to replace her... Her insides revolted at the thought of him making love to someone else. Artie forced herself to concentrate on her embroidery rather than torturing herself. The weeks since coming home, she had decided to pour her energy into her craft and had even set up a social media page and website. To take it from a hobby to a business. She had orders coming in so quickly she could barely keep up. But it gave her the distraction she needed to take her mind off Luca and their broken marriage.

Rosa came in carrying a tray with their refreshments. She set it on the table in front of Artie and then sat down beside her, taking a cup of tea for herself off the tray. 'I'm thinking about taking a little holiday. I know my timing isn't good, given the situation with you and Luca, but I thought it was time I saw a bit of the world outside these walls now you're a little more independent.'

Artie put the christening gown to one side, wrapping it in the white muslin cloth she used to protect it. 'Oh, Rosa, I feel bad you've been stuck here with me for so long. But you don't have to worry about me now. I've been to the village several times this week on my own and even had coffee at the café a couple of times. I can't say it's easy, but I do it and feel better for it.'

'I'm so glad you're able to do more.' Rosa sighed and continued, 'While you were staying with Luca, I realised I might have been holding you back. Don't get me wrong—I wanted to help you, but I think my reasons were not as altruistic as you think.'

Artie frowned. 'What do you mean?'

Rosa looked a little shamefaced. 'When I got my heart broken all those years ago, I locked myself away here working for your family. It was my way of avoiding being hurt again. But I worry that I might have inadvertently held you back by allowing you to become dependent on me.'

'You haven't done any such thing,' Artie said. 'I held myself back and now I'm moving forward. But I can't thank you enough for being there when I needed you.'

Rosa's expression was tender with concern. 'Have you heard from Luca?'

Artie sighed and shook her head. 'No. Nothing.'

'Have you called or texted him?'

Artie leaned forward to reach for a teacup. 'What would be the point? I told him how I feel and he didn't feel the same, so end of story. I have to move on with my life. Without him.'

Rosa toyed with the hem of her flowered dress in an abstracted manner. 'What will you do if or when he sells the *castello*?'

'I'll find somewhere else to live. I can't live in a place this big. It's not practical.' Artie's shoulders went down on a sigh. 'I'll always have wonderful memories of being here with Mama and Papa before the accident but it's well and truly time to move on. Someone else can live here and make their own memories.'

Rosa straightened the folds of her dress over her knees. 'The holiday I was telling you about…? I'm going with a…a friend.'

Artie's interest was piqued by the housekeeper's sheepish tone. She put the teacup back down on the table in front of her. 'Who is the friend?'

Twin spots of colour appeared in Rosa's cheeks. 'Remember I told you about the love of my life who got away? Well, Sergio and I met up while you were staying with Luca. We've been seeing each other now and again since. He's asked me to go away with him for a short holiday. I won't go if you need me here, though.'

Artie leaned over to give Rosa a hug. 'I'm so happy for you.' She leaned back to look at her. 'I will always need you, Rosa, but as a friend, not as a babysitter.'

Rosa grimaced. 'You don't think I'm too old to be galivanting off with a man?'

Artie smiled. 'Not if you love him and he loves you.'

If only I should be so lucky.

Luca put off telling his grandfather about Artie leaving him for as long as he could because he didn't want to say the words out loud. *She left me.* But when Nonno was released from hospital and transferred into a cancer therapy unit, Luca had to explain why Artie wasn't with him. *She left me.* Those three words were like bullet wounds in his chest, raw, seeping, deep.

Nonno's distress at hearing Luca's news about his marriage was almost as bad as his own. 'But why? She's perfect for you, Luca. Why haven't you gone after her and brought her back?'

'Nonno, gone are the days when a man can carry a woman back to his cave,' Luca said. 'I can't force her to stay with me. She made the choice to leave.'

Nonno scowled. 'If you loved Artie like I loved your grandmother, nothing would stop you from doing everything in your power to get her back. A man in love is a force to be reckoned with.'

The silence was telling.

Luca loosened the collar of his shirt and leaned forward to rest his forearms on his thighs. 'Enough about my dramas. Is there anything I can get you?'

Nonno shook his head and closed his eyes. 'No. I just need to sleep.'

Luca stood from the bedside and laid a gentle hand on his grandfather's weathered arm. 'I'll be in again tomorrow.'

He was on his way out of the hospital when his phone rang with his mother's ring tone and his chest seized with the all too familiar dread. But instead of letting his phone go to message service as he often did, this time he answered it. 'Mama.'

'Luca, how is Nonno? I tried calling him but he must have his phone off. His carer rang to tell me he had a fall a week or two ago. She also told me you're married. Is that true? Why didn't you invite me to your wedding?'

Guilt gnawed at his conscience. 'Nonno's doing okay. As to my marriage—it's a long story and I hate to tell you it hasn't got a happy ending.'

'Oh, Luca.' His mother's sigh only intensified the pain riddling his chest. 'What's happened to us that you didn't want me to be there on your special day?'

Luca cleared his suddenly blocked throat and stepped out of the way of visitors coming through the hospital entrance. He pinched the bridge of his nose, scrunching his eyes closed briefly. 'It's not you. It's me. It's always been me that's the problem.'

'You're too hard on yourself,' his mother said. 'You're so like your father it's uncanny.' She sighed again and went on, 'It's why I found it increasingly difficult to be around you as you grew into a man. I couldn't look at you without seeing him. It reminded me of my role in what happened.'

Luca frowned, his hand going back to his side. 'Your

role? What are you talking about? I was the one who entered the surf that day. You weren't even at the beach.'

'No.' Her voice was ragged. 'I wasn't there. I went shopping instead of spending the day with my family as your father wanted. Do you know how much I regret that now? It's tortured me for years. What if I had gone along? I could've called for help instead of you trying to do it on your own. I can't bear to think of you running along that deserted beach, half drowned yourself, trying to find someone to help.' She began to sob. 'Whenever I've looked at you since, I've seen that traumatised, terrified young boy and felt how I let you and your papa and Angelo down.'

Luca blinked away stinging moisture from his eyes. He swallowed deeply against the boulder-sized lump in his throat. 'Mama, please don't cry. Please don't blame yourself. I'm sorry I haven't called you. I'm sorry I've let you suffer like this without being there for you. It was selfish of me.'

'You haven't got a selfish bone in your body,' his mother said. 'Your father was the same. Too generous for words, always hard-working, trying to make the world a better place. But tell me, what's going on with your marriage? It breaks my heart to think of you missing out on finding the love of your life. I'm so grateful I had those precious years with your father. They have sustained me through the long years since. I live off the memories.'

Luca gave a serrated sigh and pushed his hair back off his forehead. 'I'd rather not talk about it now, but next time I'm in New York do you want to catch up over dinner?'

'I would love that.' His mother's voice was thick with emotion. 'Give Nonno my best wishes.'

'*Sì,*' Luca said. 'I will.'

Luca tried not to think about Artie in the next couple of weeks and he mostly succeeded. Mostly. He blocked his memories of her smile, her touch and her kiss with a punishing regime of work that left him feeling ragged at the end of each day. One would think he would stumble into bed and fall instantly asleep out of sheer exhaustion, but no, that was when the real torture got going. The sense of emptiness could be staved off during the day but at night it taunted him with a vengeance. He tossed, he turned, he paced, he swore, he thumped the pillows and doggedly ignored the vacant side of the bed where Artie had once lain. He did his best to ignore the fragrance of her perfume that stubbornly lingered in the air at his villa as if to taunt him. He did his best to ignore the pain that sat low and heavy in his chest, dragging on his organs like a tow rope.

She left you.

But then more words joined in the mocking chorus. *You let her go.*

He allowed them some traction occasionally, using them as a rationalisation exercise. Of course he'd let her go. It was the right thing to do. She wanted more than he could give, so it was only fair that he set her free.

But you're not free.

What was it with his conscience lately? Reminding him of things he didn't want reminding about. No, he didn't feel free and—even more worrying—he didn't *want* to feel free. He wanted to feel connected, bonded to Artie, because when he was with her, he felt like a fully functioning human being. He felt things he hadn't felt before. Things he didn't think he was capable of feeling. Things that were terrifying because they made him vulnerable in a way he had avoided feeling for most of his adult life.

He had shut down his emotional centre.

Bludgeoned it into a coma.

But since his conversation with his mother there were tiny flickers of life deep in his chest like the faint trace of a heartbeat on an electrocardiograph. A pulse of something he had thought long dead. A need he had denied for so long he had fooled himself he wasn't capable of feeling it.

The need to love and be loved.

Three more words popped into his head like a blinding flash of light.

You love her.

Luca let them sit for a moment, for once not rushing to block them or erase them or deny them.

You love her.

And then he tweaked them, substituting the 'you' for 'I'.

I love her.

Bringing himself inexorably closer to the truth, step by step.

I. Love. Her.

He embraced the truth of those words like someone sucking in oxygen after near strangulation.

I love her.

His chest ballooned with hope, positive energy zapping round his body.

I love her.

Luca snatched up his car keys and the wedding and engagement rings from the bedside table. He'd placed them there as a form of self-torture but now he couldn't wait to see them back on Artie's finger where they belonged. Nonno was right. Luca's love for Artie was a force to be reckoned with—nothing would stop him from bringing her home.

Artie heard a car roaring through the *castello* gates and her heart turned over. She peered through the window in the sitting room and saw Luca unfold his tall, athletic figure from his car. Her pulse picked up its pace, her heart slamming into her breastbone, her skin tingling all over.

He's here.

She walked as calmly as she could to open the front door, schooling her features into a mask of cool politeness. After all, there was no point setting her hopes too high—he hadn't made a single effort to contact her over the past month. 'Luca. What brings you here?' She was proud of her impersonal tone. It belied the tumult of emotions in her chest.

He stepped through the open doorway with brisk efficiency, closing it with a click behind him. 'You bring me here, *cara*. You and only you.' He stood there with his hands by his sides and his expression set in grave lines. He looked tired around the eyes and his face hadn't seen a razor in a couple of days. 'I need to talk to you.'

Artie took a step back, her arms folding across her chest, her chin lifting. 'To say what?'

He unpeeled her arms from around her body, taking her hands in his. 'I've been such a fool. It's taken me the best part of a month to realise what's been there all the time.' He squeezed her hands. 'I love you, *mia piccola*. I love you so damn much it hurts. I can't believe I let you go. Can you ever forgive me?' He blinked a couple of times and she was surprised to see moisture in his eyes. 'I made a terrible mistake in not telling you sooner. But I wasn't able to recognise it until it was too late.' He drew her closer, holding her hands against his chest. 'Tell me it's not too late. I love you and want to spend the rest of my life with you. Please say yes. Please say you'll come back to me. Please give me another chance to prove how much I adore you.'

Artie brought one of her hands up to his prickly jaw, stroking it lovingly. 'I never thought I'd hear you say those words to me. I had given up hope, especially over the last few weeks.'

He grimaced and hugged her tightly to his chest. 'Don't remind me what a stubborn fool I've been. I can never forgive myself for that. I was in such denial that I couldn't even bring up your name on my phone. I knew it would hurt too much, so I didn't do it. Classic avoidance behaviour.'

Artie eased back to smile up at him. 'You're here now, so that's the main thing. I've missed you so much. I felt only half alive without you.'

He framed her face with his hands. 'You're everything I could ever want in a life partner. You complete me, complement me and challenge me to be the best man I can be. I can barely find the words to describe how much you mean to me.'

'I love you too, more than I can say.'

Luca lowered his mouth to hers and happiness exploded through her being. He was here. He loved her. He wanted to spend the rest of his life with her. His kiss communicated it all, passionately, fervently, devotedly. Even the steady thud of his heartbeat under her hand seemed to say the same. *I love you. I love you. I love you.*

After a moment, Luca lifted his mouth off hers and took something out of his trouser pocket. He held the wedding and engagement rings between his fingers. 'I think it's time these were put back where they belong, don't you?'

'Yes, please.' Artie held out her hand for him to slip them back on her ring finger. 'I'm never taking those rings off again.'

Luca smiled. 'I want you to meet my mother. Will you come to New York with me as soon as possible?'

Artie raised her eyebrows in delight. 'You've spoken to her?'

His face lit up with happiness. 'We had a chat about things and I realised how blinkered I'd been all these years, reading things into her behaviour that weren't accurate at all. You've taught me so much about myself, *cara.* I can never thank you enough for that. I hope you won't mind sharing my mother with me? I should warn you that she'll very likely shower you with love.'

'I won't mind sharing her at all. I can't wait to meet her.' Artie lifted her face for his kiss, her heart swelling with love. Her sad, closed-off life had somehow turned into a fairy tale. She was free from her self-imposed prison, and Luca, the man of her dreams, her Prince Charming, had claimed her as the love of his life.

Luca finally lifted his head and looked down at her with heart-stopping tenderness. 'Will you come away for a honeymoon with me after we visit my mother?'

'Just try and stop me.'

He stroked the curve of her cheek with his finger. 'I wasn't going to sell Castello Mireille.'

Artie smiled and gave him a fierce hug. 'I think on some level I knew that.' She eased back to look at him again. 'But I don't need it any more. What I need is you. It doesn't matter where I live as long as you're there with me.'

His eyes shimmered with emotion and her heart swelled with love to see how in touch with his feelings he was now. 'I've spent most of my life avoiding feeling like this—loving someone so much it hurts to think of ever losing them. I was in denial of my feelings from the moment I met you. You woke me to the needs I'd shut down inside myself. The need to love and be loved by an intimate partner. I can't believe how lucky I am to have found you.'

Artie pressed a soft kiss to his mouth. 'I'm lucky to have been found by *you*. If it hadn't been for you, I might still be locked away from all that life has to offer.'

Luca smiled, his eyes twinkling. 'I know it's early days, but maybe we can think about having those bambinos Nonno was talking about?'

She beamed with unfettered joy. 'Really? You want to have children?'

'Why not?' He kissed the tip of her nose. 'Building a

family with you will be a wonderful experience. You'll
be the best mother in the world.'

'I think you'll be an amazing father,' Artie said. 'I
can't wait to hold our baby in my arms. I never thought
I wanted to have a family until I met you. I didn't allow
myself to think about it. But now it's like a dream come
true.'

Luca gazed down at her with love shining in his
eyes. 'Thank you for being you. Adorable, sweet, amazing you.'

Artie gave him a teasing smile. 'So, you don't think
I'm too naïve and innocent for you now?'

'You're perfect for me.' He planted a smacking kiss
on her lips. 'And as to remaining innocent, well, I'll
soon take care of that.'

Artie laughed and flung her arms around his neck.
'Bring it on.'

* * * * *

GUILTY PLEASURE

TARYN LEIGH TAYLOR

Thanks for helping me with my homework, Crystal.
And for Jo. We made it. Thank you for everything.

CHAPTER ONE

SOMEONE WAS GOING to pay.

Wes Brennan just had to figure out who.

Accepting the lumpy manila envelope the guard slid under the Plexiglas barrier, Wes ripped into it and dumped the contents on the stainless steel counter.

He grabbed his watch first, fastening the platinum band around his left wrist. His blue silk Brioni tie was unceremoniously shoved into his pants pocket, along with his keys. After a quick inspection of his billfold—one hundred dollars and all his plastic—it, too, was tucked away, this time in the breast pocket of his suit jacket. If he'd known he was going to end up in jail, he would have stopped at an ATM first. A hundred bucks probably wouldn't even cover his cab ride home if traffic was bad, and in LA, traffic was always bad.

Wes picked up the last item on the counter. He barely recognized his bearded reflection in the black screen of his phone. Well, what was left of his phone, anyway. He'd watched an FBI agent strip it of its SIM card, which was still evidence in his active and ongoing case, the day they'd put him in cuffs. He pressed the power button a few times, but to no avail. Clearly no one had thought to turn his phone off after whatever the hell they'd seen fit to do to it during his incarceration. With a sigh, he slid it into the same pocket as his wallet.

The mandated hiatus from the digital world was probably for the best, he decided. *Cybersecurity expert rips off his clients.* Yeah, he could see the press getting some mileage out of that. He'd take the reprieve while he could get it.

Then he tossed the empty envelope in the designated bin and walked out of prison.

Ten days he'd been held like a mongrel at the pound, focused on this moment—liberation—but when he stepped beyond the squeaky metal door and back into the world, what he felt was not so much relief as wariness. A haunting certainty that the dog catcher loomed around the next corner, or the one after that. He wasn't out of this nightmare yet. Not by a long shot.

It didn't help that California's famous sunshine was nowhere to be seen, swallowed by dank, gray clouds that reflected his mood. The air was foul with smog. Wes took a deep breath anyway, inhaling the tainted scent of freedom.

He wanted to incinerate the suit he'd been arrested in with a blowtorch.

He wanted to scald any remnants of the experience from his skin with a blistering shower.

But most of all, he wanted vengeance. With every cell of his being.

Odd, then, that he was so easily and thoroughly distracted when he caught sight of the woman who was waiting for him at the end of the sidewalk.

She'd been wearing a red dress the first time he'd seen her, at an overstuffed party, in a frat house that reeked of booze and pot and hormones. Her dress now was the same color, but streamlined and structured, tailored to perfection to skim the long, sleek lines of her body. Back then it had been short and flowy, fluttering around her thighs in a way that made his fingers ache to inch it higher.

Gone, too, were the wild brown curls of her youth, replaced by an angled bob that showed off sharp cheekbones and made the generous curve of her mouth look even softer and more inviting in contrast. Her lips were painted the same red as her dress.

Vivienne Grant.

The *last* person he wanted to witness his personal and professional nadir, and yet, an oddly fitting choice.

After all, what was hell without your very own devil incarnate?

"Hello, lover."

Her voice still grabbed him by the balls. Throaty. Sexy. Poisonous.

Wes's chuckle held no mirth as he stopped in front of her. "And to think I thought things couldn't get worse."

The slow curve of her mouth was mesmerizing.

"I knew you'd be surprised." Vivienne's eyes glittered, hard and sharp.

Beautiful. She'd always been so fucking beautiful.

"Did Whitfield send you?" Just saying his former client's name made anger surge in Wes's veins, and he had to actively relax his fists. For the last two months, he'd poured all of Soteria Security's time and resources into figuring out how someone had bested their top-of-the-line security system and hacked Max Whitfield's tech empire. As thanks, Max and his business nemesis, Cybercore CEO Liam Kearney, had joined their considerable forces and accused Wes of the crime before siccing the FBI on him. Not that he and Whitfield had ever had the fuzziest feelings for one another, but he'd deluded himself into believing there was respect there.

Now, all bets were off.

"Hardly. He's still very upset with you."

Wes hiked his pant leg high enough to reveal his state-of-the-art, tamper-proof ankle monitor. "You can tell him the feeling's mutual."

"I can't actually. I quit last week. Max is no longer my concern."

The announcement surprised him, though he masked it. Lead counsel at Whitfield Industries was the sort of power gig Wes had assumed would need to be pried out of her cold, dead, lawyerly hands. Vivienne's career had always been priority number one. Six years ago, he'd been stupid enough to test that theory, and his hubris had resulted in an incisive verbal flaying, a glorious breakup fuck and her walking right out of their place and onto a plane bound for Yale.

The resulting years of radio silence had come to a crashing halt a year ago, when she'd returned to LA to accept a position as Max Whitfield's legal consigliere.

The current state of their relationship consisted of little more than the coldest of professional acknowledgments and an undercurrent of venom whenever they sporadically ended up in the same meeting.

Of course, now that neither of them worked for Whitfield in any capacity, the thin layer of civility that had coated their professional interactions for the last twelve months was no longer required.

"Then to what do I owe the distinct lack of pleasure?"

Icy amusement arched Vivienne's brow. "I was in the neighborhood."

Dread settled cold and flat in his gut at her ill-timed appearance in his world, but he kept his expression bland. "Terminal Island seems a little outside your usual radius. Are you in the market for clients? Or dates?"

There was no reason it should bother him that her laugh sounded rusty.

"Invectives, Wesley? And to think I was expecting a thank-you for using my kick-ass lawyer skills to get you out on bail."

Not good. Not fucking good at all. "You're not my lawyer."

She wasn't his anything. Not anymore.

"Well, I believe you were made aware that Deni-sof Price Goldberg is no longer interested in repre-senting you going forward."

Ha. The bastards couldn't disassociate fast enough. DPG had dumped his ass almost the moment he'd been arrested, citing conflict of interest with their ongoing role as counsel to Soteria Security.

Proof that his company, the one he'd built with brains and sweat and sacrifice, was disassociating. It was what he and his partner, Jesse Hastings, had agreed to when they'd been making contingency plans, something they'd written into the contract when they'd incorporated. Just one of many business-first precautions—a *what-if* that was never supposed to happen.

Wes gave a terse nod. "I was."

That, he'd been expecting. What he *hadn't* been expecting was the hesitancy by several other large law firms—all directly or indirectly affiliated with some of Soteria Security's biggest clients—to also balk at the idea of representing him.

Blackballed. Whitfield and Kearney wielded their clout with devastating precision, he'd give them that.

"I wasn't, however, made aware that I had new representation."

Something flashed across her face that he might have labeled remorse if he hadn't known that Vivi-enne was incapable of it.

The odd look was replaced with haughty disdain as she straightened to her full height. In her heels, she was only about two inches shorter than his six-three. "So how did you think you got released today? Magic legal fairies?"

"I figured my assistant had finally hired someone." Wes aimed for an offhand shrug. "We had a very promising meeting scheduled with one of LA's most elite attorneys. You might have seen his picture on some of the bus stop benches downtown."

He was only half joking. Because every cell in his body was screaming at him to back away from the woman in front of him, his freedom be damned.

The two of them had imploded in spectacular fashion last time they'd been in each other's orbit. It had fucked him up for longer than he cared to admit. And if he was going to clear his name, if he was going to get his company back, he couldn't afford even the slightest distraction.

"So you're saying you'd rather hire some hack ambulance chaser who will be thoroughly outmatched by the elite law team representing your former company than be represented by me?"

"Yes." That was *exactly* what he was saying.

She blanched, and against his will, Wes found himself trying to soften the blow. "You're a corporate lawyer, not criminal defense."

So fucking weak, and she knew it, too.

Determination manifested itself in the set of her chin. "I can do this, Wes."

The use of his name threw him off. Slipped beneath his defenses. Crawled under his skin.

His blue eyes cut to her dark ones. "As a rule, I

don't like to mix current business and former plea-sure. Things tend to get messy."

Vivienne pressed the remote starter in her hand, and the glossy Vanquish S Coupe behind her purred to life. It was a gorgeous car. Sleek and sexy, just like its owner.

Tendrils of unease fisted around his spine as she pulled the door open for him.

"Doesn't matter if you like it, Brennan. I'm all you've got."

And *that* was exactly what he was afraid of.

Wes looked good.

Vivienne sent a covert glance at her passenger as they zipped over the suspension bridge that led to the 110 and back into LA proper.

In fact, he looked better than good, considering.

She had to strangle a macabre laugh. *Considering*. A bland euphemism for being arrested, having your assets seized and losing your cybersecurity business and your reputation in one fell swoop.

She'd worried that he'd look different, that prison might have irreparably changed him. It was the one thing he'd vowed would never happen—ending up in jail, like his deadbeat father. But now it had.

And yet, as far as she could see, the only outward evidence of his ordeal was ten days' worth of facial hair and a slightly wrinkled suit that fit him to per-fection—an ode to both the breadth of his shoulders and the skill of his tailor.

Wes had come face-to-face with his greatest fear and emerged sexily disheveled.

An unwelcome heat prickled across her skin, some kind of carnal nostalgia, and she shifted against the black leather bucket seat like it was a lightning rod that could dissipate the sudden charge of attraction inside the Aston Martin.

She was desperate to pop the bubble of awareness that had so easily consumed her, but her haste made her careless and the conversational pin she chose was a mistake.

"How is…everyone?"

Bland pleasantries with anyone else, but between them, the question felt shockingly personal.

Wes's shoulders stiffened. He obviously hadn't expected her to go there either.

The fact that Vivienne found she cared about the answer—after so many years of purposefully not thinking about his mother, his sister, *him*—stung more than she'd expected. Like she'd accidentally ripped a scab off her heart.

"What are you doing?"

She didn't know. She'd returned from her annual three-day pilgrimage to the Phoenix Inn, a little B&B in Connecticut, to the news that her boss had put Wesley in the FBI crosshairs. She'd quit her dream job and spent the last week pouring everything she had into getting him out of jail. She'd called in every favor, pushed her legal acumen to the brink, wheedled, cajoled, outsmarted and insomnia-ed in anticipation of this moment. And now that it was here, now that he was free...*ish*...she had no answer to his question, no explanation that wouldn't reveal more than she wanted to give. He was a weakness she couldn't afford. He always had been.

"It's called small talk. It's a form of politeness that acquaintances use to fill the silence."

Wes's sudden grin dominated her peripheral vision and tightened Vivienne's hands on the steering wheel. She remembered a time it wasn't quite so mocking.

A time when a flash of it was all it took for her to surrender her panties in the unisex bathroom at Señor Taco's a mere two hours and three tequilas after her roommate had dragged her across campus to the lamest of frat parties. Then they'd headed back to her dorm room for orgasms two, three and four, and woken up the next morning wrapped around each other and well on their mutual way to orgasm number five.

Wes hadn't been wearing a suit then. Just a white T-shirt that seemed to glow against the tan he'd acquired doing manual labor in the California sun, a pair of faded jeans that were soft from washing, the worn fabric hugging thighs thick with muscle, and *that smile*. The one that gave her the kind of XXX butterflies that skipped her abdomen altogether and headed straight for her—

"Oh, is that what we are? *Acquaintances?*" He sneered the word.

Viv forced air into her lungs and kept her glance dismissive. "Would you prefer something more colorful?" After a quick shoulder check, she maneuvered the sports car into the far left lane. "Former paramours? Scorned exes?" Her voice broke, and she had to clear her throat to finish her list. "Star-crossed lovers?"

Wes blew out an audible breath, tinged with defeat. "Acquaintances it is," he conceded. "You going to tell me where we're going?"

The moment of truth.

"My place."

For the first time since he'd gotten in the car, she was in his sights. She could feel the burn of his stare on her profile. "I don't think so."

Vivienne's spine hardened with resolve. She wasn't that idealistic, lovestruck girl anymore, and he was no longer the object of her affection. No amount of reminiscing—sentimental or erotic—was going to change that fact. She was a lawyer. He needed a lawyer. And that was that.

"As a computer wizard and a flight risk, there were a couple of provisos I had to agree to in order to get you out on bail."

He resettled his big frame against the passenger seat, a whisper of fabric on leather, but the flex of his fist against his muscled thigh belied his calm exterior. "No tech. No internet. No travel beyond the range of my ankle monitor. I got the speech, Vivienne. Stop stalling"

The sound of her full name on his lips was a bullet to the heart. Taciturn and austere, with no flicker of the heat that used to burn strong and insatiable between them.

Tangible proof the past was gone.

And the present was a cold, hard bitch.

Just like me, she reminded herself, buoying her resolve.

"In addition to those stipulations, you've also been remanded into my care until the trial."

"Fuck that."

There was no particular emphasis in his words, but that didn't make his shock less palpable. It was a living thing in the confines of the luxury car. The air around them crackled with the restless energy of it.

"Should I turn around then? I can call ahead to make sure your cell is ready by the time we arrive."

She felt him bristle at the constraints of his current situation, as though his essence was pacing the car like a caged lion, testing the bars for weaknesses. It didn't take him long to realize there was no escape. Wes had always been a staunch realist.

The charged silence of his acceptance oozed over her skin, thick and uncomfortable, unbroken aside from the soft rush of the air-conditioning and the muttered curse that crossed his lips.

She refused to label the loosening in her chest, because it felt a little too much like relief for her own peace of mind. She arched an eyebrow in his direction. "Good to know my company still ranks higher than incarceration."

"Just barely," he mumbled, and with that unflattering summation, he purposefully and studiously ignored her for the rest of the trip which, thanks to the notorious LA traffic, took three times as long as it should have.

Not that it mattered. His opinion didn't concern her, and he'd proven a long time ago that he wasn't susceptible to anything as basic as human emotion, so the state of his *feelings* was irrelevant. Vivienne was going to set things right, and his cooperation was neither essential nor desired. She would do what needed to be done, and once she had, she could finally lance this painful, recurring boil that sprang up every time their lives intersected.

Besides, Vivienne reasoned, flipping on the signal light, his silence was no more than she deserved.

She was, after all, the reason he'd gone to jail in the first place.

CHAPTER TWO

WES HAD SPENT a lot of years convinced that prison was his worst nightmare.

He'd had only a vague notion of what it meant to be locked up back then, but he was intimately familiar with how it affected those you left behind. He'd watched his mother wait for his father, first with dreamy idealism, then with stalwart resolution, and finally with glassy, narcotic-numbed indifference. At six years of age, Wes had promised himself he'd never end up like his dad, never do that to his own family.

His scoff was silent and self-directed. He'd managed to keep only half that bargain, and on a technicality, no less. Because he didn't have a family of his own. Ironic, then, that his punishment was to be a court-enforced game of playing house with Vivienne Grant.

Maybe jail hadn't been so bad after all.

The erroneous thought hit him just as Vivienne glided the luxury automobile into its designated spot in the underground parking garage of her high-rise condominium.

The building was posh. Top-of-the-line. The kind of place he'd been determined to be able to afford for her one day. Their relationship had been long dead by the time he'd reached that goal.

She'd changed a lot since then, a lifetime ago, but not this. Not her easy familiarity with the best the world had to offer.

There were some physical differences, of course, but nothing that couldn't easily be attributed to the passage of time.

A sleek, straight haircut, a rigidly professional wardrobe, and the daring glint in her eyes had mellowed and morphed into confident determination.

But the shift from the girl he'd loved to the woman he resented wasn't in her surroundings, or her appearance, so much as a tectonic shift in her *essence*. As though some part of the Vivienne he'd known had not made it through the carnage.

She was still a force to be reckoned with, but there was nothing scattershot about her anymore. She was laser focused. Precise. A corporate warrior who'd abandoned the volatile bow and flaming arrow of her youth in favor of the cold, exact steel of a scalpel. And her new weapon of choice suited her well. So well that Wes wondered if his memories of her, wild and reckless and overwhelming, were mistaken. The woman getting out of the car seemed impenetrable to him, an avatar.

Wes closed the door on his useless musings and followed her through the parking garage toward the elevator, the staccato beat of her heels bouncing in the cavernous structure lined with expensive cars. He watched as Vivienne swiped a small fob in front of the receiver before dropping her keys into her purse. The brass door slid open to reveal the elevator car, paneled in dark, carved wood that had been polished to a gleaming shine. An intricate brass handrail bordered the interior, glinting in the diffused light of the crystal chandelier.

Since he was closer, Wes lifted his hand to press the button before realizing that he didn't know where she lived.

Vivienne slanted him a glance that felt significant, before she reached past him and pressed the button numbered 37 with a perfectly manicured finger. Scarlet.

The spicy, sultry fragrance of her signature scent hit him in the gut. Made especially for her at the same little French *parfumerie* that her mother used to frequent. He wasn't sure if he liked the fact that the stranger beside him still smelled like Viv.

Wes took a self-preserving step backward. "I promised you the day we met that I'd never use my tech skills to find out anything about you," he reminded her.

He knew it was the wrong thing to say the second it came out of his mouth, even before her spine stiffened and accusation flooded her eyes. Despite his best intentions, all he'd managed to do was conjure the ghost of another vow he'd made to her, one that he'd reneged on.

Promise me, Wes, that no matter what, I'll always

be more important to you than work. That we'll al-
ways put each other first.

Stupid, childish notions that had been selfishly
asked and callously disregarded.

But obviously not forgotten.

"How very chivalrous of you, Wesley." His name
on her lips dripped with scorn.

She wasn't so bad with invectives herself.

Any other time, he'd be glad the building was
too distinguished to subject them to Muzak, but not
today. Not when the silence between them was thick
with tension. With history.

Hell, he'd have given his left nut for a little soft
jazz right now, and he *hated* soft jazz.

This wasn't going to work. Them. Together.

Not if the past was going to haunt them like this.
And how could it not?

You've been remanded into my care until the trial.

What the hell had she been thinking accepting
that deal? And what the hell was he doing, going
along with it, like the proverbial lamb?

When they passed the twentieth floor, Wes pulled
the shell of his phone out of his suit jacket.

He popped it open and removed two thin plastic rods that could pass as part of the casing in any
reputable scan.

As they approached the twenty-fifth floor, he
screwed them together and stepped up to the elevator controls, inserting the tool into the small hole at
the bottom of the brass panel. With a quick push, the

latch released. From there, he popped open the plate
and set to work.

Wes could sense the moment that her interest
piqued, could tell that she was leaning to the side in
an attempt to see around him. Even pissed at him,
Vivienne's curiosity had always gotten the better of
her. He shifted his shoulders to block her view—and
the security camera's—so neither could see what he
was doing. Wes disabled the coax cable for the camera first, then bypassed the alarm. They'd just passed
the thirtieth floor.

"What the hell are you doing?"

"I'm pretty sure that's my line," he countered, his
fingers on the wires as he watched the floor count
tick upward. Then he unplugged the twisted-pair
cable—blue and white—just as the thirty-sixth floor
lit up, and the elevator juddered to an early halt. The
chandelier swayed above them, tinkling in the silence
as he shoved the pieces of his phone back into his
pocket and turned to face his quarry.

"Why'd you get me out?"

She owed him that answer, and they weren't going
anywhere until he got it.

"This couldn't have waited until we got to my
apartment?"

No way was he giving her full home-court advantage. Hell, he never should have gotten into her
vehicle in the first place. In his desperation to get
as far from FCI Terminal Island as possible, he'd
failed to play this obscene scenario out to its obviously doomed conclusion.

Sloppy.

And if there was one thing he prided himself on, it was not being sloppy.

"I'm more comfortable in small spaces these days."

If Wes didn't know better, he'd have thought she flinched at the bleakness of the jibe, but before he could be sure, her expression deadened. She shook her head. Disappointed in him.

Well, welcome to the fucking club. He'd let someone get the drop on him, and he'd ended up in handcuffs for that oversight. Now he was out for himself, and the rules no longer applied.

"I'm so glad you enjoyed your time in the slammer, because if you keep this up, you'll be going straight back." She lifted her fingers to her temple, as though a sudden headache had struck.

"My God, Wes. You've been out for less than an hour, and you've already hacked an elevator!" Viv's helpless laugh held a note of desperation as she gestured at the missing control panel. "And here I thought maybe, just maybe, you'd care that you're the target of a federal investigation. That for once in your damn life, you wouldn't flout the rules just to prove that you could."

That's what she thought this was about? A jab at authority?

"I'm sorry. Am I not being rescued right? I'd hate to deviate from your script. I know how much you hate it when your plans go slightly awry."

"What I hate is your single-minded devotion to

making sure everything ends up awry, whether it's my plan or not!" Her brown eyes were sharp with accusation. "Do you have any idea how serious this is? Max Whitfield is a very powerful man. Never mind that Liam Kearney has joined forces with him to end you. They think you screwed them both over. This is personal to them. They can ensure your whole life falls apart. Do you get that?"

"My whole life has already fallen apart!" The words snapped in the tight confines of the elevator car with a heat he couldn't contain. Fury sparked in his blood, lightning in search of a conduit.

He wasn't afraid of Whitfield and Kearney. He didn't give a shit about the FBI. His life's work was about to be taken from him, the company he'd built out of nothing and sacrificed everything—*everyone*—for. And he'd be damned if he'd stand by and watch it all go to hell.

"And how is being in jail for the rest of your natural life going to help that?"

"I'm not going to sit around and let this happen!" And if she didn't understand that about him, then she'd never really known him. The realization that maybe she hadn't lent a dangerous edge to his voice. "If I don't fight this, I will have *nothing* left. Do you understand that? Nothing to show for all the years I poured into building Soteria Security from the ground up." He didn't want to look at her in that moment, but he couldn't look away. "I gave up *everything*."

The word was layered in the bitterness that always

coated the resurrected memories of her, of *them*, he'd worked so hard to bury.

"Oh please. As if anything in your life has ever meant more to you than work."

His body vibrated with the fight, and he stepped closer, exploiting his height advantage.

"I'm not asking for your permission, Vivienne, and you'd do best to stay out of my way. Someone fucked me over, and I *will* make them pay."

He was riled up now, chest heaving, every breath fueling the fire, the anger, inside him. But Vivienne didn't heed the warning. Instead, she fed the flame.

In the span of a heartbeat, Wes's shoulders hit the elevator wall, and before his brain had fully registered that she was clutching a fistful of his shirt, her purse hit the ground and she surged onto her toes, crushing her mouth to his in a bruising, rage-fueled kiss.

Yes. The word blazed through his blood. Through his body.

Wes dragged her close as he reversed their positions, shoving her back against the carved wood. He opened his mouth over hers, angling for more, more of her tongue in his mouth, more of the heat coursing through his veins, more of the way she consumed him.

He'd been expecting fight.

Prepared for flight.

And then she'd gone and blown his mind by choosing fuck.

Her hands were frantic, shoving at his jacket, and

he let go of her to help pull it down his arms, fighting free of the confines.

She broke the kiss as she yanked his shirt out of his pants, and Wes tried to catch his breath, to slow the roar of his blood and the heaving of his lungs, but he was too far gone. Too far in. He needed it. Needed this.

Her hands worked the buttons on his shirt and he shoved his fingers in her hair, anchoring his palms on either side of her face so he could taste her again.

High voltage.

Lit gasoline.

It had been too long since he'd touched her.

He craved this, the slide of her tongue against his, the rake of her nails down his bare chest.

The confines of the elevator filled with the harbingers of sex: the rasp of their breathing, the clank of his belt, the rush of his blood in his ears, the scrape of his zipper.

Fuck yes.

Her fingers galvanized him, and his cock pulsed in time with the thick beat of his heart.

She made a sound in the back of her throat, a needy hitch that he recognized, and just like that, they were *them* again. It erased the distance, the fights, the years between them, and he hated her for the power she held over him. But he couldn't resist it, either.

He'd never been able to resist her.

With a growl, he pulled his mouth from hers and spun her to face the wall. Her hands came up to press against the wood and she turned her head. Despite the desire pounding through his veins, he was transfixed for a moment by her profile, her long lashes at half-mast, the quick tug of her teeth against her full bottom lip. He did his best not to ruin the gold zipper that ran the length of her spine as he yanked it out of his way with less finesse than he'd have liked, but he was desperate for her skin, for the constellation of beauty marks high on her shoulder blade, just to the right of her bra strap, that he used to idly connect into a star pattern, sometimes with his finger, sometimes the tip of his tongue, back when they used to kiss and talk and fuck the night away.

He shoved the material out of the way to reveal them, tracing them with his thumb before dipping his head and blazing the same trail with his mouth. Vivienne shivered under the hot swipe of his tongue before turning to face him, her delicate shoulder blades pressed against the dark wood, and just like that, she was pulling her top down, revealing her black mesh bra with strategically placed seaming, and he was pulling her skirt up, baring creamy thighs and matching panties. The red dress bunched around her waist as they met in the middle.

There was relief bound up in the heat that slammed through his body. She'd always had a thing for delicate, sexy underthings, the kind that could send a man to his knees. Not everything about her had changed.

Wes grasped her by the back of her thighs and hoisted her up until she was balanced on the brass railing. She wrapped her legs around his waist, high heels digging into his ass, urging him closer. His hips lurched forward, and she bit his lip as their bodies made contact, skin to skin.

Everything got mixed up then. Past. Present. Anger. Desire. Right. Wrong.

And Wes was powerless to do anything but feel it all as he tugged her delicate panties out of his way and slid deep into the slick heat between her legs.

It was heaven. The kind that would invariably end with a long, slow descent into hell, but in that moment, in Viv's arms, he didn't care. He just gave in to the burn.

God, it had been forever since she'd had sex like this. The hard punch of lust. The bittersweet edge of desperation. Just the right amount of rough.

Wes had always had a knack for just the right amount of rough.

She'd gotten wet in an instant, the second their mouths had met. Proof that, despite her best efforts to erase the past, her body remembered him—the spiraling ache, the dark, hot friction of them together.

Why it surprised her, she couldn't say. Chemistry had never been their problem. Not back when they'd dated, and not now when she hated him and craved him in equal measure.

She didn't care that she was kind of his lawyer.

She didn't care that she still bore the scars from their breakup.

She just wanted this, the wild that he brought out in her.

The heady pleasure of having Wes hot and hard between her thighs overwhelmed her senses. She breathed him in, tracing the ridges of muscle that lined his shoulders and flexed in his back as they moved together. The rock of his hips made her whole body come alive, pulsing with need.

Vivienne let her head fall back as his mouth traced the sensitive skin of her neck, shocking her with his tongue, surprising her with his teeth, soothing her with his lips.

Heat, wicked and delicious, twisted inside her, peaking her nipples. Every part of her ached to be closer to his big body and she tightened her legs so she could grind against him with each thrust, needing more. More pressure. More everything.

"Harder." The plea fell from her lips, and the answering shift of his muscles as he drove into her with more force blurred the edges of thought until all she could do was feel him. Feel the power they'd unleashed between them.

He'd always done this, pushed her so high, so fast, it made her head spin. She was dizzy with lust and it was so good. So damn good. Then he lifted his head and seized her mouth, and the sharp throb and catch of her inner muscles caught her off guard.

No.

Her imminent pleasure was edged with panic as Viv dragged her right hand down from where it had accidentally ended up tangled in his hair, and shoved it between them to touch herself, working her clit to ensure that later, when she remembered this devastating lapse in judgment, her climax couldn't be traced back to his kiss, but to her own fingers.

Because she wouldn't give him everything. She couldn't. Not again.

And yet, as pleasure swamped her, consumed her, it was his name she cried out, drowning in the intensity. Wes dropped his forehead to her shoulder and gave in to the same pulsing drive that had caught her in its maelstrom. He swore as his hips jerked with his own release. The low, guttural curse imprinted on her brain.

Somewhere at the edge of her consciousness, she knew everything was different between them now, but with her eyes closed his body felt the same, and Vivienne let herself stay there a moment, clinging to memories, as she dragged air into her lungs and settled back into her body.

He lifted his head as her feet touched the floor, and the scrape of his beard against her jaw vanquished the haze of nostalgia and catapulted her back to the present.

Because the Wes in her head didn't have facial hair.

The Wes in her head didn't exist anymore.

Viv loosened the arm she'd anchored around his broad shoulders, and his fingers dug into her waist for a moment before his touch disappeared altogether.

He pushed a hand through his disheveled hair and set to work on the buttons of his shirt as Vivienne slipped her arms through the sleeves of her dress and pulled the top into place, readjusted the skirt so it covered her thighs.

Less than an hour alone with him, and *this* had happened. It was a tale as old as time—an addict and her fix. Six years of personal growth down the tubes, and all she had to show for it was an orgasm.

The soul-melting kind that erased time and space, leaving her wobbly kneed and desperate for more.

God. She needed to get her clothes back on before she begged him to do it again.

"Could you…?"

She turned her back to him, glancing over her shoulder in question. He finished tucking his shirt in before giving her a brusque nod, stepping forward to tug her zipper back up.

Vivienne made a swipe to move her long hair over her shoulder and out of his way, momentarily forgetting she was currently rocking her sleek, angled bob.

The past version of her, the one with long hair, didn't exist anymore either, she reminded herself, ignoring the rasp of her zipper and a thousand memories of other times his big, capable hands had skimmed the curve of her spine…before moving on to more interesting places.

Wes stepped away from her, bending to pick his suit jacket up off the floor. She faced him as he pulled it on.

He frowned, reaching out to tip her chin up and to the left.

"I didn't hurt you, did I?"

Vivienne shook her head, dislodging his finger and tucking her hair behind her left ear. It wasn't completely a lie. She was fine, except for the lurch of her heart when he touched her, but that was entirely of her own doing. Romantic residue that she should have put out of its misery long ago.

Wes's eyes shuttered in the space of a blink. "I should have used a condom."

His words were a jarring crash back to reality.

It was silly to be upset by them, to have wished, for just a brief, foolish second that he'd say something dreamy and quixotic instead.

Vivienne straightened the seams of her dress and notched her chin up, brushing off the bleak reminder that they weren't lovers anymore. Just people who'd given in to baser passions. Strangers. To counteract that weakness, her tone was brusque and business-like. "Is there anything I should know?"

His head snapped up at that, brows drawn together, and his eyes turned to blue flame…not lust anymore. Anger. "You think I would've—" He cut himself off, shook his head. "No." The word reset his expression to neutral, like he'd flipped a switch. "I'm clean."

"Same. And I'm protected," she added, hating that she'd lost control. Despite her IUD, it bothered her that she hadn't learned her lesson all those years ago. Despised that he still held the power to override her better judgment. That she still liked it when he did.

He gave a curt nod.

She ran her hands over her stomach, smoothing imaginary wrinkles from her dress, hating the sympathy clench of her abdominal muscles over the tragic consequences of the last time one of their fights had devolved into a bout of vertical-surface rage sex.

The doomed pregnancy that had heralded the end of them. And Wes didn't even know.

Guilt gnawed at the lining of her stomach, acidic and vile, as it always did when she remembered her own cowardice.

She should have told him. Should have told him before there'd been nothing to tell.

Wes's gaze remained steady on hers as he fixed his collar. It felt for a moment like he could see into her soul, read her darkest secrets and most painful memories. She dropped her eyes, in case he could, and busied herself with retrieving her handbag from the floor. But when she stood up, she could still feel the weight of his stare.

"What?" She wished the question had sounded defensive at least. Not so…searching.

Wes dropped his hand to his side, shook his head like he was clearing the lingering cobwebs of a dream. "Nothing. You just…you kiss different now."

She wanted to ask how. To tell him that he did, too.

To understand exactly why he'd met her mouth with an edge of desperation that she'd been compelled to match and what it meant that kissing him still made her weak in the knees.

Her fingernails dug into her palm around the leather handle of her purse, just enough pain to bring her back to reality. "That's a pretty nuanced take on a hate fuck in an elevator."

"Yeah. I guess I've grown as a person since we were together."

The wry answer brought her head up, but Wes had already moved to the control panel so Vivienne couldn't gauge his expression. Within seconds, everything was back in place, and the elevator had resumed its course. The bell dinged as the car drew to a smooth stop on the thirty-seventh floor.

CHAPTER THREE

HAD SHE ALWAYS lived this damn far from the elevator?

The tastefully bland hallway felt never-ending with Wes following along behind her. Especially when they both smelled like sex. Amazing, animalistic sex. It was almost enough to make her forget that they'd broken up years ago. Or that she'd just picked him up from his unjust stint in prison.

Almost, but not quite.

Her pace slowed as they approached the last door on the left, just as it always did since that day, a little over two months ago, when she'd walked down this hallway, blissfully unaware that her life was about to change. That her security panel had been overridden, and a nondescript envelope was waiting for her on the other side of the door her mysterious visitor had left slightly ajar.

She'd had a brand-new door installed the next day, complete with a dead bolt and a chain lock, as well as a state-of-the-art security camera in the foyer, in case anyone managed to bypass her upgrades. Too little, too late, of course. Her life had already been irreparably thrown off course when she'd curiously ripped into the manila packet.

No, not then.

A moment after that, when she'd decided to follow the neatly typed instructions that accompanied a thumb drive with the Whitfield Industries logo emblazoned on the side of it and a copy of the medical records detailing the lifesaving surgery she'd underwent in the dangerous wake of her ectopic pregnancy that would be made available to *interested parties* if she failed to comply.

The realization that she was being blackmailed turned quickly to panic in an instant, and she'd doubled down on the same decision she'd made years earlier, when she was a scared, pregnant twenty-two-year-old bound for law school. Installing the program on one of Whitfield Industries' computers had seemed so much easier than letting Wes back in her life in any capacity.

And now she had to deal with the consequences of her cowardice—forced proximity with the man she'd been trying so hard to avoid—ironic though they might be.

Vivienne stopped in front of her condo and glanced over her shoulder at her court-appointed houseguest.

Whatever he saw on her face made Wes haul up short. He lifted his hands in surrender, hanging back to give her more space, unaware that inside, she was crying out for the comfort of his arms around her, for just a moment where she could set down her burden and rely on his strength to hold her up.

But that was solace she didn't deserve.

Viv let the misinterpretation stand, accepting the extra distance between them as her due as she stepped up to her access keypad.

She automatically angled her torso to block the numbers from his view — a move he'd taught her— but she realized the pointlessness of it a moment later. After all, he'd built his fortune on testing for weaknesses.

"What did I tell you about using your mom's birthday as your passcode?"

Her shoulders drew tight at the rebuke. "That I might as well not lock the door at all." There was a liberal amount of snark in her voice as she parroted back part of the lecture he'd given her when they'd first started dating.

Which pissed him off, just as she'd intended. "It's a—"

"—top ten guess," she finished, shoving her key in the lock with way more force than was necessary.

"Top five if the thief did the barest amount of research on me," she added, just to goad him. "I remember, okay?" Then the heat left her voice and the dead bolt disengaged with a twist of her wrist. "I just miss her."

The words stole all his righteousness, and she heard him sigh. "Habit," he said, by way of non-apology.

She stole another glance over her shoulder, watching him drag a hand down his beard.

"It's none of my business."

"No. It's not." Vivienne pushed the door out of her way, dropping her keys into her purse so they wouldn't give away the tremor in her hand. This had all seemed so simple when she'd embarked on her plan to get him out of jail. Now that he was here, there was nothing simple about it. "Are you coming in?"

He started, as though he hadn't realized he still hadn't crossed the threshold, as though maybe he was having second thoughts about doing so. Which was fair enough. Because when he finally stepped into the foyer, closing the door behind them, it felt like the whole world had shifted.

Wes was here.

He reset the dead bolt with a thunk.

Slid the chain into place with a rattle.

Ominous sounds that sealed their fate inside these four walls. It hadn't turned out well for them the last time they'd cohabitated. And as she'd proven moments ago, being alone in confined spaces with this particular man had never resulted in her most brilliant decision making.

"You'll have to sleep on the couch." The words fell out of her mouth like a challenge, blunt and abrupt. "I turned the spare room into an office."

Wes just nodded.

His subdued acceptance made her feel churlish,

and she did her best to sound conciliatory. "Make yourself at home. I'm just going to freshen up."

"Sure. Yeah." Wes's gaze had migrated up to the pinhole in the crown molding, where she'd had the camera installed post-envelope. Figured that's where his attention would go. Work had always been the first thing on his mind.

"Motion sensor, or constant feed?"

"Both. Motion alerts come straight to my phone."

When his blue eyes met hers, she could feel his silent approval at that particular security upgrade, and the fact that it warmed her, even now, set off a different kind of alarm in her brain.

How in the hell, after everything they'd been through, could she still care what he thought of her choices?

It took everything she had not to run from the room at the realization.

She counted her steps to keep the strike of her heels against the hardwood floor even, though she granted herself the concession of using the main bathroom, because it was closer than her en suite, and because she was afraid her knees might give out with the effort of appearing unconcerned if she had to fake it for even a second longer.

She slammed the door shut behind her in her haste for privacy. Once it was locked, Vivienne blew out a breath and set her purse on the counter.

Get your shit together, she lectured herself.

Leaning forward, she met her own eyes in the

mirror. Her pupils were large, her hair was mussed, and her lipstick was smeared.

She looked like she'd just been ravaged in an elevator.

She lifted her hand, restoring order and precision to the sharp angle of her bob.

It was just sex with the ex, she assured herself.

No big deal.

Digging into her purse, Vivienne pulled out her small makeup case and extracted a travel pack of makeup wipes and her signature red lipstick, laying them with precision on the marble countertop, as though she was about to scrub for surgery, rather than tackle the faint crimson stain that had migrated outside her lip line.

Tugging one of the disposable cloths free, Viv set about restoring the cool, controlled facade she was known for.

She'd curated a very precise version of herself in the years since they'd been *Wes and Viv*, but today was the first time she'd considered how much he'd changed, too. With his expensive suit and his fancy watch.

All the trappings of his success, so different from the boy she'd known, and yet…

He still had this way of sucking up all the oxygen in the room, dominating her thoughts without even trying. Hell, the aftereffects of him were still fizzing in her blood. Not that she was surprised. That body of his had always affected her like a narcotic.

Even the first time she'd laid eyes on him.

God, he was beautiful. So intense that she couldn't look away.

A tiger in a room full of hyenas. Or more accurately, a man in a room full of drunken frat boys. She'd be surprised later that night, over tacos and tequila, to learn that he was a mere two months more experienced with being twenty than she was, but in that moment, he'd seemed so mature and so above the frat party that Jesse Hastings had all but begged her and her roommate to attend. And the way he'd filled out his white T-shirt and worn jeans hadn't hurt, either.

She'd never believed in instant lust before that night. She'd seen plenty of hot guys who hadn't affected her beyond the clinical acknowledgment of their good-lookingness.

She'd never been desperate to taste any of them.

Mesmerized, she watched him survey his surroundings as he lifted the red plastic cup full of foamy keg beer to his mouth. Frat party booze was cheap and utilitarian, the path of least resistance to drunkenness. Even in the awful lighting—a bunch of neon beer signs and some bargain-basement, light-up disco ball provided by the delusional frat brother with visions of DJ stardom in his future who had cranked up the bass to teeth-jarring levels—she was entranced by his throat, the bob of his Adam's apple as he swallowed, and the way his tongue darted out to catch the remnants of the foam that had dotted his upper lip.

Something warm throbbed to life between her thighs.

Then, as though he sensed her single-minded fascination with him, he turned his head, and their eyes met with a jolt of instant attraction that, a split second earlier, she'd thought only existed in the dirty-sexy romance novels she favored when she could afford to take a study break.

Viv dropped her gaze immediately, heat washing over her skin at being caught staring like some perverted stalker. As much as she wanted to blame the burn on embarrassment, it wasn't *just* that. Beneath the fabric of her short, flirty red dress, her nipples had drawn tight so quickly that it hurt. In the best possible way.

Composing herself, she ventured a peek at him, relieved to find the full weight of his attention remained on her. Whatever the undeniable force that had sprung up between them, he wasn't immune to it either.

Something dark and hot slid through her as he started toward her. He walked with the loose-hipped ease of someone who was comfortable in his skin, and the crowd seemed to part for him as he drew closer. Vivienne couldn't help but notice that there was none of the boastful swagger of a college jock in his approach. Just quiet, determined confidence.

Bam! Lust-struck.

She was thoroughly seduced before he even reached her.

"Seven out of ten." Viv raised her voice to be heard over the thudding bass.

He quirked a brow at the assessment.

"Your approach could use some work. Most guys would have brought me a drink to break the ice."

"Are you here with one?" he asked. His voice was deep and sexy.

"One what?"

He leaned closer under the guise of being heard over the music, and his breath on her jaw was like the lick of a flame. "One of those guys who would have brought you a drink?"

Touché. She dipped her head, hiding her smile. "Maybe I'm keeping my options open." Vivienne looked up at him through her lashes, pouring it on thick. "Or maybe I was waiting for you."

He, on the other hand, didn't even try to hide his lopsided grin, and the flash of white teeth hit her veins like nitroglycerin. "I find that hard to believe."

She shrugged in a way she hoped was mysterious. "Daddy issues. He never put me at the center of his world, so now I sit in the shadows, waiting for someone to notice me." Viv shook her head melodramatically so that he'd assume it was a lie. "It's all very tragic," she assured him.

"Somehow I doubt that you wait around for much."

"Oh yeah?" She reached for his beer, which he relinquished with a smirk, his eyes fixated on her mouth as she took a long sip of the slightly too-warm brew. When it was her turn to lick the foam from her lips, she milked it for all it was worth, reveling in the role of the daring seductress in the short red dress. "Why's that?"

"Because you strike me as the kind of woman who doesn't let anything stand in her way." He tipped his chin to the beer she'd commandeered. "You take what you want."

Oh, and she intended to.

"So?" he asked, taking the cup back from her. Her belly fluttered as he lifted it to his mouth, sipping from the exact same spot that she had. "Do I pass?"

The smile that curved her lips was genuine. He'd run her gauntlet with style and wit. It was exceedingly rare to encounter such advanced verbal chess moves at a frat party, let alone from someone with muscles like his.

"That was a very good answer. I haven't heard that one before." She lowered her voice just enough that he had to lean in to hear her. "Most guys just ask me what I want to drink."

"Maybe that's because you've been wasting your time with slick college douchebags who regurgitate what their textbooks tell them to think." He cast a cursory glance over the drunken crowd. She'd forgotten they weren't the only two people in the world. "Not a truly original thought among them."

Vivienne reminded herself that it was ludicrous to fall a little bit in love with someone whose name you didn't know. Then she gave him a pretty moue. "That's not a very nice way to talk about my friends."

He stepped closer. "Tell me they don't bore you."

"If I confess they do, will you whisk me away to somewhere that will delight and amaze?"

He reached up and set the half-empty beer on the trophy shelf a couple feet above her right shoulder. "I guess that depends."

"On what?"

"On how much you value the artistic merit of tacos."

It might have been the most sublime pickup line she'd ever heard.

"A fellow taco-lover, huh? With so much in common, you'd think we would have crossed paths before now. How come I've never seen you around?"

"Because I'm not a student here."

Interesting. This big, beautiful man was just full of surprises.

"Then what are you doing crashing frat parties and luring co-eds off campus with the promise of delicious Mexican cuisine?"

"Jesse Hastings invited me."

Vivienne grinned. Jesse Hastings was your typical narcissistic son of a senator, nice enough if you got past his penchant for schmoozing and namedropping. The thought of Jesse hanging out with this guy was like imagining a chihuahua hanging out with a Doberman.

"And how do you know Jesse?"

"I landscaped his family's estate."

Well, that certainly explained the muscles.

"And he's my business partner."

Vivienne's eyebrows shot up at the announcement. She hadn't seen that one coming.

"I didn't know Jesse knew how to handle a lawn mower."

"He doesn't. But I know how to bypass a lot of high-tech systems to siphon internet access from a senator's mansion, and Jesse assures me that he has the kind of contacts who can fund talents like mine, if I choose to use them for good."

Vivienne would be lying if she said she wasn't a little turned on by his white-collar, bad-boy tendencies. It was just the right amount of disreputable.

"And do your talents extend beyond hacking into senators' mansions?"

His slow grin made her knees weak. "I consider myself a man of many talents."

And Vivienne was suddenly desperate to experience all of them.

"I'll let you take me for tacos on one condition. You have to promise that you'll never use your computer skills to find out anything about me."

"Well, if I'm not allowed to hack your phone, how am I going to impress you with insider knowledge of all your favorite things?"

"Guess you'll have to find out what I like the old-fashioned way."

His gaze darkened in a way that unleashed a rush of heat in her abdomen.

God, flirting was fun. She sent him her best look of prim admonishment. "I meant with small talk."

He leaned close again, and the world faded away. "No, you didn't."

Perfect. He was absolutely perfect.

She extended her hand and sealed her fate. "I'm Vivienne."

"Wes."

If she hadn't known she was a goner already, she would have the second their palms met, and first contact jolted through her like she'd picked up a downed power line. A mere two hours of small talk later, replete with tacos and tipsy on cheap tequila and lust, they'd consummated their inability to keep their hands off each other in the bathroom at Señor Taco's, before they'd kissed and groped their way back to her dorm room and had their way with each other until the sun rose.

A rather quixotic beginning for where they'd ended up, mired in the technicalities and intricacies of the law.

Vivienne tipped her chin up, examining the whisker burn that had marked up the underside of her jaw.

I didn't hurt you, did I?

She ran her finger along the patch of reddened skin.

They'd hurt each other.

But things didn't have to play out the same way they had. They were older now. Presumably wiser. And this was strictly business.

She'd do well to remember it.

With a reinforcing breath, Vivienne threw the

makeup wipe into the trash bin and straightened the seams of her dress.

It was probably best they'd gotten this out of their systems, she decided, squaring her shoulders as she reached for the tube of lipstick.

She wouldn't let it happen again.

CHAPTER FOUR

YOU KISS DIFFERENT NOW.

Jesus Christ.

Wes barely held back an eye roll at his idiocy.

Hell, she'd all but run from him the second she got inside, leaving him to wander around her place as though he gave a shit about home decor.

As though he didn't still have lust coiling in his belly. As though his fingers didn't itch to pull her close. *Jesus.* He was so wound up you'd think they hadn't just screwed each other senseless. He wanted her all over him. Naked. Panting. Begging him for more. Or hell, he'd do the begging...

Wes raked a hand through his hair and did his best to focus on something less dangerous than his rekindled lust for Vivienne Grant.

Predictably, his mind turned to work. Or at least what he would have considered work before he'd become a disgraced cybersecurity specialist with nothing to his name.

The cameras in the hallway were almost undetectable, which impressed him, but the coverage pattern left a lot to be desired.

So far, he'd rate the building's security as *decent*. Which wasn't nearly good enough considering the caliber of vehicles in the parking garage. The elevator had been laughably easy to override, and the security panels on the doors they passed wouldn't take much more effort to crack. A skilled burglar could clean up.

He'd shore up a few things while he was here. And change her goddamn password.

Christ. Dead mothers' birthdays could get you into houses, safes, bank accounts...especially if the mark had lost hers young, like Vivienne had.

Not that he was that surprised by the reversion. Viv had always been sentimental—to the point of packrat-itis.

That was probably why he still hadn't made it past the foyer.

"Make yourself at home," she'd said, but the words struck a dissonant chord in his brain.

They'd shared a tiny apartment while she was finishing her undergrad at UCLA and he was still busting his ass landscaping, trying to get Soteria Security off the ground. Back then, when being with her had been his version of "home," Vivienne had stuffed their space with nostalgia—framed photos of friends, mementos from trips, the blanket her mother had knit.

This place was sterile. Barren.

It had less personality than some hotel rooms he'd been in.

Wes ventured farther into the condo, reminding himself that she wasn't his concern anymore. She hadn't been for a long time now.

But the truth of that didn't stop him from taking in her home through the lens of their past. To his left was a professional chef's wet dream—way too much kitchen for a woman who used to pride herself on how many take-out places' numbers she knew by heart. Straight ahead sat a spacious living room/dining room combo with a killer view of the city. Vivienne had always been a sucker for a view.

Dark wood floors, light taupe walls, an uninviting, high-backed cream couch. Nothing in the bold hues she used to favor.

Hell, even the meticulously hung abstract paintings that dotted the walls were drab. Which, he assured himself, was the only reason his gaze snagged on the single punch of pigment in the bland suite—a vase of wilted tiger lilies centered on the fancy dining room table.

It certainly wasn't because he'd given her some before their first official date—Viv insisted that the night they'd met at that stupid frat party, which they'd bailed on to get drunk at a divey little Mexican joint before consummating their lust in the unisex bathroom and then groping their way back to her dorm room so they could love each other until the sun came up, didn't really count as a date.

Either way, it still ranked as one of the best nights of his life.

So when he'd shown up the next night to take her to a movie, armed with a bouquet of orange blooms, it had been a joke, a callback to her taco-and-margarita-fueled rant about flowers being a cop-out gift. "The pinnacle of generic present giving," she'd called them. "Little more than socially accept-able thoughtlessness."

He'd been hooked on her right from the start.

The way she'd stared down her nose at them when she'd opened the door.

"Flowers?"

"The perfect flowers, yes." He held them out to her, but she made no move to accept them.

"You're pretty, but you don't listen so good, huh?"

"Oh, I listen just fine. And what I heard is that the wrong guys have been giving you flowers."

The unimpressed arch of her eyebrow stoked his competitive streak. "Because *you're* the right guy to give me flowers?"

"No." Wes stepped closer. "I'm just the guy who's giving you the *right* flowers."

Something subtle shifted in her eyes at the dis-tinction. She finally accepted them. "And how come these made you think of me?"

Wes held up a finger. "Because they're beautiful."

She didn't bother to temper her eye roll. "And the same color as cheese, apparently."

Undeterred, he held up a second finger. "Because they're named after a sleek, dangerous predator."

She was adorable when she scoffed. "So I'm a tiger, and that makes you what? My helpless sex antelope?"

Smart and smart-mouthed. The desire to kiss her was overwhelming, but he couldn't afford the distraction. Not when she was so close to being charmed.

"And last but not least—" Wes raised a third finger "—they're ballsy as hell."

Heedless of her present, she crossed her arms, and the cellophane crinkled as it got trapped under her elbow. "Oh, this I can't wait to hear."

"These flowers are cat-killers. Notoriously toxic for felines and yet they're named after one. That's some hard-core badassery, right there."

She uncrossed her arms and looked at the flowers, as though reassessing. "That's the story you're going with? That I remind you of a sleek, dangerous, pet-murdering predator?"

Wes placed a hand on either side of her door frame and leaned forward, waiting until she lifted her gaze from the bouquet to him. "A *beautiful*, sleek, dangerous, pet-murdering predator." He took a step closer. "Don't forget beautiful."

Something sparked in her chocolate-colored eyes, the heat of it turning them melty and inviting, and his blood picked up. "Is it weird that I'm kind of turned on by that description?"

God, this woman. Wes hoped his shrug looked casual, even as his knuckles whitened against the jamb, his restraint as thin as a razor's edge. "I mean, I dared to hope."

"Also, I have a very strong urge to donate a large sum of money to a local cat shelter."

"We could stop on the way to the movie," he suggested, his voice low and rough with anticipation born of the way she was sizing him up. Like a tigress.

"Definitely. We should definitely do that. But I have to take care of something first."

Heat arced between them, and Wes dropped his hands to his sides. It took everything in him not to reach for her. "I'm pretty tall. You want help reaching a vase?"

Her answering smile was slow and naughty. "Not exactly." She fisted a hand in his T-shirt and tugged him through the doorway. "C'mere, sex antelope. I feel an ambush coming on."

They never had made it to that movie.

And they'd celebrated every birthday, every anniversary, every *just because* with tiger lilies and sex for the next two years.

Until it had all shattered under them...

The sound of Vivienne's heels against the hardwood yanked him out of his reverie in time to see her striding toward him in pristine condition.

Her hair had been smoothed, erasing any hint that he'd had his hands in it, and the whisker burn he'd left on her jaw seemed less red, thanks to her stellar makeup skills, he assumed, taking in her precisely applied lipstick, no longer smeared from his mouth. In seven and a half minutes, she'd managed to erase the past.

He'd do well to follow her lead, he realized, as she stopped in front of him.

Instead, Wes gave in to the perverse urge to reach out and stroke a finger down the cold glass of the vase that contained the six drooping lilies, their orange petals limp and curling as they wilted in the murky, fetid water. Not unlike their relationship.

"Is this symbolism for my benefit?"

Something stark flashed across Vivienne's face. "It's been a long time since 'your benefit' played any role in my life decisions."

Wes tried not to let it bother him when she slid the bouquet out of his reach. He shoved his hands into his pockets, but he ignored the warning to drop the subject. "And yet my presence here would suggest the opposite."

Silence crowded the space between them, so thick that Vivienne had to punch through it. Unlike him, she'd never liked the quiet.

"Are you hungry? I think there's some leftover takeout in the fridge."

A slow, mocking smile tilted the corner of his mouth at the dodge, but he followed her as she retreated into the high-end galley kitchen. "So this is how it's going to be now?"

She lifted her brows, feigning ignorance over her shoulder, but he didn't buy it for a second. Vivienne was way too smart to play dumb.

"That might work on strangers, but I know you better than anyone."

She froze with her hand on the refrigerator door,

and a wry smile twisted her lips. "And you don't know me at all. Not anymore."

The stark truth of that settled around them, like ash. It was all kind of poetic, Wes decided. That they'd end up here, as fun house–mirror versions of themselves. Older and wiser but shoved back into the same constraints—her with some grand plan; him with nothing to his name. The first time they'd been alone together in years had ended up just like the last time they'd been alone together.

When she'd given him the *your-business-or-me* ultimatum and called him "a money-obsessed workaholic," and he'd chosen his business over her and told her she was "so goddamn selfish," and then they'd banged each other's brains out up against the wall of their cozy apartment one last time. Before he'd walked out of her life. Before she'd hopped a plane out of his.

It had been a long time since he'd let himself think about their spectacular crash and burn, but today, he couldn't stop thinking about it.

He realized, in that moment, with his body still buzzing from the contact high, what a colossal mistake elevator sex had been. Instead of getting her out of his system, it made him want things he'd thought he'd exorcised ages ago.

"Don't do that." Vivienne let her hand drop from the stainless steel handle and stepped away from the fridge. "Don't reassess how we ended up here. This isn't one of your security systems. You can't work backward through the problem and figure out where it all went wrong. You can't reset this. We were hot for each other, and it flamed out."

Her shrug was insultingly dispassionate. "The experiment failed. It's time to accept it and move on. We didn't even last long enough to get to the part where we got bored with each other."

"Is that what you think? That if we were this far in, I wouldn't want you anymore?"

Something raw and painful crossed her face. "Please. By now we'd be scheduling sex. Every second Friday, like clockwork. I'd have to break out the sexy panties."

Lies. If nothing else, the elevator had proven that. "All your panties are sexy," he offered, trying to diffuse the uncomfortable tension vibrating between them like an out-of-tune guitar string.

"Life gets in the way." Her voice was soft. "We're nothing if not proof of that."

The philosophical detachment stoked his anger, and his words held more heat than he'd intended. "So that's it, then? We just pretend like what happened didn't happen?"

Something almost wistful flitted across her features, but she tamped it down. "We're not pretending it didn't happen, Wes." When she met his eyes, hers were stone-cold. "We're just not pretending that it meant anything."

Back to the status quo. Cool politeness. Respectable distance.

He had to remind himself that was how he wanted it.

"Now," she tucked her hair behind both her ears, "am I your lawyer, or not?"

The challenge was quintessentially Viv. And despite the excuses he'd flung at her in the prison parking lot, he knew there was only one answer for a smart man in immense legal peril. "You are."

Her nod was almost...relieved? "Then if you'll excuse me, I have a lot of work to do on your case. There's bedding in the linen closet beside the bathroom if you want to make up the couch."

And with that, she turned and disappeared around the corner, leaving Wes with the distinct impression that, despite the square footage, there was no space in her house for anyone else.

CHAPTER FIVE

AND PURSUANT TO these charges, legalese, legalese, blah, blah, blah.

With a silent scream of frustration, Vivienne braced her elbows on her desk and dropped her head into her hands. Her legendary ability to plow through piles of legal documents had abandoned her, as though her tireless obsession with Wes's case had fallen victim to her less welcome preoccupation with the man himself.

He took up space. In her house. In her mind. And because he didn't fit there anymore, it was distractingly noticeable. She'd been at this for hours, trying to figure out how to get the charges dropped, but she couldn't focus. Couldn't forget that there was only a wall between her and the defendant.

Well, a wall and six years of growing in opposite directions.

With a sigh, she glanced at the clock in the lower right corner of her screen. It was just past midnight.

Shutting everything down, she undocked her laptop and stuffed it into its padded case. Wes's release was contingent on her not giving him access to any electronics, although the precaution of hiding her computer felt like too little too late, considering that he'd already bypassed an elevator...not to mention her newest lingerie.

Vivienne squeezed her thighs together at the inconvenient flutter low in her belly and shoved the dirtier bent of her thoughts aside. Great sex might have been enough to sustain a relationship when she was twenty-two, but it wasn't enough for her now. And there was too much history between them to entertain the notion of the strictly carnal, no-emotions-allowed fling that her hormones were currently begging her to consider. Best to forget their lapse in judgment altogether.

Reaching beneath her desk, Viv fished her Louboutins out from under her desk, where she'd kicked them off earlier, and got to her feet.

She wasn't proud of the tentative way she opened the door. The exhale of relief when the living room was dark and silent.

Wanting her visitor to get some sleep was just being a good hostess, she assured herself. It certainly had nothing to do with avoiding any further run-ins with her big, sexy houseguest.

And she repeated that lie to herself over and over as she crept silently down the hallway, with her laptop under one arm and her shoes in the other hand.

Only after she'd pushed her bedroom door closed behind her with the softest *click* she could manage, did she allow herself a full breath. It had been a hell of a day.

Vivienne padded across the plush beige carpeting and into her walk-in closet. She placed the nude pumps back into their designated spot—third from the left on the rack allocated for work-appropriate shoes with heels three inches or higher—before crossing to a rainbow collection of handbags. Although she was alone, guilt lent a furtiveness to her actions as she reached up to pull her blush Chanel 2.55 handbag down from the shelf so she could hide her laptop behind it. The chain caught on something, and a black shoebox came crashing down, spilling its contents beside her feet.

She froze, heart pummeling her ribs as she tried to listen for Wes over the sound of her racing pulse. After a long, tense moment of silence that assured her that the noise hadn't disturbed him, she lowered herself to the floor.

And came face-to-face with her and Wes's past. Various sundries littered the carpet, including a pressed tiger lily from their official first date, a Señor Taco's matchbook from their unofficial first date, a bunch of silly photos of them and their friends that she'd removed from frames years ago, and the reason she was mired in this court-mandated Greek tragedy in the first place—a hospital bracelet with her name on it.

Ghosts of a future that wasn't to be.

Vivienne stuffed the offending mementos into the box and put it back on the shelf, next to her laptop. She didn't need to linger over them to know that she'd made a lot of mistakes in her life. But getting Wes's bogus charges dropped would make everything okay. Even the score between them. Her lie had gotten him into this mess. Her skill would get him out. And then she could cram all these unwanted feelings back in that damn shoebox with the rest of the things she couldn't bring herself to let go of and get back to her normal life.

With a nod, she shoved her designer handbag up on the shelf, blocking the memories and her computer from view.

Vivienne reached behind her, tugging on her zipper as she walked back into her room. She stopped in front of the ornate cheval mirror in the corner and stepped out of her dress. But even as she tossed it over the nearby antique chair, her gaze remained fixed on the mirror.

Her body looked different to her, tonight. Softer somehow. In addition to the whisker burn along her jaw, Wes had left his mark on her right breast. She lifted her hand and ran the pad of her finger across it, wondering if she'd left traces of herself on him, too.

It had always been like that between them— incendiary—even that first night.

She'd had sex only with her high school boyfriend before Wes—and while Rob had been sweet and kind and she had no regrets, they'd mostly fumbled around in the dark, equal parts nerves and hormones. Too young, she thought in retrospect, and not equipped to deal with the emotional ramifications of what they'd done. But Wes…

Vivienne let her finger drift along the curve of her cleavage.

Wes had been a different level all together. While she hadn't fully felt like a woman that night, he'd seemed all man to her. Their frantic fuck in the ta-queria bathroom had been hot and sexy and panty-meltingly good, but it was later, back at her dorm room, when they'd had the time and space to worship each other's bodies that crept back into her fantasies every now and again.

She hadn't been ready for the sight of him, the rush of warmth between her legs that had come from watching him take off his clothes.

Goose bumps broke out across her décolletage as Vivienne removed her bra, and her breasts tingled at the memory.

She'd been mesmerized by his body, his shoulders thick with muscle, his hands, roughened by work and tanned by the sun, veins prominent along the backs of them, and up his forearms. He used to landscape back then, to help take care of his mom and his lit-tle sister and to fund his dreams of world domina-tion, and the hours of manual labor showed in all the best ways. His abs were a masterpiece, and while his chest was smooth, there was a trail of hair that drew her eyes downward from his navel toward the bulge of his erection.

Vivienne let her hand wander down past her own navel, watching the flush of her skin in the mirror as her fingers trekked lower. She licked her lips as she breached the gathered waistband.

He'd touched her like he knew what he was doing, like he wasn't in a hurry, like she was safe with him…but not too safe.

That edge of danger was like catnip. Addictive. She'd tried to make it into a cliché in the intervening years, tell herself it was nothing more than dating a guy from the wrong side of the tracks. The thrill came from the fact that her father wouldn't approve…or at least he wouldn't have if Harold Grant had cared enough to notice anything going on in her life. If he'd cared about something besides his eponymous law firm. If he'd looked up from work for even a second to see how much she'd needed him, needed someone to help her through the loss of her mother.

But it had been a long time since she'd given a damn what her father thought.

Then again, she'd thought it had been a long time since she'd given a damn about Wes, too, and look how that had turned out.

That try as she might, she couldn't banish Wes from her body, let alone her brain. Which, she thought wryly, might have something to do with the fact that she was touching herself to a mental highlight reel of their greatest orgasms.

The elastic snapped against her abdomen as she yanked her hand free.

She needed a goddamn drink.

Viv stalked over to her dresser and grabbed an

oversize T-shirt from the drawer, tugging it over her head as she headed for the door.

She wasn't some starry-eyed, hormone-infused college junior anymore, she reminded herself as she headed for the kitchen, doing her best to wrestle her weird sexual obsession with Wes into submission through sheer force of will. They'd lived separate lives. They'd grown into different people. They had nothing in common anymore, no ties to one another.

"Is that my shirt?"

Vivienne started at the sound of his voice, swearing as her hand flew to the base of her throat and she whirled to face the couch. "God! You scared the shit out of me."

"Sorry."

But he didn't look sorry, propped indolently on her designer couch, his back against the armrest, his beautiful chest bare, and the blanket pulled up just high enough to make her wonder if he still slept in the nude.

In the interest of distraction, she focused on his original question and glanced down at herself.

Wes's shirt. One she'd stolen from him a lifetime ago.

Considering the name of the landscaping company was emblazoned across the front of it, she figured plausible deniability had left the building.

Hoping the blush prickling up her neck wasn't visible in the dimness of night, she lifted her chin to an angle that was all bravado. "As for this being your shirt, I guess that depends."

"On what?"

"On whether you subscribe to the idea that possession is nine-tenths of the law."

Wes's deep chuckle raced along her skin as he threw back the blanket and planted his feet on the plank flooring.

Boxer briefs.

White.

And tight.

He'd always had the sexiest thighs.

Viv cleared her throat. "Sorry I woke you up."

"You didn't." He dragged a hand through his hair, leaving it sexily disheveled. And right then, in the intimacy of the shadows, the living room lit faintly by whatever moonlight managed to join the light pollution of Los Angeles at night, it was easy to slip back to a time when midnight conversations with Wes, her in his T-shirt, him in his boxers, had been normal.

And all she had to do to maintain the illusion was ignore the electronic monitoring device blinking on his left ankle.

He stood up, stretching, and Vivienne took a step backward in self-preservation.

"This couch sucks."

Glad for the distraction, Vivienne frowned, taking more offense than his words warranted. "It cost ten grand."

"Well, none of that cash was funneled into adding cushioning to the cushions, I'll tell you that much."

She stared at the mod-style cream monstrosity, realizing for the first time that she didn't really like it. Funny that she'd never noticed before. "Is it that bad?"

"Back in the day, you dragged me across the entire city, made me sit on fifty-seven couches before you would commit to one, and now you're trying to tell me you've never sat on this overpriced torture device once?"

"A designer picked it out." She glanced around the pristine, muted apartment, suddenly aware of how blank it was. "When I'm not at Whitfield, I'm sleeping. And if I can't sleep, I'm in my home office. Working."

That was her life since she'd come back to LA. And if she were being honest, she liked it that way. Being busy with work was much safer than being alone with her thoughts.

"So what are you doing out here now?" Wes's voice sounded deeper in the dark, and the question stymied her for longer than it should have.

"Alcohol," she blurted, remembering herself. "I need alcohol. Do you want a beer?"

He cocked an eyebrow. "I just got out of prison."

"Whiskey it is."

His mouth twisted with bleak humor, and her heart did the same as he followed her into the kitchen.

CHAPTER SIX

SHE MIGHT NOT be much of a cook, but he was damned impressed with her bartending skills. Wes leaned a hip against the counter and watched her. Within minutes, she was handing him a crystal tumbler of top-shelf whiskey, complete with a spherical ball of ice.

"Fancy." He lifted the glass in a wordless toast, and she clinked hers against it before they indulged.

The smooth burn was exactly what he needed.

"Your taste in alcohol has definitely improved over the years."

"Hey. Señor Taco's cheap tequila Tuesdays will always hold a special place in my heart," she countered.

The reference to the night they'd met charged the air, stealing the jaunty smile from her lips. She hadn't taken off her makeup yet, so they were the same deep red they'd been in the elevator. Except now they'd taste like whiskey and sex, instead of just the latter.

Wes drowned that dangerous thought with another swallow of premium liquor. He should walk it back. Hit the eject button. But as she stood there, in his shirt, her pale thighs dappled with shadows, he said what he was thinking instead. "Mine, too. Señor Taco's changed my life."

Their gazes held in the darkness of the kitchen, and for a second, she looked like the fearless, passionate girl he'd known, before she'd smoothed it all out into precise angles and lines.

She opened her mouth, probably to make some excuse and retreat, so Wes kept talking, unwilling to let her disappear quite yet. "Jesse dragged me to that party at his frat house. He wanted me to see this girl he had a crush on."

She relaxed a little at the promise of gossip, even though this particular secret was in the rearview mirror. "How did I not know that?" Vivienne took a sip of her drink, and he used the moment to admire the graceful line of her throat as she swallowed. "Did he make a move?"

"Nah. She bailed on the party to get tipsy on cheap tequila with some blue-collar lawn jockey before he had the chance."

Dawning understanding tightened her fingers around her glass. "I never thought… I didn't know he… Jesse and I were just friends."

Wes nodded, twisting his wrist so the ice sphere rolled around in his glass. "I figured that out when you left with me. And I wouldn't have gone into business with him if I didn't believe he was cool with it. Can't build a solid company with someone you don't trust…" He set his drink on the counter. "Or someone you want to beat the shit out of."

The not-quite confession sharpened her gaze, and for a split second, something flared in her eyes. Like she understood that that night, the night they'd met, he would have dumped Jesse—all his money, all his business connections—in an instant for her. Would have shoveled decorative rocks and schlepped Bermudagrass sod for the rest of his life, if that's what it took for a shot with her.

Then she blinked and it was gone, like the failed strike of a match.

Considering that, in the end, he'd chosen Soteria Security over her, it was a fair reaction.

"It's getting late."

She brought the glass to her mouth. Finished it in one go. The tumbler seemed loud when it met the counter, even though she set it down carefully.

Retreat mode activated. "It was late before you came out here," he reminded her.

Their eyes met, and lust sizzled along his spine. It was still there. The connection between them that he'd thought was lost. Or at least that's what he'd been telling himself since the day she'd hopped a plane to Yale. But he couldn't deny it anymore.

Vivienne shook her head, and it was edged with desperation. "The elevator was a mistake. It shouldn't have happened. A memory," she added, her voice trailing off into nothing.

"It was a hell of a memory," Wes countered.

He stalked closer. One careful step, then another.

Her lips parted on a shaky exhalation, and the answering snap of hunger made his body hum.

In the space of a breath, he'd become the tiger. "You felt it, too."

Her tongue darted out, leaving a sheen on her matte-red lips. "And you have evidence to back up that claim, counselor?"

Such a badass, even when she was the antelope. As true now as it had been then.

His eyes dropped to her chest, her nipples hard beads against the soft cotton of his old T-shirt. His hands itched to feel them pressing against his palms.

She glanced down, a frown creasing her forehead. "Don't flatter yourself. A woman's nipples aren't like a pop-up thermometer in a turkey. You can't gauge a heat level from them."

There she was. His tigress.

It was his turn to lick his lips. "And what do you know about cooking a turkey, Viv?"

Pride lifted her chin, her color gloriously high with that potent combo of anger and lust that they both excelled at. "I know you can order delicious, apricot-glazed turkey breast from Whole Foods that's so good, no one cares who cooked it." He saw her struggle to stop herself, saw the moment she lost her inner war and veered off the high road. "You'd probably love it. You always *were* a breast man."

Wes's grin was all male satisfaction. Sparring with her had always been the best aphrodisiac on the planet. "Still am. Which is how I know that, while that might be true for women in general, *your* nipples have always been incredibly accurate at predicting your heat level."

She crossed her arms over her chest to conceal the evidence. "It's not so tough to read your thermometer either." She dropped her gaze to his crotch, but the ploy backfired. Because he wasn't embarrassed. And there was nowhere to hide when all you were wearing was a pair of white boxer briefs. He didn't miss the way her eyes flared at the result of their exchange of innuendos.

"I wouldn't think so," he conceded, and Vivienne swallowed as he drew closer still, so fucking hard for her. "Being around you always gets my temperature up."

"That's close enough," she warned, flattening her palm against his chest, and the burn of skin on skin almost sent him to his knees.

His heart thudded hard on the other side of his ribcage. "Not by half."

"Why?" She breathed the question and it rippled along his skin, raising goose bumps. Her fingers flexed against his skin. "Even after everything we've been through, why is it like this?"

Her elbow relaxed a fraction of an inch and he leaned into the concession.

"Because I still know your body. I know what you like. What you need."

Her laugh held a note of desperation. "God, you're so full of yourself."

"That's not bragging. It's fact. I spent two years learning you. Studying you. Logging every catch of your breath, every clench of your muscles. I know what makes you shiver. I know what makes you wet."

He lowered his voice. "I know you're wet for me right now."

Her exhalation was a familiar breathy sigh that slid down his spine and wrapped around his balls. She'd made that sound before, in bed with him. Wes clenched his fists against the urge to touch her, to take too much too fast. Desire beat thick and heavy in his veins.

"And that's after a six-year hiatus from you. Imagine how it could have been if I wasn't so rusty."

Viv shook her head against his words, against the persuasive heat pulsing between them, but her arm lost all rigidity, and her fingers slid down his sternum in an inadvertent caress that set his skin ablaze.

"This isn't real."

"Fuck real."

His blunt rejoinder widened her eyes.

"You know what's real? Two billion-dollar tech firms are out for my blood." Anger got tangled up in the lust. "I'm out on bail, and one spectacle of a trial is all that stands between me and prison for the rest of my life. In the meantime, I have no money, no clothes, and no job. Not to mention, my reputation is in shreds."

He was desperate for her, even if it couldn't last.

"Maybe I'm not looking for real. And I know you didn't come out here for a drink."

Fuck real.

Vivienne let the sentiment quiet the inner turmoil that was raging in her gut.

She'd let herself be blackmailed and, as a result, an innocent man had gone to prison.

She'd quit her dream job in a desperate attempt to clear his name.

The odds of any of it working out were miniscule at best, and nonexistent at worst.

But right now, he wanted her. And she wanted him.

Tonight, that could be enough.

After everything, they deserved the illusion. Just for a moment, they could forget the rest. Pretend they were who they used to be.

And she might get there, if she disregarded the beard, dismissed the hardened glint in his blue eyes. If she ignored the million things that had gone wrong between them and the years that had intervened since.

She spread her fingers over his heart, his skin hot beneath her palm, his heartbeat strong and steady. His body shuddered when she stepped closer, lifted her chin.

"Viv." He breathed the words against her lips a split second before his fingers slid into her hair, and the edge of pain as he tugged her head back made her gasp even as he claimed her mouth in a scorching kiss that sent pleasure surging through her. She clutched his shoulders, desperate to get closer.

His other hand fisted her T-shirt in the small of her back, lifting the hem and baring her thighs. Wes opened his mouth over hers again, kissing her, consuming her, as he walked her backward until the curve of her ass bumped up against the edge of the tabletop.

The chill of the marble was a shock against the heat of her skin, and her pelvis jerked in surprise. Wes growled as their hips collided, and the sound, combined with the brief, electric contact with his erection, had her all keyed up.

God, she'd forgotten how much she loved sex.

She gave him her prettiest pout, looking up from beneath her lashes. "It's cold."

His tiger smile revved her estrogen, and her belly clenched with a pulse of heat.

"Let's get you warmed up then."

He slid the T-shirt up her torso, and Vivienne bit back a moan. He hadn't been wrong about her breasts. They were tight with need, her nipples hard and sensitive from the drag of the cotton as she lifted her arms so he could pull it over her head.

Her fingers toyed with the elastic waistband of his underwear as she pressed herself against him, flattening her breasts against his chest, burying her face in his shoulder so she could breathe in his skin. The scent of him was so familiar it made her ache, but she ignored the moment of weakness, bit his shoulder as she slid her hands inside his boxer briefs and palmed his ass.

Wes's reaction was instantaneous, and there was a flurry of motion as he slipped her underwear down her thighs before stripping off his own. Then he was kissing her, lifting her onto the table, stepping between her legs.

It took a second for her to realize that she was sitting on his T-shirt, that he'd covered the cool marble surface before lifting her onto the table, and that funny little ache reared up again, trying to make this more than it was.

But Wes saved her from herself, sliding clever fingers through the slick heat of her, making her buck against his hand. She was drenched for him, and the rasp of his breath let her know that he'd noticed. That he was pleased. That he was on the edge.

And just like that, the slow glide of his fingers wasn't enough anymore.

"No more teasing," she ordered, reaching for his cock, taking him in her hand. Vivienne traced her thumb along the prominent vein that ran the length of his shaft and he went completely still. He was all leashed power in that moment. She owned him, owned his pleasure, and it was intoxicating.

She swiped her thumb over him, spreading precum across the sensitive head. Wes's thighs shook as she guided him right where she wanted him, and then, mercifully, he was pushing inside her.

Vivienne's eyes drifted shut, blocking out reality, and she let everything go back to the way it was. When being with him had been full of possibilities. Her world narrowed to the heat of him, and she clung to his body, biting back a moan as he rocked his hips, plunging into her, driving her higher.

She breathed his name, trying to get closer, even now, when they were as close as two people could be. Physically, anyway. And that's all this was about.

The sturdy table shuddered beneath them as Wes picked up his pace, until each of his thrusts was harder and faster than the one before.

Vivienne gave herself over to the wild sensations building inside her as he pushed her back on the marble, half on top of her, so far inside her. The promise of climax was within her grasp, but when she reached between them to take it, he caught her wrist and pinned it above her head and her eyes flew open at the show of dominance.

"Not this time."

His pupils flared, ringed with blue the color of stormy seas, and he thrust into her again, and again, hard and deep and perfect. It was too much sensation, too much everything, and Viv squeezed her eyes shut even as her body clenched in response to his precise invasion. And then she was drowning in the sharp, roiling pleasure that rushed through her with so much force that she was helpless to do anything but cling to him as they crashed together a final time. Light fractured across the backs of her eyelids and she held him close as she cried out, their bodies shuddering with shared release.

She was still panting as he straightened his arms, lifting his chest from hers.

"Shit."

She frowned up at him at the assessment, but his gaze was focused over her left shoulder, and she shoved up onto an elbow to look behind her.

A pool of murky water dripped off the edge of the table, and on the floor, the vase lay splintered in a million glittering shards, dangerous and beautiful and dotted with dying tiger lilies.

Something shivered down her spine as she and Wes remained perfectly still, catching their breath as they stared at the resulting chaos of their mutual orgasms.

Goddamn symbolism.

CHAPTER SEVEN

WES SQUEEZED HIS eyes shut against the intrusion of the morning sun and pulled a hand down his face, though it didn't feel like his. He still wasn't used to the beard. But he was keeping it—a tangible reminder of his time at Terminal Island. Something to aim his focus where it belonged. On figuring out who'd framed him.

Not that the beard had helped much last night, when the only thing he'd been able to think about was how sexy and responsive Vivienne was, and how damn good it felt to be so deep inside her again. The primal satisfaction he got from making her come had been enough to set off his own climax.

Of course, after they'd cleaned up the botanical carnage, Vivienne had disappeared so quickly and completely that he might have thought it had all been a dream...if he'd actually been able to fall asleep. The couch from hell had done everything in its power to make sure that didn't happen.

He cracked open an eye at the faintest whisper of sound to find Vivienne trying to sneak past him.

Not that he'd been listening for her.

"Pretty sure it's not a walk of shame if your name's on the mortgage."

Bare feet aside, she looked far more untouchable in her charcoal power suit with a pair of high heels in her hand than she had last night in his T-shirt.

She sent him a distracted smile. The kind you gave a stranger.

"You're up early." Viv stopped at the end of the couch, resting a hand on it for balance as she tugged one shoe on, then the other, now that the click of her heels wouldn't wake him.

He pushed himself into a sitting position. "I could say the same."

"I have some research to do on your case. It will probably take all day."

He could read her stubborn determination to make sure that it did in the set of her shoulders. Wes tugged the blanket, baring his left calf so that his ankle monitor was visible. "I'll just stay here."

She ignored the jibe. "Help yourself to whatever's in the fridge. I'll order some Thai for dinner."

His favorite.

"If that's okay with you."

It was a purposeful hedge, an attempt to distance herself from him. The pretense rankled.

"Sure, sounds good," he assured her, playing his role in this pantomime of pleasantries she seemed determined to enact. Not that he gave a shit. He had enough problems to worry about without his cock in the mix. She wanted to pretend they were polite strangers? He could do that.

In fact, that was better for his plan. If they were nothing but compulsory roommates, then he had no reason to feel guilty about his intention to loot her home office for whatever device he could jury-rig into internet access as soon as she left.

He listened to her go through her morning kitchen routine, which judging by the delicious smell wafting from the kitchen, still consisted solely of coffee. Like old times, he thought, and instantly regretted it when his mind used that moment of nostalgia to segue into a series of unwelcome flashes of morning seductions past. Steamy showers where they got dirty before they got clean, quickies where they raced the snooze button timer to climax, the dozens of debauched ways he'd tempted her into being late for class and the dozen more variations she'd used in retaliation to make him late for work.

And today she couldn't get away from him fast enough.

He did his best not to look annoyed by that platonic turn of events as Vivienne appeared just long enough to bid him an awkward goodbye.

He was on his feet the second the door closed behind her.

Her home office was as colorless as the rest of the place, and just as precisely organized. *Everything in its place* was a religion to Vivienne.

Wes's eyes went straight to the wooden rolltop desk that had been converted into a twenty-first century workstation, and the empty laptop dock that sat atop it.

Viv had left with nothing but a small purse and a travel mug's worth of caffeine this morning. Which meant that her computer was somewhere. He just needed to find it.

He went through the room with a meticulous hand—who said you couldn't learn anything from a father who spent most of his time in jail?—careful not to disrupt Vivienne's things in his search for the key to the online kingdom.

There was nothing, he realized, after he'd been through every filing cabinet and carefully stacked box in the joint. He'd even lowered himself to tugging open the desk drawer, in hopes she'd left an older model cell or abandoned battery that he could use to boot up his currently useless phone. Unfortunately, the only thing it contained was an impressive collection of Post-its, a box of paper clips, a stapler, a couple of pilfered pens and a USB drive emblazoned with the Whitfield Industries logo.

Wes shut the drawer with more force than he'd intended.

Shit.

The room was clean. And that could mean only one thing, he realized, stepping out of the office. His gaze snagged on the door at the end of the hallway.

The woman he'd known was a sentimental creature of habit, and he hoped, somewhere beneath her slick haircut and structured dresses, some of that woman still existed. Because *that* woman would have something hidden away that could help him.

Wes's conscience reared up before he'd even put his hand on the knob.

If there was any other way, he promised himself. And then he opened the door and walked into Vivienne's bedroom.

Her king-size bed dominated the room, and it took a good amount of effort not to let visions of her in it dominate his thoughts, as well.

Statistically, people were most likely to keep items that were of value to them in relatively obvious places. Under the mattress, for instance, or— he swung his gaze toward her antique dresser—in the sock drawer. But Vivienne wasn't a statistic. At least not to him.

He turned his head again.

She'd always hidden his presents in the back of her closet. Even after she knew he'd cracked the location.

When he stepped inside, his hands balled into fists. *Jesus.* She had all her pretty underwear on display like a lingerie shop, and Wes swallowed against the surge of lust that swamped him. He remembered her, wrapped around him in the elevator, their bodies rocking in unison, the feel of her beneath him on the kitchen table as she took him to paradise, the way that only Vivienne could—with a naughty smile and total abandon. There'd always been something electric between them.

Wes shook off the memory.

With renewed determination, he forced himself

to take in the scene before him. Everything was perfectly in place, color coordinated to within an inch of its life, folded, stacked and hung with precision... except...

His eyes lit on one of her purses, a pale pink one that was slightly askew. He reached past it, shoved a black shoebox to the side and hit pay dirt. Vivienne's laptop.

The faster he figured out who'd gotten him into this mess, the sooner he could get himself out of it, and out of Vivienne's orbit.

Wes pulled her bedroom door shut behind him and headed back to the living room, pausing to assess his options.

Tiger lily–less marble sex table? No.

The devil's sofa? Hell no.

He settled for pulling an ottoman up to the coffee table and booted up Viv's computer. Bypassing the fingerprint lock was easy. Setting up a bit of a smoke screen in case any eager-to-please FBI agents were monitoring her internet usage took a little longer. But in truth, the mindless task made him feel like himself again. He'd missed the work. The work cleared his head.

Even so, when he'd set up a secure connection for himself so he could make contact with the world's foremost expert on his case, he hesitated for a moment before connecting the video call.

There was a lot riding on this, not the least of which was his freedom itself. He couldn't think of anyone who hated his guts more than the hacker on the other end of the secret number that she didn't know he knew. Except maybe Vivienne.

Unfortunately, he didn't have the luxury of being discerning right now. Because if he'd had that luxury, he certainly wouldn't be calling the woman who'd put him in jail out of blind loyalty to Max Whitfield, a man determined that Wes spend the rest of his days rotting behind bars.

With a deep breath, Wes connected the call. It only rang twice before she answered.

"Max, what are you…" The woman's voice trailed off as she recognized him and she rolled her eyes. "Oh, you have *got* to be kidding. How the hell did you get this number? Max is gonna be so pissed when he—"

"Are you alone?" AJ was a rambler…a rare trait for an elite hacker, and he didn't have time for it right now.

"What the hell does that mat—"

"Are you alone?" Wes repeated.

"Geez. Yes. I'm alone." She scowled at him when he stayed silent, shoving her raven curls back from her forehead. "If you think I'm picking up this phone and showing you my place like some virtual real estate agent, you can go to hell. You're the one wasting my time right now."

Oh well. Worth a try. "Is this line clean?"

She crossed her arms over her black T-shirt. "That's why you picked it, isn't it?"

Fair point.

"I need your help."

AJ laughed. "You're joking, right? Why would I help the evil mastermind who fucked over my former boss *and* my current sexual obsession?"

Wes let his surprise show. Last he'd heard, the boss was up close and personal with Emma Mathison, a former Whitfield Industries employee and the original suspect for the hack that had landed Wes in prison. "You and Max, huh? How's his girlfriend taking that?"

"Ew. No. I worked for Max, you perv. It was never like that between us. Liam is my boyfrie—my sex toy," she corrected, but not fast enough.

The fact that she'd quit working for Max intrigued him, but the Cybercore connection was a total blindside. Her screwing the CEO would have been…less than ideal on its own, but the fact she obviously considered Liam Kearney more than a fling did not bode well for his mission.

"Not to mention, I'm the one who caught your ass."

Oh. And there was that.

Wes forced himself to maintain a casual tone. "Yeah. You really fucked that one up. Consider this your chance to atone."

She leaned toward the screen, a Cheshire cat smile curving her lips. "For a man who's not supposed to be anywhere near the internet, I'd think you'd want to watch how you talk to me right now. One press of a button, and I can have you back on Terminal Island so fast your head would spin."

"Really, AJ?" His voice was laced with irritation.

"Isn't all this behind us? You tried to hack Whitfield Industries, and I caught you fair and square. I know that pisses you off, and that putting me away for this breach feels like revenge, but do me a solid and put the bloodlust aside for a second. Think it through. How'd you find me? Was it just a little too easy to connect the dots? And did the path lead straight to me?"

She glared at him, and he knew he had her.

"You know I'm better than that," he said simply. "I wouldn't have caught you if I wasn't."

AJ crossed her arms. "You called me sloppy."

His words rushed back to him, the ones he'd said to Max Whitfield five years ago.

She's got skills, but she's impulsive. Lets her ego get in the way of her work. That's how I caught her. She's talented, yeah, but she's fucking sloppy, and sloppy gets you caught. If you're not careful, you're going to end up bailing her out instead of the other way around. You need a hacker, not a hack.

Not the most flattering assessment, he had to admit. Wes scratched his bearded jaw. "I didn't know you were with him when he called me."

Her frown deepened. "Try again."

"It was a bad day."

"Thanks for the oversimplified recap, dickwad."

"It was a bad day for *me*," he clarified, figuring he owed her at least that. "Jesse had sunk everything we had into scoring Whitfield Industries as a client."

One big client, Jesse had insisted. *Once one*

*mega-corp takes us seriously, the others will have
no choice but to follow suit. You'll see.*

He'd been right, too. But AJ had almost fucked
it all up.

"Our contract was one week old when you bur-
rowed through our defenses." Wes shook his head.
"You were almost all the way in before I even noticed
you. The first real test of my tech, and you were this
damn close to breaching it."

Because Wes hadn't been watching. Not like he
should have been. No, he'd been too preoccupied
with revenge. With showing Vivienne what a colossal mistake she'd made, leaving him before he'd had
a chance to prove his worth.

But if Soteria Security was successful? That
would be hard evidence he was destined for more
than landscaping and manual labor. Proof that unlike his father, he could take care of a family. Proof
that unlike his mother, Viv's money had nothing to
do with why he wanted to be with her.

And AJ's elegant hack had almost cost him the
contract. Which would have cost him his company.
And his company was all he'd had left. It had never
been AJ he'd been angry at. She'd just been convenient. A stand-in for the woman who'd breached his
heart and taken everything.

"I was mad at Vi—" He bit back her name just in
time. "—at someone else, and I took it out on you."
His jaw tightened. "And the truth is, the only person
I should have been mad at was myself. I'm the one

who didn't do my job, and I didn't want Whitfield to know it. I shouldn't have said what I did."

It was as close to sorry as he was willing to get, considering she'd landed him in the pen.

AJ stared at him, and he could see her seeing too much. Reading between the lines. It felt like shit to let her, but what choice did he have? And he might not *know* her, but he'd *studied* her—and her hacking style—in the years since well enough to know that the driving need to prove himself against all comers was a motivation this woman understood.

AJ lifted her brows and leaned back in her chair. "Well, this just got uncomfortably honest."

Her version of *apology accepted.*

Wes exhaled with relief. "Yeah, well. I'm on kind of a tight schedule here. I need to know exactly what led you to me. Someone laid that trap you found, and you're going to help me take the bastard down."

"Remind me again why I'm going to do that?"

"Because besides me, you're the best, AJ. And I need the best."

She gave him a hard look, the kind that said she was trying to figure out if he was bullshitting her or not.

"Look, clock's ticking here. What do you want? A show of good faith?"

His fingers flew over the keys, preparing an offering that no hacker worth her keyboard could refuse.

It was the biggest gamble of his life, putting his fate in enemy hands, but there was no alternative. He wasn't going back to jail.

Desperate times, he assured himself as he hit the enter key on Viv's laptop, deploying the nuclear option.

A moment later, AJ's eyes widened. "No way."

He could hear the quick staccato of keystrokes as she verified the gift he'd just given her. "Did you just...was I just granted carte blanche access to Soteria Security? Why the hell would you do this?"

"Because I was framed. And considering you're the one who followed the evidence that led to me in the first place, I figure you're my quickest route to freedom. Thanks to you, I don't have a lot of equipment at my disposal to get to the bottom of this, which means I'm in the market for a contractor."

Her gaze was shrewd as she stared into the camera. "This is a paying gig?"

"You clear my name, I'll meet your going rate. You don't, you get nothing." Mostly because if she didn't, his assets would remain frozen indefinitely.

"Okay, hold up. Let me see if I've got this right. Not only are you going to pay me, you've given me a free pass into the inner workings of the best cybersecurity firm in the business *and* you're telling me that someone framed you?"

"Yes."

"Cash, computers and conspiracy theories." She leaned forward and her face took up the entire screen. "You know those are like, three of my favorite things in the world, right?"

He did. Because Wes made it a point to know everything about people who had the ability to destroy him. "So you're in?"

"Oh, I'm in. I'm all the way in."

Wes took his first easy breath since AJ had answered his call. One good thing about hackers, they were always jonesing for a bigger target, a better takedown, which meant their loyalty could be malleable, if the price was right. "Have a look around. Check Soteria's original assessment of the hack on Whitfield Industries against your own. Let me know if anything rings any bells. I'll be in touch."

"Sure. Whatever." Her attention was already back on her computer screen, and the rhythmic click of the keyboard let him know she was digging into her present with the gusto that made her such an ace hacker in the first place.

"Before you go, I need a secure connection that will keep any heat off me and my current location." He could have done it himself, but why waste the time?

"God. If I'd known you were so needy, I wouldn't have agreed to take your money." A couple more clicks of her keyboard and he had what he needed. "If this is for porn, I'm going to be so grossed out. And next time you call me, put on a shirt."

Wes lifted his head at the rebuke, wondering why the idea that had just struck hadn't occurred to him earlier. "Yeah, about my current wardrobe situation..."

With a few curt instructions for AJ, Wes disconnected the video chat, and used his shiny new untraceable internet access to pull up the latest about Soteria Security. According to several news sites, there was a press conference starting in about an hour, and everyone was all atwitter at the prospect of watching Jesse Hastings announce the future of the company now that his scummy ex-partner was out of the picture.

Which gave said scummy ex-partner just the right amount of time to try to convince the building's concierge to loan the stranger squatting in Vivienne Grant's apartment some tools. Wes glanced at his ankle monitor, then over at Vivienne's Roomba docking station.

He needed a screwdriver.

CHAPTER EIGHT

IT WAS LATE afternoon when Vivienne stepped tentatively into the men's department at Neiman Marcus in Beverly Hills.

She'd filed everything that needed filing before noon and spent the rest of the time looking for reasons not to go back to her place. And then she'd remembered that Wes had nothing but the suit he'd walked out of prison in. And he really needed to start wearing more than boxer briefs to bed if this roommate situation was going to continue. That was how she'd ended up in the T-shirt section, wondering if XL was big enough for his shoulders, and debating the merits of crew necks versus V-necks. And the fact she cared at all was so stupid that she—

Something brushed against her purse, and she whirled around at the slight movement of the strap to find Jesse Hastings tucking his phone into the breast pocket of his stylish navy suit.

"Jesse!"

He looked almost angry for a moment, but it gave way to a smile. "Vivienne."

She stepped woodenly toward him, exchanging de rigueur air-kisses with her former classmate and Wes's business partner. Also *former*, she reminded herself, and the familiar churn of guilt turned over in her stomach.

"Fancy meeting you in Neiman's men's department. What are you doing here?"

"Nothing." The lie came out too sharp. "Just, ah, running some errands," she prevaricated, pushing her hair behind her ear. "My dad. His birthday is coming up so, yeah, I thought he could use a new tie."

"That's funny. I thought your dad's birthday was in January."

Vivienne started. Her father's birthday *was* in January, but she couldn't think why Jesse would know that specific piece of trivia. The two men had never even met.

"I like to stay ahead of things," she offered. "If I'm not four months early, I'm late."

It felt like a long time before Jesse nodded. "You've always been very...proactive."

The adjective choice struck her as odd, but she couldn't say why.

"How are you holding up, anyway? You know, with Wes in jail and everything?"

Vivienne didn't let herself flinch at the question. So, he hadn't heard Wes was out yet. And he definitely hadn't heard she was the reason.

"It's been a long time since Wes and I were together," she lied.

"Well sure, but that doesn't change the fact that you'd never do anything to hurt him. Right?"

Vivienne's stomach dropped as her mind cataloged the multitude of her offenses against the man she'd once loved. "Right," she agreed weakly. Shame ate at her. Seeing Jesse was a stark reminder that Wes's life wasn't the only one she'd ruined when she'd chosen blackmail over telling the truth.

"And after what he did…" Jesse trailed off, shook his head. "It's okay to feel betrayed. I'm still in shock myself."

"You think he did it?" Guilt oozed through her chest, black and sticky. Wes had already lost so much. Viv hated to think he'd lost his best friend, too. Because of her. Because of her cowardice.

"I mean, I don't want to, but it all fits. Still, Soteria was his baby."

Viv flinched, ignoring the squeeze in her abdomen at the choice of words.

"I'm as sick about it as you are. But I can't give up without a fight. Especially not after the big press conference this morning. Paperwork's all gone through. I'm officially the bigwig in charge of Soteria Security."

The announcement blindsided her, and her gut ached for Wes.

Jesse's friendly smile dimmed. "You don't look happy for me."

"Just a little taken aback. Congratulations, Jesse. Truly."

"Thanks. That means a lot, coming from you.

As my first official act as CEO, I've got a meeting at Whitfield Industries this afternoon." Jesse straightened his tie. "Hoping I can convince Max to see reason and keep Soteria on his payroll, now that the guilty party is behind bars. You work for him." His eyes narrowed slightly. "How do you like my chances?"

He hadn't heard she'd quit, either. And for reasons she couldn't explain, now didn't feel like the time to volunteer that information. "I've always found Max to be a reasonable man," Viv offered, a little off balance at the whole exchange.

"Well, I hope you're right. If I can keep even a few high-profile clients, then maybe I can stay solvent enough to take the company public. Wes would have wanted that." He shoved his hands in his pockets. "Despite everything, we were friends. Wes dedicated everything he had to Soteria Security. The least I can do is keep it afloat."

Vivienne had shot a hole right through the hull of Wes's dream, and this was the result. Jesse was doing everything he could to right the sinking ship. And now it was up to Vivienne to prove Wes's innocence and put everything back to normal.

"Are you heading back to Whitfield? I can give you a ride back to the office if you want."

"Oh. Thank you. That's really sweet of you, but I actually... I have a doctor's appointment in an hour. So..."

She could have sworn his gaze dropped to her stomach, and a shiver slid through her.

"Nothing serious, I hope."

Viv shook her head. "Just a checkup."

"I see." Jesse's expression cleared and he took a step back. "Then I'll leave you to it. It was good seeing you, Viv." He reached out, gave her shoulder a friendly squeeze. "If you ever need to talk about Wes, about what he did, you know where to find me."

Vivienne forced a smile as he left, trying to shake off the weird vibes of their interaction. She'd known Jesse for years, and he'd never made her uncomfortable before. Obviously, her guilty conscience was tainting everything, from interactions with old friends to Wes's whole life. Still, she watched until Jesse disappeared from view before she turned in the opposite direction and walked directly out of the store. She needed to get out of there before she ran into anyone else she knew.

An hour and a half later, Vivienne walked into her condo, hands laden with take-out bags. The Thai food she'd promised, because she knew it was Wes's favorite. Which felt like the least she could do, under the circumstances. She made a quick stop in the kitchen to set the burden on the counter, before she continued into the living room.

Wes stood up abruptly at her arrival, stepping in front of the coffee table. To her dismay, he was still bare chested. And as if that wasn't enough on its own, his dark hair was shower damp and his lean hips were swathed in nothing but a white towel.

She really should have bought a couple of those

T-shirts before she'd fled the department store. Viv dropped her gaze from the delectable sight under the guise of hunting through her purse for her phone. "I know that they confiscated your razor in the clink, but you could have opened the pack in the bathroom."

"This is what unemployed people do, Vivienne. They grow beards."

She glanced up as her hand closed around her device, and she checked to make sure she hadn't missed any calls about Wes's case. "And clothes? Do unemployed people not wear clothes?" She set her bag on the couch and toed off her shoes.

"My wardrobe has been seized by the US Government." Wes crossed his arms, and she did her best not to notice all his muscles, or the way they flexed beneath his damp skin.

"I bribed your door guy to take the only suit I own to the dry cleaner with my last hundred bucks. And my unmentionables are currently in the dryer."

More guilt, this time over her aborted shopping mission, swirled in her gut, but she tamped it down. She'd gotten him out of jail. And let him stay here. And she was going to make sure that she got the charges dropped so that he—

Her train of thought was disrupted by a soft, familiar whir.

Vivienne watched with astonishment as her Roomba appeared from the direction of the bathroom, chugging its way down the hall and back toward the couch, where it stopped as abruptly as if someone had ordered it to. Wes's ankle monitor sat atop it, its green light flashing rhythmically.

Her gaze cut to Wes. "What have you done?"

He kept his attention on his robotic henchman.

"If you're asking about the monitor, *tamper-proof* is just code for a challenge. You know that. As for the Roomba, the feds get suspicious if you don't move around a little."

"You programmed it to go to the bathroom?"

"And the kitchen." His eyes grew dark with determination. "I told you. I'm going to clear my name."

"What about my name?" The words ripped from her chest, jagged and sharp. "This is my career on the line, do you understand that? You've been remanded into my care. I'm supposed to make sure you're following the rules. I can get disbarred for this."

"They'd have to catch me first."

Anger bubbled up in her chest. She needed to move. Needed to burn off this frantic, anxious electricity crackling in her muscles. "In case you've forgotten, they already caught you! That's the reason that we're in this mess! How did you even…"

Her eyes lit on her laptop, and all the color drained from her face. Her blood turned to liquid nitrogen in her veins, so cold it burned. "Where did you get that?"

But she knew. Knew it had been stashed in her closet, behind vintage Chanel, right next to a shoebox full of secrets that Wes didn't know.

That she didn't want him to know.

"You went snooping in my bedroom?" When she

turned on him, there was still white-hot anger, yes, but it was the kind that was laced with terror. Had he seen the shoebox? Poked inside it? "You had no right!"

Emotions whirled inside her, banging up against each other, with nowhere to go. She made a move to shove him, but the second her hands met his skin, he caught her wrists, and his fury rose up to meet hers.

"Then why the hell did you get me out of jail?"

The question hung between them, both of them breathing hard, her palms pressed against his chest, her wrists manacled by his hands.

When Wes spoke again, he was dangerously close, and his voice was dangerously soft. "You knew I would do this. Tell me you knew I would do this."

Vivienne was helpless to do anything but nod. Because she had. Her attempts to find her black-mailer and deal with the mess she'd made herself had gotten her nowhere. And the idea of him rotting in prison for a second longer than he already had broke her heart.

Her throat burned, and to her mortification, she could feel her eyes welling with tears that she was desperate not to let him see. But it was too late. She couldn't hide them. Not anymore.

CHAPTER NINE

"DON'T CRY, VIV."

Wes had meant it to sound soothing, but it came out hostile.

Angry.

Because he was.

He was fucking furious, but he shouldn't be taking it out on her. The only person who'd offered him any sort of help when he needed it the most. The last person he wanted to see him like this…at his lowest.

And now he'd dragged her down with him.

Like he always did.

You can't make things better, so stop trying!

His mother's words echoed through his brain. She'd said it to him every time he'd found her crying her eyes out at the news that his father had pulled some new, boneheaded stunt that had landed him back behind bars. Every time he'd discovered her passed out in a pool of vomit after another failed attempt to erase the pain with booze. Every time he'd come upon her rocking in the corner, strung out on whatever cut-rate product one of the many men who wasn't his dad was willing to part with in exchange for whatever she had to do to get it.

He'd promised himself that one day he'd have enough money, enough power, to prove his mother wrong. To make things better for his little sister so that she didn't have to grow up like he had. To make himself worthy of the smart, beautiful, challenging woman he'd fallen half in love with the night he'd met her.

And for a little while, he thought he'd managed to fool Vivienne into loving him back.

But the truth was that she'd seen him for what he really was early. She'd bailed before he'd even gotten Soteria Security up and running.

To punish her for not believing in him, for not giving him a chance, he'd spent the last six years working himself—and Jesse—into the ground, taking the company from nothing to market dominance in record time.

And as the money rolled in, he thought he'd broken the curse. Proved his mother wrong.

But the truth was, Lorraine Brennan had been right all along.

Because despite his best efforts, he'd ended up in jail. Lost his company and his reputation. He was broke. And ostracized. And he'd just managed to alienate his only ally.

But then Vivienne lifted her chin, eyes still glittering with tears that she wouldn't let fall, and all the vulnerability of the moment before had morphed into sheer force of will. A broken angel. She was absolutely magnificent.

"Why didn't you come to see me?"

"What?"

Vivienne met his eyes without flinching. "At Yale. Why didn't you come after me?"

The question collapsed his lungs, like she'd landed a good hard punch to his solar plexus.

"I thought about it." A million times. Maybe more. But there'd always been one more milestone to reach that he'd thought would make him ready to go after her. Make him worthy of her. "God, Viv. I thought about it, about you. All the time. But I couldn't... I needed to make Soteria a success before I saw you again."

Her brows dipped in an offended frown. "You thought I'd care about that?"

"Of course, I thought you'd care about that! Every moment of being with you felt like a test. From that first night of verbal foreplay to the last night, when you shoved that goddamn plane ticket in my face and forced me to choose."

"And you did." She dropped her gaze.

To his surprise, when she lifted her head again, the anger looked a lot more like pain.

"I guess I just hoped, after Jesse showed up that—"

Everything in him went still and sharp. "Jesse visited you? When?"

"Right after—" Viv cut herself off. Shook her head. "It's not important."

"Then why'd you bring it up?"

"Because it should have been you!"

It hurt to fucking breathe. "You're the one who left."

"And you're the one who let me go."

Wes shook his head, weary. "Don't say it like I had a choice. I thought you were going to Stanford. You *said* you were going to Stanford. Jesus, Viv. We were together two years and you didn't even feel the need to mention that Yale was a goddamn option." The ache of old wounds pulsed in his chest. "I watched my mom give up everything to make my dad love her, and it was a losing game. I swore I wasn't going to make the same mistake."

"Is that what we were? A mistake?" Her eyelashes were tear-damp and spiky, but her voice didn't waver.

"I don't know what we were. I just knew I had to make Soteria a success. To finally do something to prove that I could take care of you."

Anger flooded her cheeks. Not broken anymore. Avenging. "I didn't need you to take care of me."

Something cracked and splintered behind his ribs. "You think I didn't know that? Of course, I knew that! Do you know how many sugar momma jokes I endured from your college friends? How it felt to have your dad look down his nose at me because of the calluses on my hands?"

"And that mattered more to you than how I felt?"

"Not more. But it mattered. What they thought was just one part of it—do you get that? It was about what *I* thought. I needed to prove to myself that I was responsible enough to show up for you in all the ways that mattered. That if we ever got married, or had kids, that I could be better than my con man, absentee-dad role model."

Viv blanched at the confession, and Wes cursed himself. *Jesus.* Why were they even talking about this stuff? It was dead and long buried. Resurrection at this point wouldn't revive anything but a slimy, rotting mess.

"Let me go."

Wes looked down. He'd been so caught up in the moment that he was surprised to see he was still holding her hands against his chest. But when he obeyed the order, she didn't call him an asshole and storm away like he deserved.

She took off her blouse.

"Viv…" He wasn't sure if it was a warning or a plea.

And when her skirt hit the floor, he found he didn't much care.

"I don't want to fight anymore." She reached behind her to unhook her bra.

That hum of awareness that had started yesterday in the elevator was back, arcing between them, charging up his cells. So fucking beautiful.

She slid her panties down her thighs, stepping out of them when they hit the floor. "I'm so tired of fighting."

And just when Wes thought he couldn't get any luckier, she reached out and his towel hit the floor. He had a moment to wonder at the power she wielded over him before it surged bright and hot, and she crushed her mouth to his, clutching at his shoulders as he yanked her up his body. Then she moaned into his mouth as she wrapped her legs around his waist and he was lost. The realization rang an alarm bell in his head.

He was too much like his mother, so desperate to escape reality, to trade everything for a moment's pleasure.

Despite the need coursing through his body, and how good she felt pressed up against him, Wes forced himself to break the kiss.

Vivienne's fingers tightened on his shoulders in protest. "Wes," she breathed. "Please don't stop."

But she wasn't looking at him. Her eyes were closed. Just like they'd been in the elevator. And on the dining room table.

Fucking to forget.

And the thought that she might be pretending he was someone else, even some former version of himself, was more than he could handle.

"Not like this." The words scraped against his throat as he unhooked her ankles from around his hips and set her down.

"Not like what?" she asked. Her eyes were open now, wide with confusion as he stepped back from her.

"I just got out of jail."

The slightest crease marred her forehead. "I know."

"You know, but do you understand what that

means? I'm not the same guy you used to screw in the bathroom at Señor Taco's for kicks." Wes dragged his hand through his hair. "Everything has changed, and we're way past that. So if you want to fuck me, you're going to have to do it with your eyes wide-open. Because I'm done pretending."

Vivienne stared at him for a long time. So long that when she finally spoke, her words didn't make sense in his brain. "Challenge accepted."

"What?"

"Sit down, Wes."

He obeyed, dropping his big frame onto the couch, watching in awe as she crawled on him, planting a knee on either side of his hips. When she'd settled, her breasts were at eye level, pretty pink nipples drawn tight, begging for his mouth. But before he could decide where to start, she curled a finger under his chin and angled his head higher.

"My eyes are up here," she teased. "We haven't even started yet, and you're already breaking the rules. You sure you can handle this?" she asked.

A moment ago, he'd been positive he could. But then she reached between them, and his hips canted the second her hand made contact with his cock, and suddenly, he wasn't so sure.

No one touched him like Viv. Literally. Figuratively.

God, she was beautiful.

He loved the way her eyes widened and her breath caught as she took him inside. The slow, sweet slide of her down the length of him was the most exquisite torture. No better feeling in the world.

And then she sucked her bottom lip between her teeth and started to move and made a liar of him.

Wes ran his hands up her torso, palming her breasts, watching the pleasure ripple across her face as he flicked his thumb across her nipple.

Her mouth parted, and she ran her palms up the sides of his neck until she held his bearded jaw between her hands as she increased her pace.

The pressure was mind-blowing, and when he dropped his hands to her waist, he tried to remind himself that he was the one who'd wanted to slow things down, even as he flexed his thighs, driving his hips higher, burying his cock deeper every time she was on the down stroke.

Her legs trembled with effort as she rode him, staring deep into his eyes, and then she broke with the sweetest cry, melting all over him as her body pulsed around his shaft, squeezing him until he couldn't help but follow her over the edge.

She was breathing hard as she leaned forward, pressing her forehead against his, and he ran his hand up her back, until he reached that constellation of beauty marks. He didn't need to see them to trace them into a star pattern with his finger. He knew them by heart.

"You were right." She breathed, before catching his lips in a long, slow kiss.

"About the benefits of fucking me with your eyes open?" he asked when she finally pulled back.

"No."

Her Cheshire cat smile hit him in the gut.

"About how much this couch sucks." She nipped his bottom lip, and he groaned in protest as she pulled away, getting to her feet in front of him. "Maybe it would be best if you slept in my room tonight."

She held out her hand, and after a long, charged moment, Wes took it, letting her tug him to his feet before he followed her to her bedroom.

CHAPTER TEN

SOMEONE WAS IN the apartment.

Wes's heart rate jacked up, and he was instantly alert at the sound of the front door unlatching. He looked down at the sleeping woman beside him and his fear doubled. Vivienne gave a sleepy moan as he slid her carefully off his chest.

Grabbing his underwear, Wes yanked it on, searching the room for some kind of weapon, considering the merits of stabbing someone with a high-heeled shoe, but then the burglar shut the door with a complete lack of finesse, and he rolled his eyes.

Wes pulled the bedroom door shut behind him as quietly as possible, crossing his arms as he came around the corner. "The reports of your stealthiness are greatly exaggerated."

AJ turned away from the dull wall art to face him. "Hey, I was just giving you a heads-up so you could make yourself presentable." Her gaze slid dismissively over him, from head to foot. "But obviously you suffer from a raging case of chronic shirtlessness."

"That's why you're here. Did you get the stuff?"

"Of course, I got the stuff."

AJ tossed the bag in her right hand at him, and he caught it against his chest. "Your clothes, sir. Because apparently, I'm a fucking personal shopper now. I just brought you a bunch of black stuff."

Wes side-eyed her black Doc Martens, black jeans, black T-shirt and black leather jacket. "We'll match. How exciting."

She held up the duffel in her other hand. "Also, one air-gapped laptop, one burner phone and a bunch of other gadgets you should have asked me for but didn't."

Wes dug a pair of sweatpants out of the tangle of clothes before he gestured vaguely at the couch, and AJ set the tech equipment on it.

"The suits didn't take it easy when they searched your place. They tossed it. And you've still got a few reporters snooping around."

Wes's jaw tightened at the news. "I assume you took adequate precautions. Liam Kearney's current girlfriend showing up at Max Whitfield's ex-lawyer's place isn't quite the low-profile operation I'm trying to run right now."

"You're the one who dragged me into this. You don't like how I operate, then find someone else." AJ joined the duffel bag on the couch, flopping onto the nearest cushion. "What the hell, man? Is this thing stuffed with broken glass and lace thongs or something? It's like they corporealized *uncomfortable* and made a couch out of it."

Wes pulled the sweatpants on before reaching back into the bag for a shirt. "I've never worn a lace thong, but your hypothesis seems plausible. And as I already explained, I chose you because you're the best."

She shot him a saccharine smile as he dragged a T-shirt over his head. "I know. I just like hearing you say it."

Vivienne walked into the living room just then, looking sex mussed and gorgeous in his landscaping T-shirt. She paused as she took in the woman sprawled on her inhospitable furniture. "Oh, hello. I didn't realize Wes had company."

AJ tipped her chin up in greeting, but her shrewd gaze moved from Vivienne's state of undress back to Wes. He ignored her knowing look.

"Nice place you got here. You should change your security code. Mom's birthday isn't even going to keep the amateurs out, let alone the pros."

Vivienne's gaze snapped toward him, but he was already shaking his head. "I did *not* tell her to say that."

Viv turned the unimpressed look away from him and back onto their visitor. "So are you an amateur, or a pro?"

"I'm not really into labels. And I go where I want."

Vivienne frowned slightly, pointed at AJ. "I know you. You were in Max's office."

"When you quit, yeah."

Viv's eyes found his, and Wes nodded, setting

her mind at ease that that connection wasn't news to him. Her shoulders relaxed.

"I apologize if I was rude. I wasn't myself that day."

"No big." AJ waved off the apology.

"Coffee?"

The Roomba zipped back into the room, and AJ's eyes widened with tech envy as she took in the blinking ankle monitor riding atop it. It was the look of eager hacker geeks everywhere. She wanted to play. "I could be talked into staying for a bit."

"Latte okay with you?"

AJ nodded, already reaching for the ankle bracelet.

"Wes?"

"Sure. Please."

Vivienne disappeared into the kitchen, her bare feet quiet on the hardwood floor.

"I didn't know it was like that between the two of you."

Wes didn't acknowledge his visitor with a look, though he kept tabs on her in his peripheral vision. AJ's many talents included an almost preternatural ability to size up situations in an instant, and Wes didn't like the smug set of her body language. "Like what?"

AJ rolled her eyes. "I mean, I probably should have. She was pissed the day she quit. Ripped into Max for ruining you, going on about how you would never betray him."

Something clenched in his chest, and his head

came up with enough speed that AJ's expression turned to one of vindication. He didn't care anymore. "She quit because of me?"

"Uh, yeah, dude. She went *off.* Said her loyalties were with you, chucked her keys on the boss's desk, and stormed out. It was pretty magnificent, if I'm being honest."

He glanced toward the kitchen, where he could hear the faint whir of the espresso machine. *Magnificent.* An apt description of Vivienne Amelie Grant if ever he'd heard one.

"AJ?"

"Yeah."

"Get out."

She grinned at him. "You know, it's kind of sad I wasted so much time hating you. You're all right, Brennan. I'll be in touch when I have news. But you owe me a crack at this ankle bracelet." She set the monitor back on top of the Roomba and headed for the front door.

The second it closed behind her, Wes stalked straight into the kitchen.

"Is your little techie playdate over already?" Vivienne turned away from her fancy espresso machine and held a steaming cup in his direction.

"You quit to take my case?"

She didn't have to answer. He could read the truth of it in the rigidness in her spine and the way the latte sloshed dangerously close to the lip of the mug. Wes took it from her and set it on the counter.

"Why the hell would you do that? You loved that goddamn job!"

She looked startled for a moment, like she didn't think he'd noticed. Granted, their paths didn't cross at work all that often—until the hack, they'd probably only been in the same boardroom three or four times, since Whitfield had an army of lawyers, and Wes tended to bow out of the site visits anytime he could get away with sending Jesse by himself. Wes had always preferred being behind the scenes, focused on the tech. He left the parties and the wooing to his more personable partner.

But he'd seen Vivienne enough, paid attention enough, to know that she was killing it as Whitfield's chief legal counsel. That she excelled at what she did. That she was confident and kick-ass in equal measure. That Whitfield had been lucky to have her on his side.

Which was why it haunted him, the way she was looking at him right now.

Unsure. Uncomfortable.

"Max is the one who sent the FBI after you. He was hardly going to keep me on while I was trying to get the charges dropped," she said simply. But her matter-of-factness was not reassuring in the least. Something dark lit in Wes's belly.

"Is that why you left? Because that son of a bitch was going to fire you? Was he trying to push you out?"

"No. Wes, just…drop it okay?"

"Not until you tell me why the hell you'd give

up your career for me after everything that's gone down between us."

"I know you're innocent!"

Her voice echoed in his ears. The vehemence. The way she believed in him. He'd be lying if he said it wasn't exactly what he wanted to hear. Wished he could take it at face value and use it to block out the shitstorm that was swirling around them.

But this situation was way too complicated for such a simple happy ending.

And the fact that she wasn't looking at him right now, wasn't standing her ground, told him everything he needed to know.

"How? How do you know that?"

She wrapped her arms around herself in a way that struck Wes as self-protection, like an animal trying to shield its soft underbelly. Still, he pressed on.

"How can you be so sure that I didn't do exactly what they say?"

"Because!"

"Not good enough, Viv."

When she raised her brown eyes to his, what he saw there almost sent him to his knees.

"I'm the one who hacked Max's company, okay? I know you didn't do it, because it was me."

CHAPTER ELEVEN

THE CONFESSION WOULDN'T compute in his brain.

"I installed the malware on Emma Mathison's computer. She'd put in her notice. She was supposed to be gone. No one was supposed to notice anything before you—"

"Before I what?" he demanded.

"Before you stopped it. I knew you'd stop it." There was a faraway look in her eyes, like she was somewhere else in that moment. "I never meant for this to happen."

And just like that, everything slid into place. Wes shook his head at his own stupidity. "I should have known." He scraped a hand down his face.

"I should have known that first day, when Max called us all into his office to tell us Whitfield Industries had been hacked. You gave yourself away."

She looked so vulnerable then. So small in his old shirt, her long legs bare. He watched as her toes curled against the dark floor tiles, before she crossed her right foot over her left, her heel bouncing in time with her nerves.

"First, you jumped to Emma's defense, even though she was the obvious suspect. Then you uncrossed and recrossed your legs. Which is your tell when you're uncomfortable." He stepped closer, and despite the two feet of distance between them, she pushed back against the counter.

She'd already uncrossed her legs, out of habit, and he saw the second she caught herself, the way her muscles tightened against the instinctual need to cross them again.

Wes cocked an eyebrow and took another step in her direction.

Vivienne's breath picked up, as he placed his hands on the counter on either side of her and leaned close, so close that he could smell that alluring French perfume of hers, the embodiment of wine and tangled sheets and desire. Distinctly, deliciously Vivienne. Her tongue darted out to moisten her lips. "That doesn't prove anything." The protest was barely more than a whisper.

"And then you tucked your hair behind your left ear," he told her, reaching up and doing it for her. The feel of her beneath his fingers, even a touch as innocuous as this, sent heat through him. "Which is your tell when you're lying."

She flinched at the word, but he didn't stop.

"At the time, I didn't know why, but now I get it."

She curled away from him, hands still protecting her stomach, and it hurt him to see her like this, it did. But he had to know.

"What do they have on you?"

Her eyes snapped to his, wide with shock. "What?"

"You're a lot of things, Vivienne. Brilliant, beautiful and ballsy as hell. But you do not have the computer skills to have done this to me on your own."

Anger flared in her eyes and tightened her jaw. "You don't know that. You have no idea what I'm capable of. You still think I'm that naive, wide-eyed girl who threw herself at you at a frat party. But I'm not, Wes. I'm not her. I haven't been for a long time."

Naive. Not a word he'd ever associated with her. She'd been optimistic, and determined and sexually explosive, but she'd never been naive.

She just hadn't been this jaded. This brittle. The change was startling, and now that he'd seen it, he couldn't believe he hadn't noticed it before. "You're not like I remember you."

The idle observation startled a bitter laugh from her. "I guess it shouldn't surprise me it took you this long to notice. I mean, that was always our problem, wasn't it? Good at sex, bad at communication? Sorry to shatter your illusions, but we all have to grow up sometime."

She brushed past him, and he let her, but he followed her out of the kitchen, through the living room, around the corner to the hallway that led to her bedroom.

He didn't speak until her hand was on the doorknob. "And what made you grow up, Vivienne?"

She stopped dead at the question, but she didn't answer.

She just shut down, wilted right in front of his eyes.

* * *

Vivienne's hand trembled on the doorknob.

She wanted him to scream at her. To feel the anger he didn't know was his right. To be furious at her for all her secrets and how they'd ruined his life.

Why wouldn't he scream at her?

She could feel Wes at the other end of the short hallway, feel the burn of his gaze on the back of her neck as he started to approach.

Vivienne squeezed her eyes shut until colors danced behind her eyelids. She needed him to blame her so she could repent. But there was nothing, no punishment to absolve her guilt. Wes was angry, yes, but not at her. On her behalf. And that was more than she could take.

Forcing herself to turn around, Vivienne channeled the frosty demeanor that had held her together for the last six years and faced the man she'd ruined.

The concern in his blue eyes almost sent her to her knees, confusing the situation, melting her resolve. Wanting him. Missing him. It all got jumbled up as they stood there, and she grabbed hold of defensiveness, because angry seemed like a safer option than sad. Especially in the face of his pity.

"Don't look at me like that. Like I'm innocent."

She planted her hand on his chest, and Wes looked down at the point of contact before meeting her gaze, his eyes full of questions.

Angry sex had always been a forte of theirs. He knew she was provoking him, but he couldn't figure out why. And that was good. She wanted him a little off balance. Not so in control.

With a raise of her brow, she gave him a hard shove. Hard enough that he took a step back, but still there was no anger in his voice. Just resignation. "What are you doing, Viv?"

"I did this to you."

She moved to push him again, but he grabbed her by the upper arms, and just for a second, his fingers bit into her flesh before he loosened them. She was getting to him, the flash of pain proved it. A glimpse of the loss of composure that she craved.

"But not by yourself."

She couldn't atone without his censure. Couldn't banish the black tendrils of guilt that snaked through her chest, wound around her lungs, squeezed her heart. There was no catharsis in his kindness.

"Why not? You don't think I can hurt you? You don't think I have the power?"

His hands tightened on her arms again.

Yes. This was what she needed. What she deserved for keeping the truth from him. His rage. She could feel it now, pulsing just beneath the surface.

"Who else knows you like I do?" she goaded. "Who else knows your worst fear is ending up like your father?"

She could feel the leashed emotion rushing through him, and the darkness of it called to her, made her blood run hot.

"I ruined your company. I put you in jail."

The lash of her words had the intended effect.

She could read it in the darkening of his eyes, the way his breathing picked up. His chest heaved as he stared at her. His fingers dug into her skin as he jerked her closer.

Vindication surged through her blood at the lapse of his control.

There was barely any space between them, but it was still too much.

"Stop it," he warned, his voice low and dangerous.

"Make me." Vivienne lifted her head a fraction of an inch, and when he didn't move, she leaned forward and bit his bottom lip.

He sucked in his breath and went still, and then everything happened at once. Wes hauled her close, crushing her to him, first with his arms, and then she was pinned against the wall so tightly that it knocked the breath from her lungs. Rough. Perfect.

Vivienne clutched at his shoulders as he ground his hips against her, and when he grunted into her mouth, she was enraptured.

Elemental. Animalistic. She wanted him to use her. Wanted to use him right back.

Fucking to drown out the emotion that threatened to consume her if she let it.

Straightforward, and simple, and so damn good.

And if he wouldn't give her what she needed, she'd take it from him. She'd push him until he begged her to take what she needed.

She rubbed against him, glorying in the rough sounds her sensuous movements dragged from his throat. "Take off your shirt."

Something wicked and powerful suffused her body when he obeyed, pulling the black T-shirt over his head and revealing his gorgeous muscles.

"Good boy." Vivienne leaned forward, pressing a soft, openmouthed kiss against his pec even as she raked her nails down his abs, and he swore at the dueling sensations.

Vivienne bared her teeth, not quite a smile. "I've been very bad, Wesley. I've done things that I need to be punished for."

Emotion crowded her heart, seeped through her chest like an ink stain, but she held it down, strangling it until it loosened its hold. Nothing mattered right now but the dark heat in Wes's eyes. The rush of fire in her blood.

"Viv." Just her name, but she heard everything in his voice. The question. The anger. The confusion. The desire.

He was so close to giving in.

She needed him to give in.

"What is this?"

"You don't like it?" she countered, running a hand across his chest, tracing the flat disc of his nipple before pinching the sensitive skin. He inhaled sharply, pulling her close, his hips instinctively grinding against hers for a few blissful seconds before he got himself under control again. "I like it," he conceded, his voice husky. "I just don't understand it."

"I thought you liked things a little rough." Vivienne took a step back, pulled her T-shirt off and dropped it on the floor beside his. His gaze dropped instinctively to her chest, now that she was bared to his gaze, and Vivienne egged him on, biting her lip as she ran her hands up her torso.

He swore softly as she squeezed her sensitive flesh, before pushing her breasts together to exaggerate the swell of her cleavage.

The rasp of his breath, the complete focus of his attention, was heady. Vivienne pinched her nipple, not bothering to hide her gasp of pleasure, and she was rewarded as Wes shoved his hand down his sweatpants to readjust himself.

"So what do you say, Wes?" She stepped backward, reaching behind her to push her door open without breaking eye contact with him. "Wanna play?"

CHAPTER TWELVE

"FUCK YES."

Viv's lips curved with satisfaction at his answer, and she hooked her finger into the elastic at his waist, tugging him along as she walked backward to her bed.

Once she'd gotten him where she needed him, she dropped to her knees and stripped off the rest of his clothes with one swift tug.

His cock was so hard it slapped against his abs when she released it from its confines, and the proof that he wanted this almost as much as she did made her bold. She dug her fingernails into his muscled thighs as she leaned forward and licked up the length of his shaft before lifting her gaze to his.

His eyes were dark, more pupil than iris, and she could feel the quiver in his thighs as he stared down at her. She exhaled against his skin, damp from her tongue, and his cock twitched.

"Please."

She shook her head. "Don't ask. Take it from me. I want you to."

He shoved his hand into her hair, and she could feel the effort it took him to hold back. His body knew what she craved right now. She just needed his brain to give in to baser urges.

Vivienne leaned forward, running her tongue along the flared head of his penis without giving him the pressure she knew he craved.

Then his hand fisted in her hair, guiding her, demanding more from her, and her victory pulsed between her thighs.

She took him in her mouth, reveling in the taste of him, seducing him with her tongue until he couldn't help the rock of his hips. But when she would have swallowed him deeper still, he pulled free.

"Get up."

A frisson of desire slid down her spine at the hoarseness of the order. Wes was losing control, and it was exactly what she wanted.

She stopped him when he bent his head to kiss her, tried to pull her into his arms.

Wes straightened to his full height, but his gaze never left her as she moved closer to the bed.

She turned from him, crawling on her hands and knees onto the mattress. She sent him a coy look over her shoulder, enjoying the stark hunger in his expression.

Wes stepped closer, and she shuddered as he reached out and ran his hand along her spine, tracing it from her nape to the lacy band of her panties.

Too gentle. He was being too gentle.

Vivienne pressed back against his cock, until his

hand tightened on her hip and he ground his hips against her ass.

"God, Viv. I need to be inside you."

She wasn't sure if it was the fact that the words sounded like they'd been tortured out of him, or the haste with which he was dragging her black lace undies down her thighs, but whatever the reason, everything was working for her in a big way.

"Do it."

Her inner muscles clenched with need at his answering growl as he positioned himself at her entrance.

"Fuck me, Wes."

His hands gripped her hips and she reveled in the strength of him as he drove into her with more force and less finesse than his usual style. Still, she knew he was holding back.

"Don't be careful." Vivienne pushed the heels of her hands deeper into the mattress, anchoring herself to increase the force of his thrusts. "I want you to punish me."

His hips stuttered at the plea, and Vivienne looked over her shoulder again. "Spank me."

His fingers loosened on her hip, and after a moment of hesitation, he gave her a light swat.

It wasn't enough. Not even close.

"Don't tease. Make me feel it."

The vehemence in her voice surprised her, but not as much as the sudden, sharp smack of his palm against her flesh. The resulting sting made her muscles clench, igniting a ripple of pleasure deep in her core.

"Is this what you want?" Wes's voice was rough. Hoarse.

Jesus. "Yes."

She'd never felt anything like it.

She stole another look at him as their bodies slammed together. God, he was gorgeous. Intense. There was something so erotic about having all that focus on her. Wes always made her feel like the one, the only, and it was a potent sensation, to feel like someone's whole world.

Too soft. Now she was being too soft.

"Harder."

The command made Wes groan. His hand came down again with more force.

The sting spread, like a crackle of electricity across her skin, and the burn of it focused her back in her body. No regrets. No past mistakes. Just Wes. Just her.

"Yes." The cry came from somewhere deep inside her, a place she'd sealed over long ago.

She could feel the way her blood raced to the surface to meet his hand, knew that he was marking her, turning her skin pink.

"Again," she begged.

This time, the smack landed on the other cheek, and she bit her lip as something dark and hot throbbed to life within her.

"Tell me you're with me. Tell me you want this."

Her voice was almost a sob. "I need this. I need you."

Wes's large hand landed between her shoulder

blades, pushing her upper body into the mattress before tangling in her hair and pinning her there. The sting brought a smile to her face. She turned her head to draw in a shuddering breath. The comforter pressed into her cheek as he held her in place and drove deep inside her. She reveled in the way he dug his fingers into her hip as he sped the cadence of his thrusts.

Vivienne pushed back against him, chasing the rush that was building so quickly, afraid to lose the promise of benediction that was coursing through her.

The sound of them, the slap of flesh against flesh filled her ears, set her blood on fire. She was drowning in sybaritic delight as Wes took her to the brink of pain-edged pleasure.

And then his cock hit her G-spot and his palm came down on her ass, and Viv was consumed as her body erupted in a sensation so intense, she wasn't entirely sure she hadn't blacked out.

For a split second, everything was perfect. But perfect never lasted.

As the pleasure receded, it left a gaping emptiness behind, and in the resulting void, there was nothing holding her together anymore. It hurt. It hurt so goddamn bad, like her heart had burst.

She tried to get it back. To concentrate on Wes's rhythmic thrusts. To stay grounded in the physical.

There was nothing titillating about the anguish burrowing in her chest. It wasn't muddled with pleasure, like before.

This was a dark chasm that threatened to swallow her whole from the inside.

"I need you."

It wasn't what she'd meant to say. It had been far too romantic for the moment.

But in the middle of the most darkly desperate fuck of her life, those were the words that had spilled out of her.

Brutal in their honesty, leaving her flayed to her emotional core.

The physical marks he'd left would disappear, she knew that, but the emotional marks were forever. Not even the six years between then and now had faded them. She'd just buried them deep enough to fool herself for a little while.

And now everything she'd pushed down, refused to feel, came rushing out to fill the empty space in her.

The tears caught her by surprise, dripping onto the comforter before she'd realized she was crying. It was impossible to breathe through the violent sobs that racked her body.

She cried for the lost pieces of her heart.

The piece she'd surgically carved out so her mother's death and her father's disinterest had no hold on her.

The piece she'd salted and burned so that her time with Wes would stop haunting her.

The piece that had been ripped from her when the promise of life inside her was extinguished without her permission.

What was left of her heart ached.

Behind her, Wes went dead still.

"Viv?"

His voice sounded distorted and far away, as if she were submerged in her tears, as if they were trying to drown her and steal what was left of her tenuous physical connection to Wes.

"Jesus, Vivienne." He pulled out of her, leaving her empty on every possible level.

Viv shook her head, lamenting the loss of his body. Trying to reassure him through her sobs, but she couldn't stop.

Suddenly, Wes was beside her, his arms tight around her, pulling her close. "What's wrong, baby? Did I hurt you?"

She hated him for comforting her even as she buried her face against his chest and let him rock her.

"I'm sorry. I'm so goddamn sorry. Please don't cry. Tell me what you need."

She didn't want solace. That wasn't why she'd gone after him, pushed him to the brink. Why couldn't he understand that?

He wasn't the one who should be apologizing. She had to tell him that. He had to know.

"I've done such awful things." The words burst from her, desperate and soaked in self-recrimination. "Things you should hate me for."

He didn't push her away though. He just kept soothing her, whispering her name against her hair, and it hurt so badly because she didn't deserve any of it.

"Why don't you hate me?" The question was physically painful, like it had been ripped from her throat.

In answer, he pulled her closer still, and she couldn't fight him anymore. Because in that instant, his arms, the strength of him, were the only things holding her together.

CHAPTER THIRTEEN

Wes woke up alone in Viv's bed. He wasn't sure if
it had been minutes or hours since the most intense
sexual experience of his life, and its emotional fallout.

All he knew was that when Viv had finally cried
herself out, she'd fallen asleep in his arms as he
stroked her hair. And it had changed something monumental between them.

He shoved himself up on his elbows, wondering
where she was. The faint sound of the shower flipping on in the en suite answered his question.

Wes rolled out of bed, padding to the end of the
mattress to grab his discarded sweatpants, but he
paused with them in his hand, and his gaze wandered
back toward the bathroom door. He spent a pleasurable minute indulging in visions of joining her in the
shower, of having Vivienne, slick and soapy, beneath
his hands. Despite the pleasant throb in his groin at
the prospect, he decided against it, stepping into his
sweatpants instead.

She'd been through the wringer earlier, and the

fact that she'd snuck out of bed without waking him was probably a sign that she could use a little time alone to sort through all the same stuff that was swirling in his own head.

His stomach rumbled, and he decided he'd see what she had in the fridge that wasn't takeout. He could whip them up a little something and they could talk over food. Figure out what came next, now that... well, now that things had changed between them.

Wes headed into the living room, following along in the Roomba's wake until it veered right and whirred back to its spot by the couch, while he continued on to the kitchen.

One o'clock in the afternoon, according to the digital screen on the convection oven. The perfect time for the culinary masterpiece that was the grilled cheese sandwich. Wes rooted around the kitchen for the ingredients, relieved and strangely touched that she'd set it up almost exactly the way he'd stored things in their old place.

He'd just flipped the first sandwich when the sound of her heels on the hardwood brought his head up.

She was fastening an earring in her left lobe as she came around the corner all buttoned-up in another of the tailored dresses she favored for the office...and stopped dead.

"What's all this?"

"Lunch." He thumbed toward the pan. "Fair warning, you only have one kind of cheese, so if it's not as good as you remember, that's probably why."

There was a moment of awkward silence. And then: "I'm actually not that hungry. But thank you. That was…"

Shit. Wes's shoulders tightened, bracing for impact. Whatever she was about to say, he didn't want to hear it.

"Nice."

Nice. Wes set the spatula on the counter with a lot less force than he would have liked to use. *She thought he was being nice.*

"My fault," he said, as she placed her purse on the edge of the counter. "I should have asked if you had plans." He didn't bother to mask the sarcasm in his voice. "You going somewhere specific? Or will anywhere do?"

The verbal swipe got her attention.

"What's that supposed to mean?"

"You tell me. I'm the one making you lunch so we can talk about whatever the hell just happened between us. You're the one bailing."

"I'm not bailing." Her attempt at blasé failed miserably as her entire body went rigid. "There's nothing to talk about."

"Really? Because I've got a list going. Screwing. Spanking. Sobbing." He held up a finger for each verb. "And that's just the *S*'s."

"I knew this would happen," she muttered, digging through her purse for something that never materialized.

Now it was his turn to play defense. "And exactly what do you think is happening here?"

"You're turning this into something it never was. Assuming too much." She gestured at the kitchen in general. "Trying to make things better by staging this trite, Dickensian tableau!"

You can't make things better, so stop trying!

The paraphrase of his mother's favorite refrain caught him where he lived, but he took the hit without staggering. Much.

"I can never remember, is the doggy-style spanking scene in *A Tale of Two Cities* or *Great Expectations*?"

Her eyes told him to fuck right off, and there was poison in her voice. "You're the one out here making grilled cheese sandwiches. Because that's what we used to do. But this isn't a Ghost of Christmas Future kind of situation."

She inflicted the cut with surgical precision.

"I'm not your girlfriend. I'm your lawyer. I'm trying to keep you from going to jail. You are here because the court ordered it. This is *not* some magical glimpse into the future we could have had if we'd stayed together." That desperate little laugh of hers made his fists clench, even before she added, "I knew you'd read too much into this."

"Okay. Right. That's all this is. Me, reading too much into things. I guess I missed the memo on which rule book you're using today."

She crossed her arms, like she was above the fray, but he wasn't the only one with white knuckles right now.

"So to recap, when you shove me up against the

wall and fuck my brains out in the elevator, that doesn't mean anything. But when you seek comfort in my arms while you cry your heart out, and then beg me to forgive you before you fall asleep on my chest, that also doesn't mean anything. Got it." His nod was curt as he shoved the pan off the burner and killed the flame with a turn of the dial. "I don't know how I could have screwed that up when it's so obvious to me now."

"Wes."

There was a softness in the way she said his name, a note of pleading, that caught him off guard after their heated exchange. It took him a second to realize her hand was on his bicep. When had she moved so close?

"Please. Don't be mad. We're—"

Her phone buzzed in her purse, and he used the interruption to steel himself against her touch.

"You should get that."

The phone vibrated again, and her hand dropped away as she turned to retrieve it, bringing it to her ear.

"This is Vivienne Grant. Yes. That's correct." Her forehead creased slightly with concentration. "So what does this mean for my client?"

Her client.

That's what he'd been relegated to. All he was to her.

"Okay. That's great news. We can definitely make it there in an hour." Vivienne nodded. "I'll tell him. Thank you so much."

"Tell me what?" he asked as she disconnected the call.

Vivienne dropped the phone back in her purse. "You're free."

"What?"

"The charges have been dropped."

Wes frowned at the sudden reversal. "Max changed his mind?"

"Not Max. New evidence exonerating you has come to their attention, and they are *pursuing other leads*," she told him, obviously quoting whoever had been on the other end of the call.

Wes's brain scrambled to keep up with what she was saying. "But how...that's not... It doesn't make any sense."

"It doesn't have to make sense. When the result you want comes up, you take it."

A soft whirring drew both of their attentions down to the floor, as the Roomba made its scheduled appearance in the kitchen, just like he'd programmed it to.

"Guess you'd better put that ankle monitor back on so you can get rid of it for good, huh?"

He leveled his gaze at her, felt the jolt of connection when her eyes met his. "So that's it?"

He wasn't talking about his case.

Her shrug was barely discernible, even with all his attention focused on her. "That was the plan from the start, right?"

Wes didn't have an answer for that. Right now,

"the start" felt like a million years ago, and he couldn't remember it with any clarity.

Vivienne glanced at the clock on the microwave and cleared her throat. "You'd better eat fast, so you have time to change. This judge is a stickler for punctuality."

Wes grabbed the pan and tipped the contents into the trash, before dumping the Le Creuset in the sink with a loud clatter.

"I'm actually not that hungry either," he mocked, before heading off to don his freshly dry-cleaned suit.

CHAPTER FOURTEEN

IT HAD BEEN a week since his ankle monitor had been removed. Well, in an official capacity and not just as a Roomba attachment, anyway. A week of being haunted by memories of Vivienne, of having her in his arms again, of feeling her beneath him.

He'd tried to drive all that shit from his mind by going through every bit of the evidence AJ had used to bring him down in the first place.

He pored through his own notes and analysis of the hack on Whitfield Industries that had set the entire chain of events in motion. Compared them to AJ's take on how the hack had derailed SecurePay, Max Whitfield's digital crypto-currency app.

He wasn't surprised to find they both thought it reeked of an inside job.

Then he dug into AJ's discovery that the phone that Wes had given to Whitfield's little sister and PR guru, Kaylee Whitfield, after she'd broken hers had been bugged. Wes hadn't done it, obviously, but sifting through AJ's timeline of events, he understood that if he *had* orchestrated the whole thing, a prebugged phone would have been the way to go.

The flaw in the plan, of course, being that there would have been no way for him to ensure Kaylee had shown up that day with a broken phone, eager to make an exchange for the one that had been doctored.

Wes filed that discrepancy away in the back of his brain and kept going.

Next up was the knock-off version of The Shield, Liam Kearney's competing entry in the digital crypto-currency market. Instead of an app, Kearney's company, Cybercore, had opted to create a status symbol, embedding his payment system in a wearable piece of hardware that doubled as a fashion accessory. The specs for which, inconveniently, had been leaked shortly after Cybercore had started testing Soteria's commercial antivirus product for installation on some of their products.

AJ had found a version of the program on Kearney's laptop with a back door installed, which would have made accessing the top-secret plans the digital equivalent of taking proverbial candy from proverbial babies.

All together, it looked bad. Really bad.

And most damning of all, every piece of infected tech had the exact same code in it, a garbage string of eight digits that marked them all as related. And every single one of them could be traced back to him and Soteria Security.

AJ's notes suggested she'd started off thinking it was a date, but like her, he couldn't find any significance. May 10, six years earlier yielded nothing of consequence when plugged into a search engine.

The fact that the code had infected every avenue of her investigation had led her to the working theory it must be some kind of signature. The hypothesis remained theoretical though, since it didn't match the calling cards of any of the well-known, or less well-known, hackers that either he or AJ were familiar with.

By the end of the analysis, Wes was half-convinced he'd done it.

He pushed back from his desk and scrubbed his hands over his face. The only piece of the puzzle he could bring to the case was the knowledge that Vivienne had been blackmailed into installing that original program. And that was just one more link that pointed directly at him.

What he couldn't figure out was who had the talent, and the motive, to have set this up. What he needed was to unleash the full force of Soteria Security on this case, but in order to do that, he needed his impossible-to-get-ahold-of partner to push his reinstatement papers through.

He grabbed his cell and connected the call.

He couldn't say he was surprised when he got shunted to voice mail.

"Jesse, man. It's me. Again. We need to talk. Call me back, okay? Or text me. Or answer one of the million emails I've sent."

Wes disconnected and tossed his phone beside his computer. AJ hadn't figured out the meaning of that garbage code that appeared on all the affected devices. That was the key, he knew it. If he could figure out the significance of that, it would tell him—

"Do you not own a shirt? Is that the problem?"

"Jesus!" He banged his knee on the underside of his desk as he spun around in surprise, frowning as he caught sight of his black-clad interloper. "Don't you knock?"

AJ's grin was smug. "Guess the reports of my stealthiness aren't so greatly exaggerated after all, huh?"

"You shut down a wall of infrared and broke into my place in the middle of the day just so you could throw my comment back in my face?" Now that his heart rate had slowed some, the ballsiness of that struck him. He gave a philosophical shrug at his own summation. "That's a level of petty that I can respect."

He also respected the fact that she'd bypassed his system. He'd have to shore up whatever loophole she'd found to get into his place. Maybe Max had been on to something when he'd hired her after all. Once he exacted revenge on whoever had ruined his life, he might have to see if AJ wanted a job at Soteria.

Wes got to his feet. In deference to his visitor, he dragged an abandoned black T-shirt over his head before joining her in the kitchen area of his swanky loft. "You want a victory beer?"

Her smile faded. "Sure. But you might want to change your order to a beer of the 'drown your sorrows' variety. You're not going to like the reason I'm here."

Unease prickled along his spine as she followed him at a distance. "What am I not going to like?"

"The reason you're off the hook."

Well, shit.

Grabbing two longnecks from the fridge, he twisted off each of the caps with a satisfying hiss and lobbed them into the sink. Then he slid one of the beers across the butcher-block island to her, and his own personal harbinger of doom caught it with ease.

The brown-glass bottle in his hand had already begun to sweat when he tipped it against his lips and indulged in a long swallow. A little fortification couldn't hurt. "Talk."

AJ picked at the edge of the label, as she erased a drop of beer from her cupid's bow with her tongue.

The fact that she was stalling made his shoulder blades itch.

"You know how when Whitfield Industries got hacked, the surveillance footage was missing?"

Wes nodded. While he'd been hauled into Whitfield's office to give a preliminary damage report, Jesse had worked tirelessly to try to unscramble the feed. To no avail. And thank the gods for that, because otherwise Vivienne would be rotting in jail.

"Well, when I was looking into it on the down low for Max, I found that it had been clipped."

Wes set his beer on the counter with a loud *thunk*. "What?"

"The section that would have revealed our perp wasn't scrambled. It was missing. *Poof.*"

A litany of swear words rolled through his brain, even as a hit of adrenaline jacked up his senses.

"I haven't poked too deeply, but chatter is that the G-men have gotten their hands on the footage and—"

"Shut up."

AJ's brows dove low over brown eyes glittering with venom. "Listen up, dickwad. In case you've forgotten, you came to me. I didn't ask to help you ou—"

"I'm serious. Stop talking, AJ." Wes stalked over to his desk.

"What the hell is your problem?"

He rooted through the jacket he'd slung on the back of his chair, liberating his wallet and keys. "My problem is that if you say what I think you're going to say, then you're taking away the only possible course of action I have to protect the woman I lo—" He cut himself off. "Someone who matters a lot to me."

He shoved his phone in the pocket of his jeans as he met her eyes. "So don't say what you came here to say. Once I take care of things, then we can finish this conversation." He could almost see the pieces of his plan clicking together in her brain, and AJ's mutinous expression cleared when they did. "Tell Vivienne I said congratulations."

Wes nodded curtly, hoping it conveyed even a fraction of the gratitude coursing through him right then.

No one understood how to work around the law

like a former thief…except maybe a kick-ass lawyer. He hoped the future Mrs. Brennan would accept the necessity of his plan as easily as AJ just had. But Wes would worry about that hurdle when he came to it. First, he had to get her to open the door.

Vivienne was at loose ends, dressed casually in jeans, a white T-shirt and bare feet. In her kitchen. In the middle of the afternoon. On a weekday.

Unemployment didn't suit her, and now that she didn't have Wes's case to distract her…

And she could definitely use some distraction, because as soon as her brain was left to its own devices, it kept turning doggedly back to the same subject.

He'd been gone a week, but the sexual specter of him lingered.

In her bed. On the couch. On her dining room table. But worst of all, in her head.

Vivienne took a deep breath, staring at the sink where the Le Creuset pan still sat at the same awkward angle that he'd left it in.

She should have cleaned it up, but something kept stopping her. Vestiges of the sentimentality he used to tease her about.

Maybe today was the day she'd be able to erase the last evidence of their time together.

A loud rap at the door saved her from having to follow through.

She hurried over to answer the summons, though she wasn't expecting anyone. But even with no expectations, her visitor shocked her.

"Wes?"

Her synapses stuttered at the sight of him, and for a moment, she couldn't be sure if he was really there, or she'd just conjured him with her single-minded preoccupation.

Then he pushed past her, barging into her place and sanity returned like a punch in the face. As did her snark.

"No, please. Come in." Vivienne shut the door behind him.

"Put this on."

She caught the small box he'd lobbed in her direction against her chest. Tiffany blue with an iconic white ribbon.

Unease slithered between her vertebrae.

"What is this?"

"*Absolute perfection.* At least according to the sales associate who assured me she had 'just the thing' before putting a sizable dent in my credit limit."

Her hands shook at that announcement. She wasn't sure what felt worse—the way her heart kept throwing itself against her ribcage or the fact that her lungs refused to fully inflate. Her gaze ping-ponged between Wes and the box as she undid the ribbon, lifted the lid, opened the hinged jewelry case inside.

Twinkling up at her was a huge, flawless princess-cut diamond set in platinum with a fleet of smaller diamonds flanking it.

It was, indeed, absolute perfection.

She hated everything about it.

"What is this?"

"Exactly what you think it is." Wes sounded grim.

Vivienne had wasted enough youthful dreams pondering this moment, and to have them acted out in this macabre pantomime felt cruel.

"You can*not* be serious. If you think I'm going to marry you because of a couple of glorious orgasms then—"

"Eight." Her would-be fiancé glared at her. "You had eight glorious orgasms, but we don't have time to go over our highlight reel right now. City Hall closes at five."

"This is ridiculous." Vivienne snapped the box shut on the sham of a ring and held it in his direction. "I'm not marrying you."

Wes remained completely still. "Yes, Viv. You are."

The deadly seriousness of him finally penetrated her shock, centered her. Something was very, very wrong. "What's going on?"

"I can't tell you that."

"Why the hell not?"

"Because the less you know the better!" His words were harsh, but there was something tortured about them, as well. Like he no more wanted to be saying them than she wanted to hear them. "Hell, the less I know the better. Something bad is coming, and after what you did to help me, what you gave up…" Wes raked a frustrated hand through his hair.

"A week ago, it wouldn't have mattered. But we don't have attorney-client privilege going forward. And now I know things that can hurt you."

I'm the one who hacked Max's company, okay? I know you didn't do it, because it was me.

Her foolish confession pulsed hot in her brain. Shame burned through as she came to grips with what an untenable situation she'd put them both in.

"But you know things that might be able to help me figure this out. And now that they've let me go, the investigation is...pursuing new leads."

Oh, God. Her knees shook as she read between the lines. At the realization she was in the crosshairs.

"Now we need to improvise. The faster the better. Get your purse."

She couldn't drag him any further into this than she already had. Not when spousal privilege was black-and-white, and his plan was soaked in so much gray. Vivienne shook her head, trying to make him understand. "This will never hold up in court if it comes down to it. There are a million ways to poke holes in what each of us knew and when we knew it. It won't keep either of us safe for long."

She could see she wasn't getting through to him. That his mind was set.

"We were together for two years," he countered. "We lived together, and we broke up when you got accepted to Yale. Now work has thrown us back in each other's lives, and old feelings have resurfaced. Just stick to the salient facts. Let people assume the rest."

Hearing her inner feelings laid bare made Vivienne tremble. She tried to make him see the truth wasn't enough.

"If they have the kind of evidence that would send you to Tiffany's before knocking on my door, then things are too far gone to fix. I'm guilty of what they think I am, Wes. Best-case scenario is that this buys a little extra time while they figure out how to prove our marriage is a sham designed to keep us from testifying against each other."

"Time is exactly what I need to figure out who did this to you. Why the blackmailer targeted you to get to me. How it all fits together. And I will do whatever it takes. I swear it. I will get us both out of this, but I need your help to make it work."

Her breath shuddered from her lungs, as though it was filled with razor-sharp ice crystals. Not exactly the "I need you," she used to dream of when she'd been sure Wes's proposal was inevitable. The fun house–mirror version of it sat like a rock in her gut.

"You've got two choices here."

Vivienne dropped her gaze to the ring box.

"It's me, or prison. And orange isn't your color."

He stepped close, and his finger was warm against her chin as he tipped her head up, blue eyes boring into hers. "Let me protect you this time, Viv."

The shift of it prickled through her veins, mixing past memories with present in a way that warmed her blood, that made her want impossible things.

Wes's fingers brushed hers as he gently tugged the forgotten ring box from her grasp. He opened it and held it between them, a silent offer, not of love, but of momentary safety.

It wasn't nearly enough, and yet it was so much more than she deserved.

With a trembling breath, she pulled the ostentatious solitaire out of the ring box and slid it on her finger, ignoring the way his shoulders loosened when she did. Because this was going to be painful enough without letting emotions and foolish what-ifs into the mix.

Vivienne dumped the Tiffany packaging on the table beside the door before grabbing her purse. "We should get going."

Wes nodded, pulling the door open for her.

"And for the record," she rallied, squaring her shoulders as she stepped into the hallway, "I look great in orange."

CHAPTER FIFTEEN

THE PROCESS OF procuring a marriage license seemed absurdly easy, Vivienne thought, strangling her purse with sweaty palms as they sat on a bench outside the room where she would become Vivienne Brennan. Just as soon as the ceremony scheduled before theirs was finished.

A couple of signatures and a few dollars was all it took to change your life irreparably. That and the possibility of a prison sentence.

"We should have a contingency plan."

Wes looked up from his phone at the sound of her voice. Calm and cool as ever.

How he could be so blasé about this was beyond her.

"What are you talking about?"

"Divorce papers, in case I end up going to jail." Her voice wavered, and she hated the show of weakness. It took more effort than she'd have liked to swallow it down. "I could presign them so you can just file them if they have enough evidence to lock me up even without your testimony. Or maybe an annulment would go faster for you. We could say I coerced you into marrying me…"

She didn't realize her knee was vibrating with nerves until the heat from Wes's palm seeped through her jeans, stilling her leg. But not her brain.

"Fraud might be better, actually. You could tell them that I—"

"Hey. Take a breath."

He squeezed her thigh in silent acknowledgment as she took his advice.

"How about we get married before we worry about the divorce?"

She nodded jerkily. The bleakness of the situation stained her heart.

Then the doors beside them burst open, and a grinning band of revelers appeared. The bride was radiantly happy, and very pregnant, garbed in a silky white dress and birdcage veil, one hand full of fuchsia peonies, the other hand laced with her groom's. He wore a vintage blue tux and a megawatt smile.

Viv's stomach twisted at the happy scene, and she reflexively clenched the cotton of her T-shirt, her nails digging into her abdomen and the cold, empty feeling there.

What could have been was a knife to her heart.

Still, she couldn't look away from them, her throat tight as the newlyweds kissed and giggled and oozed optimism all the way down the hall, surrounded by their merry entourage of friends and family.

"Wes and Vivienne? We're ready for you now."

They stood in unison, and the gray-haired justice of the peace introduced herself and the hired witness Wes had paid extra for, before warmly inviting them into the room where they would become man and wife.

But when Wes would have followed, Vivienne grabbed his forearm, stalling him on the threshold.

"I can't do this. I can't do this to you."

"And I can't do this without you." Wes stepped close, lifted his hand to cradle her jaw. She leaned into the warmth of his palm, trying to steal just a little bit of his strength. "But we're out of options here. So we're going to have to do it together, okay?"

His lips brushed her hairline. "All you have to do is close your eyes and pretend with me, just a little longer."

Pretend. Yes. Viv nodded. She could do that for him.

With a deep breath and her cold hand engulfed in Wes's warm one, she followed him inside.

You may now kiss your bride.

He could still taste her on his mouth. The fake sweetness of whatever she'd used to make her lips glossy. Their kiss had been brief, little more than a chaste peck, punctuated by an unrelenting awkwardness that had caused the justice of the peace to clear her throat before hurrying them through the document signing and sending them on their way to register the union so that Los Angeles County could do their part in making everything legal and official. So he could keep her safe.

His bride.

His wife.

How surreal was that?

Not the title so much as the way it had all gone down. Nothing like either of them had thought when they were young and in love. When he'd thought marrying her was kind of a foregone conclusion— not an *if*, but a *when*.

Looked like he hadn't been wrong on that front.

Vivienne was quiet in the passenger seat of his tricked-out Range Rover, staring contemplatively out the window as he navigated the start-and-stop traffic, toying with the gaudy ring on her finger. But he knew it was a temporary lull. That her brain was churning, looking for dots to connect, ways to fix things.

He wanted to kiss her again. A deep kiss that would make her forget, for just a second, that they were no closer to finding their puppet master. A slow kiss that would stop her brain from spinning in circles and remind her that she wasn't in this alone.

She'd gotten him out of prison, and he intended to keep her out in return. To finish his quest for revenge on whoever had blackmailed her into this debacle in the first place. Because if he'd doubted for even a second that he was being framed for this, the fact that she'd been dragged into the fray let him know that this had been an intensely personal attack.

"Can I ask you something?"

She straightened in the black leather bucket seat at the sound of his voice, but it took another second before she tore her gaze from the window and shifted it to him.

"Why didn't you come to me? When you got blackmailed?"

She stiffened like he'd hit her with a cattle prod and looked away from him, staring straight ahead.

He pushed again, even though her body language screamed at him to leave her alone. But he needed to understand. "I founded a cybersecurity firm. I could have helped."

"It was my problem." Her voice was as stiff as her spine.

The answer was so Vivienne that he almost smiled, despite the minor traffic jam that was messing with his attempt to get in the other lane. "You always were the most stubbornly independent woman I ever met."

"We were broken up! And I wanted to take care of it on my own because I don't need to run to a man every time something in my life goes wrong."

"I meant it as a compliment."

Vivienne twisted her new accessory around her finger. "Oh."

Since he'd penetrated her bravado, Wes kept talking. Viv always took a little while to open up.

"My mom used to fade into nothing when my dad was serving time. I thought that's what love was for most of my life...staggering codependence. And then

I met you, and it was, I don't know, kind of refreshing that you didn't need me like she needed my dad."

He felt her gaze on him as they inched their way past the fender bender that had been holding things up, and Wes maneuvered the vehicle into the right lane.

"You were smart, and vivacious, and you had your whole future planned out. And for some reason, you wanted to be with me. That made me want to be better. *You* made me want to be better."

His words had been meant to soothe her fears, but her anguished response let him know they'd had the opposite effect.

"God, Wes. If I'd known what I did would end up with you in jail…"

The threat of tears was there, wavering on the edge of her voice. He knew how much she hated that. Wes blew out a breath. It had been a long day, and she'd earned a break. They both had. They could get into the details tomorrow.

"It was nude photos, wasn't it?"

Her gaze whipped to his profile. "What?"

"You shouldn't have been embarrassed to ask me for help. If you think about it, I'm basically the most qualified person on the planet to help you deal with that kind of thing. Not only am I great with computers, I've seen you naked a *lot*. I'm sure I could have gotten them back for you. After an in-depth verification process to make sure all the photos were legit, of course."

She gave him a shove, but laughter lurked at the

corner of her lips, and relief poured through him that she'd smiled at least once.

It was their wedding day, after all.

"You hungry?"

Her eyes lit up, but she tried to mask it with a stoic shrug. "I could eat."

Wes shoulder checked as he flipped on his signal light and snaked through traffic. "I know just the place."

CHAPTER SIXTEEN

STEPPING INTO SEÑOR TACO'S was like stepping back in time.

"Man. This place hasn't changed a bit."

Vivienne nodded at Wes's assessment as they walked into their old haunt.

The gray brick walls, scarred wood floor and dim ambient lighting gave the place a cozy feel. Washes of color came from the fluorescent signs that dotted the walls, advertising a multitude of Mexican alcohol, from Montelobos to Don Julio, and there was a cluster of intricate iron-work chandeliers hanging from the industrial ceiling over the small open area where people sometimes danced when they had live bands on Saturday nights.

They approached the dark wood bar that was inset with tile mosaics and lined with bottles of booze, backlit by blue spotlights.

"Hey. I'll take a Corona and two shots of house tequila. And two orders of the street tacos," Wes glanced over at her. "*Al pastor* and *carne asada*?"

She nodded at their standard order, feeling stupid

that menu items seemed poignant to her. As did the offhand way he'd confirmed before ordering, even though they'd never had anything else off the menu. She fiddled with the ring on her left hand as Wes turned back to the guy at the cash register.

"You can add a side of guacamole and *pico de gallo* to that."

After Wes paid, the guy rimmed two shot glasses with coarse salt, filled them with tequila, and laid a lime wedge across each of them. Then he added the Corona and a metal stand with a laminated number six clipped to it.

"Someone will bring out your tacos when they're ready."

Wes passed her his beer before he grabbed the shots in one hand and their table number in the other and they turned to face their old stomping grounds. Vivienne's gaze migrated directly to the back corner, the table she thought of as "theirs."

There were a couple of big guys with long, wiry beards sitting at it. Internally, she rolled her eyes at the pang of disappointment. She'd accused Wes of trying to summon the Ghost of Christmas Future, and here she was channeling the spirit of Christmas Past.

"Hold these for a second, would you?"

Vivienne accepted the shots in her empty right hand, even as she shook her head. "You don't have to...there's a table right over there. It's fine."

"I got this."

She chewed on her bottom lip, watching as he

walked over to the two burly, trucker types. No way were they just going to concede the spot when there was an empty table right in front of them. Vivienne turned to scope out anywhere else they could sit. There seemed to be a vacancy on the other side of the dance floor, as well. But much to her surprise, by the time she looked back, the truckers were on their feet, nodding chivalrously at her as they moved their giant burritos to the neighboring table.

Wes's grin was smug as she approached, and he planted their number on the table like he was Neil Armstrong raising the flag on the moon.

"How'd you manage that?"

"I told them we're on our honeymoon."

Vivienne's hand tightened around the beer bottle at the reminder, and the ring cut into her skin.

"And I gave them five hundred bucks," Wes confessed, relieving her of the shots and setting them on the scarred wooden tabletop.

"Expensive tacos."

"Yeah, well. I figure we saved a lot of cash on our wedding garb," he motioned at her T-shirt and jeans, then his own, "so why not splurge?"

Wes's attempt to keep things light was appreciated, but even so, her stomach gave a weird little bump as he tugged the stools to the same side of the table. The best formation for people watching, taco sharing and intimate conversation. She wondered if it was only habit, or if he'd made the conscious decision to set the table up like they had the night they'd met…and every other night they'd eaten at Señor Taco's since.

She set the Corona on the table and they settled onto their seats.

Wes grabbed his tequila. *"Salud."*

Vivienne followed suit, lime wedge in one hand, drink in the other. With a quick clink, they downed the pungent liquor. Then the sharp, sour tang of citrus made her scrunch up her nose. She and Wes dropped the rinds into their empty glasses in unison.

Wes. Her husband.

She was suddenly struck by the fact that she barely knew anything about him anymore. That little business venture he'd gotten so obsessed with toward the end of their relationship, the one he'd poured all that time and effort into, had grown into something incredible.

Not that she was surprised. Wes might not have gone to college, but he'd always been the smartest guy she'd ever met. She'd known he was destined for big things, even back then.

"So how long have you wanted to take Soteria public?"

Wes frowned slightly, shook his head as he ran a thumb along the condensation on his beer. "I don't. I like not having to answer to anyone. The freedom of being able to try things without the pressure of it having to turn massive profits."

"Oh, sorry. For some reason I thought Jesse said…" Vivienne flicked her hand, dismissing the thought. "I was pretty distracted that day. Must've misunderstood."

Wes stilled. "You saw Jesse?"

"I ran into him the other day in the men's department at Neiman's. He came over to say hi."

There was something about the sudden tautness in his body as Wes crushed the lime wedge against the neck of his beer bottle before pushing it inside.

"It was a quick conversation," she assured him, though she wasn't quite sure why she felt the need to do so. "He was on his way to Whitfield Industries to try to woo Max into sticking with Soteria."

"I've been trying to get in touch with him since the charges were dropped."

"I'm sure he's just really busy. He knows how much the company means to you."

Wes nodded. Took a sip of beer. She was relieved that he looked more relaxed.

"So what were *you* doing at the men's department at Neiman's anyway?"

Vivienne cast around for a reason not to admit that she'd considered buying him clothes because his constant shirtlessness had been wearing down her attempts to keep her hands off him. Since she'd failed so spectacularly at the clothes buying and at keeping her hands to herself, the point was moot. In the end, she went with a classic subject change.

"The real question is, what was Jesse doing there? When was the last time that guy bought anything off the rack?"

Wes chuckled, relinquishing his beer when she

reached for it—a habit so old and engrained that she hadn't even realized she'd done it until the bottle was in her hand. "He does love to blow money on pretentiously expensive custom-made suits."

"And country club memberships," Vivienne added. "Vintage Corvettes. Rolexes." Jesse had always loved a good status symbol. Or eight.

"And a luxury schooner."

Vivienne's eyes widened at the addition, Wes's beer arrested halfway to her mouth. "He did not." She took a long swallow. "Does he even sail?"

"No. He was at some auction and just wanted to outbid that douchey frat brother of his. The one who stole his girlfriend during spring break. Trina What's-her-name. The heiress to the bagged salad fortune."

Vivienne laughed as she handed back the Corona. "I remember that guy! He wore so much cologne." She shook her head. "Jesse really bought a vengeance boat? That is a level of retribution I didn't even know existed."

A pretty raven-haired server with a high ponytail and the most perfectly winged eyeliner arrived with their tacos, and they both dug in with gusto.

Vivienne closed her eyes and hummed at the gustatory pleasure that was Señor Taco's. "Oh, God. How have I stayed away from this place for so long?" she mumbled through the bite of heaven. "Still the best thing I've ever had in my mouth."

Her heart clenched hard at his lazy white smile. "I'll try not to take offense at that."

The sexual innuendo slipped under her skin.

He turned back to his taco, giving her leg a teasing bump under the table, but her body misinterpreted the casual contact as something far more charged. Her muscles clenched at the jolt of heat that Wes so easily unleashed in her.

They people watched as they ate. It was a good crowd. Lots of college students, judging by the number of T-shirts with school logos on them.

Vivienne watched in fascination as a couple of UCLA students stole past them hand in hand, all flushed cheeks and furtive giggles. The fact that they thought they were being sneaky in their quest for a quickie had her rolling her eyes.

"Nice to know Señor Taco's restrooms are still seeing their fair share of action."

"Is that censure in your voice?" Wes shoved their empty plates to the middle of the table. "Because if I remember correctly, you and I were responsible for a good portion of that action."

"That was a long time ago."

Wes stared at her for a little too long, and she wondered exactly what he saw in the dim light. His voice was low when he spoke again. "Not that long ago. And action has its charm. Sometimes talking's overrated."

He shifted on his stool, and their shoulders touched. "Those two agree with me."

Vivienne followed the tip of his chin to find that, at some point during their conversation, a few couples had migrated to the dance floor to take advantage of the sensuous Latin beat. She didn't need to ask who he was talking about.

They were mesmerizing—practically glowing with sexual energy as they used dancing as a thinly veiled metaphor for foreplay. Their bodies moving in unison, brushing against one another, only to retreat before coming together again. It was absorbing, the illicit heat of them.

This time, Wes's leg didn't bump hers so much as slide along it, and Viv sucked in a breath at the unexpected contact that turned watching into something more visceral.

"You remember what that was like?"

His voice was husky, seductive, and it prickled along her spine like a touch.

"Being so into someone that you can't think straight. That undeniable pulse of desire that makes you want to push the limits."

Wes pushed his stool back a little, angling his big body toward her. "That overwhelming rush of lust that makes your skin come alive."

She shivered when his thumb traced the length of her arm. Vivienne was definitely alive in that moment. It was like someone had plugged her into a power source. Her cells vibrated with it. With him.

The scrape of wood on wood echoed in her ears as he grabbed the leg of her stool and tugged it in front of his. And just like that, she was between Wes's legs, his chest at her back, his voice in her ear.

"That's the kind of heat that makes you forget where you are. Who's around."

His hand came to rest on her hip, and her eyelids drifted shut as he traced his thumb along the waistband of her jeans, stopping just beneath her belly button.

"His world is just her right now."

The reminder of the dancing couple made her open her eyes in time to watch the guy's hands as they migrated up from the girl's waist. His fingers were dangerously close to her breasts, flirting with that intoxicating line between PDA and public indecency charges.

"All he can think about is touching her."

With the flick of Wes's thumb, the button on Viv's jeans went slack. She swallowed against the rush of warmth between her thighs.

"About getting his hands on her."

She couldn't hear her zipper over the music, over the beat of her own heart, but she felt the denim grow even looser.

Wes's mouth was so close that his breath tickled her ear. Her lips parted on a silent sigh.

"That buzz is everything. The build of anticipation. The throb of it in their veins."

The thrall of lust wound through her, consumed her.

"He's so hard it hurts, and do you know why?"

"Why?" she breathed the word so softly, she wasn't sure if Wes heard it over the bar din, or if he was just so deep in his story that her answer was irrelevant.

"Because he knows she's wet for him."

She sank her teeth into her bottom lip. So, so wet for him.

"He can smell her arousal. Feel the way she trembles beneath his touch."

Her whole world had narrowed to the burn of his fingers on her abdomen.

"Until they're so turned on, so wild with need, that they can't handle the tease for another second."

Vivienne squeezed her eyes shut as Wes slipped his hand in her panties. The stroke of his finger, precise and unerring, as he circled her clit with just the right amount of pressure.

An involuntary moan escaped her lips at the contact, half relief, half desperation.

"God, you feel so fucking good, Viv."

She bit her lip as he pushed his hand deeper, so he could slip a finger inside her. *Yes*. It was too much, and not nearly enough. She mewled in frustration.

"You want more?"

Thankfully, he didn't wait for an answer before pressing a second finger inside her. Her body stretched to accommodate the slow, slick slide of his hand, and she leaned back against his chest, something solid as the promise of pleasure began to make the rest of the world go a little wavy.

She could feel the heat of his chest seeping into her back, the jut of his erection pressing against her ass.

Before long, she was rocking her hips in time with the steady drive of his fingers in her mindless quest for climax.

"Jesus. You make me so hard. I wish I was inside you."

Wes finally gave her what she wanted, and with the twist of his wrist, the pad of his finger brushed her G-spot with every thrust.

Vivienne bit her lip, working herself against his hand, desperate for release. She was close. So damn close.

The rasp of his breath in her ear let her know he knew it, too. "That's right. Come apart for me."

Her body tightened at the sexy order, squeezing around his fingers, and then Wes pressed the heel of his hand against her clit and caught her earlobe between his teeth. The weightless free fall of orgasm rushed through her with unstoppable intensity.

CHAPTER SEVENTEEN

"LET ME TAKE you home."

That's what he'd said when she could finally breathe again. When her heart rate had returned to normal operating parameters and she'd settled back into her body to find they were still at Señor Taco's and that she hadn't transcended into another plane of existence all together.

Which was why she shouldn't have been surprised when Wes pulled up at his place, not hers. And as much as she wanted to look around the ritzy loft, with its big windows and manly, brown leather furniture and surprising sense of hominess, that was going to have to wait.

Right now, she needed to get Wes's pants off.

She would have, too, but he impeded her progress by shoving her up against the door the second it closed and pinning her arms over her head so he could capture her mouth with his. The flavor of beer and tacos on his tongue might not do it for some women, but Viv figured their youthful antics had classically conditioned her to drop her panties faster for that taste than any response Pavlov had managed to get with his stupid bell.

With a groan, Wes pulled his mouth from hers, let go of her wrists.

"Not here."

Since she disagreed with that assessment, Vivienne slid her hand between his legs, and did her best to change his mind. "Not exciting enough without the taco crowd? We could move this in front of the window and hope a bunch of people walk by."

His answering chuckle loosened something in her chest. "Tempting, but this time I want you all to myself."

Before she'd realized his intentions, Wes ducked down and hoisted her over his shoulder in a fireman's carry. Her stomach hurt from laughing by the time he'd marched her across the floor and dumped her on his mattress.

He dragged his T-shirt over his head. "I mean to have you in my bed, wife."

Vivienne froze at the pronouncement. Wife. She was his wife.

He was her husband.

She watched as he shucked his jeans and underwear, revealing the perfection of his body. Strong. Sexy. For two years of her life, he was all she'd ever wanted. And tonight, he was really hers. Boyish and eager, with mussed-up hair and sex on his mind.

Despite everything that had brought them to this point, all the guilt and wasted time, she didn't want to miss the moment. She could worry about the rest tomorrow.

"You're falling behind there, Mrs. Brennan." He grabbed the hem of her shirt and pulled it up over her head. "Let's get you naked," he said, giving her a playful shove to make her lie down so he could do the same with her jeans and underwear.

When he was done, Vivienne sat up and scooted to the middle of the bed so there was room for Wes to join her. He positioned himself on his back, with his head on the pillow, watching as she reached behind her back to unhook her bra.

There was something about the look in Wes's eyes when he watched her undress that did it for her every time. With a coy smile, she crawled toward him, leaning down to catch his mouth in the kind of kiss that let him know exactly what she was thinking.

When she lifted up, his eyes were that dark, swirling blue that let her know he was on the same page. Or at least she thought he was, but when she made a move to slide down his body to take him in her mouth, he stopped her.

"Grab the headboard."

"Wes…"

"Do it." There was a little bit of darkness in his voice as he issued the order, and she was helpless to disobey. He grabbed her by the hips, once she'd complied, and she had to admit, it was kind of sexy the way he manhandled her, positioning her with a knee on either side of his head.

"I'm calling the shots this time."

She should hate it. At least that's what she told herself.

She was independent. She'd built herself a life and career without him. Without anyone. And that's how she liked it. Because if there was one thing she knew, people never failed to let you down. To leave. Wes had done both already.

Then his breath trailed along her inner thigh. And it made her want what she shouldn't.

Him.

But it felt good to let go of the control, just for a second. To rely on someone else with no worry that it might end in heartbreak or disappointment. Because the truth was, though she might struggle to trust him with her heart, he'd always been the master of her orgasms.

When his tongue touched her, the shock of pleasure sizzled through her. He was the one who growled, though. "It's been way too long since I've tasted you."

She tipped her head back in ecstasy as he licked straight up the center of her. Her fingers tightened on the headboard as Wes alternated between slow, open-mouthed kisses and then switched it up with surprising moments of suction that had her on the precipice in no time. Vivienne tightened her thighs, and the novelty of the rasp of his beard against her sensitive skin drove her even higher. The heat built fast, almost too fast considering she'd come so recently. This time was different though. In the bar, the steady drive of his fingers against her G-spot had unleashed something deep and pulsing in her belly. But this, the swirl of his tongue against her clit, was a shallower kind of pleasure. Not worse, just different, like static electricity crackling across her skin. And then Wes did that thing she liked where he pressed his tongue hard against her and moved his head just so—oh God, it felt even better than she'd remembered—and the myriad sensations coursing through her culminated in a flash of heat and light as her pelvis jerked and she came apart with Wes between her thighs.

She was boneless as he helped her slide down his body, until she was lying on top of him. With a satisfied sigh, she pressed a kiss to his talented mouth as he traced the length of her spine with his knuckles.

His cock was hot and hard between them, and she teasingly wiggled her hips. "You didn't want to come, did you? Because I'm all tired out."

"No problem," he assured her. But before she could tell him she was only joking, he'd rolled her onto her back with a swift, hard kiss.

"You just lie back and let me do all the work." The offer was made with a cocky grin that convinced her libido that she could probably muster the energy for round three. The slide of his body as he eased himself inside her dispelled any doubt, and Vivienne wrapped her arms around him, sure she would never get enough of the way he made her feel.

He was gorgeous when he fucked. Predatory. She'd forgotten the intensity of him. The focus. How he turned straight-up missionary into the most consuming, intimate kind of pleasure.

She drank in the familiar sight of him as he thrust into her, the feel of his muscles bunching and releasing beneath her questing fingers. She'd missed the feel of him, exciting and familiar, all at once. Vivienne bent her knees, sliding her heels closer to her thighs, because she knew what he likcd, too, and she wanted to thank him for the thing he'd donc with his tongue.

Digging her heels into the mattress, she countered his thrusts, circling her hips and wringing a curse from him. Yeah. He loved that. And she loved giving it to him. Wes's muscles drew tight and his hips started to speed up as he hit the point of no return. Then he was groaning her name as his body convulsed with the force of his release. Vivienne wrapped her arms around him, pressing her lips against his neck and holding him close as he shuddered with the aftershocks of their desire, hoping that he'd felt even an echo of what he'd made her feel.

When his breathing returned to normal, he pushed off her, rolling onto his back, and they lay side by side in his giant bed, staring up at the ceiling.

After a moment, Wes grabbed her left hand with his right and began idly stroking his thumb across her knuckles. It was hypnotic, and surprisingly electric considering how tame it was compared to all the ways, all the places, he'd just touched her. The memories distracted her, and it took her a second to realize that he was twisting the ring off her finger.

Something like panic fisted her heart, squeezing to the point of pain.

"Done with me already?" It was supposed to be a joke, but it held no levity. The symbolism of it was a fissure in her heart, growing wider by the second.

He turned his head toward her on the pillow. "I know you don't like it. I saw your face when you opened it."

Shame washed through her. She'd been a total bitch to him after the intensity of what had happened between them that last day at her place. Being spanked had pushed her to the physical brink, made her more vulnerable than she'd ever been, and she hadn't been able to process the emotional fallout. Or the inescapable connection that had sprung up between them. From the second Wes had pulled her into his arms and held her while she cried, she'd known something monumental had shifted between them. Something she couldn't undo. And so after she'd used him, slaked her need for punishment, she'd discarded him without explanation. Pushed him away with brutal efficiency, intentionally hurt him in an attempt to avoid dealing with the shift in their relationship.

And still he'd shown up at her door to help her.

"I was just…surprised." Terrified. Desperately happy.

"Uh-huh." To her amazement, he sounded amused, not offended. "I've got something for you."

Her shriek of shock turned to a laugh as he rolled his big body on top of her, before bringing her along for another half turn. When they were done, he'd usurped her side of the bed, and she was on top of him.

Planting her knees in the mattress on either side of his torso, she pushed herself up so she was straddling his stomach. The expensive ring clattered against the end table as he dropped it there before lowering his hand to the drawer pull and tugging it open. "Can you grab that red box for me?"

Vivienne leaned slightly to the side, her gaze snagging on a red velvet ring box tucked against the back corner of the drawer. Her fingers shook as she reached for it, turning it over in her hands, avoiding the next step.

"Open it."

Swallowing back her fear, Vivienne complied. The hinges were tight, and the box snapped open. For a moment, she thought her heart had stopped.

"Wes…"

A small diamond was set in matte white gold that reminded her of vines. It was like nothing she'd ever seen before. Too modest for a man of Wes Brennan's current means, too thoughtful for a stand-in ring for this sham of a wedding, too perfect for any of that to be a mistake.

"It's yours."

The wording struck her as odd, ringing an alarm bell deep in her bones.

And she knew. Without question. That this ring was hers. It had been intended for her all along.

Her chest felt tight, crowded with emotion, as her gaze found his.

"You were going to propose?"

His embarrassed grin sent her heart careening into a free fall. "I mean, one day. Once I'd made something of myself."

"I told you I didn't care about that."

"Because you grew up with a father who was a named partner of a corporate law firm. My mom was trying to support two kids and a raging drug habit as a grocery store cashier. When she bothered to show up for work, that is. And I didn't know how to make you understand that I needed to be able to provide for you, not because you couldn't, but because not being able to would make me too much like him."

His dad. Wes had described him as a low-budget con man who only showed up when he needed money, who only called when he needed bail.

Wes's self-recriminating laugh broke her heart as he took the little box from her numb fingers. "When I bought this, I didn't think this moment would be so far in the future."

Then, before Vivienne could even fathom what he was doing, he lifted her hand and slid the ring onto her finger.

I, Wesley James Brennan, take you, Vivienne Amelie Grant...

She replayed the vow he'd made her at City Hall in her head, his voice solemn and deep, as she stared down at her hand and the unique, perfect ring that completely eclipsed the generic princess-cut diamond she'd worn earlier.

Vivienne leaned forward, bracing her forearms on his chest so she could catch his mouth in the kind of kiss they hadn't shared in a very long time. One that lacked the crackling heat and promise of deep, drugging pleasure. One that, instead, promised something far more profound and lasting than physical pleasure.

As if he'd sensed the difference, there was a question in Wes's blue eyes when he opened them, and the difference in the way he was looking at her gave her chills.

Wes lifted his hand, his fingers tracing the curve of her cheek. "Viv?"

"Yeah?"

"The last time we were together, when you wanted to be spanked?" His fingers stilled against her face. "Was I...was I not giving you what you needed before? Would you have stayed if the sex had been dirtier? More adventurous?"

The sheer vulnerability of the question was enough to rip her heart out of her chest, to break through the wall of bravado and ice she'd constructed to keep it safe after she'd driven him away six years ago. The layer of shame that kept her from admitting how desperately she wanted this fake marriage to be real. The bone-deep knowledge that she still loved him. Dirty, sweet and every which way in between.

"You're enough for me, Wes. Just this. Just us."

He always had been. Always would be.

And to prove it to him, she leaned forward, press-

ing a kiss to his chest, right above his heart as she slid
her other hand down his body, taking him inside her
so they could rock together until the heat between
them raged out of control again.

CHAPTER EIGHTEEN

"Where do you think you're going? I'm not done with you yet."

Vivienne laughed as she slipped out of his grip and made a break for it, crawling toward the edge of the bed. "I need to hydrate or I won't last the night."

"I'll allow it," Wes decreed. "But be quick," he advised, with a smack on the ass that made her giggle, but also made her want to hurry back and explore the pulse of heat that flared in her belly. Grabbing his T-shirt from the floor, she pulled the black cotton over her head.

His lips twisted with wry humor. "Yes. Modesty is key after how we've spent the last four hours."

In response, she pulled the pillow from beneath his head and smushed it on his face.

"There's some bottled water in the fridge," he advised, his voice muffled by her feather-filled retribution.

Vivienne padded her way across his loft, eyes roving over the decor, his possessions. It was a classy place, for sure, but it didn't scream tech billionaire. It

was more understated than that. Cozier. It took her a
second to realize the reason for that was all the little
personal touches that he used to tease her about. The
ones, she suddenly realized, that she'd phased out of
her own life in the intervening years.

Picture frames on the table, a shelf full of books,
things he used to be far more utilitarian about.

"Oh my God. Are these throw pillows on your
couch?" she teased with faux horror. When they'd
lived together, he'd been adamantly anti–throw pillow since beading and tassels and fringe made them
uncomfortable, which, he'd argued, robbed them of
their pillow destiny. Granted, his were plain, but it
was still a big step for Wes.

"What can I say? I guess you rubbed off on me."

The idea of that pleased her more than it should,
but her grin faded as she approached the kitchen and
her eyes lit on his stainless steel fridge.

Or more accurately, on the crayon drawing that
was proudly displayed on it.

To Uncle Wes, it said. *From Jeremy.*

The sudden buzzing in her brain was disorienting, and she braced a hand against his butcher-block
island as she tried to catch her breath.

Reality was not to be denied though. It seeped
through all the cracks in her heart, reminding her
that there was no happy ending for her and Wes.
They'd tried this once, and it had all gone to shit.

They were only here now because she'd lied to
him.

The vilest of lies.

She looked down at her finger. At the perfect ring. Perfect because he'd chosen it for the old her. The one who hadn't known yet what a coward she would become.

"Viv?"

His voice was too loud, and the realization that he was behind her snapped her head up.

She swiped a hand across her cheek to erase the tear that had escaped against her will, wondering just how long she'd been standing there.

"You okay?" There was concern on his handsome face as he stepped up to the fridge, pulling open the door and grabbing each of them a plastic bottle from the door rack.

He'd pulled on his jeans, but he hadn't done them up. Her throat ached at the sight of him as he set the water on the counter beside her.

"I was just looking at your picture." Her voice sounded small, but it echoed in the empty feeling in her chest.

He glanced over his shoulder as he cracked open the lid on his own bottle. "Nice, right?" He was grinning with pride when he turned back to her, but there was something else there. Something that sliced at her heart. Love. "You might not recognize me, but that is actually a very accurate depiction of my backyard soccer skills."

"Erin had a baby." A little boy that Wes obviously adored. He was an uncle.

"Yeah. She found herself a good guy. Peter's a high school chemistry teacher." Wes took a long swallow before putting the cap back on the bottle and setting it next to the one she hadn't touched. "But Jeremy, that kid's the best. You're gonna love him."

It was the worst possible thing he could have said. Including her like that, like part of the family, brought everything roiling to the surface, past and present clashing in such a painful, disorienting way.

"We didn't use a condom."

He frowned at her abrupt announcement, and she braced for his fury before she realized it was just confusion. And concern.

"I know. We haven't used one since we established we were both clean after the elevator, remember? Do you want to sit down? You look a little pale."

Wes lifted her onto the counter before she had a chance to protest. Not that she could have even if she'd wanted to, because other words started spilling out of her mouth instead. Words she should have said to him a long time ago.

"Not now. Then. That night in your car." About a month and a half before everything had gone oh so wrong. "Our second anniversary."

They'd been driving to dinner to celebrate when Wes's hand had wandered far enough up her thigh to ruin his anniversary present—a black lace garter belt and thigh-highs that Viv hadn't been able to resist. Wes had felt the same way. They'd pulled into an alley so he could unwrap his gift right away, which had resulted in them missing the window of their fancy reservation. They'd ended up improvising their anniversary dinner with fast-food burgers and milkshakes in bed, followed by a couple more rounds of dessert.

She could see the memory solidify behind his eyes. Then he went deathly still.

"So?"

But as nonchalantly as he might have meant for it to sound, the syllable was cocked and loaded. Viv could actually feel him processing the news, the way his body braced against the unwelcome realization.

Her tears stung, salt on a wound that had never healed quite right. That she knew now never would. But she made herself say the words she'd never said aloud before.

"I was pregnant." The words hollowed out her chest, like someone had dug her heart out with a spoon, leaving her raw and scraped up.

Wes shook his head, like his body couldn't process what his mind had already pieced together. "When you shoved that goddamn ticket to Connecticut in my face and told me that if I really loved you, I'd drop everything to go with you? You were pregnant?"

"Yes."

He staggered, like the word was a blow.

"You didn't tell me." He shoved his hands in his hair, looking helpless for a second, before anger flashed in his eyes. "How could you not tell me?"

"Because I was terrified!" The words came out with more force than she'd intended. "More scared than I'd ever been in my whole life. You'd been so distant, so focused on Soteria."

She couldn't hold back all the old feelings. "I needed you, Wes! I needed you to want me. To want to be with me. Not because I was pregnant, but because I was important to you. More important than all those investor dinners Jesse kept dragging you to. More important than your business plan and your goddamn computer."

"Are you fucking kidding me right now? You think that's a good enough reason?" He stepped back from her.

It wasn't. She knew it. She'd known it then. While they'd fought. While they'd had sex. While she'd boarded the goddamn plane.

"I meant to tell you. After I left, I spent weeks trying to figure out the best way to tell you."

Wes sneered at the flimsiness of her defense. He stepped back again. "Oh, you meant to tell me. You meant to fucking tell me that we had a baby."

She shook her head, and her throat constricted at the prospect of telling him now. "There was no baby."

The anger had been a good distraction, but now the overwhelming sadness was back. Tears dripped down her face.

"I'd made an appointment for a ten-week ultrasound to find out the sex."

An appointment she'd had to cancel. For a baby that would never be.

"I thought that's how I'd tell you, because you'd want to know. I practiced it so many times. 'Wes, I'm pregnant. It's a girl,' or, 'It's a boy.' But three days before, I woke up and everything hurt so badly. I remember calling 911. Then I passed out."

Vivienne stared at the ring on her left hand as she twisted her fingers in her lap.

"When I woke up from surgery, I asked about our baby. I swear to you, it was the first thing I asked. But the doctor explained that I was in the hospital because I'd had an ectopic pregnancy and my fallopian tube had burst."

She forced herself to meet Wes's eyes, even though he was blurry through her tears.

"It was all for nothing." The words clawed at her throat. "Our whole lives changed and there wasn't even a baby." *Breathe*, she reminded herself. "There wasn't even the chance of a baby. And so I told myself it was better if you didn't know, because when I asked you to come with me, you turned me down."

The stricken look on Wes's face hurt her all the way to her bones, and she hopped down from the counter at the sudden need to go to him. To erase the distance that had sprung up between them. But when she would have reached for him, he stepped back from her, did up his jeans.

"I need to get out of here." He stalked toward the door, grabbing the hooded sweatshirt from the coat rack and shoving bare feet into his sneakers.

Vivienne watched as the man she loved walked out the door, flinched as it banged shut behind him.

Her greatest fear made manifest. Again.

Everyone who'd ever mattered to her left her when she needed them most. Her mother. Her father. Wes.

She'd known they were destined for this. It was why she'd fought her feelings so desperately. Because if she and Wes were meant to be, it would have worked out the first time.

CHAPTER NINETEEN

PREGNANT.

When she'd first said the word, it was like some-one had shoved a spike through his skull. Disori-entation. Nausea. Agony. He couldn't get his brain to focus.

Now, after an hour of walking aimlessly down the street in the middle of the night, he was just numb.

He couldn't feel anything anymore.

Wes jammed his hands deep in the pockets of his hoodie.

Pregnant. But not pregnant.

Wes walked faster, hoping motion would help dis-sipate some of the toxic emotional cocktail that was swirling in his gut. He was trying so goddamn hard to hold on to the anger, but other stuff kept getting in the way. Especially after he pulled his phone out of his pocket and googled *ectopic pregnancy*.

Vivienne had never been totally sold on the idea of having children. She'd told him that once, a few weeks into their relationship when she'd asked him if he wanted kids and he'd said yes. One day.

She hadn't quite been able to squelch the fear in her eyes.

"I'm not sure if I do," she'd confessed. She was worried that she wouldn't be a good mom because no one had taught her. Cancer had stolen her own mother before she'd had a chance to learn anything.

The memory chilled him.

Vivienne had been knocked up and terrified, and instead of turning to Wes, she'd fled across the country alone.

It broke his fucking heart to think he was the greater of two evils for her in that moment. A moment when he should have been there for her.

And that wasn't even the worst of it.

Burst fallopian tubes, according to what he'd read, could be life-threatening.

She'd almost died and he hadn't even known. How could he not have known something like that?

Jesus. No wonder she'd left him.

At the time, her sudden announcement that she was going to Yale instead of Stanford, that stupid ultimatum with the plane ticket, had struck him as incredibly selfish.

But he'd been selfish, too. She wasn't wrong. He'd been caught up in Jesse's plans to schmooze investors and turn Soteria into something big, right out of the gate. Maybe if he'd been paying better attention, he would have realized that something was going on with her.

Because he knew. He knew what losing her mom had done to her. How abandoned she'd felt by her father afterward. She'd told him how she used to dream about her father choosing her over work, how she used to scan the hall during piano concerts and dance recitals in hopes that just once, he'd pick her instead of a meeting, or a business lunch or golf game. She'd trusted him with that knowledge, and then he'd acted just like the son of a bitch who'd raised her. Let her fly across the country without him. Abandoned her when she'd needed him the most.

Just like he was doing right now.

The realization hauled Wes up short. She'd trusted him again, and he was fucking it up. Walking away when what she needed was his understanding. The realization disgusted him, and he cursed himself silently as he turned around and started the long walk home.

He knew she wasn't there the second that he opened the door. Not that he blamed her for leaving. God, he was such an asshole.

He considered going to find her right then, had his keys in his hand, but he stopped himself. Set them back down. Dismissed the idea as he pulled off his hoodie and draped it over the back of his desk chair. If she'd wanted to discuss things further tonight, she wouldn't have left. They could both use some time to let what had just happened settle and get a couple hours of sleep.

Tomorrow, he'd go and get his wife.

"Viv? C'mon. Open up."

Wes knocked again, ignoring the tingle at the base

of his spine that was turning into a bad feeling about the fact that she hadn't answered the door yet.

He punched the eight digits of her mom's birthday into the security panel and burst inside. "Viv?"

He strode past the kitchen, through the living room, into the bedroom.

Empty.

Memories of the last time he'd come home to find her gone assailed him, twining the past and the present together in a way that constricted his breathing.

His heart started to thud against his ribcage with more force, but he swallowed the panic. He wasn't going to lose her again. This was just a problem in need of a solution. He was good at finding solutions. She was somewhere, even if she wasn't here, so all he had to do was—

The vibration of his phone in his pocket interrupted his train of thought, but any hope that it was her was dashed as he glanced at the screen.

"What the hell, man? I've been trying to get in touch since the charges were dropped."

"I know." Jesse's voice was calm. Eerily so. "My lawyers advised I shouldn't speak with you."

Wes's fingers tightened on his phone. He didn't like the sound of that. "Your lawyers," he repeated, matching Jesse's composure. "Don't you mean our lawyers? Because I'm pretty sure the esteemed law firm of Denisof Price Goldberg represents Soteria Security. Or at least that's the way they made it sound when they told me to fuck off after I was put in handcuffs and hauled off to jail. But now that my legal woes are behind me, we've got some reinstatement paperwork to sign. Isn't that right?"

The long silence on the other end of the line told Wes everything he needed to know, even before Jesse spoke again.

"This isn't how I wanted this to go down. We've been partners, friends, for a long time. But Soteria is hemorrhaging clients since you went to prison. And I've been doing everything I can to keep us afloat!"

Not so calm anymore.

"You're a goddamn liability."

"The charges were dropped," Wes countered.

"And then you turned around and married the goddamn enemy! How do you think that's going to play in the media? That the second you're cleared of wrongdoing, you hitch yourself to the FBI's next target!"

"She didn't do this." Wes's voice was flat and hard with conviction.

"Tell that to the video surveillance footage. I've got to go. I have a joint meeting with Max and Liam in a couple of hours, and I need to prepare. If I can keep them on board, then this media storm will stabilize, and I can finally implement my plan to take Soteria Security public by the end of the year."

The announcement blindsided Wes.

"What the hell are you talking about? I thought we agreed no IPO. We always said Soteria could be more innovative, and do better work, without having to answer to shareholders!"

"We didn't agree. You used your fifty-one percent share to cock-block me, and what I've wanted, for years. I'm the one who sacrificed for your genius. I'm the one who parceled out my shares to get new investors, to take Soteria to the money-making behemoth it's become. Now that I have controlling interest, you honestly think I'm giving it back to you?"

Wes realized in that moment that his plan to preserve the business by signing his shares over to Jesse before he went to jail had turned out to be Soteria's death knell instead.

"You're freezing me out of my own goddamn company?"

"Don't act all hurt. You brought this on yourself. For once in your life, you're going to see what it's like when everything doesn't go your way. And Wes? Don't call me again. From now on, any communication between us needs to go through my lawyers."

Wes was still reeling from the precision of Jesse's vindictive attack, the intensely personal nature of it, after he'd hung up the phone. Between the two of them, Jesse Hastings was the gregarious one, the figurehead who was out front, drumming up business and dealing with clients, while Wes preferred to stay behind the scenes, creating.

Jesse was always the guy scouting for new opportunities, trying to grow their coffers, and with every big monetary milestone they'd reached, he'd broached the subject of taking the company public one day. But Wes had always managed to talk him down, to convince Jesse that it was the work that mattered most, not the money, but the innovation. At least he thought he had.

Apparently, he'd been wrong.

Wes ran a hand down his face and shoved his phone back in his pocket.

He'd worry about the professional blow later. Right now, he needed to find Vivienne.

As he stalked back through her condo, something bright and orange on the kitchen table caught his eye, drawing him over.

A tiger lily in a vase.

Along with the flower, there was a black shoebox, a nondescript envelope, some official-looking papers, her wedding ring, and a handwritten note from Vivienne. His hand shook as he reached for the sheet of blue stationery.

Wes,
If I'm going to jail, there's somewhere I have to say goodbye to before that happens. In the meantime, I hope that, whatever you came here for, you'll find it on this table.
Viv

Wes glanced at the legal documents—a set of presigned annulment papers and a set of presigned divorce papers. Viv always was an overachiever.

The envelope contained the blackmail letter, which ended up a little crumpled when anger made his hand clench, and a thumb drive with the Whitfield Industries logo on it.

Despite the note's strict instructions to dispose of the thumb drive once the program was installed on Whitfield's system, Vivienne had found a way to preserve this key piece of evidence.

That's my girl, he thought, turning it over in his fingers before dropping it back in the envelope with the now-mangled note. *So fucking smart.*

He lifted the lid off the shoebox, and the contents were like a gut punch of sentimentality. A bunch of photos of the two of them, looking young and fresh faced and in love. The frame with the pressed tiger lily that used to sit by their bed—she'd made it with one of the flowers in the bouquet he'd given her the night of their first date.

There was a notebook, too, and Wes had to leaf through only a couple of pages to realize it was a diary of sorts. The dates on the tops of the pages told him these entries spanned her nonviable pregnancy, from terrified start to tragic end.

He snapped the book shut at the realization. Because as desperate as he was to know, to understand what she'd gone through, he wanted to hear it from her. Face-to-face. But when Wes slipped her diary back in the shoebox, something else caught his eye.

Not the hospital bracelet itself, but the number sequence printed beneath her name. The date she'd been admitted for emergency, lifesaving surgery.

May 10. Six years ago.

The exact eight numbers in the string of garbage code that had popped up repeatedly throughout AJ's investigation. She'd been right on both counts. It was a date and a signature.

What had Viv said? Something about *"...after Jesse showed up...right after..."*

The realization of what she'd left unspoken hit him like a lightning bolt. Jesus Christ.

Precise. Vindictive. Intensely personal.

Wes glanced over his shoulder, through the kitchen to the foyer where Vivienne's security camera was logging the comings and goings of all her visitors and transmitting them to her phone...and anyone who might have bugged her phone.

His partner's out-of-the-blue phone call suddenly made a lot more sense. The bastard had watched him walk into Viv's apartment.

A cold rage flooded Wes's veins at the betrayal.

Poaching Soteria Security was one thing, and if Jesse wanted to punch below the belt in some desperate attempt to hurt him for whatever slights and transgressions he'd already found Wes guilty of, well, Wes could take care of himself. But exploiting Vivienne's trauma in some sociopathic attempt to twist the knife in Wes's back a little deeper? Monitoring her phone and her security feed? Hurting the woman he loved?

Jesse would pay dearly for that.

Wes pulled his own phone out and waited for his call to connect.

"AJ? Never mind how I got this number. I need you to get me into that meeting with Whitfield and

Kearney that's happening later. I know who fucked me over, and I'm going to bury the bastard."

Grabbing Vivienne's ring from the table, Wes shoved it in his pocket.

Then he gathered up the rest of the evidence she'd left him.

He needed to pay a little visit to the FBI before his meeting.

CHAPTER TWENTY

WES STRODE INTO the lobby of Whitfield Industries at precisely 2:00 p.m. and headed straight for the elevator. A familiar black-clad figure hit the button as he approached.

"They're expecting me?"

AJ slid him a look drenched in annoyance. "You know, you really need to stop second-guessing my methods. It makes me not like you."

"You never liked me," he pointed out reasonably, straightening his tie. There was a certain poetic symmetry to ending things as they'd begun. Which was why he'd changed back into the gray suit he'd been wearing when he was arrested before arriving at Whitfield Industries to deliver the coup de grâce.

The silver doors dinged open, and once the herd of office drones disembarked, AJ and Wes stepped inside. A harried, balding guy tried to join them, but AJ stopped him.

"Sorry, this one's full."

The doors slid shut on the man as he gaped at

the two of them, alone in the twenty-eight-person-capacity elevator.

Wes lifted a brow as he hit the button that would take them to the top floor.

"What? These elevators are the worst when people are hopping on and off at every floor. Especially when you're trying to get to the penthouse." AJ reached into her leather jacket and retrieved her phone. Her thumbs flew over the screen, and then she looked up at the elevator control panel.

Wes followed her line of sight in time to see a small light in the upper right-hand corner switch from green to red. Override complete.

"There. Isn't this better with no one bugging us?"

Since he couldn't disagree, he changed the subject entirely. "For the record, I wasn't second-guessing you. I actually thought we worked pretty well together."

AJ frowned at the commendation. "Why does that sound so leading? It's like you're *this* close to offering me a *fabulous opportunity* that's going to end with me hawking shady pyramid scheme products and drinking a lot of Kool-Aid."

"Because you're very jaded and don't know how to take a compliment. How do you feel about IPOs?"

"Are you kidding?" She scoffed. "The whole reason I'm starting my own thing is because I don't even want *one* boss, let alone a team of rabid shareholders pestering me about dividends and shit."

"We should talk after I've got this situation under control."

Her whole body grew wary. "Are you gonna try to convince me to work for you?"

"Not exactly. I'd like to work with you."

AJ's eyes widened at the prospect. "Like partners?"

He shrugged, letting the possibility hang out there. He didn't want to spook her.

It took three more floors before her posture switched from cagey to contemplative. The second it did, Wes pounced. "We'll talk after?"

"It's under consideration," she hedged, just as the elevator drew to a stop.

The doors slid open to reveal a gleaming modern lobby that offered spectacular views of Los Angeles thanks to its floor-to-ceiling windows, but neither of them spared a moment's thought for the scenery. Heedless of the executive assistant's protests, they strode across the white-tiled floor, directly to their destination.

The office was brimming with hostility. Whitfield was on his feet the instant they breached the door, which caused the two men who sat in the visitor chairs facing him to whirl around to see who dared intrude on their meeting.

Max's voice was as cold and harsh as the arctic tundra. "What the fuck is he doing in my building, AJ?"

Goddammit.

Wes slanted her a glare. "Oh, good. They were definitely expecting us."

Her shrug was unrepentant. "They were expecting me," she said, walking straight to Kearney. Wes didn't miss the moment of silent communication between them, the way the man dialed it back from wanting to rip Wes's throat out to casually speculative with nothing more than her slow nod.

Jesse, on the other hand, had molten rage bubbling inside him. It glowed in his eyes.

Wes unbuttoned his suit jacket. "You guys should really see your faces. You'd think I just got released from prison for betraying you all or something."

Slowly, purposefully, Jesse rose to his feet. With his gregarious facade ripped and torn, Wes could see the anger pulsing just below the surface. He barely recognized his partner. The man he'd considered his friend.

And for the first time, Wes realized that what was in front of him now was the truth, and it was the rest of it that had been lies.

In that moment, betrayal cut both ways.

"Give me one reason I shouldn't hit this button, Brennan."

Max's voice startled him, snapped his attention back to the now.

"It will have security here in under a minute."

Wes nodded, pointed at him. "Keep your finger on the trigger. I just wanted to talk to my buddy Jesse here in person, because it's been hell trying to get a hold of him lately."

"I have nothing to say to you."

Wes's chuckle held no mirth. "Great. Fewer interruptions. Since the charges were dropped, I've spent the last week poring over the evidence AJ used to put me away. Pretty damning stuff. I mean, think about it."

He shoved his left hand in his pocket, dragging the right one contemplatively down his beard. Max settled back into his chair, wary but intrigued, too.

"First, Whitfield Industries gets hacked and thanks to some modifications I made, we catch the breach and ring the alarm. But when we get here, *I'm* the one who delivers the bad news to the client, and my outgoing, personable second-in-command goes to investigate the surveillance footage."

Jesse's skin was mottled, his anger manifesting as red splotches against his tanned skin. "It was a massive security breach. I'm a stakeholder in the company. Of course I wanted to help figure out what went wrong. Whitfield Industries is our flagship client, and I'm the one who landed the account," he added smugly.

"Next up, the phone that I gave to Kaylee Whitfield after she broke hers starts misfiring. And when they crack it open, it turns out it was bugged— monitoring her location, logging her calls and transmitting her conversations."

"I'm sorry. Are we all supposed to stand here while you list off all the reasons you should be back in jail?" Jesse raked an agitated hand through his blond hair.

"Hey, I get it, man. You're the CEO of Soteria Security now. Shopping at Neiman's to do, private medical records to hack."

Precise. Vindictive. Intensely personal.

The attack straightened Jesse's spine. "I don't know what the fuck you—"

"I thought we agreed, no interruptions. I don't want you to miss anything. Especially since I think you're really going to like the twist ending. And I don't want Kearney here to feel left out."

The CEO of Cybercore stiffened up at the sound of his name, and AJ set a comforting hand on Liam's shoulder.

"He tests out Soteria's commercial antivirus software. Coincidentally, counterfeit versions of his latest product start flooding the market not long after you show up to install some updates, on my behest."

Jesse slow-clapped, four loud cracks of sound in the otherwise silent office. "You're really nailing this performance, Wes. You sure you don't want me to get the FBI in here so they don't miss the drama of this confession?"

"Sounds like one, right? But that's when I realized that I'm not the only one who looks bad here. Because you're the one who volunteered to check the surveillance footage after Max got hacked, which gave you the opportunity to make it disappear. And Kaylee's bugged phone? That was the new business phone that you configured for me. It was never meant for her. I screwed up your plan when I gave it away. And let's just be honest, since we're among friends here—I never sent you to update Liam's test software like you told him I did."

"I'd like to see you prove any of it."

Wes's smile was feral. "I already have. You got

sloppy, and AJ found your fingerprints all over this case. She couldn't figure out what that string of garbage code that linked all the attacks meant. But I did."

For the first time since he'd walked into the office, Wes saw fear in Jesse's eyes. An involuntary confession.

"I'm not going to stand here and listen to bullshit accusations." Jesse turned to stalk from the office, but the second he drew even, Wes pounced, shoved him up against the frosted glass of Max's office wall by the lapels.

"I know what you did, you son of a bitch." He angled his forearm across Jesse's chest, his elbow dangerously close to the bastard's windpipe. "I'll bet if I look at her phone, I'll find the same goddamn bug that was on Kaylee's phone. That's how you found Viv at Neiman's. That's how you knew we got married. And that's why you phoned me this morning, to threaten me. Because you have control of her phone, which means you can watch the feed whenever the mood strikes. And when you saw me on it, you were worried your little plot might unravel, since it only works if Viv and I aren't sharing secrets."

Wes applied a little more pressure against Jesse's trachea, and the bastard clawed at his arm.

"You want to take me down, fine. But you should have left her out of it, because you might have gotten away with it if you hadn't blackmailed her."

There was a dawning horror in Jesse's eyes, and it was all the confirmation Wes needed.

"Yeah, that's right. She told me what happened

after we broke up. In fact, she's the reason you're going to spend the rest of your life in prison. She kept a diary, one that proves she never told me about the pregnancy. Which absolves me from being the blackmailer. There's also an entry in there about the day she was rushed into lifesaving surgery. A date that I think the feds are going find very interesting when they compare it to that garbage code AJ found. And then there's my favorite—the story of how you went to visit her at Yale, shortly after she'd been released from the hospital. Did you already know what had happened before you went? Or was it the visit that made you curious enough to do some digging?"

Jesse opened his mouth to reply, but Wes cut him off. "You know what? Don't tell me. It'll make the trial so much more compelling if I have some surprises to look forward to. But I'll bet the FBI agents I gave it to this morning will get a kick out of it.

"Viv kept it all in a box, with a pressed tiger lily and some framed photos from back in the day. You're even in a couple of them. You know how sentimental she is."

Wes couldn't help his mocking grin. "You poured the time and effort and the resources of an elite cybersecurity firm into screwing the two of us over, and she took you down with a diary entry and a hospital bracelet, you dumb fuck."

And courage, Wes added silently. So much damn courage that she'd quit her job to get him out of jail. Sparred with him. Driven him to unparalleled heights of frustration and desire. And despite their complicated history, she'd never given up on him.

Jesse's forced laugh was all bravado. "Tell me it hurt. Tell me it killed you when you found out what she'd done. The secrets she kept from you."

The dig had no power, and Wes's muscles relaxed slightly at the realization.

Because it had hurt. It had hurt them both. But it hadn't killed them. In that moment, Wes recognized that they were stronger for it. *Bad at communication, good at sex.* That's why they'd broken up the first time. But not this time. This time was different.

Because it wasn't his computer prowess that had solved this case. It was the fact that he and Vivienne had actually talked to each other. Laid the ghosts of their pasts to rest.

He refocused on Jesse. "How the hell did I not know what a malicious son of a bitch you were?"

"You're like a goddamn cat, you know that? Always landing on your feet. You get all the credit for Soteria, even though you'd still be working out of your junkie mother's basement if it wasn't for me! For my connections and all the investors I brought in. But you're the one the magazines write about! You're the one they praise. Like I'm nothing. I just stand by and watch you get everything I want. More of the money. More of the fame. The only reason you even met Viv is because I took you to that party, and then you got her, too!"

Jesse's chest heaved with fury.

"I knew the only thing that would hurt you more

than losing your precious company would be to know that the love of your life betrayed you. Got to admit, I didn't think Vivienne would crack. She's usually such a cold hard bitch."

Wes increased the pressure of his arm. "You're going to want to watch what you say to me right now."

Jesse's smile was a little manic. "Keep it up, tough guy. You want to strangle me? Punch me? Put my head through the glass? Go for it! I'll press charges so fast you'll be back in the slammer faster than Vivienne dropped her panties for you the night of the frat party."

Wes's muscles shook with the control it took not to take him up on the offer. He shoved Jesse back against the glass one last time, with enough force to make him feel it. But he'd made the wrong decision six years ago, when he'd chosen Soteria over her, and again the night before, when he'd walked out on Vivienne after she'd confessed her deepest, darkest secret to him. He wouldn't do it a third time.

"I thought I wanted revenge on the person who framed me more than anything in the world. You took my company from me, and I planned to savor every second of watching you get frog-marched out of here in cuffs as they hauled your ass to jail. But thanks to you, I've got more important things to do."

Because Jesse, and Soteria, were his past, but Vivienne? She was his future. She always had been.

Somewhere behind him, Whitfield's voice penetrated Wes's consciousness.

"Sherri, can you please send security to my office immediately. And then get Special Agent Behnsen on the phone. Tell her there's been a break in the case."

"Guess he wasn't kidding about that button, huh?" Wes pried his hands from Jesse's suit and adjusted his own jacket, just as two burly security guards entered the office.

"Looks like you'll be in good hands after I leave. And Jesse?" He waited until the prick met his gaze with a seething glare. "When Max and Liam are done with you, you'll be hearing from my lawyer."

He just had to find her first.

CHAPTER TWENTY-ONE

VIVIENNE SAT ON THE porch swing, one foot tucked beneath her, the other skimming along the painted wooden deck planks as she swayed back and forth. The rhythm of the movement was slow and soothing for her frayed nerves. She stared contemplatively through the railing at a bed of tiger lilies on the edge of the gorgeously landscaped property.

The first time she'd fled to the Phoenix Inn, she'd been young, and terrified, nursing a broken heart as she recovered from the emergency surgery that had both saved her life and changed it irreparably. Like a desperate philosopher, she'd spent hours on this very porch swing, convincing herself that a nonviable pregnancy was basically the same as not being pregnant at all. Which meant there was no real reason to tell Wes. Because there was nothing to tell.

The irony that the decision she'd made then was the reason she was here now, and that she was on the precipice of jail time because of it, was not lost on her. She'd chosen to keep a secret, which had turned septic so quickly that she couldn't remember what it was like before it had seeped into her bones and become part of her. One more experience in a long line of experiences she'd used to justify to herself that she was better off alone. That loving people hurt too much.

But then she'd reconnected with Wes.

And she'd finally accepted that, no matter how much it hurt, she couldn't stop loving him.

The burn of tears threatened, but through sheer force of will, she held them back. She'd given in to tears the last time, and they hadn't helped. This time, she'd be stronger.

The back door creaked open, and Vivienne kept her eyes stubbornly forward, not quite ready to give up her solitude, no matter how well-intentioned the innkeeper was.

"I'm not really in the mood for company right now, Sally."

"She said you'd say that."

The sound of Wes's voice brought Vivienne to her feet. But even though she recognized that he was standing with her on the porch where she'd spent so much time thinking about him, it still took everything she had to turn and face him. To make it real.

He was gorgeous in a light gray suit, pristine white shirt and dark gray tie. His thick brown hair was the perfect amount of mussed, and he'd trimmed his beard back from "verge of unkempt" to "dangerous bad boy."

It was too much, having him here with her, and she turned toward the yard, grabbing the railing and focusing on the tiger lilies instead of the nerves that jittered in her stomach.

"What is this place?"

She closed her eyes, letting his deep voice wash over her. "It's where I came after…everything." Lost pregnancy. Lost love. Lost self. "To heal. And clear my head."

"Serendipitous choice of flowers."

"Not really."

Wes joined her beside the railing, and she made herself look at him.

"I planted them. When I came here the first time." She turned back to the profusion of orange blooms. "Part of the healing I was talking about."

He was quiet for a long time. When he spoke again, his voice was solemn. "Thank you."

She looked up in surprise. "For what?"

"For letting me be part of that piece of your life."

A poignant smile tipped the corner of her mouth up. She'd never thought of it like that. That planting tiger lilies had been a connection to Wes. That in some small way, he'd been here with her even as she'd been so desperately trying to push him away.

He shoved his hands in his pockets and rocked back on his heels. "So why are you here now?"

"The threat of jail made me contemplative, I guess. And I can breathe when I come here. No matter how bad it gets."

"Well, it might not get as bad as you think."

She frowned at the riddle.

"As of this morning, you're no longer suspect

number one. I'm sure Whitfield won't press charges against you, and even if he does, you can dust off those kick-ass lawyer skills of yours, turn state's evidence, and testify against Jesse."

The announcement blindsided her, dropping her heart into her stomach. "What?"

"It was Jesse." Wes's voice was laced with a hint of rancor.

Of course, it was. All of the evidence, so inextricably tied to Soteria…everything pointing just a little bit more toward Wes and letting Jesse off scot-free. Because Jesse had his finger on the scale of justice.

The realization that someone she'd considered a friend had betrayed them both like that quaked through her. But to her surprise, the bitterness that usually rushed in when someone she cared about let her down didn't overwhelm her. Instead, her heart was full of concern for the man standing in front of her.

"Are you okay?" She almost reached for him then, but she stopped herself just in time. "What's going to happen to Soteria?"

For a man who might have just lost his life's work, his shrug was more laissez-faire than she'd expected. "It doesn't matter. I've got other options in the works, and I'll land on my feet. I didn't stick around to sort through the details. I had something more important to do."

Vivienne's heart melted at the look in his steely blue eyes. The meaning behind his words, as evidenced by the fact he was here now. With her.

"How'd you find me?" The words scraped her throat.

"I hacked your phone."

His self-effacing smile nearly sent her to her knees. God, she'd missed him so much.

"Since not tracking you was the only promise I ever made you that I kept, I thought maybe if I blew that one up too, we could start over. Try this again without all the baggage."

Something inside her cracked open, and all the hope she'd buried so deeply when she'd fled here at twenty-two bloomed in her chest, riotous and color-ful, like the bed of tiger lilies she'd planted all those years ago.

"You remember how you said we're good at sex and bad at communication?"

Viv bit her lip, nodded.

"I didn't catch Jesse because I outwitted him or because of my coding skills. I figured it out because of you. Because we finally talked to each other. And I am so fucking sorry I walked out after you told me what happened."

Wes's forehead creased slightly, as if he was searching for the right words to say. As if he didn't understand that he'd already found them.

"If you hadn't shared what you went through with me, he might have gotten away with it. But he didn't. And that got me thinking about us. About what we've been through. I know things didn't work out between us last time…"

He trailed off, and the silence was overwhelming.

She took a step forward because she needed to be closer to him. "Last time isn't this time."

Wes nodded at the assessment. "Well, in that case, I've got a question to ask you."

The air got thick and hard to breathe as Wes reached into his pocket and pulled out the ring. He took her left hand in his, and it was like plugging into an electrical socket. Her skin came alive. Her heart thudded against her ribs.

But that was nothing compared to the jolt of unfiltered emotion that buzzed through her when he lowered himself onto one knee in front of her.

The tears she'd held back earlier spilled freely down her cheeks now.

"Vivienne Amelie Brennan, I am desperately in love with you. Even when I'm trying really hard not to be. And if you're up for it, I thought we could give this another try, because I want to spend the rest of my life being good at sex *and* good at communication with you."

Her heart squeezed as she watched him slide the ring, *her ring*, back onto her finger. She looked into the eyes of the man who had seen all of her—the good and the bad—and yet he'd flown across the country anyway. Because he loved her.

"So, what do you say? Want to stay married to me?"

Viv was nodding before he'd finished the question, and he surged to his feet, catching her around the waist and lifting her up as she wrapped her arms around his shoulders and whispered her answer against the soft, warm skin of his neck. "I do."

When he finally set her back on her feet, Vivienne stared up at her husband. Having him with her, here at the Phoenix Inn, where she'd endured so much sadness, went a long way to making her heart feel whole again. "I love you so much," she confessed through the emotion clogging her throat.

Tenderly, Wes pulled her closer and pressed a kiss to her forehead.

Vivienne stood there in his embrace, letting it all sink in. But as was often the case in Wes's presence, it didn't take long before the heat of him worked its way into her blood, morphing the sweet relief of having him here into the sultry desire to have him naked.

"I don't want to alarm you," she teased, even as she pressed closer, stoking the fire between them, "but we may have officially crossed into old married couple status."

Wes looked down at her with sham horror. His fingers dug into her hips, and she could feel his body start to harden. "I'm not taking the blame for that. You're the reason we're at a bed-and-breakfast right now, instead of somewhere sexy."

He backed her up against the railing, and the press of his growing erection against her stomach gave the porch some triple-X street cred in her books.

She slipped her hands beneath his jacket and ran her hands up his chest. "Sure, but you're the one who sealed our true love vow with a forehead kiss."

He pressed his lips to the edge of her jaw, and her head fell back, granting him better access. "You're right," he conceded, wringing a low moan from her as he worked his way down her neck with soft, open-mouthed kisses.

"We'd better do something dirty, stat." He rocked his hips against hers and her knees went weak. "Breathe a little life back into this dying relationship. Do they have an elevator?"

She shook her head with faux solemnity as she loosened his tie. "Afraid not."

"How about a sturdy kitchen table?" he asked, as the button on her jeans went slack.

"They do, but it's in a communal area."

His naughty grin made her heart stutter. "Since when has that ever stopped us?"

"This is a respectable bed-and-breakfast, sir. Not some sexy West Coast taqueria where people get freaky in public."

"Then I guess we'd better get to your room before I can't control myself anymore."

Vivienne shrieked with surprised laughter as he swept her off her feet and into his arms. "What are you doing?"

"Carrying you over the threshold so I can have my way with you."

She snuggled against his chest, the ring on her finger glinting as she started unbuttoning his shirt. "Because you're so desperately in love with me?"

Wes shoved the door out of their way in his quest for her bedroom.

"Guilty as charged."

EPILOGUE

One Year Later...

"Come here, baby."

Vivienne smiled to herself as Wes stepped close behind her and dropped a kiss to her exposed shoulder.

"You know I don't know which one of us you're talking to when you say that, right?"

His arms came around her to cradle the six months' worth of baby bump she'd crammed into a red floor-length gown to celebrate the official launch of Wes and AJ's new joint venture, DBS Security.

"I was talking to the kid. But since you're here, too, what do you say we get out of here?"

"This is *your* party," she reminded him, motioning toward the glittering crowd schmoozing in Liam Kearney's palatial Beverly Hills mansion. "The who's who of the wealthy business elite are here to celebrate, and be wooed by, you. Look. There's Aidan Beckett, right over there. I thought it was your mission in life to land him as a client."

Wes tightened his arms around her, pulling her closer so her back was laminated to the front of him. "I mean, I probably shouldn't show AJ up at our launch party by scoring a bigger client than her. Especially not in her own house." He nuzzled her ear, and her knees went a little woozy. "I'll get Kaylee to introduce me to him next week, at Max and Emma's engagement party."

"Prioritizing getting laid over getting clients?" Vivienne's head lolled back against his shoulder as he worked his lips down her neck. "That can't be good for business."

"True, but if we stay and I have to explain DBS stands for 'don't be sloppy' to one more person, I might lose it, and that won't be good for business either. I never should have let AJ name the company." Wes's hand slipped up her torso, skating dangerously close to her breast, making her crave more pressure there.

"So how about you save me from myself and we go check out how swanky Kearney's bathroom is?"

Vivienne feigned shock, even as the promise of sex slid along her spine and pooled low in her gut. "You want to have your way with me while my boss is right over there?"

Wes followed her gaze toward Max Whitfield. His dark head was bent close to his fiancée's blond one. An intimate smile dawned on Emma's face in response to whatever he'd said, and she reached up and wrapped her fingers around the man's tie, tugging him even closer.

"Yeah, he definitely gives a shit that I'm dying to ravage you. Those two are going to beat us to the upstairs bathroom if we don't get a move on." His voice rumbled through her, and she couldn't quite hold back her moan as he caught the edge of her earlobe between his teeth and gave it a slight tug.

"Like you're going to be able to lift me onto the counter," she teased, turning to face him and looping her arms around his neck. "Though I suppose the slit in this dress is immodest enough that we could make doggy-style work."

His eyes darkened at the suggestion. "And I thought you were horny before you got pregnant." His large palm landed with a muted smack on the curve of her ass.

Her smile was decadent. "I could say the same about you."

Wes stepped back from her, cocking an eyebrow in invitation. "Come with me? I promise to make it worth getting fired for."

God. All he had to do was look at her, and her body turned hot with longing. Would she ever not want this man?

With a furtive glance, Vivienne slipped her hand into his, letting him tug her along in his wake, through the glittering crowd and up the stairs. The bright chatter and pulsing music muted instantly when Wes pushed the bathroom door shut behind them.

The click of the lock sent a ripple of anticipation across Vivienne's skin.

"Not bad." Wes pulled out his phone, sending a

cursory look around the exquisite fixtures and high-end finishings as he thumbed the screen. He glanced over at Vivienne and stowed the device back in his pocket.

"I mean, it's no Señor Taco's—" he stripped off his suit jacket and laid it on the countertop "—but I think we can make it work. C'mere, you."

He pulled her close, seducing her with a deep, drugging kiss as he worked her dress up her thighs.

"Mmmm." She smiled when he finally let her up for air. The hem of her gown had migrated all the way to her waist. "You're in a hurry tonight."

"Because it drives me crazy when you wear red," he confessed, voice rough with arousal.

"And I can't wait to be inside you," he added, turning so that she was flanked by his big body and the bathroom vanity.

Without warning, her feet left the ground, and she gave a startled gasp as Wes lifted her onto the bathroom vanity, her hands grasping at his shoulders to steady herself at the sudden movement. His jacket was warm beneath her bare thighs.

"Also, we've got about six minutes, tops, before AJ figures out what I just did to the security camera in the hallway, so we need to get this show on the road."

Vivienne was still laughing as she wound her arms around her husband's neck and pulled him close.

* * * * *

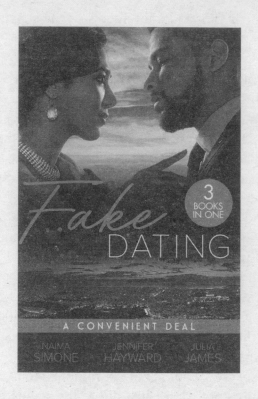

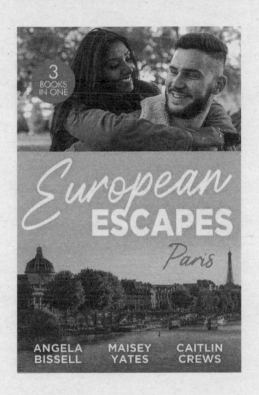

LET'S TALK

Romance

For exclusive extracts, competitions and special offers, find us online:

- MillsandBoon
- @MillsandBoon
- @MillsandBoonUK
- @MillsandBoonUK

Get in touch on 01413 063 232

afterglow BOOKS

Introducing our newest series, Afterglow.

From showing up to glowing up, Afterglow characters are on the path to leading their best lives and finding romance along the way – with plenty of sizzling spice!

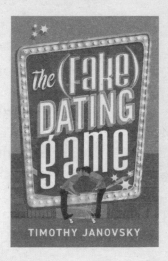

OUT NOW

Two stories published every month, find them at:

millsandboon.co.uk

MILLS & BOON

THE HEART OF ROMANCE

A ROMANCE FOR EVERY READER

MODERN

Prepare to be swept off your feet by sophisticated, sexy and seductive heroes, in some of the world's most glamourous and romantic locations, where power and passion collide.

HISTORICAL

Escape with historical heroes from time gone by. Whether your passion is for wicked Regency Rakes, muscled Vikings or rugged Highlanders, awaken the romance of the past.

MEDICAL

Set your pulse racing with dedicated, delectable doctors in the high-pressure world of medicine, where emotions run high and passion, comfort and love are the best medicine.

True Love

Celebrate true love with tender stories of heartfelt romance, from the rush of falling in love to the joy a new baby can bring, and a focus on the emotional heart of a relationship.

HEROES

The excitement of a gripping thriller, with intense romance at its heart. Resourceful, true-to-life women and strong, fearless men face danger and desire - a killer combination!

From showing up to glowing up, these characters are on the path to leading their best lives and finding romance along the way – with plenty of sizzling spice!

To see which titles are coming soon, please visit

millsandboon.co.uk/nextmonth